**Praise for *New York*** ...
**Lor**...

"Count on Lori Foster for sexy, edgy romance."

—Jayne Ann Krentz, *New York Times*
bestselling author, on *No Limits*

"A sexy, heartwarming, down-home tale that features two captivating love stories... A funny and engaging addition to the series that skillfully walks the line between romance and women's fiction."

—*Library Journal* on *Sisters of Summer's End*

"Foster fills her scenes with plenty of banter and sizzling chemistry."

—*Publishers Weekly* on *Driven to Distraction*

## Praise for *USA TODAY* bestselling author Jules Bennett

"Jules Bennett writes heartwarming and passionate characters guaranteed to grip your heart."

—*New York Times* bestselling author Lori Foster

"Jules Bennett is the queen of small-town romance."

—*New York Times* bestselling author Maisey Yates

"Jules Bennett has a gift for creating warm-hearted, emotional stories of love, friendship, and romance set in small towns readers will want to return to again and again."

—*New York Times* bestselling author JoAnn Ross

# SWEET SURRENDER

*NEW YORK TIMES* BESTSELLING AUTHOR

## LORI FOSTER

Previously published as *Messing Around with Max*
and *Single Man Meets Single Mom*

Recycling programs
for this product may
not exist in your area.

ISBN-13: 978-1-335-40640-8

Sweet Surrender
First published as Messing Around with Max in 2001.
This edition published in 2021.
Copyright © 2001 by Lori Foster

Single Man Meets Single Mom
First published in 2014. This edition published in 2021.
Copyright © 2014 by Jules Bennett

This edition published by arrangement with Harlequin Books S.A.

For questions and comments about the quality of this book,
please contact us at CustomerService@Harlequin.com.

Harlequin Enterprises ULC
22 Adelaide St. West, 40th Floor
Toronto, Ontario M5H 4E3, Canada
www.Harlequin.com

Printed in U.S.A.

# CONTENTS

**Lori Foster** is a *New York Times* and *USA TODAY* bestselling author of more than one hundred titles. Lori has been a recipient of the prestigious *RT Book Reviews* Career Achievement Award for Series Romantic Fantasy and for Contemporary Romance. For more about Lori, visit her website at lorifoster.com.

## Books by Lori Foster

### HQN

#### *Road to Love*

*Driven to Distraction*
*Slow Ride*
*All Fired Up*

#### *The Summer Resort*

*Cooper's Charm*
*Sisters of Summer's End*

#### *Body Armor*

*Under Pressure*
*Hard Justice*
*Close Contact*
*Fast Burn*

#### *The Ultimate series*

*Hard Knocks* (prequel ebook novella)
*No Limits*
*Holding Strong*
*Tough Love*
*Fighting Dirty*

Visit the Author Profile page at Harlequin.com for more titles.

# MESSING AROUND WITH MAX

**Lori Foster**

# Chapter 1

Rain and hail hitting the door was one thing. A woman was another.

She ran into it at full speed, and Max stared, seeing long blond hair stick wetly to the glass panel, a small nose smooshed up hard, red and looking miserably cold. The rain came down in a curtain, muffling her grunt but not obliterating it entirely.

Cleo took an instant dislike to the intruder.

Hurrying around the counter of his sister's bookstore, Max opened the door. The small feminine bundle tumbled limply inside. At first Max thought she'd been shot or bludgeoned on the back of the head. In a fury he stepped over her and peered through the downpour, looking for another body, for any type of threat. There wasn't anyone there. Just the miserable rain.

Cleo continued to complain and snarl and as Max knelt down by the felled body, which now moaned loudly, he said, "Pipe down, you mean-tempered bitch."

The woman on the floor gasped, rolled over onto her back, and started to open her eyes. She moaned again instead.

"I'm wounded," she snarled, every bit as ferocious as Cleo. "I could certainly do without your abuse!"

"I wasn't..." Max stopped when she got one eye peeped open. It was a startling, dark blue eye, fringed by dark brown lashes. It was just the one eye, not even both, but he felt the impact of her gaze like a kick.

Cleo snuffled closer, poking her wet nose against the woman's face while emitting a low growl.

"Where are you wounded," Max asked, still not sure why she'd thrown herself against the door, or why she was still on the floor.

"All over." That one eye regarded him steadily. "Even my teeth are rattled, so the least you can do is not insult me while I'm still down."

Max wondered if that meant he could insult her when she got up. *If* she got up. She didn't seem to be in any rush to do so.

"Cleo," he explained, more quietly this time, "is my dog. And she is mean-tempered, but not really ferocious. She won't hurt you."

"I'm not afraid of dogs." Even in her less than auspicious position, she managed to appear affronted by the very idea, then she turned her disgruntled one-eyed frown on Cleo, who whimpered in surprise. "I just don't want snout tracks on my cheek."

Max hid a grin. "C'mere, Cleo. Leave the lady alone." Cleo obeyed—a first as far as Max could recall. She came immediately to his side, but continued to grumble out of one side of her mouth, making her doggy lips vibrate, while keeping her watchful attention on the downed female.

A puddle had formed around the woman and since she continued to recline there on the tile floor, apparently at her leisure, Max looked for injuries. He found instead a rather attractive if petite bosom covered in a white T-shirt that read I Give Good Peach.

His brows rose. What the hell did that mean?

The shirt, now soaked through, was practically transparent and put on display a lacy pink bra beneath. Not that he was looking. Nope. He'd made a deal with Cleo, and he intended to keep to his word. He stroked his fingers through Cleo's ruff, just to reassure her.

The damn dog looked beyond dubious.

Maybe she knew him better than he knew himself.

"Are you okay?" Max asked the woman, in lieu of what he was really thinking, which had to do generally with her wet shirt and specifically with what it was molded to. He *would* distract himself. But it'd be easier if she'd just get up.

With what appeared to be a lot of undue effort, she got both eyes opened and stared at him. "I'm seeing two of you," she muttered in surprise, "and surely that's a fantasy, not reality."

"A fantasy, huh?" Maybe she was delirious. Maybe she was drunk.

Maybe she was fodder for his next advice column. No sooner than he thought it, Max discarded the idea. It was just a tad too far-fetched to be believed. Even for his eclectic audience, who so far seemed to believe anything he told them.

One small hand lifted to flap in his face, the gesture making Cleo positively livid. The female human ignored the female dog.

"Well, you *know* what you look like, I assume. Two of you would be…never mind." As if just realizing what she'd said, she cleared her throat. "Yes, I think I'm okay."

Max had never met a woman like her, and that was saying something since he'd known a lot of women. He was so knowledgeable on the subject of females, in fact, that his column was a rousing success—written anonymously, of course. Even his family had no idea that he wrote it.

They all thought he was jobless.

This woman was most definitely different. She was flirting, then withdrawing—all while stretched out in sodden disarray on the tile floor. "You're sure?"

"My pride is permanently damaged," she admitted, "but beyond that I believe I'll live." She pushed herself into a sitting position, long legs stretched out before her. Cleo again tried to sniff her, but when the woman turned that blue-eyed stare on her, Cleo whimpered, backed away, and from a safe distance, started snarling again.

Max could understand that. Her eyes were incredible. Not the color, the shape or the size. But the intensity.

"Where's Annie?" the woman asked, looking around the bookstore with an air of familiarity.

"You know my sister?"

"I've bought tons of books here," she explained, "to use in my work. Annie and I've gotten to know each other pretty well over the past year. Now we're friends." Then she asked, "Why was the door latched?"

Cleo, suddenly acting brave, inched one paw closer and the woman absently petted her. Outraged, Cleo yapped and howled, and the woman ignored her bluster while continuing to stroke the dog's too-small head.

Amazed, Max could do no more than stare. No one other than he had ever ignored Cleo's hostile swagger to give her affection. Max looked the woman over again, this time with a different type of interest. His heart beat just a little too fast.

He was on a bride hunt, and since his bride absolutely had to get along with his dog—he was marrying for the dog, after all, to give Cleo a stable home and the love and acceptance she'd never had—he couldn't help taking note of the somewhat tenuous friendship forming right before his eyes. It amazed him.

It warmed his cynical heart.

In a way, it even made him horny. But then, the rain had made him horny, too. Hell, he'd been so long without, a smack in the head would have turned him on. The only action he'd seen lately had been in the damn newspaper column, and that sure as hell wasn't enough to appease a man of his appetites.

The woman snapped her fingers in front of his face. "Where'd you go, big guy?"

Max laughed. "Sorry. My mind wandered."

"I could see that." She looked him over slowly, brazenly, then asked, "Why are you in here with the door latched?"

Max remembered that his sister had the habit of leaving the door cocked open, something both he and Daniel had grumbled about endlessly, which was probably why Annie continued to do it. She lived to irritate her brothers.

"Annie isn't here, and the storm kept whistling through the door, so I closed it. I hadn't figured on many people shopping today anyway. And of course, I hadn't counted on a woman throwing herself against it." More softly, because she had that effect on him, he said, "That must have hurt."

She sluiced water off her arms, and wrung out her hair. "I nearly knocked myself silly, but I'll survive."

Cleo, still looking ferocious so no one would realize her real intent, nudged the female's hand for another pet. Max nearly gawked. "What are you doing out in this storm?"

"I needed a book. I was running to keep from getting soaked, but obviously I hadn't planned on hitting a closed door." Suddenly she grinned, and it made her face go crooked, made her eyes squinch up. She looked adorable, even with her smeared makeup and rain dripping from the end of her red nose.

And she was still petting his dog.

And Cleo was still allowing it.

Max settled himself more comfortably on the floor, where it appeared their conversation would take place. The woman showed no signs of rising any time soon.

Doing his best to ignore her clinging T-shirt and the equally enticing long legs displayed by her tight rain-soaked jeans, Max asked, "Do you need a doctor?"

"Oh, no. Really, I'm fine." She continued to grin, then added, "I'm Maddie Montgomery." To Cleo's dismay, she stuck out a slim wet hand, now slightly coated with dog hair.

Max took it, felt how cold her fingers were and held on. "Max Sawyers. You're freezing."

"And you're Annie's most disreputable brother."

"Her brother, yes, the rest is debatable." Especially lately, Max added to himself. His life as a monk was not an acceptable one.

Maddie pulled her hand away and struggled to her feet. "You know, I've heard tales about you that could curl a woman's hair. You look different from how I'd imagined."

She'd imagined him? Max walked toward the back room where he could find a towel, deliberately removing himself from temptation. Sexual excitement, the thrill of the chase, the discovery, had already begun a heady beat in his heart. After so many years of indulging his basic nature, his actions were often instinctual. He'd find himself seducing a woman without even realizing it, as if he went on automatic pilot or something.

A woman commenting on his reputation just naturally left herself open to a firsthand display of that reputation. Only now he needed a bride, not merely a temporary bedmate. Which meant he had to move slower than he preferred.

But he couldn't stop himself from asking over his shoulder, "How did you expect me to look?" *And,* he added silently, needing the information if he hoped to succeed in his new altruistic plans, *whom did you hear it from?*

"I dunno." She followed on his heels, the squishing and squeaking of her sneakers echoed by the tapping of Cleo's nails. "I thought maybe you'd have long hair, like the guys who model for the women's magazines. Maybe gold necklaces. Something along the lines of the gigolo look."

Finding her description absurd, Max shook his head. He picked up a towel and turned to face her. "Here you go."

She swiped at her face and throat. "You're not offended, are you?"

"More like amused. And curious." No woman he'd ever been with would have described him as anything less than macho, virile...but never a gigolo.

Intrigued, he asked, "Who's been talking about me?"

"Your sister, mostly."

Max almost tripped over his own two feet. "Annie?" Well, hell, that wasn't in the least exciting.

"Yes. Your sister loves you dearly, and she's very proud of you. But she claims you're a reprobate."

"Annie told you I wear gold chains?"

Maddie laughed. It was a nice laugh—natural, warm. Cleo stared at her as if confused, her doggy lips rolling and shuddering as she gave a low growl. "No, that part I imagined all on my own. Annie just told me what a romancer you are, how women seem to find you irresistible."

Max nodded. As many women as men read his column. And they sent him letters of appreciation. He knew women, inside and out, body and soul.

Which was why his weekly column was so successful. He liked it that no one knew he wrote the thing. Anonymity was his friend, otherwise he could just imagine the women who'd be chasing him. It was bad enough that his reputation was so well known, but if women found out he was the weekly love expert...

"I've heard about you from some other women, too."

Her statement drew Max out of his reverie. "Is that right?"

Maddie blotted at her hair as she spoke, oblivious to the sexy display of her breasts beneath the transparent tee. For the most part, Max kept his gaze fixedly on her face. But he was human and male and that combination made it impossible to ignore her tightened nipples completely. He couldn't *not* look every now and then.

"You're the world traveler," Maddie claimed with

fanfare, "the lover extraordinaire, the prize every woman wants to win."

Her candid banter charmed Max. He couldn't quite decide if she was coming on to him, or poking fun at him, but she did it in such a way that either was okay. It was a unique approach, one he was unfamiliar with.

He leaned in the doorway, Cleo by his side. "Every woman?"

That crooked grin appeared again. "Certainly. I feel ready to faint just being in your presence. The sexual vibes are all but knocking me over. Why do you think I spent so long on the floor?"

Biting back a grin, Max asked, "Because you'd nearly knocked yourself out?"

"*Au contraire.* Because I opened my eyes—"

"One eye."

"—and saw you and the world tilted. I was far too dizzy to sit up straight."

Those beautiful eyes—both of them for double the impact—twinkled at Max, keeping him from knowing how serious she might be.

She started to dry her shirt, looked down and gasped. "Good grief!" She shielded her breasts with the towel and glared at Max. "You could have said something!"

Purposely being obtuse, Max asked, "About what?"

"About…about… I'm showing through!"

He shrugged. "It didn't bother me."

Grumbling under her breath, Maddie turned her back on him and tied the towel around her upper body, knotting it at the side like a sarong. Cleo barked, the sound far from playful.

"There, you see?" Maddie said over her shoulder. "The dog agrees that despite your reputation, you should have been gentleman enough to let me know that more was showing than should have been."

"Actually," Max explained, "Cleo just hates people to turn their backs on her. She distrusts anyone who does."

"Oh." Maddie shifted slightly toward Cleo, tilted her head, and said with real sincerity, "Sorry girl. But Max was rude for not saying anything."

Apologizing to his dog?

Cleo snarled.

"Aha!" Maddie said. "She obviously agrees that you're lacking in manners."

"Because I didn't tell you that your breasts were showing?" Max watched her closely, waiting for her to blush. She was far too cocky to suit him.

Maddie nodded at him instead. "Exactly."

Her lack of embarrassment disappointed him.

"You should have told me. A gentleman always lets a lady know when her modesty is threatened. And being a gentleman doesn't detract from your reputation, I promise."

"Okay." Glancing down at her plump bottom in the snug jeans, Max said, "You've got a rip."

She blinked at him over her shoulder, not understanding. "I've got a…?"

"Rip. In the seat of your jeans. Your panties, which match your bra and are really quite pretty, by the way, are showing."

Max watched as she slapped her hands over her behind. It was a generous, well-rounded behind and her hands weren't adequate. He added, "Just being a gentleman."

Maddie back-stepped to a chair in the seating area of the bookstore and plopped down. "I don't suppose you have another towel?"

"Nope. Best I can do is offer my shirt."

She flashed that silly, endearing grin. "Now, I certainly couldn't turn that down. But not yet please. I need to keep my wits about me for a bit longer, at least until I've gotten what I came for."

"Which is?" Max pulled out his own chair and straddled it to face her. The storm still raged, rain lashing the front windows and lightning splitting the dark afternoon sky. Thunder belched and rolled.

The lights in the bookstore flickered once, and all three occupants looked up to see if they'd go out. When they stayed on, Cleo settled herself nervously at Max's side, her head on his foot.

Max absently patted the dog while watching Maddie. She really was cute, though he hadn't thought so at first. And he enjoyed chatting with her. The things she said took him by surprise—not that he'd ever admit it to her.

It was a cozy scene, comfortable, until Maddie said, "Annie told me about *Satisfying Alternatives to Intercourse*."

Max almost fell off his chair. He did jerk to his feet to tower over Maddie, disbelieving what she'd said, not about to hear this concerning his baby sister, never mind that Annie was getting married soon.

His reaction startled Cleo who howled like a hungry wolf.

"Now I see where she gets it," Maddie muttered, eyeing Max's antagonistic stance.

Startled, Max wondered if she was right, but he didn't relax one bit.

Shaking her head, Maddie gave an aggrieved sigh. "Well. It's obvious you know nothing about it."

Max choked. "Ha! I know a great deal as a matter of fact!" If he hadn't sworn off casual sex, Max thought, he'd show her just how much he knew.

"No." Maddie shook her head, looking somewhat pitying and utterly positive over her conclusions. "You're clueless."

Heat rose up Max's neck. He felt his male consequence pricked, challenged. In a tone caught between menace and sultry promise, he said, "I can name any number of alternatives. As to how satisfying they are, I suppose that'd depend—"

She actually laughed at him. "Down boy."

Cleo sat.

Maddie laughed again. "At least the dog obeys."

Ready to strangle her, Max shook his head. "Only when she wants to, which isn't often." Then he added, "And never for women. Cleo hates women."

"She doesn't appear to hate me."

"I know. Strange."

Maddie leaned forward, teasing glints in her blue eyes and whispered, "It's a book, Max."

"What's a book?"

Her eyelashes were spiked from the rain, her collarbone still dewy, and she smelled nice. Like the fresh air outside and a sexy woman inside. His muscles tightened. She was teasing and bold and funny...and she liked Cleo.

He wanted her, dammit, but he had made that ridiculous vow to his contrary dog.

"I work at the women's shelter," Maddie said, "teaching classes and counseling various groups. One of our biggest problems used to be unplanned pregnancy, but with one of the groups I have now, there's more to it. I mentioned this to Annie, and she ordered me a book that she'd heard about."

So she was a counselor, Max thought with admiration, and decided her extra empathy and area of expertise had a lot to do with why she'd so easily understood Cleo, and gotten past the dog's bluster. An amazing woman.

And an amazing reaction for him. He could never recall having such an instant liking and respect for a female.

On the heels of that thought, comprehension dawned. Max resumed his seat. *"Satisfying Alternatives to Intercourse."*

"Yes, that's the title." Maddie bit her lips, and Max thought she was trying to keep from laughing at him again. He appreciated her restraint. Of course, he also enjoyed the sound of her laughter.

"Annie left me a message last week saying the book was in, but I haven't had a chance to pick it up until now."

Max continued to watch her, a variety of thoughts winging through his mind—most of them now centered around why an attractive, intelligent woman would need a damn book to tell her such things. She had to be, oh, maybe twenty-six or so. Old enough to have learned plenty of alternatives by now. Heck, he'd even invented a few, and that was while he was still a teen.

"So you're going to use this book for…research?"

"More as a reference. It's nice to be able to state documented facts to back me up when I give information or make recommendations. Also, what I learn in the book will help make me more credible in some situations. Despite my four-year degree, two years specialized and two years in the field, I still get teased for being a newbie."

Fascinated, Max asked, "Wouldn't women accept what is said more readily if it came from…experience?"

Max hoped she'd give a clue as to whether or not her brazenness was derived from experience or just plain old cockiness. With women you could never tell, and he'd long ago learned never to make an assumption about a lady.

But his question backfired on him in a big way.

"That's an excellent idea! It's so nice of you to volunteer!"

"But I never…" Max faltered. "Volunteer for what, exactly?"

"Why, to talk to the women, of course." Leaning forward, her damn towel gaping a bit, she elbowed him in a show of conspiracy. "I can imagine you'd hold their attention, at least."

Max leaned back in his chair in appalled denial. "Absolutely not."

"You're refusing?"

"Yes!"

Scrunching up her face with a dark frown, Maddie grumbled, "Then it was worthless advice."

Max glanced down at Cleo and they shared a look. Strangely enough, the dog was silent. Her tongue lolled out one side of her mouth, and there was a look of confusion on her furry face that mirrored Max's. He cleared his throat. "Uh, *you* could tell them."

She seemed to give that a lot of thought. "After you tell me?"

He supposed that answered his question about experience. Maybe. With this one he couldn't be certain. But his curiosity grew by leaps and bounds with every word she uttered. "I'll be glad to…discuss things with you."

"Hmm. I'll think on that. Now—" Maddie tilted her head "—do you happen to know where Annie might have put it?"

"It?"

She made a sound of exasperation. "You do have trouble following along, don't you?"

"Not usually, no." In fact, he was generally the one guiding the conversation. He wasn't sure if he liked this new development.

Maddie drummed her fingers on the chair arm. "The book? The reason I'm out in this miserable storm in the first place?"

"I'll look." In fact, he'd be glad of the opportunity to gather his wits and get his thoughts back in order. But just as he said it, another rumbling boom split the air with deafening force. The lights flickered and went out.

Max, slowly sinking back into his seat, said, "Then again, maybe I won't."

They weren't in total darkness. Though the sky was gray and threatening, it was still midafternoon and some light penetrated the thick, ominous clouds. Added to that was the continuous flash of lightning, strobing across the sky. But the sudden obliteration of every noise—no humming light fixtures, no air-conditioning, no buzz from the small refrigerator in the back room—left them in a cocoon of silence.

Cleo yowled and launched her rotund body into Max's lap. Since she wasn't exactly a small dog, and in fact bordered on fat, she was an armful. Fur went up his nose, into his eyes, and a wet snout snuggled frantically into his neck.

Max caught her close, but couldn't prevent his chair from tipping sideways and both man and dog went sprawling flat.

Over Cleo's panicked rumble, Max explained, "She's jittery in storms anyway, which is why I have her with me today, but she's especially afraid of the dark."

Max expected some criticism from the woman. But as he attempted to soothe Cleo, crooning to her and rubbing her ears, Maddie left her chair and knelt beside them. Her knee bumped Max's chin.

"Poor doggy. It's okay." Cleo whimpered and barked and snarled, but still Maddie stroked her.

Her understanding was seductive. And Max could smell her again, that fresh sexy smell of woman and rain. He cleared his throat, afraid he was fighting a losing battle.

Maddie straightened. "I'm going to go lock the door. It's never a good idea to leave your shop open in a blackout."

Since she'd evidently forgotten about the tear in her jeans, Max got to glimpse those satiny pink panties again as she rushed across the room to the door. She should have looked ridiculous, he thought, what with her hair wet and a towel tied around her breasts.

Instead, she looked oddly enticing. At her ease, obviously very familiar with the shop and his sister, with soothing fractious creatures, human and animal alike. Maddie flipped the many locks and turned the Closed sign around.

When she faced Max again, there was a funny expression on her shadowed face. A look of mixed anticipation, wariness and greed. Yes, it was definitely greed. *Strange.*

"I suppose," she whispered, her eyes never leaving his face, "we should both be heading out."

Max nodded and sat up, Cleo's quivering, lumpy body held protectively in his lap. "Yeah. I need to get her home. She'll be more comfortable there."

Maddie bit her bottom lip. "The thing is, I took the bus here. And now—"

"You don't relish sitting at the bus stop in this storm and with no lights."

She nodded. "And wearing a towel and with a rip in my pants. I don't suppose I could impose on you for a ride?"

That look was still in her eyes, driving Max beyond curiosity. No matter what he told himself, he simply couldn't let her walk away. Not yet. "I can take you home. No problem."

And maybe by taking her home he could learn a little more about her. If she'd be suitable as a wife, well then, he owed it to himself to find out.

Her smile was blinding in the dim room. "Thank you."

"About your book…"

"It'd be hard to find in this darkness, I'm sure. Unless you know exactly where Annie put it?"

"Nope. Afraid not." Doggy slobber ran down his neck and into his collar. Did Cleo have to drool when she was nervous? But then again, she was always nervous. Which was why Max felt compelled to give her a stable home, to show her the good side of life.

Max hugged her closer to his heart—and he saw a very discerning, sympathetic smile on Maddie's face.

"I can come back tomorrow and get it from Annie," she said in a soft voice that made his muscles clench.

"Annie may not be here." Readjusting his bundle, Max stood and faced her, trying to ignore the rushing of his pulse. "I'm minding the shop for her while she and Guy make wedding plans."

Maddie's frown reappeared before she forced a smile. "That's right, she's getting married, isn't she? That's, um, wonderful." In a stage whisper, she added, "Guy *is* a hunk."

Max scowled both at the compliment to another man, and the attitude she couldn't hide. "Annie's marrying him because they love each other."

"Of course."

Max glared at her. "You sound skeptical and you aren't even hiding it well."

Maddie lifted one shoulder in a negligent shrug and brightened her smile another watt. "I'm sure they'll be blissfully happy. I just don't happen to believe in matrimony."

Cursing under his breath, Max asked, "Care to tell me why?"

"Sure, why not? But let's do this on the ride to my house." She turned away, again forgetting about the rip in her jeans. But Max noticed big time. He hoped she wasn't serious about not believing in marriage, because if she were, he'd have to stop noticing.

And he'd definitely have to put his lust on hold.

# Chapter 2

He has a dog, Maddie thought with a wistful sigh. A fat, ugly, needy dog that he treated like a queen. Her heart thumped with unnamed emotions; suddenly, Max Sawyers no longer seemed like just a sexy body, but also a very compassionate and sensitive man. Those extra qualities only added to his appeal—but they also made him something of a risk. She didn't want to be drawn to him in any way but sexually!

Annie should have told her more about him. She'd said Max was good-looking, but she hadn't explained that he was devastatingly gorgeous. And she'd said he was cavalier about life, but cavalier men did not commit themselves to mutts.

Annie had claimed Max would be perfect—in that she was correct. Except that he was *too* perfect.

Maddie looked at his profile as he drove. The wipers worked double time clearing the windshield, but still the rain·was blinding. Thunder rocked the truck.

Maddie felt oblivious to it all.

The man was too attractive for words. Just thinking of the things he knew, the things he could do to her, teach her... Her skin tingled into goose bumps that had nothing to do with the cold and everything to do with Max. She had expected to be attracted to him; she hadn't expected to like him so much right off the bat.

Despite her innate timidity, Maddie would have brazenly sat close to Max, and had intended to do just that. But when they'd dashed through the rain to his truck, Max had left her to fend for herself while he strapped Cleo into a doggy seat, located right between them. And anytime she tried to lean closer, to see him better, Cleo snarled. The dog was already so upset by the turbulent storm, Maddie couldn't bring herself to cause the poor creature more distress.

She understood Cleo on a gut level. The dog's defensive attitude was similar to those of the women she dealt with in her job, and her heart just naturally went out to the canine. Not that Cleo needed Maddie's understanding when she had Max fawning all over her.

Cleo watched her with a jaundiced eye, curling her lips every so often in what might have been a silent threat, though Maddie thought that was just the dog's way of mumbling, since she hadn't actually done anything vicious.

Cleo was about the ugliest dog Maddie had ever seen.

Yellowish fur with streaks of white and gray, a head far too small for such a corpulent body, and squat legs, made her look like some botched scientific experiment—something between a dog and a pigmy sow, maybe a furry ball with a head and feet.

The whiter fur circled the dog's tiny head, making it appear that her head had been morphed on in the wrong spot. Maddie thought the dog's tail was long, but because it stayed curled up between her hind legs and glued to her belly, it was impossible to tell for sure.

"Why is your dog so mean-tempered?" she asked cautiously, and watched Cleo show a few more pointed teeth.

Max glanced at her, but gave most of his attention to the road, which now resembled a large puddle with the rain water pooling on it. "Whoever had her before me didn't treat her well."

Maddie nodded in understanding. The dog tried to fend off all friendly overtures, rather than trust anyone and risk more hurt, just as Max traveled the world, searching for meanings he couldn't find at home. When Annie had told her of Max's penchant for traveling, especially during the holidays, she'd naturally begun ruminating on his psyche.

Her specialized education and work experience made it easier for her to understand others.

Understanding herself hadn't been quite so easy. It

had taken her friends to point out the obvious to her, that she was now determined to arm herself with specialized knowledge so no man could ever humiliate her or take advantage of her again, due to her naiveté.

Looking at Max now, seeing the tender way he smiled at Cleo, her heart thumped. Though she knew she was getting in over her head, she still insisted to herself that it was a good plan. "How long have you had her?"

"I found her in the middle of the road about a month ago. She was just lying there and I thought she was…" He dropped his voice to a whisper, and spelled, "D-E-A-D."

Horrified as she was by the picture he painted, Maddie bit back a smile. "I gather your dog doesn't spell?"

In all seriousness, Max said, "Just a little. There are some words I can't say, hint at, or spell without her going nuts on me."

"Like what?"

"Like another word for inoculation, if you get my drift. Or the professional who might give her that inoculation."

"Ah. She hates medical personnel?"

Cleo howled. Obviously, Maddie had used words she recognized.

"That's about it," Max confirmed.

"So how do you get her there?"

"I speak to her in French." He sent Maddie a devilish grin, and added, "All females are partial to having French softly crooned to them. Makes them mellow."

Maddie snorted. "I don't understand French, and if a guy was going to croon to me, I'd darn sure want to understand what he was saying."

Why that made Max laugh, Maddie wasn't sure. His reactions left her confused as to whether he found her to be laughably odd, or appealing.

"She used to hate baths, too," Max said around his chuckles, "but I changed all that."

At the word bath, the dog's pointed ears lifted off her skull and she barked. Max laughed and rubbed her head.

"Should I ask?"

His grin was pure wickedness, but all he said was, "She especially loves bubbles."

Another bark.

Maddie found herself grinning, too, charmed by Max and his eccentric dog. So what that things weren't working out quite as she had meticulously planned? Annie had said nothing about a dog being at the shop, but then maybe she hadn't known. Perhaps Max only brought the dog along, as he'd said, because of the storm.

The unplanned rip in her jeans and the unfortunate transparency of her T-shirt had certainly gotten his attention.

She cleared her throat as they neared her street and said, "I'd like to repay you by cooking you dinner."

Max skipped another look her way. His eyes were so dark, so intense, they made her shiver.

"Not tonight." He answered slowly, as if coming up with an excuse—or because he didn't really want to say no. Maddie wasn't sure which but she hoped it was the latter. "I need to get Cleo home and out of the storm so she can settle down."

"Exactly. My apartment is close and quiet," Maddie urged. "Why make Cleo ride farther when you can come in for a spell and relax, eat a little, and maybe by then the rain will have stopped."

Max looked undecided, so Maddie worked on Cleo. Leaning close to the dog, she asked, "Would you like to come in, girl?"

Cleo snarled at the invasion of her personal space. Her lips rolled and undulated, her teeth dripping as growled threats escaped.

"There, you see," Maddie said, not the least put off by the surly dog. Cleo's reaction this time was based on jealousy, Maddie was sure. She had things all worked out and there was no way a possessive pooch would thwart her. "She likes the idea."

Max chuckled. "You really aren't afraid of her, are you?"

Maddie shrugged. "I think I understand her. She doesn't dislike me so much as she's afraid to like me."

"It took me two weeks," Max admitted, "just to get her to trust me enough to let me pet her."

Hearing that, Maddie felt tears at the back of her throat. No wonder Cleo was possessive! On impulse Maddie threw her arms around the dog and hugged her tight. Both Max and Cleo looked stunned.

"Well," Maddie said in a slightly choked voice, ignoring them both as she pressed her nose into Cleo's soft, clean fur, "she certainly loves you now."

Had Cleo been abandoned and ignored, Maddie wondered, much like the ladies she worked with?

Max interrupted her thoughts. "So why are you set against marriage?"

Startled, Maddie blinked at him. "That was a quick change of topic."

"You looked ready to cry," he explained with a shrug. "I can't abide whimpering women."

"I never whimper." Maddie sniffed, wiped her eyes, and said, "I'm not exactly against marriage, not really. It's only that I'm in no rush to get tied down any time soon. I tried that and it was humiliating in the extreme."

Max perked up. "Humiliating? How so?"

"You really want to hear this?" She no sooner asked the question than she had to instruct him to turn onto her street. Within minutes she'd be in front of her apartment building. It was either gain his interest now, or possibly lose the opportunity.

Max turned the truck, then said, "Yeah, I want to hear it."

Drawing a deep breath and doing her best not to blush, Maddie confessed, "I came home early one day and found my fiancé tied spread-eagle and naked to my bed while a woman I'd never met tickled him with a feather."

Choking, Max said, "You're kidding?"

"Turn here. This is my apartment building." Maddie felt the heat in her face, the remembrance of deep humiliation, and lifted her chin. "Nope, I'm afraid there's no joke. The feather was a huge lemon-yellow one."

"So what did you do?"

Maddie smiled. If he was curious enough, perhaps she could use that against him. She'd already sensed that his male pride was a good lever as well. When she'd teased him about being clueless on the book, he'd all but vibrated with sensual menace. It had made her heart pound.

"Come inside," she offered slyly, "and I'll tell you."

"Said the spider to the fly?"

Maddie gave him a cocky grin. "Afraid of getting eaten?"

His eyes heated, grew even more intense. "A double entendre if ever I heard one."

"I'm surprised you realized it, after all your admitted confusion about things sexual."

His teeth locked with a snap. "That sounds like a challenge."

"So it is." Annie had sworn to Maddie that forced seduction worked quite well on men. It certainly had worked for Annie! Guy had been resisting her for years, but once Annie got him alone and she could have her way with him...

Maddie grinned at the thought of having her way with Max. After she got him in the door, she'd make her move.

Max pulled into her parking garage and turned off his truck. Cleo was none too happy with the situation at all, and her menace was aimed at Maddie. The thick fur around her miniscule head bristled and stood on end. Maddie patted it back down, knowing good and well how important styled hair was to a female, even a mean female dog.

Through the impromptu grooming, Maddie continued to grin. Or was a grin considered a leer when one had lascivious thoughts on her mind? And how could her thoughts be any other way when Max was sitting beside her? He smelled good, his hot scent detectable even over the heavier smell of wet dog. And he looked good, his dark hair clinging to the back of his neck, his damp shirt showing off an impressive array of chest and shoulder muscles.

He was surprisingly kind for a Lothario, strong and gentle and understanding with Cleo, patient with Maddie herself.

Max smiled at how silly Cleo looked with her fur parted in the middle and brushed to the sides. Then he sighed in resignation. "So tell me, Maddie. What are we having for dinner?"

Maddie thought about saying *beefcake,* but curbed herself in time. Her mind moving a mile a minute, she climbed out of the truck while Max unlatched the dog and hooked Cleo's leash onto her collar. "How about chicken? I can cook that pretty quick." And then they could get onto better things.

"Chicken is fine."

Cleo woofed, for once in agreement. Her vocabulary, Maddie thought, was surprisingly varied. "We'll have to debone yours, girl. I wouldn't want you to strangle on a bone."

Max paused with Cleo held high in his arms. "You intend to feed Cleo, too?"

Appalled that he would suggest otherwise, Maddie said, "I certainly wouldn't eat in front of her!"

"And you'll even debone her meat?"

Maddie shuddered. "Can you imagine how she'd look gagging on a chicken bone?" She shuddered. "Please Max, it's not a pretty picture."

Max smiled. Then his smile spread and the next thing Maddie knew he was laughing.

"What?" His laughter had a curious effect on her, warming her from the inside out, making her toes curl. She led the way through the parking garage to the building entrance, while Max continued to carry Cleo rather than let her walk. Cleo looked as if it were perfectly natural for him to cart her around in such a grand style.

"Maddie."

His voice was so soft, so compelling, Maddie froze, then shivered. If he could do so much with just a word, she could only imagine what he'd do with his hands, his mouth.

"Are you sure you're against marriage?"

Looking at Max over her shoulder, Maddie saw his teasing smile, the sexy twinkle in his dark eyes, and she waved off his comment. Everything his sister had told her proved Max was a confirmed bachelor who intended to remain that way.

According to Annie, women chased Max daily, beautiful women, young women, mature women, wealthy women and women of lesser means. He'd traveled the world and everywhere he went, women wanted him.

Yet Max was still single.

That said a lot. And it told her that if she wished to gain her education, she'd have to keep things casual.

"Oh, I imagine I'll make a fine wife *someday*. But not for a long, long time."

"So if you don't want marriage, what *do* you want?"

Keeping her back to him, Maddie said, "To understand the attraction of a feather. To understand the lure of sex." She took a deep breath. "To notch my bedpost."

There was a pause behind her, no footsteps, no breathing. Even Cleo was silent. In a rush, Max again caught up. He didn't say another word.

She reached her door on the second floor, well aware of the fact that Max had carried fat Cleo up the stairs and still he wasn't breathing hard. He was in such superb shape.

She could barely wait to get a bird's-eye view of his body.

"Here we are," she said, trying to sound cheerful instead of triumphant. She stepped inside and waited, ready to pounce the moment she had the door closed behind him, barring his escape.

But Max hesitated on her doorstep.

"It just occurred to me," he said, looking down at Cleo who stared back in unblinking worship. "I should let her take care of business first. I wouldn't want her messing your apartment."

Maddie nearly panicked. Was he trying to escape already? And she hadn't even tried anything yet! Maybe she had come on too strong, maybe she shouldn't have mentioned that part about notching...

But then Max said, "You should change out of those wet clothes. We'll be back in five minutes or so."

Some of the tension eased from her muscles. He sounded sincere enough. "All right. I'll leave the door unlocked for you."

His eyes narrowed. "As soon as I get back, you can start explaining."

He made it sound like a threat, but Maddie was just glad he'd promised to come back.

The second he was down the stairs, she ran into her bedroom and shuffled through her closet, wondering what to change into. Not another pair of ultra tight jeans, she decided, unwilling to take the risk of a new rip. Tearing her clothes had *not* been part of the plan.

Of course, slamming into a closed door hadn't been on the agenda either. Still, she was working with what she had.

For late April it could still get cool, so she decided against a sundress, and instead pulled out a snug, long sleeved dress of beige cotton. It fell to midcalf, but hugged her bottom and her breasts. Across the bodice was a colorful mauve rose and the words In Full Bloom. And on the back, Freshly Plucked.

She rushed to the mirror, then gasped at her bedraggled appearance. It was a toss up who looked worse—her or Cleo. She grabbed a comb and attempted to get the tangles out of her hair in record time.

She heard the front door open and close. "Maddie?"

"Be right there." Quickly, she creamed off her ruined makeup and opted not to bother with more.

She'd heard sex, when done right, was a hot, sweaty business. Surely Max would do it right, so perhaps makeup would be useless anyway.

Trying to look sexy and tempting, she floated out of the bedroom toward where Max stood at her picture window overlooking the main street. Both he and the dog were now more wet than ever. Cleo saw her first and got so outraged at the sight of her that she began bouncing as well as barking.

Max turned and attempted to calm the dog. *"Cleo."* Then he caught sight of Maddie and whatever else he'd intended to say never came out. She was sure she saw him gulp.

Cleo subsided, but not without a lot of grumbling. Almost defiantly, she went to Maddie's old, floral couch and climbed up—with a lot of effort—to spread out full length on the cushions. Even as her eyes closed, she continued to snarl.

Max cleared his throat. "I'm sorry. I'll get her down…"

"She's fine."

"She's wet."

Maddie shrugged. "The cushion covers are washable." Maddie looked at the dog, so worn out from all her nastiness and her fright of the storm. Even in her exhaustion, with her eyes closed and her round body looking like a boneless pile of scruffy fur with a head, her teeth showed in a low warning growl.

Maddie's heart softened. Speaking softly so as not to disturb Cleo, Maddie asked, "Do you think she's cold? I could get her an old blanket."

Looking a little bemused, Max walked toward

Maddie. "She's got plenty of fur to keep her warm."
Max stopped about a foot in front of her, well within
range, she decided. Doing her best to repress all her
old inhibitions, Maddie thought of what she might
learn tonight. Never again would a man take her by
surprise with his sexual preferences—like yellow
feathers. She looked at Max's mouth for added courage, took a couple of deep breaths, then launched
herself at him.

Taken off guard, Max fell back a step with the
impact of her body. "What the—"

Maddie clasped his face, held on tight and found
his mouth with her own.

*Not bad at all,* Maddie thought, and scoffed at
her initial hesitation. He tasted even better than she
expected. He tasted of experience, of sin incarnate,
of a man who knew what he was about. A man who
loved women and his dog.

He tasted hot.

Maddie waited for raging lust to take control of
Max's body. She waited for his sexual instincts to
kick in. Her ex had always told her that men could
only take so much provocation, which was why he'd
been driven to cheat.

So she waited.

Then she felt Max's smile against her mouth.

Well heck! Maddie opened her eyes to look at
him. Not only wasn't he overcome with lust, it appeared he was about to laugh.

Max's first thought was that she knew next to
nothing about kissing, and his second was how soft

she felt. His third thought was that if Cleo woke up, there'd be hell to pay.

Cleo didn't like other females to touch him.

Of course, the fact that she had gone to sleep in a stranger's place showed she was somewhat at ease with the newly introduced woman, and that shocked the hell out of Max.

If only Maddie wasn't against marriage.

Max held still, a little surprised, a little amused, a little turned on. He didn't kiss Maddie back as she smooshed her mouth against his, but neither did he push her away. He smiled, thinking how determined she seemed.

Around panting breaths, Maddie asked, "What's wrong?"

The words brushed his lips, heated with excitement, touched with anxiety. It was a potent combination. Max clasped her shoulders and held her back enough that he could breathe. "Oh, did you require my participation?"

"Well…" She looked uncertain. "Yeah."

He couldn't stop himself from caressing her, feeling the smallness of her bones, her softness. For such a gutsy, outspoken woman she was amazingly lacking in knowledge. "I take it my sister has been filling your head with her astounding seduction tactics?"

Maddie nodded.

It was almost laughable, only he couldn't quite seem to get so much as a chuckle past the lump of lust in his throat. It was like the blind leading the blind. "Why, Maddie?"

"Why what?"

"Why are you attacking… I mean *seducing* me?"

She blinked uncertainly. "Because I want you?"

"You aren't sure?" Max struggled to ignore the feel of her soft body against his while he tried to figure out what was going on. Even as brazen as she behaved, Maddie didn't strike him as the type of woman to jump into bed with men she barely knew. Not that he knew her well. But he knew enough. She said she'd been engaged, and he'd already witnessed what a giving, understanding woman she was. She treated Cleo as gently as he did.

Max narrowed his eyes. He was beginning to think he'd been set up from the start.

"I'm positive." She nodded again for good measure. "I want you."

He felt compelled to tell her the obvious. "I know women really well, Maddie."

Her lips parted. "I'm counting on it."

She looked so damn ready, Max shook her. "I mean, you little schemer, that I know when they're conspiring. You, Maddie Montgomery, are up to something."

If a man had written to him in the column with this exact situation, his advice would be to run like hell. But then, Max was only good at giving advice; he'd never been any good at taking it.

Maddie shrugged. "As you said, seduction."

Max was still skeptical. "And that's all?"

She took him completely by surprise when she said, "Why else would I have been out on such a miserable day like today? I planned the whole thing. Well, not the *whole* thing. I hadn't figured on hitting a closed door and ending up at your feet, or having my clothes play peekaboo. I just thought, what with the rain and all, I'd be stranded and you could offer me a ride home...."

"And we'd end up exactly where we are?"

"Sorta. I had figured on having you naked and in my bed by now."

Max forced himself to laugh. A nice, hearty male laugh of superiority that hid his surge of lust. "Your plans went a tad awry, didn't they?"

"I wanted to meet you face to face. After all the wonderful stories Annie's told me about you, I already felt like I knew you. I definitely knew I wanted you. So I suppose I can't complain."

She just kept knocking him off guard, Max thought, disgruntled. "So you didn't really want the book at all?" He was almost relieved. The thought of any woman reading such a ridiculous text made him shudder.

"Of course I want the book. It sounds fascinating and I'm looking forward to every word."

Max groaned.

Hearing the sound of his frustration, Maddie leaned forward and touched his shoulder, her eyes earnest. "But I wanted to meet you more than I want the book."

Max rubbed a hand across his forehead. "So you could seduce me?"

"Yeah."

Plenty of women had come on to him, but none had thrown themselves against a door, gotten drenched in the rain or cozied up to his dog.

It was the last that was getting to him more than anything else.

It ate him up to see how loving she could be; she was just what Cleo needed—another person to care about her, to make her feel loved. Yet Maddie said she didn't want marriage. What a situation. A suitable woman was close at hand, begging for sex, loving his dog, and Max felt forced to reject her because she didn't want a lasting relationship. Talk about the vagaries of fate!

"It occurs to me," Max pointed out, "that you could have just about any man. You're attractive—"

"Why thank you."

"And nicely built."

She beamed at him.

"So why chase me?"

Maddie took another step closer to him. "Because you're not just any man, Max. You're a man of experience, a man with an awesome reputation. I've been good all my life and look what it got me. A guy who preferred kinky feathers to me. Now I want to know about feathers! I want to know…*everything.*"

"I hate to break it to you, but feathers aren't really all that kinky."

"You didn't see where she was tickling him!"

Max coughed, then decided to let that one go. "So, you want to use me to notch your bedpost, huh?"

She bobbed her head, her look endearingly sincere.

The idea should have been appealing to just about any red-blooded male, so why did Max feel so offended?

"All because your idiot fiancé fooled around on you?"

"It was so humiliating. I just didn't have the experience to deal with it, so I stammered and stuttered and made an idiot of myself." She shuddered with the memory. "I wish I had just left him tied there."

Her grumbling tone made Max smile. "What *did* you do?"

She snorted. "I'm ashamed to say I just stood there, staring. I couldn't think of a single word to say, and then the woman screeched and grabbed her coat and ran off."

"Just like that?"

Maddie nodded. "She left the feather behind. Troy was, as I'm sure you'll understand, in a rather awkward position."

Now that was a picture Max could enjoy. It was no less than the dishonorable blockhead deserved. "How long did you make him suffer?"

Maddie blushed.

"Maddie?" Max bent to see her averted face. True, he hadn't known her long. But he had a gut feeling that despite her declaimed lack of experience with such situations, Maddie would have found a way of getting even. "C'mon. Give."

She cleared her throat. "I went out to dinner."

Max grinned, pleased by her creativity.

"And a movie," she added with a wince.

Laughing, Max asked, "What'd you see?"

"I don't remember. I barely paid any attention. I was just trying to decide how to get Troy out of my apartment." She peeked up at him, all big blue eyes and innocence. "I thought about calling a friend to untie him, but then I didn't think Guy would appreciate it if I asked Annie to get that close—"

"No! That would have been a bad idea."

"I know. You're protective of your sister. I think that's nice." She patted his chest absently in approval, then said, "I finally just decided that I had to be adult enough to deal with it. So I went back. Troy started cursing me and threatening me the second I walked in, so I went to the kitchen and got a big butcher knife."

"You didn't...?" Max saw her wicked smile and relaxed.

"Scare him to death? Sure. It was no more than he deserved. He went from cursing to pleading. But then when I cut his right hand free and he realized he was safe enough, he went right back to being obnoxious."

Max saw something in her eyes, something wounded. Of course her vanity had been crushed. Gently, he touched her chin. "What did he say to you?"

"Typical drivel coming from a man who's had to hold his bladder for four and a half hours. He blamed me for everything." She shrugged. "Not woman enough, not sexy enough, too naive, too prim, blah, blah, blah."

Max flexed his fists, wishing he could get alone with the jerk for just a few minutes. It was no wonder Maddie was out to prove her sexuality. "I hope you didn't give his words a second thought."

She shook her head. "He was scum and I told him so. It took a lot of nerve for him to try to fob the guilt off on me." Her face red, Maddie started to raise her voice, and Cleo yawned. She cast an affectionate glance at the dog and began whispering again. "I decided to look at the nasty scene—and the nasty man—as an omen."

Max was touched by her feminine strength. No doubt about it, Maddie Montgomery was one helluva woman. "An omen, huh? How so?"

"Troy's faux pas was nature's way of telling me that I need to expand my horizons before I think about settling down. Without experience, it's no wonder I made such a bad mate choice. I mean, it takes practice to figure out what you really want. And with more experience, I'll be better able to empathize on the job with the women I talk to, and better equipped to handle the men I might see in the future."

"I see." He didn't see at all, and he didn't like the idea of her with other men. "You want to start practicing with me?"

Looking pleased that he understood, Maddie smiled. "Yes! You'll be the first of my wild oats!"

A thought occurred to Max. "Will you tell your fiancé what you're doing?"

"No, why?" She appeared puzzled by the question. "And Troy's not my fiancé anymore. He's an ex. What I do or don't do isn't any of his business."

"Are you sure you aren't planning to make him jealous?" Not that he'd blame her, Max thought, but he hoped she was well and truly over the fool.

"Well, I'd certainly accomplish that! I mean, look at you." Her gaze drifted over Max from sternum to knees, like a sensuous lick. She took a deep breath that mirrored his own. "You'd sure make any guy jealous."

"Uh, thank you."

Maddie shook herself. "But that's not what I'm going to do. Why should I? I'm not an idiot. Troy can indulge in all the feather tickling he wants, so long as he does it away from me. He's of no concern to me at all anymore."

Max accepted her sincerity.

"But," she added, "if you're worried about getting into a hostile confrontation with him, you don't need to be. I would never let him bother you, I promise."

Max immediately rebelled. "I wasn't worried about a confrontation and I certainly don't need you to protect me." He probably weighed a hundred pounds more than Maddie, and he sure as hell wasn't concerned about some idiot who indulged a feather fetish.

Maddie patted his chest again, then caressed him, then sighed. "I understand. You're a lover, not a fighter." Her patting hand was now stroking, driving him to distraction. "But that's all I want you for anyway, so it's not a problem."

That was *all* she wanted him for? How insulting! He was good for more than just sex, dammit. Feeling more like his dog by the second, Max growled, "I am *not* afraid of a fight."

"Shh." She attempted to soothe him, her small hands gliding over his chest, lower...

Max caught her wrists. He was breathing hard, his muscles aching. She stirred him, aroused him and annoyed him. "Dammit, Maddie." How the hell did she affect him so easily?

There was no easy way to break it to her, except to be brutally honest. The sooner the better, before he lost his thin hold on control. "I'm sorry, sweetheart, but the simple fact of the matter is, I'm not interested."

She snorted. "Yeah right. Annie says you're always interested."

He would strangle Annie when next he saw her. "Maybe a month ago I would have been. But things have changed."

Maddie's face fell. "You don't want me."

He cupped her cheek, let his thumb brush the soft fullness of her lower lip. "Oh, I want you all right. You can be sure of that." Max felt her uncertainty all the way to his bones. Here he was, shaking with lust, and she doubted her allure.

She stared at him, not comprehending for a long moment, and then suddenly she smacked her head. "I understand now!"

He almost hated to ask. Her assumptions had been so far off the mark all along, he wasn't sure he wanted to hear her newest revelation concerning his character. Resigned, he asked, "What is it you think you understand this time?"

"When we were discussing the book! You were totally confused about the whole thing."

"I was not."

"Don't look so indignant." She gave him a pitying look. "I know how reputations can get blown all out of proportion. I should have realized that no man could be so awesomely adept. It's almost absurd."

Max was ready to defend his awesome adeptness, but Maddie wasn't done explaining things to him.

"You don't have to worry about my expectations, Max. If you don't know everything, that's okay. It's not like I'm going to keep a scorecard. Heck, I don't know much, either, so I doubt I'd even notice if you screw up."

For the first time in years, embarrassed heat ran up the back of his neck. "Why, you little—"

She waved away his umbrage. "I'm sure we'll muddle through." Then, as if getting a brainstorm, she added, "The book could probably help! Besides, I just want to experiment and you're gorgeous and there must be at least a little truth to your reputation, right? So I know I'll be inspired."

Max saw her through a red haze. He squeezed the words out of his tight throat. "You expect us to… muddle through?"

"If need be, you can just lie there. I won't expect you to perform."

Max stared at the ceiling while he counted to ten. And then to twenty. Oh, it was *so* damn tempting to show her everything he knew, methods of seduction he'd learned in foreign countries and at home, all the different ways he could make her body sing.

And all the ways he could make her beg.

Men who read his column wrote to him for advice, and got the very best. Then women sent him letters of gratitude.

And this woman expected him to *muddle through?*

He met her gaze again, outwardly calm while inside he seethed. "You're not even close, honey."

"Uh-huh."

His temper cracked, then crumbled. "Stop sounding so damn skeptical!"

She pursed her lips in a wasted attempt at obedience. Max wasn't sure if he wanted to kiss her or throttle her. Both choices seemed equally appealing. "I have valid reasons," he managed to say with a semblance of calm, "for not wanting to get into another purely sexual relationship, and not one of them has to do with lack of expertise or fear of a physical confrontation."

"Is that right?"

"Damn right."

"And those reasons are?"

Max opened his mouth twice, but nothing came out. What could he possibly tell her? That he wanted to settle down for his dog? That one mangy beat-up mutt—a mutt now snuffling and snoring loudly on the couch—had accomplished what no woman could?

Even to his own mind, it sounded ludicrous.

He stalled for time until his brain started functioning again, then said with laudable nonchalance, "I don't travel anymore."

That took the wind out of her sails. "Why ever not?"

"I've been just about everywhere, seen just about everything."

She looked fascinated, a sentiment that reflected his own when it came to exploring the world. "Annie says you sometimes stayed gone for months. How did you support yourself?"

Such a personal question, although he appreciated her candor, her honest interest. "I worked."

"In foreign countries?"

"And in the States." He shrugged as he explained, "There's always something to be done, new building efforts in war-torn or natural disaster areas, odd jobs here and there. I've signed on to fishing vessels and cargo ships and done excursions for tourist kayaking in Alaska. And I've been an interpreter at the Olympic Games in Japan."

Her eyes were so huge, so impressed, Max felt himself puffing up. The only thing he'd ever missed in all his traveling was someone to share it with. He wondered if Maddie knew how much money he'd saved over the years, that he thrived on traveling without luxuries, living off the land instead. It was a cheap way to go, and because of that, he had quite a healthy savings account.

"Recently I decided it was time to settle down. And," Max said, expounding on his explanation though he wasn't certain why, "I have new responsibilities that keep me closer to home."

Her mouth formed an O. "Annie said something about Guy needing you to take your rightful place in the family company, but she didn't think you ever would. I'm glad she was wrong. She said it really hurt your father that you didn't want any part of the business."

Poleaxed, Max went speechless. It was true that Guy had asked him to come to work in the company, but he'd repeatedly refused. What could he contribute that his father and Guy hadn't already given? Max would only be another warm body, and there were plenty of those to go around. He had nothing unique, nothing special that the company *needed* from him. In fact, he'd never felt needed there, and he refused to feel needed now just because Guy was marrying.

"Actually," he said, slightly annoyed, "it's not that I have no interest in the company. It's just that I already have a job."

"Doing what?"

Max ignored her. His column was personal, and anonymous. And it took up very little of his time, so it wouldn't be a good example anyway. "With each new development comes another. I'm no longer traveling, and I'm no longer looking for meaningless relationships."

She drew herself up. "I don't think I like being referred to as meaningless."

"I didn't mean..." Max knew if he lived to be a hundred, he'd never be this frustrated again. "Maddie, getting together just to notch bedposts would be meaningless."

"A relationship based on devastating sex would be very meaningful to me!"

Exasperated, Max said, "So now I'm supposed to make the sex devastating when seconds ago you promised me I could just lie there?"

She blinked in surprise, then shrugged. "So I lied. I was trying to convince you. Truth is, I want you mobile and participating."

"You want me to be devastating?"

"Could you?"

Max almost smiled at the sweet, polite way she asked that. Droll, now that he felt in better control, he said, "It'd be a tall order—not that I'm not up to it, you understand."

"I'm not sure what to understand! One minute you claim all this great prowess, and the next you're running shy and saying you're not interested in a sexy affair."

"To a man who's had his fill of them," Max explained with ruthless and entirely false candor, "it sounds boring." She started to speak again, so he reiterated, "I-am-not-interested."

"I don't believe you."

Stubbornness made her eyes darken to midnight blue. Max cursed because he found her expression oddly appealing. Would her eyes go that dark when she was in the throes of a climax? When he was buried deep inside her?

Would she be this talkative, this argumentative, in bed? Or would she be sweetly submissive when he gave her the awesome sex she'd requested?

Those thoughts caused him to overstep himself, to admit more than he'd intended. "Look, it's not like I said I was becoming a monk or something. It's just that I want to settle down, to find a wife—"

She slapped her hand over his mouth. "That's not funny!"

Max pried her hand away, noticing how slim and cool her fingers felt in his. "Not funny, but true. I want a wife."

"Then why aren't you married already? According to Annie, women throw themselves at you."

"I have very precise requirements."

"Oh."

She looked crestfallen, but he had no idea why. "I'm sorry to disappoint you, sweetheart. I really am."

He started to tell her she'd have no problem finding someone else to play with, but the words stuck in his craw. She shouldn't be playing with anyone. She should be a man's wife so she could share all that fire, all that caring, for a lifetime, not just for the duration of an affair.

Maddie turned around and paced away. Max watched the slight sway and bounce of her rounded behind, the way her hips moved seductively, and called himself ten times a fool. The woman was delectable, no doubt about it.

He also reread the decorative letters on her back. *Freshly Plucked.*

Just what the hell did that mean?

"If you want to get married," she said, sounding strangled, "that's fine with me. Hey, more power to you. But why not have fun until you've found your paragon to wed? Unless of course—" She didn't turn to face him while she made her gibe "—I managed to scare you off?"

She waited, not looking at him, and even though Max knew it was a tactic meant to make him relent, he couldn't stand the challenge. She'd struck at the core of his manhood one time too many.

It was past time he got control not only of his raging libido, but little Maddie Montgomery as well.

# Chapter 3

Max crept up behind her, determined to set her straight, to make her learn the error of taunting his testicularity, which he had in spades. Hell, he *oozed* testicularity, blast her—and the loyal followers of his column could swear to it.

She was still unaware of his approach when Max whispered near her ear, "You could hardly scare me off when you kiss like a nervous schoolgirl."

Maddie gasped, her shoulders stiffening.

It was his own form of attack, and though he'd only known her a few short hours, he already knew she had pride and gumption—which was why she was determined to win with him. Her fiancé had wounded her, and she wanted to reassure herself the only way she knew how.

It was a contradiction of sorts, but he was glad she'd chosen him rather than some other man. The thing to do now was to reel her in for more than a quick tussel.

"I never claimed to be overly experienced," she stated, then asked worriedly, "Was I really that bad?"

"You showed no subtlety, sweetheart. No finesse." Determined to hide the tenderness he felt, Max added, "I felt mauled."

She started to turn to face him, but Max caught her shoulders and held her still. "Don't berate me. You claimed I was running scared, but you know that's not true. In fact, I'd say you're the overly nervous one, given the awkward, rushed way you jumped my bones."

"They're such nice bones, Max, I couldn't resist."

With comments like that, *she* was the one who was hard to resist!

Hesitation lacing her voice, she said, "I promise I'll control myself in the future."

Max didn't really want her to control herself. No, he wanted to get to know her better, to talk to her—and *then* she could jump his bones.

He needed to find a way to make her feel as intrigued as he did. He needed her to want more from him than just his sexual techniques—stellar as he knew those to be.

Close to her ear, he whispered, "I'm not afraid of any woman putting her hands on me. That's not it at all. In fact, I already told you the reason—lack of interest in a brief fling." He could feel her tension, her excitement, vibrating all along his nerve endings.

He stroked her arm. "But now I feel challenged to set you straight on your assumptions."

He heard her swallow. Good. "Should I demonstrate my lack of reserve, Maddie?"

Expecting outrage at his taunt, she surprised him by saying, "Yes."

Laughing softly at her wholehearted agreement, anticipating his little lesson more than he should have, Max bent to press his mouth to the side of her throat in a barely there kiss. He was starting to realize that Maddie would always manage to take him by surprise. It wasn't an unpleasant realization.

"Always go slow," Max whispered. "It helps to heighten the expectation."

He kissed her again, this time letting his tongue slip over her madly racing pulse. Her need to reassert herself, to prove her appeal, was mixed with the sweetest vulnerability he'd ever witnessed. She was audacious but caring, honest and earthy. Her skin was warm and getting warmer by the second, and she tasted nice.

Maddie braced her hands, fingers spread wide, on the wall in front of her. Max saw that she was trembling and more than anything he wanted to simply hug her, to tell her that there was no real rush. But he gave her just a little of what she'd asked for instead. With any luck, she'd realize on her own that a little more time would only make things better.

He skimmed her ear, his tongue briefly touching just inside, teasing. He heard her breath catch.

"You put your tongue in my ear!"

Max hesitated. "Yes."

Her sigh was long and heartfelt. "That was...nice. I hadn't realized..."

Shaking his head at her ex-fiancé's apparent stupidity, Max licked her ear again. Goose bumps raised on her skin. "A smart man always knows to take his time. The more frenzied stuff," he breathed, "can come later."

"More frenzied stuff?"

Her voice was hopeful. Max peeked at her face and saw that her eyes were squeezed shut. He smiled, and loosened her right hand from the wall. Lacing his fingers with hers, he brought her hand up to his mouth. "Sexual tension should build and build, and yes, it often ends up frenzied. Didn't you and your fiancé...?"

"Ex-fiancé. Yes, we did, but it wasn't *frenzied.* More like..." She searched for a word, then settled on, "Mundane." Her voice was low, breathy. "I guess I liked it okay."

Max vowed she wouldn't be left in his bed *liking it okay.*

Her hand tightened on his. "The thing is, Annie swears to me—"

"Forget about my sister and whatever harebrained things she told you. Annie likely has even less experience than you." Under his breath, Max muttered, "Or at least she did before Guy succumbed."

"She's read a lot of books," Maddie pointed out.

"And has been suggesting them to you?"

"Yes, but I like the idea of firsthand experience much better."

*I just bet you do,* Max thought, then got started

on his instruction again. "Never neglect the less obvious places."

"Okay, right." She looked at him over her shoulder. "What less obvious places?"

Biting back a chuckle, Max cuddled her closer to his body. He drifted his free hand up to cup just below the soft weight of her left breast. "Everyone knows that women's breasts are sensitive, right?"

"Yes."

Max could feel her heartbeat thumping, knew she was nervous because despite her bravado, she wasn't accustomed to throwing herself at men. If her fiancé hadn't done her wrong, she wouldn't be here now.

Slowly, tantalizingly, he coasted his fingers down to her belly. "And here." Damn, she felt wonderful. Soft and firm and her musky female scent was beginning to get to him. Her hair, still slightly damp, felt cool and silky against his jaw. Max was aware of her stomach muscles clenching, of her suspended breathing.

"And lower?" she rasped hopefully, bringing him out of his fog of sexual need.

"Definitely lower." His voice was too rough, too affected by her nearness. "But that comes much, much later." Like in a week or more, he thought, if he could last that long! "There are other places to visit first, places that can really excite, too."

"But not like lower." She tried to sound insistent and even went so far as to squirm against him.

She sorely tested his resolve. But Max could hear Cleo snoring in the background, which helped to keep his purpose at the forefront of his mind. Cleo needed a stable home, and Maddie seemed perfect to assist in that. She was the only woman he'd ever met who'd understood the dog right off. She'd make a perfect mother for Cleo.

Max wanted to move slowly enough that Maddie would insist on seeing him again. And again, until she got over her determination to be footloose and fancy-free. Until she was ready to go one further and really get to know him.

Max smiled. "Let me show you something." He lifted her arm and slowly kissed her wrist, deliberately leaving it damp from his tongue.

"Okay," she gasped, "that's great. But—"

Before she could continue, he kissed her palm, gently stroking with the very tip of his tongue, again leaving her heated skin damp, letting his warm breath fan the spot.

She gave a humming response.

He wanted to show her how nice going slow could be, but he didn't want to get overly intimate doing it. Cautiously, deliciously, Max sucked her middle finger into his mouth.

Maddie nearly jumped out of his arms. *"Oh my."*

He wrapped his tongue around her finger and tugged. Kissing her, experiencing her unrehearsed response, was a distinct joy. He wanted more, of her body, her time. Her affection for his dog.

And he always got what he wanted, one way or another.

Shifting restlessly, Maddie pressed her bottom into his growing erection. "Max," she breathed.

Realizing he'd gone a little too far, that she'd been

more susceptible to his brief seduction than he'd expected, Max released her and stepped back. He had to catch her so she wouldn't fall.

Stumbling around, Maddie faced him. "You *have* read the book," she accused. Her eyes were heavy, her face flushed. "You know exactly what you're doing."

Max caught her gaze and held it. "I don't need to read the damn book."

She didn't look convinced. "Whatever. It doesn't matter to me, as long as you agree to a fling with me."

One side of his mouth kicked up into a regretful grin. She was so persistent and so entertaining. And so sweet. He wanted to say yes. "I already explained that I can't."

Shoulders stiff, lips tight, she said, "You're a tease, Max Sawyers!" Her face flushed darkly and her eyes glittered. "They surely have a name for men like you."

"Yeah," Max said. "It's 'experienced.'" He refused to take all the blame when she'd more or less dared him. And besides, it had only been her finger he kissed, not all the places where he really wanted to put his mouth.

His heart kick-started with that thought.

While Max watched, that calculating look came into her eyes and they narrowed, the blue getting brighter, hotter. She was so easy to read.

Sort of.

"I believe you're more than up to it."

Max bowed his head, a man accepting female accolades. "Of course." Now all he needed was for her to agree to his terms.

"And it's obvious you're not immune to me as a woman." Her gaze dropped to his lap, a look that was nearly tactile and as hot as a live flame. "I mean, I don't think you're carrying a roll of dimes in your pocket, are you?"

Forget his terms! Max's growl of outrage sounded in the room. "A *roll of dimes?*"

She shrugged.

"More like a flashlight!"

"Size, I assume," she said with a sniff, "is in the eye of the beholder."

"And you haven't beheld a damn thing yet, so don't go calling a man's business 'small.'" With a low growl, Max considered showing her just how impressive his... No, bad thought. He was struggling to resist her, not give in to her.

Maddie stared at him hard, knowing she'd almost won. "Small, large, it doesn't matter when you continue to refuse my very nice offer."

It *was* a nice offer, Max conceded, and just a few months ago he'd have accepted without hesitation. "Why such a rush, Maddie?" he asked, buying himself time to think.

That endearing vulnerability flashed into her gaze again before she squelched it with a come-hither look. "I'm twenty-six. I've been good all my life and now all I've got to show for it is a broken engagement that I'd rather forget and a lot of time on my hands."

"So why pick me?" Max hoped to hear something complimentary, something meaningful.

He was doomed to disappointment.

"I know all about you! Annie has told me so much. Ever since I met her, I've been enthralled with the stories about you. You're everything I'm not."

That surprised him. "Like what?"

"Exciting, experienced, daring. I've lived my whole life being a Goody Two-Shoes, and in my profession, that isn't really a plus. Evidently it wasn't a plus in my personal life, either."

"Your broken engagement," Max said gently, "is a blessing, I'd say."

"And I agree! But now that I'm free, it only makes sense to gain my own experiences. As you suggested, I'll have a better perspective for the job, and I'll have fun, too." She lowered her lashes, her look now timid when she added, "Besides, I sort of feel like I know you, because of Annie. Being with you feels...safe."

Max suddenly realized he was taking the wrong tact with Maddie. She was reacting on the rebound, doing what she could to counteract the embarrassing feather episode. Her haste was probably due in part to the fact that she might chicken out if she didn't rush through things.

Perhaps Maddie would forget about the *brief* part of the fling if he showed her how sexually satisfying a real relationship would be.

That idea appealed a whole lot more than walking away did. He didn't want to walk away; he *did* want to make love to her.

Why not? Maddie suited his criteria. She did her

best to nurture his dog, she wanted lots of sex, and she was cute to boot.

He'd be holding up his promise to Cleo, and satisfying himself in the bargain. What more could a guy ask for?

He needed more time to consider the possibility of roping Maddie into marriage, but he had a gut feeling that once she was roped, she'd be incredibly loyal and giving. And she'd love Cleo. Maybe she'd even learn to love him.

That thought was far too heavy for his peace of mind, so Max decided to just enjoy dinner, and see what happened. For sure, Maddie wouldn't bore him.

Then his gaze again drifted to Maddie's breasts, and he got blessedly distracted. "You know, I'm just dying for you to tell me what all these suggestive slogans mean. *In Full Bloom, Freshly Plucked.* And earlier, your shirt said *I Give Good Peach.*"

Since Max was already thinking in possessive terms, jealousy nudged him and he asked darkly, "Do you want to have an affair with *me,* or are you hoping to turn on the entire male population?"

Maddie attempted to calm the mad gallop of her heartbeat. But it wasn't easy because Max was staring at her breasts and even though he sounded unaccountably annoyed, his rough voice stroked over her sensitized nerve endings like a slow kiss.

The way he'd touched her… Her finger would never feel the same. Even now, she realized she was holding it out apart from the rest of her hand. It was still damp, still tingling.

It was just a damn finger.

Maddie cleared her throat, determined to be as cavalier as Max. "Bea, one of the women I work with at the clinic, creates slogans for clothes." Talking normally was difficult, but Maddie thought she managed credibly.

"This was one for a florist, and a big hit, I might add. It was used as a giveaway when you ordered a certain amount of flowers and it drew in a lot of the younger crowd. Wedding orders came in like crazy."

Dryly, Max said, "I can imagine."

"The other one was for an independent company that created specialty jams."

"Specialty, as in peach jam?"

"That's right. And passion fruit—the slogan for that one is awesome—and kiwi, and wild blackberry, too." Maddie looked down at the dress that she knew complimented her figure but hadn't been enough to win Max over. "I think the slogans are nice."

"I think they sound downright nasty."

Maddie laughed at that, then dredged up another taunt. With any luck, he'd decide to prove himself to her again. "To a man who's afraid to submit to his baser side, it makes sense that the slogans would intimidate you."

Far from appearing amorous, Max looked ready to strangle her. "I am not intimidated!"

Maddie sighed. She knew he wasn't. He also wasn't the unconscionable playboy she'd imagined. No, Max Sawyers was a gentle man who loved his dog and had an innate honor that caused him to turn her down repeatedly.

He wanted to go slow, but going slow meant getting to know him, and already she liked him far too much. The more time she spent with him, the more risk to her heart.

She didn't want to care about another man. Glancing at Cleo snoring on the couch, Maddie decided it was bad enough to care about a man's dog. If she let it go any further than that, she could end up with her pride butchered beyond repair.

No, she wouldn't allow herself to get roped in like that again. If Troy with his limited experience had played with feathers, there was no telling what a man like Max played with—other than women's hearts. Getting overly involved with him would be like jumping from the frying pan into a raging inferno.

She was just about to let Max off the hook, to concede defeat, when he asked belligerently, "Were you just kidding about dinner, or do you intend to feed me?"

Her spirits lifted. "Can you be bribed with food?"

"No."

Despite her disappointment, she laughed. His honesty delighted her; she knew without a doubt that Max would always be truthful with her; his sister was right about that. He might be a confirmed bachelor, but he was an honorable one. "I'll feed you. Would you like to help me in the kitchen?"

"Will you behave?"

"Heavens, no!" Maddie winked at him, enjoying the banter between them. Never had she carried on so before, and it was fun. Not as much fun as she was sure an affair would be, but still very enjoyable. "I had no idea that becoming a vamp would be so enjoyable."

"You're not a vamp yet, Maddie," Max said with a growl reminiscent of Cleo in a malcontent mood. Not that Cleo appeared to *have* any other moods.

Maddie patted his shoulder. "Come on. You can tell me about your travels while I cook, and we'll both, unfortunately, behave."

An hour later Maddie had dinner ready to be served. Max had surprised her by being more help than she'd expected. Not only wasn't he a shallow playboy with only personal gratification on his mind, but the man knew his way around a kitchen. One more thing to like about him, she thought, and frowned at the idea. Liking him was *not* part of the plan.

As she set the food on the table, Maddie heard a noise from the couch and saw Cleo's nose move first. Then her front left paw. Her stubby legs started jerking as if she were trying to run to the table, but her eyes were still closed.

Maddie laughed out loud. "She's so fat, and still so attuned to the smell of food."

Max grinned, too. Softly, so softly Maddie barely heard, he said, "Cleo," and the dog's small head jerked up, her too large ears rising to attention. "Food," was his only other word, and Cleo instantly lumbered off the couch and to Max's side, to sit next to his chair.

Rubbing the dog's scruff, Max explained, "She

was near starved when I found her. Since then, she eats like a glutton."

Hearing that brought a glitter of tears to Maddie's eyes. With a wavering smile, she reprimanded Max. "She's like a little kid with too many treats. Sometimes overindulgence isn't the best way to prove love. Look at her. She needs more exercise and less food. Or at least buy her food that won't make her any heftier."

So saying, Maddie began cutting up some skinless chicken into bite-size pieces. Max watched her with a curious little grin on his face. "You should have a dog of your own, Maddie."

"I would if I could afford one," she assured him. For the longest time she'd wanted a dog and a cat and a house—and a husband and children of her own. Maddie shook her head—that plan had come and gone. She said negligently, hiding the remnant of longing, "My salary doesn't allow for a lot of extras. And I'd never get a dog if I couldn't take care of her properly."

Max said nothing to that, but he had a strange look on his face.

"C'mere girl," Maddie called, then set the plate on the floor. When Cleo growled and snarled her way over to her, Maddie smoothed down her fur. "I think the local pet shop sells special food for overweight dogs."

Max shook his head. "She doesn't like dog food."

"Then disguise it with some chicken or something she does like for a while. You know it's best for her."

His gaze locked on hers, Max said quietly, "I can't believe you're really worried about her."

"Who knows," Maddie said around a laugh, "maybe her disposition will improve when she feels healthier. Do you walk her every day?"

"In the park."

Giving her attention to her plate so Max wouldn't see her yearning, Maddie said offhandedly, "Maybe I could join you both sometime."

"Maybe."

Jerking her head up, Maddie stared at him. "You mean it?"

"Sure, why not? You, Maddie Montgomery, just keep amazing me."

Why that made her blush, Maddie didn't know. It probably had something to do with the way he said it, with a hint of admiration and a look of lust in his eyes. At least to her it looked like lust. Not that she was an expert, just very, very hopeful.

She also wasn't used to praise, and certainly not that kind of praise. So she amazed him, hmm? "Enough to give in? Enough to put me out of my misery, to want to be the first notch on my bedpost?"

To her amazement, he didn't immediately refuse. Instead, Max thoughtfully chewed a bite of chicken, then swallowed a drink of milk before finally saying, "It's possible."

Maddie's eyes widened until she thought they'd drop out of her head. *It's possible* was a whole lot more encouraging than *I'm not interested.* Progress, she decided, and throughout the rest of the meal, she barely tasted her food.

Once Cleo realized the food was all gone and the humans wouldn't be handing her any more scraps, she slunk off to sleep on the couch again. Maddie watched her go, noticing that she moved even slower now than she had before being fed. When she lay down, her body looked twice as wide, spread out on Maddie's couch. Cleo was one lazy dog.

"What are you thinking, Maddie?"

Red with guilt, Maddie turned to Max and admitted, "I was thinking of conniving a way to get Cleo on a diet."

Rather than being angry or insulted, he nodded. "Good luck. If you can find a way to get her to eat the good stuff, I'd be indebted. My vet mentioned a diet last time we were in—"

At the word "vet," Cleo jerked awake, then fell off the couch during a vehement snarling jag. She looked surprised and embarrassed to find herself sprawled on the floor.

Max just shook his head, but Maddie leaped from the table and ran to the distraught dog. Despite Cleo's furious barking, Maddie cuddled her close and hugged her. "Shh. It's all right."

Cleo, going quiet in a heartbeat, looked as flummoxed as Max. Maddie ignored them both. She hated to see anyone or anything afraid.

She pressed her face against Cleo's scruffy neck and said again, "It's all right."

Very slowly, as if half afraid to move, Cleo began crawling toward Max with her belly scraping the floor. She kept casting worried, suspicious glances at Maddie, and Maddie kept pace with her, scooting along on her knees until they were both at Max's feet.

Maddie released the dog and saw that Cleo was staring up at Max, her expression a request for aid. It was obvious Cleo had no idea how to deal with Maddie's affection, which reminded Maddie of the women she worked with, how they'd first behaved when meeting her.

Many of them had moved on with their lives, happier, more content. The few that Maddie still saw now loved her, as she loved them. She hoped the same outcome was possible with Cleo.

Max laughed out loud and Maddie sat back on her haunches, shaking her head at both dog and man. "She still doesn't trust me."

"I beg to differ. She doesn't know what to make of you at all." Max patted one knee. Maddie started to move, but Cleo beat her to it, and lumbered up onto his lap.

She sighed. Max's lap looked very comfortable. But there wasn't room for both of them.

Cleo gave Max one grateful lick on the chin, then looked back at Maddie with a worried frown. Her furry brows were pinched together, her teeth were showing, but for once, not in a snarl.

"You're covered in dog hair," Max pointed out as his gaze slipped over Maddie's breasts.

"Oh." Maddie looked down and attempted to brush herself off, but the last thing she was concerned with was a few dog hairs.

Setting Cleo aside, Max said, "Go lie down."

Maddie assumed he was speaking to the dog.

Cleo gladly retreated to the couch and again settled herself there, yawning and stretching and sighing in relaxation.

Maddie smiled. "Let's be very careful not to mention that 'v' word again. I don't like seeing her upset."

Without warning, Max caught her beneath her arms and pulled her upward until she was on her knees between his open thighs. It was a very nice place to be. Her face tilted up to his, her hands clasped his shoulders for balance.

Max stared at her mouth, and said huskily, "You've convinced me."

Maddie's heart leaped. She was half-afraid to believe what she hoped he meant by that. "Convinced you...of what?"

"That a sexual fling between us wouldn't be meaningless."

Her fingertips dug into his shoulders—nice solid shoulders—and she held on in case he suddenly changed his mind. "This means you're now willing?"

"Willing, able and anxious."

*Ohmigod, ohmigod, ohmigod.* "Tonight? Right now?"

Max glanced toward Cleo, heard her snoring, and smiled. "All right," he said gently, and his eyes seemed to be peering into her soul. "If you're certain that's what you want to do."

Maddie was more than certain. She was insistent. Fanatical even. "Yes."

Lifting her, Max brought her face up even with his. The new position caused Maddie's belly to flatten against his groin and she had to swallow back a groan. He was hard again! Or was it that he was hard *still?*

That thought made heat curl through her in dizzying intensity.

Max caught her gaze, refusing to let her look away until the very last second when his mouth touched hers. Her eyes drifted shut. The damp heat of his mouth, the sultry scent of his hard masculine body, the feel of his large rough hands, all consumed her.

Maddie's last thought was: *Finally!* And then she couldn't think at all.

# Chapter 4

Max tasted her deeply, ready and willing to fall off the deep end. Damn, he'd had no idea that watching a woman coddle his dog could be such an aphrodisiac. He loved Cleo, had loved her from the second she'd tried to bite him while he carried her off the road. Seeing someone else love her was a heady thing.

He hadn't known anything was missing from his life until he'd brought Cleo home.

He hadn't known anything was *still* missing from his life, until he'd seen Maddie press her face into Cleo's yellow fur and squeeze her so tight that the dog had no breath left to growl.

Cleo had looked helpless against the emotional onslaught. Her feelings had mirrored his own.

Something insidious and sweet and warm expanded in his chest the second Maddie went to her knees by the dog, making Max's heart feel full to bursting.

The more emotional feelings blended with the sharp sexual desire he'd been trying so hard to ignore, leaving him with no way to resist her.

Max's hands trembled as he held Maddie a tiny bit away from him. Her eyes were heavy, sexy, the blue heated to a midnight hue. Damn but he wanted her.

And he knew in his gut that it wasn't just physical desire, though physically he was so aroused his bragging about a lead pipe earlier was coming back to haunt him. He felt so heavy, his jeans were now painfully tight. But it was more than that; Maddie had nurtured his dog when no other woman even wanted to look at her, much less touch her.

Max had felt the dog's loneliness, her need for love behind her bristled warnings, and Maddie had seen it, too. She was a special woman, too special to let get away. He was already convinced that she'd be perfect to mother his dog. He had a feeling she'd be perfect for him, too. One way or another, he'd convince her to marry him.

What better way to start than by making her body need him?

Max brushed the corner of her mouth with the edge of his rough thumb. "Why don't you go get ready while I put our dishes away? I'll join you in five minutes."

Eyes wide, Maddie asked, "Umm… Get ready?"

She sounded scandalized, and Max couldn't help but grin. "You don't have to put on risqué lingerie or break out the oil. Just get rid of the excess dog hair clinging to your clothes. Maybe turn down the bed. That's all I meant." He added, "Most women like a few seconds alone to themselves."

She stared at him blankly and Max sighed. "You do have some sort of birth control on hand, don't you?"

"Uh…"

Max felt the urge to laugh with disbelief, or shout with frustration. "I gather by your long face that you don't?"

Maddie licked her lips. "I figured you carried condoms."

"Often I do. But not this time." Mostly because he knew the lack of protection would go a long way in deterring him from giving in. He was scrupulous about birth control, and didn't take chances. Period.

But now… "I could run to the drugstore."

Maddie's eyes were hungry as she stared at him. "How long will that take?"

"Half an hour, tops. Why? You have someplace to be?" The thought that another man might be waiting in the wings tonight did not sit well with Max.

Maddie shook her head so hard her long blond hair whipped against his leg. "No! I'm just…" She shrugged, then gave him a wavering smile. "Impatient."

Max touched her cheek again. He couldn't seem to stop touching her. Her honesty was another turn on, nearly driving him over the edge. "I'll be quick." *As quick as humanly possible!* "I still have your key so

I'll let myself back in. Go ahead and get ready and if Cleo wakes up, tell her I'll be right back."

Still she hesitated, and Max asked, "What is it?"

"You won't change your mind while you're gone?"

Tenderness exploded inside Max, mixing with the lust and the other swirl of emotions with combustible force until it was all he could do to force himself to his feet. He needed to join with her, and it was tempting to say to hell with protection. At the moment, lowering her to the floor and taking her right beside the table seemed like a grand idea.

"I won't change my mind," he promised.

The rain poured down in buckets soaking Max to the skin as he dashed to his truck. He drove faster than he should have, but for once it wasn't just Cleo waiting for him. No, now there was an adorable woman who displayed her brazen sexuality as often as she did her naiveté. He could barely wait to take her, to show her what her idiot fiancé obviously hadn't.

The lights from the all-night drugstore barely penetrated the constant rain. By the time Max was back in his truck with the paper bag on the seat beside him, every inch of him was dripping wet. Not that it mattered because he expected to be out of his clothes very soon. He was so hot, it was a wonder he wasn't steaming.

The apartment, as he let himself back inside, was quiet except for Cleo's snoring. Her back paws went through spasmodic jerks and her lips curled in a soundless howl as she dreamed of chasing some hapless critter. Max smiled affectionately.

In some ways, Cleo reminded him of Maddie. She was pushy and insistent one minute, in the next so sweet he wanted simply to hold her all night.

He couldn't hold Maddie all night. He'd have to leave so that Cleo was in her own home come morning. The dog had a problem that he doubted Maddie would care to experience.

If it wasn't for the doggy door Max had installed after the first two days of bringing Cleo home, all the carpets in his house would have been ruined. It wasn't Cleo's fault, so he'd never scolded her. She woke disoriented and nervous, and would run in circles trying to find her way out. Anytime she'd had an accident, she had looked heartsick about it, and strangely enough, embarrassed. So Max had ended up comforting her rather than scolding her.

As soon as Cleo had figured out the doggy door, she'd learned to hold on until she got outside. She'd still run around, baffled for a while, but eventually she'd hit the door and find herself in the backyard where trees and shrubs beckoned.

Max smoothed his hand over the dog, settling her back into a deep sleep without pesky rabbits or birds to provoke her, then he looked toward Maddie's bedroom. A bright light shone from around the partially open door. Max's stomach tightened in anticipation.

There was only one bedroom in her apartment. It was a nice place, though very small. The kitchenette led into the tiny dining room that led into a sitting area with a small television and a stereo system. Her bookshelves were filled with books, rather than photos or bric-a-brac. Her reading material displayed her intelligence, and as he imagined *Satisfying Alternatives to Intercourse* joining her other more academic texts, he winced. Perhaps after a few days of play, she wouldn't need the book at all.

Everything was decorated in floral patterns—cream-colored flowers, soft greens, hints of mauve. He liked it, and decided the small no-nonsense apartment suited her personality just right.

Dripping rain and gripping the paper bag, Max started toward that bedroom door and Miss Maddie Montgomery. He pictured her naked, in a sexy pose on the bed, her fair hair spread out over the pillow.

He pictured the smile on her face, the welcome in her dark blue eyes.

Holding his breath, Max pushed the door open—and jumped when Maddie let out a small shriek of surprise.

Clutching her heart, she said, "Ohmigod, you startled me, Max."

Max lounged in the doorway. "You were expecting someone else?"

Maddie wasn't naked, and she wasn't posed.

She wore a thin teal blue robe that fell to her knees and left the bottom half of her shapely legs bare to his view. Nice knees. And sexy calves. Small feet...

"No, of course not." She stepped away from the window where she'd been watching the storm. Nervously, she folded her hands over her flat stomach and shifted her bare feet. "You got here quicker than I thought and I didn't hear you come in."

He didn't tell her how much he'd hurried. "I was quiet so I wouldn't wake Cleo."

"She's still sleeping?"

"Like a baby."

Maddie's smile was all too obviously forced. Max knew he couldn't rush her, despite his clawing need and all her bravado. Every time she met his gaze, she blushed, so he looked toward the bed instead. She really did have a four-poster, he was amused to see. Would she actually carve a notch in the thick, smooth oak?

"I expected to find you in the bed."

The silky robe shimmered as she lifted one shoulder. "I wasn't sure you'd want me there."

Her reply surprised him, since she'd all but roped and dragged him to the ground. "So," he said, flashing her a smile, "now my wants matter?"

"I thought you might prefer us standing against the wall, or perhaps bent over the chair."

Max couldn't hide his surprise.

"I'm not looking for the conventional wham-bam here, Max." Maddie took another step closer to him. "I was thinking along the lines of adventure." She shrugged.

She gestured toward the overstuffed flowered seat that held her dress. "It has padded arms on it, and a nice soft seat."

His tongue stuck to the roof of his mouth. As outrageous as her words were, they brought with them pictures of Maddie bent at the waist, her bottom in the air for him to cuddle and pet and kiss. He could almost see her, and that wasn't good for his libido.

*Maintain control, maintain control,* he told himself, repeating the advice that often graced his column. After a deep breath that didn't do a damn thing to slow the racing of his pulse, Max asked, "So you're looking to get kinky, huh?"

Maddie bobbed her head enthusiastically. "The way I see it, if I'm going to do this, I might as well go all out."

She was making him feel cheap, Max realized with astonishment, quickly followed by annoyance. He wanted their first time together to be romantic, not merely sexual. He'd never cared overly about being romantic before, but now he did, dammit. And romance wasn't likely if she insisted on getting risqué right off the bat.

He'd always thought there was a lot to be said for good old-fashioned missionary sex.

Keeping his expression and tone level, Max said, "Kinky it is. What would you like to try first?"

"I dunno. You're the supposed expert."

*Supposed, ha!* Going for the one thing Max knew for a fact would turn most women off, he said, "What about a ménage à trois?"

Her eyes widened. "You'd do that for me?"

Max nearly swallowed his damn tongue; her willingness threw him. He was beginning to think he'd made a huge mistake, and would have to walk out on her after all.

Then she took the final step that brought her body close to his and severely weakened his resolve.

With the most innocent expression he'd ever seen on a woman, she asked, "Do you know a guy who's willing, or do I get to pick him?"

Max jerked back a step. "A guy! I meant another woman."

Maddie gave him a mock frown. "No way! This is my show." Her smile proved she'd been teasing all along. "Why would I want to share you?"

Shaking his head, Max started to laugh. Maddie came close again to cover his mouth. "Shh. You'll wake up Cleo."

"I can't help it. You're so funny." Max pulled her against his chest, which effectively soaked her robe since his clothes were still dripping wet, and kissed her hard and fast. Maddie didn't complain. If anything, she hugged him tighter.

"How about," Max whispered against her smiling lips, "we get naked and climb into bed."

"To do things the conventional way?"

"It's a nice easy way to start, honey, I promise."

That seemed to appease her. Without missing a beat, she dropped the damp robe and turned her back on Max to climb into the large bed. *What a view!*

Heat roiled and welled beneath his skin. His control slipped a little, but he reined it in, determined to make this the best *notching* Miss Maddie Montgomery would ever experience.

As Max peeled off his clinging wet shirt, he couldn't stop himself from growling, "You have a gorgeous bottom, Maddie."

"Really?" Her face bright pink from her brazen display, Maddie scurried under the covers, then gave him a beatific smile.

Toeing off his shoes, Max added, "Really."

Her cheeks remained heated, but she watched as

he dropped his pants, leaving his clothes and shoes in a sodden pile on the floor. He started for the bed.

"Turn around."

Max paused by the footboard. "Why?"

"I want to see if you have a nice backside, too."

Feeling a little self-conscious, Max obediently turned, and was startled by the sound of Maddie's low wolf whistle.

"Very nice," she said. "Now bring your hunky self to bed." She threw back the covers and patted the mattress beside her hip.

Chuckling at the uniqueness that was Maddie, Max settled himself beside her. He didn't have time to reach for her.

No sooner was he laid out flat than Maddie launched herself on top of him. Soft flesh moving against hard, silky hair against rough. Max barely had time to grab for a breath before her mouth covered his and her hands began mauling him again.

Max struggled to the surface of his turbulent lust. It wasn't easy because while his mind rebelled at a rushed, frenzied mating, his body was all for the idea.

A mauling had never felt so good.

"Maddie," he said, trying to hold her off. It wasn't easy. Maddie might be slender and delicate, but she was stronger than she looked.

She bit his neck, panting. "You're a tease, Max Sawyers. Stop teasing me and give it up."

Forcefully, Max held her back then flipped over to pin her to the mattress. "You want to wrestle, sweetheart? I'm game."

"There's no wrestling involved, you big ape, when you just hold me down."

Max knew there was a big goofy grin on his mug, but dammit, it felt good to be wanted so much.

"Why don't we talk a bit first," Max suggested, needing a distraction to regain some control.

Maddie shook her head. "I didn't get you into bed to *talk*."

He was starting to feel used again.

Being desired physically was great. Hell yes, it was wonderful.

But Max wanted to feel that she had picked him specifically, not just because of his body or his reputation. He needed to be reassured.

*How lame for a macho stud!* he thought in disgust.

Maddie had made it clear that she didn't want to get to know him, she just wanted "it."

Max seethed, wanting to tell her that he could give her more than sex, more than a warm male body in bed. But it sounded foolish. And unaccountably female. Gad. He wanted sex, for crying out loud! And up until a short time ago, sex without commitment was right up his alley.

But everything had changed.

Max rallied forth and said, "Okay, then let's decide on what type of kinky stuff you want to do."

"Everything." Maddie tried to get her arms free but couldn't. She finally subsided, staring up at Max with wide eyes shadowed by long lashes. Her hair was in an appealing tangle around her head, her cheeks were pink, her lips parted.

Max sighed. He was so hard he hurt, and he was getting harder by the second. "Spanking?"

Maddie's eyes widened even more. Good, at least *that* shocked her.

Then she said, "I doubt I could ever get you over my knees. You're too big."

That was one taunt too many.

Growling, Max abruptly sat up, making Maddie squeal as she realized she'd gone too far. But she didn't escape even halfway across the bed. With no effort at all, Max caught her by the waist and expertly flipped her across his naked thighs. Her long legs kicked and her soft white behind beckoned his hands. He couldn't resist palming her, squeezing gently.

At the touch of his hand on her behind, Maddie stiffened. "Don't you dare, Max Sawyers!"

The squirming bundle draped across his lap no longer sounded so derisive.

"Don't dare what?" Max asked. "This?"

"Max!"

His palm landed with a barely there thwack. Still she gasped and redoubled her efforts to get free.

"Max Sawyers! You stop it right now!"

Max easily controlled her. "You look mighty sexy like this, Maddie." He thwacked her again and she quit struggling to twist around and look at him.

"You think I look sexy?"

"You're naked," he explained reasonably. "Of course I think you look sexy."

She licked her lips. "You wouldn't hurt me, would you, Max?"

He turned her over and cradled her protectively

in his arms. She was flushed, nervous and inflamed. Max absorbed it all, and felt that twisting inside his heart again. "Not even if you asked me to."

No longer fighting him, Maddie drew her left hand slowly over his shoulders. She tested his muscles, tangled her fingers in his chest hair, and when she looked at him, pure lust shone from her eyes.

Max bit back a groan. "Maddie…"

Leaning forward, she kissed his throat. "Please, no more teasing. I can't take it. I've been thinking about this forever, and now I want you too much."

"All right." At the moment, teasing was well beyond him. Hell, breathing took an effort.

"I love how you smell, Max."

Max tightened his hold on her. Finally, they were moving at a normal pace toward a proper goal. He dipped down to rub his cheek over the crown of her head. "I like how you smell, too, sweetheart. Sweet and soft and so very female."

"Female isn't a smell."

"Mmm. Female is most definitely a smell, a scent unique to every woman."

Her thumb brushed his nipple, stretching his control to the breaking point. "You know what I said about a small pistol?"

Max spread one hand over her behind, weighing the soft fullness in his palm. He nuzzled her cleavage. "You wounded me to my masculine core. I doubt I'll ever forget."

"I was teasing. There's nothing small about you at all, is there?"

Max met her gaze, and promptly lost the battle.

Dropping backward onto the mattress, he allowed Maddie to settle herself on top of him. He gave himself up to her, relishing the kisses she rained over his face and throat and chest, wallowing in her tentative touch, the way she wiggled her pelvis against his straining erection.

He gave up trying to slow her down, and just went with his senses.

"Shh," Max told her when she cried out in surprise at the intimate touch of his fingers down her elegant spine, her generous bottom, and further. He traced around her most sensitive flesh with gentle fingertips.

Maddie reared up, stiffening her arms. "That… that feels good, Max."

"It should. If anything doesn't feel good, Maddie, I want you to tell me."

Eyes squeezed tight, teeth biting into her bottom lip, she nodded agreement.

"You're nice and wet." Max was so hot, his voice sounded disembodied, vague.

A groan broke past the restriction of Maddie's teeth as he continued to explore her, skimming over her delicate, swollen tissues.

Her rigid posture had brought her plump breasts right above his face and Max took swift advantage. Her nipples were dark pink, puckered and too enticing to resist. Max licked first, lazily stroking with the rough wet heat of his tongue, letting her know his intent. She trembled, her breathing now audible as she leaned forward, making it clear what she wanted.

Max drew her deep.

Maddie's hips jerked, causing his fingertips to slide over slick flesh.

"Relax for me, Maddie."

*"Impossible."*

Smiling, Max insisted, "It's very possible. And you don't want to wake Cleo."

"Okay. Okay. Okay…"

Max pushed one finger slowly, deeply inside her. Her feminine muscles gripped him in a tight silky vice.

*"Okay!"*

Using the only way he could think of to quiet her, Max kissed her hard. Maddie fell into the kiss, taking his tongue and giving back her own, consuming him, making him crazed with lust. He'd never had a kiss like this, inexperienced but so hungry, so generous and hot.

The gentle thrust of her pointed nipples on his chest was a seductive lure. Combined with her scent, stronger now that she was so excited, and the softness of her hair and skin licking over his heated flesh in dark sensual places, Max gave up. He knew she was ready, knew he was beyond ready, and decided it was time.

Getting Maddie to turn him loose took some doing though.

"Just let me get the condom," he urged.

Her fingernails bit into his shoulders, firing his lust further. "Don't leave me, Max."

"I'm not going anywhere except to the night-stand." He put her to the side and then got distracted looking at her body. She was slim but shapely, her breasts rosy now with need, her stomach tightened, trying to hold in the sweet ache of desire. Her long legs shifted restlessly on the bed.

And her blond curls…they were damp and inviting.

Max bent and pressed a kiss low on her belly.

"Max!"

He rested his chin on her thigh. "You need to stop shouting, honey. Think of Cleo as a baby. If you wake her, she's not going to want to go back to sleep. Putting her outside the door won't help. She'll howl loud enough to wake the dead."

With dawning fury, Maddie said, "You've locked her out when you were with other women?"

A woman like Maddie could quickly grab a man's heart. She was aroused, wet and ready. Her breasts rose and fell with her deep heavy breathing and her skin was warmed to a rosy glow.

Yet she had the sensitivity to consider his dog's feelings.

Max gently stroked her thigh, high near her hipbones, and then very lightly, between.

"No," he whispered, bending to kiss her again. He hadn't been with many women since getting Cleo, mostly because Cleo hated them all and wasn't shy about letting Max know it. He'd tried, but having an hysterical dog on his hands wasn't his idea of fun. And the women had complained mightily when he'd chosen to calm Cleo over bedding them.

Selfish women.

Women unlike Maddie Montgomery.

"I tried shutting her out a few times," Max explained, letting his breath fan her skin, "so she wouldn't shed in my bed. She…ah, didn't like it. She really has this thing about closed doors, especially when she's on the wrong side of them."

Mollified, Maddie pulled a pillow over her face. When she spoke, her voice was muffled. "This will help. You can proceed now with what you…started to do."

Never before had Max suffered the combination of humor and lust and tenderness. It kept him off guard with no way to protect his heart. Max gently urged her legs wider apart, then paused.

"What are you doing?" she mumbled from beneath the pillow.

With his heart in his throat and blood pulsing hotly through his veins, Max said, "Just looking at you."

The pillow lifted and Maddie's gaze met his. "Why?"

Touching her lightly with his fingertips, Max said, "Because you're so pretty and pink and ready for me."

The pillow slapped back over her face. "Oh."

Savoring the moment, Max kissed her softly, then as his hunger raged, not so softly.

Maddie's legs stiffened.

He teased her, teased himself, using his tongue, his teeth, and when she was sobbing beneath the pillow, her hands clenched in the pillowcase, Max drew her into his mouth and suckled her right over the edge.

The pillow proved inadequate to properly stifle

her wild cries, but it helped enough. Thank goodness for small favors, Max thought to himself as he moved in a rush to the nightstand and ripped open a condom package. He couldn't have waited a minute more. Not a second more.

Maddie, her pillow now limp beside her equally limp body, got her eyes open enough to watch him sleepily as he slid on the protection and moved between her thighs.

Her hand lifted tiredly and stroked his shoulder. "That was…indescribable."

"Better than okay, huh?"

"Definitely—*oh!*"

Max tried to hold back as her body softened to accept him, as his erection slid deep inside her to be squeezed by hot, moist flesh. He growled low in intense pleasure. "Oh, yeah."

"Max?"

"Easy now, Maddie. Just a little more. Damn, you feel good."

She took two gasping breaths. "So…do you."

He pulled out, felt her hands grip his shoulders, her legs curl around his hips trying to keep him close, and he drove forward again.

Maddie tipped her head back on the pillow. "This is better than any damn feather!"

"You better believe it." Max gave up the fight and began a rhythm that supplied just the right amount of pressure, just the right friction. "Squeeze me, Maddie," he rasped. "It'll make it better for you. Tighter." He moaned. "That's it."

Holding him with arms, legs and hidden muscles,

Maddie began to feel a part of him, a very necessary part.

Max meant to make the pleasure last, meant to give her a half-dozen orgasms so that she'd never be able to forget him, never be able to move on to the next man.

But it was already too late for him.

With a roar worthy of a wild beast, he came and Maddie joined him.

Unfortunately, their combined yells woke Cleo, who was highly affronted by their unseemly behavior.

And just as Max had predicted, she refused to leave the room.

Their night of debauchery was over.

# Chapter 5

"Where's the book?"

Maddie drew up short, staring back at the three women eyeing her so suspiciously. Darn, she'd forgotten all about the book!

Tossing her backpack—what she carried instead of a bothersome purse—into a seat, Maddie slumped onto the cracked leather couch. "I don't have it."

Bea snorted, making her white hair wobble precariously. Bea spent more time on securing her big hairdos than she did on anything else. "You mean it doesn't exist."

"Does, too," Maddie returned petulantly, then grimaced as Mavis and Carmilla shared a look. "I'll get the book. It's just that…well…" A big grin broke over her face and she leaned forward in excitement. "You guys were right!"

Catching Maddie's enthusiasm, all three women leaned forward. Silver hair blended with white blended with glaring red. Hands wrinkled from time and a working woman's life reached for Maddie.

Carmilla spoke first, her tone hushed with scandalized delight. *"You didn't."*

Bea laughed. "I'll bet she did! Just look at her. She's *glowing*."

"Only one thing gives a woman a glow like that," Mavis agreed, and she was grinning like a loon. "'Bout damn time, if you ask me."

"No one asked you," the other two replied, always too contrary to agree with Mavis's constant predictions.

Maddie let all three of them hold her hands, her wrists, her shoulder. "He's positively dreamy," she said. "A stud, just as you told me he should be."

"Give."

"Yes, every single detail, honey. I wait with bated breath."

Carmilla chuckled. "Mavis, there ain't a damn thing she can tell you that you haven't done a million times yourself, so forget the 'swooning young girl' act."

Mavis slanted Carmilla a venomous look that didn't mean a darn thing. Maddie knew they just loved to twit each other.

"Carmilla, darling, at sixty-eight, I *am* a girl compared to you."

Bea slapped her knee. As the oldest at seventy-five, she often played the peacekeeper. "She's got you there, old girl."

Maddie cleared her throat. "Do you three want to hear this or not?"

Mavis waved a hand. "Tell all."

"I did everything you said—well most of what you said. And he took me home just as you told me he would. It was a little rocky, but I finally won."

Carmilla blinked dark brown eyes. Her face was wrinkled and worn, but in a nice way, like a favorite pair of house slippers that only became more comfortable and appealing the longer you had them. "Whatd'ya mean, it got rocky? He didn't jump your bones?"

"Uh, no. I jumped his."

Mavis harrumphed indignantly. Her eyes spit green fire, which went well with her bright red hair. She resembled a beacon in the night, able to pull in any wayward male souls—which had been the point back when all her work was done at night. She kept the bright hair out of sentiment, and because the senior men still tended to flock to her like flies to honey. She had that special "oomph" or charisma— whatever you called it—that men never seemed to outgrow.

According to Mavis, she sometimes missed working the corner. Holding hands and behaving like a lady didn't suit her at all.

"What kind of man," Mavis demanded, "would have to be jumped?"

"He's a very good man."

"Honey, there ain't no such thing."

Bea swatted at Carmilla. "Don't tell her such a thing! Of course there are good men."

"Good for certain things, but she's not ready for love everlasting again so soon."

"For pity's sake, Carmilla, no one mentioned love everlasting!"

"Look at her eyes, Bea. That girl is smitten."

Everyone turned to stare deeply into Maddie's eyes. She squirmed and immediately felt defensive. "It's not like that at all! You know I've given up on that."

"After what your scumbait fiancé did? Hell yeah, you gave up. I still think you should let us contact a few old friends. I'm tellin' ya, Tiny would love to give your old beau a good goin' over."

Bea shook her head in exasperation. "You are so bloodthirsty, Carmilla."

Mavis snorted. "I agree with her. We should all rough him up, the miserable bastard."

Laughing, Maddie took turns giving each of them a hug. She always felt comforted by their fragile, warm embraces, given from the heart.

She'd been working as a counselor for several years now, and she'd made some friends along the way. She'd started with troubled teens, and gradually been shifted to older women. A lot of those women were now in homes with families and jobs, or doing volunteer work. But Mavis, Carmilla and Bee were aging rebels, women who refused to conform to society's strictures. They were fun loving and adventurous despite their fragile bones, and energetic in a way that belied their years.

They no longer needed her counsel, but they still liked to meet. And being with them helped temper the more stressful sessions Maddie had with abused women, or recovering alcoholics.

Maddie loved Carmilla, Bea and Mavis dearly. For her, they served as surrogate mothers, aunts, best friends and confidants all rolled into one. She admired them for what they'd survived, worried about them endlessly, and counted on them much more than they counted on her, though not a one of them would ever admit it.

She smiled at them. "Max is a good man, I promise. He's a hound dog, no doubt about that—which makes him perfect for my coming-out. But he's also honorable."

"All men," Carmilla said, "are hound dogs, some are just better at it than others."

Mavis raised a slim, drawn-on red brow. "So is this young man good?"

Maddie bobbed her head, making the women laugh. "Yeah." In a whisper, she confided, "He said I was sexy." Then, even lower, "And he seems to know all kinds of kinky stuff."

Carmilla gulped. "Kinky sexual stuff?"

Bea shook her head. "Of course she means kinky sexual stuff. What'd you think? That he wears his shoes backward?" Then to Maddie, "So what'd you do?"

"Nothing kinky," she rushed to reassure them. "He sort of lost control. But the good old conventional stuff was…well, *incredible*."

"Well then," Bee said, setting aside her round

glasses. "It's no wonder you're running a little late this morning."

Mavis signed. "I remember those mornings."

Carmilla nudged her hard enough to almost knock her off her chair. "Baloney. What you remember is the money on the nightstand, not a warm body in the bed."

Mavis grinned. "That, too."

It never ceased to amaze Maddie how open and... cavalier the women were about their hardships. To hear them tell it, life as a hooker had been a lark. But she'd talked with each of them enough to know that was simply their way of burying the past.

It sometimes broke her heart.

This time, as always, she hid her reaction with a smile. "Max didn't spend the night."

*"What?"*

"That cad!"

"I say we get hold of Tiny," Carmilla growled, "and let him teach old Max a few manners."

"It's not like that," Maddie hurried to explain. "You see, he has this dog."

Blank stares were the only response.

"The dog is adorable. Well, not physically. But she's very sweet. When she's not growling."

Mavis chortled. "Sounds like Carmilla."

"Ha ha."

Biting back her own laugh, Maddie said, "The dog has a...well, a bladder problem."

Bea leaned toward Mavis and said low, "I can certainly relate."

"Oh, for goodness sake, be quiet Bea!"

Maddie raised her voice to forestall the start of a new quarrel. "Max didn't want the dog to soil my carpet, so he went home."

"Afterward?" Mavis asked suspiciously.

Smiling, Maddie confirmed, "Yes, afterward." And in dreamy tones, "Way afterward."

"She's got that look again."

"Well," Maddie explained, "it was more wonderful than I'd ever imagined."

"Hurray!"

"'Bout damn time."

"Your damn ex-fiancé should be shot."

Maddie laughed out loud with the joy of it. She'd never imagined, never guessed, that sex could be so wonderful. Max had scandalized her with a few of the wonderful, incredible, sizzling hot things he'd done to her and with her.

But she wouldn't have had him stop a single one.

"So when are you seeing him again?"

At Bea's question, the other two got quiet, all of them waiting for her reply. Maddie forced a negligent shrug.

"I don't know."

"What the hell does that mean?"

"I'm sorry, Carmilla, but it's the truth. I'm not sure what to do now. Max is a confirmed bachelor, and I'm afraid if I get too clingy, it'll spook him."

"You assured him," Mavis asked, "that all you wanted was some good one-on-one experiences to store away for a rainy day?"

"Yes, I told him all that. I don't understand him.

He seemed to really resist me, but then once things got going, he was…"

"Into it?"

"Yes."

"Typical man. Fickle, all of them." Mavis shook her head. "Why, I knew a guy once—"

Bea threw up her hands. "You knew lots of guys in lots of ways, Mavis. For cryin' out loud, let's don't go tromping down memory's bumpy lane right now. We need to figure this out for Maddie."

Carmilla crossed her arms beneath her massive bosom and said three words. "Let's call Tiny."

"I have a better idea," Mavis said, ignoring Bea because she had obviously *wanted* to go down memory lane. "Forget about him."

Maddie bit her bottom lip. Though she knew it was probably best, and it *had* been her original plan, she didn't want to forget about Max. Not yet, maybe not for a long, long time.

Maybe not ever. *No,* she would *not* think that!

Bea patted her arm. "Now look what you've done, Mavis! You're going to make her cry."

"I'm not crying!" Maddie had no intention of getting maudlin over Max Sawyers. This was an adventure, an experience, a way to add lascivious excitement to her PG-rated life. She wouldn't let herself get hurt over it.

"Get rid of that long face, Maddie," Mavis said with a laugh. "I didn't mean forget about him forever. Just long enough to whet his appetite. If this Max fellow is anything like you say, he'll expect you to be after him now, wanting more of his sexy body and all the well-oiled parts. Well, throw 'em for a loop, I always say! Don't give him what he wants."

Carmilla gasped with glee. "Exactly! That's brilliant, Mavis!"

Mavis pretended to have a heart attack over the praise and wouldn't quit until Bea threatened to give her mouth-to-mouth resuscitation.

"Men always want what they can't have." Carmilla rubbed her hands together. "As long as you don't give it to him, he'll keep coming back."

"I already gave it to him."

"He'll want it again, and more."

"But…" Maddie wondered how to phrase her worry. Then she decided that with these three, delicacy wasn't needed. "I *want* to give him more."

"Music to my ears." Bea patted her hand and said, "You're a healthy woman, honey. Just tell him that. Sex—but nothing else," she warned. "It's the 'nothing else' that'll get his goat. I promise, it'll drive him plumb crazy and before you know it, he'll be the one chasing you."

"But wait at least a week," Mavis advised. "After a week, he won't know what to think! He'll be gnawing on his own insecurity. Oh, it'll be so sweet."

"I want to meet him," Bea suddenly declared. "Bring him around. I want to judge for myself if he's worth all this bother."

Maddie knew firsthand that Max was more than worth it, but she wanted to show him off to the ladies. She wanted them to see him and experience his charm.

"I could go to him in a week to get the book—"

Carmilla's rough laugh interrupted Maddie's plan. "A book that claims to have *Satisfying Alternatives to Intercourse* has to be drivel."

"Or an outright lie." Bea watched Maddie with a calculating eye as she delivered that insult.

Trying not to laugh, Maddie assured them, "It exists, and I have it on good authority that it's excellent."

"Bring it, and the young man. We'll check them both out."

"Yes, Mavis," Maddie agreed. "And then all three of you will owe me an apology."

There was a general round of grumbling over that prospect, then a snort of contempt, proving that not one of them planned to apologize at all. No, they just intended to meddle, but Maddie didn't mind. She could barely wait to see Max's reaction to them.

She figured if she could be cordial to his dog, dealing with Mavis, Carmilla and Bea ought to be a piece of cake.

She didn't call, she didn't write...

Max paced the small confines of the bookstore, his temper high, his mood black.

His manly ego thoroughly damaged.

He'd written three columns on the evils of women-on-the-make, then had to destroy them. Truth was so often stranger than fiction, and no one would have believed that he was actually *complaining* about the situation.

In fact, he could barely believe it himself. But dammit, he'd bought a box of condoms just for her!

He had three of the little silver packets in his wallet right now.

Yet she hadn't so much as blinked when he'd told her he couldn't spend the night a week ago. She hadn't offered him her phone number, hadn't invited him back, hadn't done anything but thank him.

And now he knew why.

Maddie truly had just been using him. One time. One lousy damn time and she was through with him. She had the number for the bookstore, and she knew Annie. She could have gotten his home number. But no. She'd ignored him without hesitation.

The hair on the back of Max's neck bristled. *How dare she?* He was no lady's conquest! He wasn't a man to be trifled with!

He had a good mind to storm over to her apartment and see for himself if she'd reduced him to a nick in the bedpost. Only...what if she was with another man when he showed up?

What if she took his visit as a sign of jealousy?

Max cursed and started pacing again. If he found a man there, he just knew he'd get rip-roaring mad and probably do something foolish—like punch the guy out.

And he sure as hell didn't want it to look like he was chasing her. Ha! The very idea was absurd. Women chased *him,* not the other way around.

Max sighed as he stalked the perimeter of the bookstore once again. It was bad enough to be in such a foul mood without having to deal with Annie's shop as well. But his little sister and Guy were off wallowing in premarital ecstasy, on a wedding planning venture that seemed to have no end in sight.

Guy insisted that Annie have the biggest and best wedding around. And his father agreed. They didn't know he had a job writing for the paper, so they probably thought they were doing him a favor, keeping him employed. Ha.

Curse them all.

Cleo whined, tilted her small head and gave Max a quizzical look. If he didn't know better—but he damn well did—he'd think Cleo missed Maddie, too. Impossible. The woman was too pushy to be missed by man or beast.

So why had Cleo been moping so much? Why had she been so maudlin? He loved Cleo, he really did, but it was almost repulsive to see her dragging her chubby little short-legged body around in a depression. He preferred her grumbling and snapping to the worried, unhappy look she'd worn since Maddie left.

Now he knew where the term "hangdog expression" had come from, because Cleo wore it all over her furry face.

"I'm fine, Cleo," Max bit out, "so quit frowning at me."

Cleo looked unconvinced. She whined again and laid her head on the floor, resting it on her front paws and staring up at Max with wrinkled brows and quivering whiskers.

"Stop fretting!" he demanded, unable to bear it a second more. "It doesn't suit you at all. Besides, I'm just stewing in my own juices."

"And what juices would those be?"

Max jumped at the soft, teasing female voice. Maddie stood there in the doorway looking sweet and sexy and happy to see him, as if a damn week hadn't gone by, as if she hadn't been ignoring him completely after taking him like a convenient body with no soul.

No, Max admitted to himself, that wasn't quite the way it had happened. She'd taken his body, yes— most thoroughly in fact—but she'd also grabbed his heart and soul with both fists.

It was unbearable.

Just looking at her hurt.

Cleo, the traitor, took one peek at Maddie and began leaping about in near maniacal excitement. Her snarls and growls actually mingled with happy woofs. Max glared at her.

Then her tail—a tail seldom seen since it spent most of its time curled safely against her belly—gave a one-thump wag of delight.

"Well, I'll be damned."

Maddie went straight to the dog, not even slightly put off by Cleo's mixed display of joy and wrath, and hugged her tightly. "Did you miss me, sweetie?"

Yellow fur clung to Maddie's hot-pink T-shirt, a T-shirt that read *Made In The Sun.* Cleo went so far as to lick Maddie's ear.

*Oh yeah,* Maddie with her long blond hair hanging free, her blue eyes smiling, would look very sweet under the hot sun. Naked. Open for him.

Max cleared his throat, angry at himself for responding to her. Sure, she loved all over his damn dog, but she'd barely said two words to him.

It was as if she hadn't missed him at all.

"Well, well," he murmured in his most sarcastic tone, "look what the cat dragged in."

At the word "cat" Cleo's ears lifted, her portly body trembled and she went bonkers. She snapped at the air and raced around the small bookstore, bumping into shelves and sticking her snarling nose into every small space, searching for the heinous feline creature.

Maddie frowned at Max. "Now look what you've done!" She rushed after Cleo, her white sandals clicking on the tile floor as she ran through a haphazard game of tag that had Maddie, too, bumping into bookcases before she finally got both hands anchored in Cleo's collar. "Shh. Shh. It's all right, Cleo. I promise, there aren't any other creatures here except us."

Cleo wasn't about to trust anyone and so the game continued. Maddie got dragged several feet before she gave up and released Cleo's collar, only to rush after the dog, explaining all the while.

Max sauntered off to the back room to get himself a cola. He was being ignored, so he figured no one would miss him. Let the two ladies have their fun. He'd ignore them right back.

He'd finished half the bottle of soda before Maddie again appeared in the doorway. The tight tee outlined her breasts and her long legs were displayed under an itty-bitty white cotton miniskirt.

She looked good enough to eat, he thought. Then in the next second, he got hard.

"What are you doing?"

Max shrugged, the epitome of a man without a care. He ruined the pose, though, by grumbling, "Not a damn thing, why?"

"My, my," she said with raised eyebrows. "Surly this morning, aren't we?"

Surly? *Surly!* Max paused, thinking, Did real men act surly? Good grief, he didn't think so.

He mentally shook himself and gathered together his lauded control.

"Sorry," he uttered, once again sounding like himself, a man without a care, a man who excelled in deception. "I had a...late night."

There, Miss Montgomery, he thought, work that over in your conniving little brain.

Yawning hugely, Maddie said, "Me, too."

Max jerked to attention and demanded, "A late night doing *what?*"

"Working."

"Oh."

She gave him an impish grin. "What did you think I was doing?"

"Notching more bedposts?"

"And that would have bothered you?"

"Not in the least."

Her smile was smug and he wanted to kiss it right off her face. No sooner did the thought enter his mind than he decided, why not?

Max stalked her, his intent gaze letting her know

exactly what he wanted, and Maddie began backing up as she chuckled.

"Cleo finally settled down." She giggled as she said it, and stopped abruptly when her back came up against the small cool refrigerator.

Max caged her in, flattening his hands on either side of her head. "She ran out of gas, that's all. Cleo can raise a racket for hours until she literally flops down exhausted."

"That exactly what she did! One second she was running around—"

Her words were swallowed up by his kiss. Damn, she tasted good. Too good. Even better than he'd remembered.

Max had almost forgotten how wonderful her soft mouth felt under his, how teasing her tongue could be, her delicious taste. "Mmm."

He lifted his mouth from hers and pressed soft, biting kisses down her throat. "You like hickeys?"

Maddie, breathing roughly, rasped, "Hickeys?"

"Love bites." He licked her throat. "Do you like them?"

"I… I don't know." Her hands clenched in his shirt, her hips pressed into his. "I don't think I've ever had one."

Max opened his mouth on her neck, right over her thrumming pulse, and sucked her skin gently against his teeth.

Maddie responded with a long, hungry groan.

Max made sure the mark would be low enough that she could cover it easily with her clothing, but she tasted so good he didn't want to let her go. He kissed her throat again and again, then moved on to her jaw, her ear.

Maddie panted. "This is wonderful."

She made him crazy. Max took her mouth hard in a voracious kiss, all the while his mind was churning. He knew he should hold back, knew he should set things straight with her. He couldn't. Not right now.

"Ever had a nooner?"

Maddie slowly blinked open her heavy eyes. "A nooner?"

Max cupped her cheek and smoothed her skin with his thumb. She was so soft. "It's afternoon. A great time to play."

Her eyes widened. "Play, as in…?"

"Make whoopee. Here. *Now.*" He wanted her so badly, just getting the words out was an effort.

Maddie glanced around the tiny back room where unopened boxes crowded the floors and file cabinets were squeezed into the corners. One small square table held a coffeemaker and was surrounded by three mismatched chairs. The miniscule refrigerator hummed against her backside. Max could feel the teasing vibration through Maddie, their bodies were pressed so closely together.

Most importantly, though, was the open door leading into the rest of the bookstore. Any customer coming in might be able to see them if they got close to the door. Max saw the confusion, the scandalized excitement that darkened Maddie's eyes.

She bit her lip. "Here?"

In one deft move, Max flattened her more securely to the refrigerator and pushed himself between her thighs. With a tilt of his head, he could see the front door, but no one coming in could see him unless they rounded the corner. Max knew she felt his erection, as well as the way his hands shook. But he didn't care. All he cared about was hearing her soft enticing groans again as she came.

"Here," he growled.

"Standing?"

"Standing. You offered this last time, remember? The only difference is that the fridge is nice and cool, and I swear, you'll appreciate that in a minute."

"Why?"

"Because I'm going to make you burn up."

"Oh." She touched his chest, looked around the room again. "I'm... I'm kind of wobbly," she said worriedly.

Max smiled. "I won't let you fall." Hell, his muscles were so tense, so tight, he was more likely to break than bend.

Maddie licked her lips slowly while her eyes searched his. "What if someone catches us?"

Kissing the corner of her sweet mouth, Max whispered, "It's an exciting thought, isn't it? Doing the forbidden? Taking a risk? But the door has a bell, remember? We'll know if anyone comes in." With a touch of demand, he added, "Trust me."

Her fingers gripped his upper arms, squeezing, caressing. "All right."

Breathing hard, Max held her gaze as he caught the hem of her miniskirt and slowly raised it. Maddie moaned.

"We need to get rid of your panties," he told her,

knowing his words would work as foreplay, "so that I can touch you."

Maddie closed her eyes.

"You want me to touch you, don't you, Maddie? That's why you're here again." He'd have rather believed she'd missed him, but he was a realist. Fingers on her thigh, he asked, "You missed *this,* didn't you?"

She nodded, her chest heaving, her thighs trembling as Max ran his fingertips up and over her legs to her hips.

With no warning at all, he cupped her through the silky triangle of underwear.

"Why, Maddie Montgomery," he said softly, "you're already hot and wet." Max moved his fingers over the damp silk, outlining her swollen folds, then higher, stroking her through the material. Maddie gasped.

"Mmm," he said. "Right there, huh?"

She didn't answer, so he paused, keeping one finger pressed teasingly to the ultrasensitive spot.

Maddie's eyes opened and she stared at him, looking somewhat dazed. "Max?"

He loved hearing her say his name. "I want you to answer my question, Maddie."

She swallowed, drew a steadying breath. "What question?"

Her rasping voice shook; Max liked that. "Is this where you want me to touch you?"

He flicked gently, then deeply, and Maddie's hips jerked against him.

"Yes!"

"I want to see your breasts, Maddie."

She stared at him.

"Show them to me." This was Max's favorite game, taking charge, making specific sexual demands. And after the week he'd been through, waiting for her, hoping she'd call, thinking she never would, he especially liked it.

And she especially deserved it.

Looking undecided about what to do, Maddie again bit her lip. It was an innocently sexual expression that turned him on even more.

Max quit stroking her, making his demand. "Show me your breasts, Maddie."

She swallowed hard, then began inching up her shirt. She had on a barely there bra of matching hot pink, transparent and sexy as hell. Max bent toward her. "Keep the shirt out of my way."

Her nipples were hard points against the thin material and Max closed his mouth around her hotly.

"Max!"

He tasted her other breast, leaving both nipples covered with damp clingy fabric. Leaning back to enjoy his handiwork, Max said, "Nice. Pretty."

He didn't want to take a chance on being interrupted, so he decided not to stall any longer. Maddie's skirt was bunched around her waist, her T-shirt up under her chin. He slowly took a step back, and cautioned her, "Don't move."

She barely even breathed.

Nodding in approval, Max knelt down and pulled her panties to her knees.

The door chimed.

Maddie started to jerk away, but Max quickly rose

and held her still. He covered her mouth with two fingers scented by her body. Against her ear, he said, "Don't you move a single muscle, sweetheart. Do you understand me?"

Panicked, her eyes huge, Maddie mumbled against his fingers.

"Shh. Trust me."

A heartbeat of silence passed while they stared at each other and the interruption he'd wanted to avoid became a real risk. Finally she nodded.

Just that quickly Max left the backroom, closing the door behind him. There was nothing he could do about his noticeable hard-on except hope the two female customers wouldn't look at him closely until he got behind the counter.

They didn't. They were too busy picking up their favorite romance novels. They discussed authors and new releases and made faces at the goofy clinch covers. In the short time he'd been filling in for Annie, Max had noticed that their biggest sellers were romances.

Luckily the customers didn't wake Cleo, but they did give her horrified stares. She was stretched out on the floor beneath a table, snoring.

Max ignored the ladies' aghast expressions and waited on them patiently. Maddie, he was certain, would have thought Cleo looked cute. She wouldn't have regarded the dog with distaste, but rather with that small, endearing smile of hers.

Max could just picture her still standing against the old refrigerator, her legs open, her hands fisted in her shirt, breasts bare, panties around her knees. She looked so sexy, so sweet. So impatient.

He had to shake those thoughts away or he'd embarrass himself.

It was a good ten minutes before the store was once again empty. Max took a deep breath, flexed his hands and rolled his head to rid himself of the worst of his tension. In the corner, Cleo lay sprawled in boneless languor, the most relaxed she'd been since she'd slept at Maddie's apartment. Since then, she'd been watching the doors, the windows, and Max knew she'd been waiting for Maddie.

Just as he had.

That sudden insight annoyed him enough that he quickly opened the back-room door and walked in.

Maddie was standing just as he'd left her.

Her tiny pink panties were still twisted around her knees and her nipples were still erect little points, telling Max that her thoughts hadn't veered from the sexual at all. She may not have missed him, but she'd missed what he could do for her. And she had come back to him. He'd build on that. For Cleo's sake.

Without a word, he knelt in front of her again. As if they hadn't been interrupted at all, Max traced a path up her thigh and asked, "You ready for me, Maddie?"

Her stomach clenched. "Yes."

Slowly, enthralled by the contrast of her moist pink flesh against his dark hand, Max inserted one finger inside her. Maddie didn't look away. Her legs parted as far as the panties would allow, straining against the bonds.

"Do you want me to kiss you?"

*"Yes."* Then, almost as an afterthought, "Please."

She no longer hesitated at all in her answers. Max's heart pounded hard, and his control was a thing of the past. Still with his finger inside her, gently probing, Max breathed in her musky scent, then opened his mouth over her in a voracious, consuming kiss meant to bring her desire to an acute edge.

Maddie's breath left her in a harsh groan. Her hands settled on his head, her fingers inadvertently pulling at his hair.

He didn't mind. He liked her unrestrained show of excitement.

Max brought her right to the edge, teasing, nibbling, kissing softly, then not so softly. He used his tongue in a never-ending, rasping stroke—then left her.

Quickly stripping her panties the rest of the way off, Max tucked them into his back pocket.

Max stroked her bare bottom as he explained, "Quickies are sometimes an elusive thing for women," Max explained as he stroked her bare bottom. "They need more…preparation. More stimulation."

How the hell he was stringing so many words together when all he could hear was the roar of his own racing heartbeat, Max wasn't sure. Maddie neither wanted nor required explanations. But he wanted her enjoyment to be a foregone conclusion, and talking not only aroused her further, it helped to calm him so that he could see to her pleasure. He refused to take a chance on leaving her unsatisfied.

"You talk too much, Max."

Max smiled at the crackle in her voice, the way she held herself so still and ready. Her back was pressed hard against the door of the fridge, her hips tilted outward, legs spread. Her little belly was so cute, so inviting.

He unzipped his jeans in a rush, then pushed them below his hips. "When I come into you now, the friction will be just right."

He felt the heat of Maddie's intense gaze, watching him as he rolled on the condom. She reached for him when he stepped between her widely spread thighs.

She held him tight when Max instructed, "Put your right leg around my waist. That's it, a little higher. Now just... Umm. That's right." She was so wet, he sank easily into her. "Tilt your pelvis toward me more."

Maddie anxiously followed his instructions. "This is fairly kinky, isn't it?" she panted.

"Yeah." He'd win her over yet, he thought. He'd make her insane with lust, make her understand that there was a special chemistry between them. Max kissed her again, and intent on making her hotter with words, he whispered, "What did you think about while I was with the customers, sweetheart?"

"You," she whispered. "What you just did to me?"

"Yes?" Max could already feel his triumph. She'd wanted him to kiss her, to pleasure her. "What about it?"

"I thought about...doing that to you."

Max froze. His vision clouded.

Unconcerned with his reaction, Maddie persisted with her arousing admission. Her breath pumped in and out, making the words stilted, as she moved against him, pleasuring herself on his rigid body.

"I thought about being on my knees in front of you, of taking you into my mouth, tasting you and sucking on you the same way you—"

With a muffled shout, Max drove into her. He was a goner, coming even as he heard Maddie's soft chuckle of success. He let her laugh, because seconds later she was climaxing, her nails biting into his butt, his arms the only things keeping her upright.

It seemed as though they stood there for hours, propped against each other, both of them gasping for breath. And then the damn door chimed again and with a dark oath, Max pulled away from her.

Would nothing ever go as he planned with Maddie? Every time he intended to overwhelm her with sex, she managed to turn the tables on him. And now, instead of being able to discuss things with her, the store had suddenly become as busy as a bus station, repeatedly drawing him away. Max disposed of the condom, pulled up his jeans, and staggered on wobbling legs out to the counter.

Unfortunately, this customer was much more observant than the others had been. She took in his disheveled state, the heaviness of his eyes, and said with characteristic cheerfulness, "Why Max Sawyers, you reprobate. You've been fooling around in Annie's bookstore!"

Lace McGee Sawyers, his sister-in-law, knew sexual satisfaction when she saw it. As a sex therapist, she was well acquainted with the subject.

Max looked at her, frowned, then said over his shoulder, "You might as well come on out, Maddie. It's just Lace, and I know without asking that she's not going anywhere without an introduction."

"At least I got here *after,*" Lace said with a grin.

Max gave her his laziest look. "You're good Lace, but not good enough to be sure of that."

"Oh, I'm positive." She laughed, then hugged him tight. "Because otherwise you'd be throwing me out!"

## Chapter 6

Maddie wanted to be a coward and hide, but more than that, she wanted to meet Lace McGee Sawyers. Lace was married to Annie's oldest brother, Daniel, the doctor. She'd never met Daniel, but Annie assured her that he was every bit as hunky as Max, just in a different, more somber way.

She straightened her clothes the best she could, considering her panties were still in Max's pocket. She could hardly believe what she'd just done; as far as memories went, that one was a keeper! But it was more than the sex, because Max was more. She would have enjoyed talking with him, asking how Cleo had been. She wanted to try to find out if he'd missed her at all because she'd definitely missed him.

But as per her original instructions, he'd shown

her a good time. She knew that was for the best, but she still wished they'd had time to…cuddle.

Shoulders back, Maddie walked out of the room. She was prepared to be adult, to be cavalier about the experience. But then she drew up short.

Lace was wrapped around Max! And he didn't seem to mind! The cur.

It made Maddie so angry to see another woman holding him so closely, that she didn't even think, she just reacted.

"Just what the hell is going on here?"

Max eyed her over the top of Lace's platinum-blond head. At first his look was questioning, then quietly satisfied. He even grinned before setting Lace away from him.

"Cursing, Maddie? My, my."

He looked mighty pleased about something, but Maddie was more interested in Lace. The woman was drop-dead beautiful. A real knockout.

Maddie felt instantly deflated.

She had no idea what to say, how to defuse the situation so she could make a hasty escape. Cleo came to her rescue.

Slowly getting to her feet, Cleo started snarling and sniping and making vague threats at Lace.

Maddie smiled.

Cleo came to Maddie, sat on her foot, and growled at the other woman. Maddie, feeling somewhat vindicated, patted Cleo's head.

"I have no idea what that dog has against me." Lace looked at Max. "She still hates women?"

Maddie answered before Max could. "She doesn't hate *me*. She *likes* me."

Lace grinned. "So I see. I suppose, considering the fact that Max seems rather partial to you as well, it's a good thing."

Maddie, surprised at how nice and reasonable the other woman was being, said, "Uh…"

Lace stepped forward, keeping a wary eye on Cleo, and offered her hand. "Hi. I'm Max's sister-in-law, Lace."

Maddie had no choice but to accept the woman's hand. "Maddie Montgomery."

"So you're Maddie! Annie has told me all about you. I understand we have a lot in common."

Maddie looked at Lace's gorgeous, perfect figure decked out in a striking black silk dress that showed off her incredibly beautiful blond hair in stark contrast and said again, "Uh…"

"I'm a sex therapist," Lace explained, "and Annie said you work with social services for planned parenthood and troubled teens on sexual issues?"

Max piped in, saying, "And I love sex. We all have something in common."

To Maddie's chagrin, Lace merely poked Max in the side, treating him like a little brother. "You're outrageous, Max. Don't embarrass your lady friend."

Max snorted. "As if that's even possible. In fact, it's generally Maddie who's embarrassing me. She's so…candid."

Maddie thought about kicking him. Cleo must have picked up on her thoughts, because she gave Max a disapproving whine.

Lace shrugged. "In our business you need to be candid. Maddie would hardly be effective at what she does if she sat around blushing and stammering."

Damn, Maddie thought. The woman was beautiful and intelligent and likeable.

Max threw his arm around Lace, making Maddie narrow her eyes. But then he said, "Maddie, did you know Lace has always treated me like I'm twelve? I swear, I'd try to flirt with her and she'd pat my head."

Lace rolled her eyes. "Don't let it bother you, Max. I was in love with your brother, remember?"

"But you didn't know it at the time."

A feline smile enhanced Lace's already perfect features. "No, but I did know that I wasn't in love with you."

"Heartless wench."

Maddie grinned. They carried on just like siblings. "It's very nice to meet you, Lace. I listen to your radio show all the time. It's wonderful."

"Thanks. Maybe we could have lunch today and get to know each other better? Are you free?"

Maddie wanted to, she really did. But she had a few things she'd already committed herself to. "Could we make it another time? I have…plans for today."

Max took a step forward, no longer looking amused. "Plans to do what?"

She couldn't tell him without ruining the surprise. Maddie peeked at Cleo, saw that the dog was on alert, and shrugged. "Just…some things."

Max ignored Lace, who stood there looking beautifully spellbound by the sudden tension in the air, and he growled, "Things involving *debauchery?*"

Maddie gasped. How dare he try to embarrass her in front of his sister-in-law. She raised her chin and lied convincingly, "Yes."

Max started to reach for her, but Maddie stepped away. "In fact," she said airily, her anger a near tangible thing, "I should be going."

It was the perfect exit line, but Maddie hesitated.

Max had her panties in his pocket. She was more than a little aware of being naked beneath her skirt. When she looked at Max, she knew he was aware of it, too. His look dared her to leave without them, and dared her to request he give them back.

Maddie lifted her chin. "Thanks for the…"

Max smirked at her, and even then he looked so handsome she wanted to drag him back into the other room.

"The what?" he taunted.

Maddie ground her teeth together. Lace silently watched them both, her gaze moving from one to the other. "Why, for the entertainment this afternoon, what else? I'd have been bored to tears otherwise."

Lace choked on a laugh.

Maddie turned to her. "How about lunch on Friday, Lace? Are you free then?"

With a beaming smile, Lace said, "That'd be wonderful. Shall I meet you here at eleven-thirty?"

Maddie nodded. "Sounds perfect. I'll look forward to it."

She waggled her fingers at Max. "See ya later, Max." Then she went to her knees—carefully so that her skirt kept her naked behind well covered—and hugged Cleo. "I'll visit again soon, Cleo! And maybe next time you'll be able to stay awake."

Cleo's growl turned into a begrudging woof.

Maddie walked out without another word to anyone.

Max waited until Maddie had rounded the corner outside the shop, then said in a rush to Lace, "Do me a favor, sweetheart. Watch the shop for a few minutes."

"Max! Where are you going?"

Max reached in his pocket for his keys, felt Maddie's silky panties still tucked in there, and smiled. "I'm going to follow her, of course."

Cleo ran to Max's side and growled her approval as Max trotted out the door.

Lace hurried behind them. "But…she looked ready to kill you, Max! Maybe you should give her a little time to cool down, after provoking her that way."

"Ha!" Max headed for his truck in the parking lot. "You should get to know Maddie better if you want to see the definition of provoking. Besides, if Maddie plans to do any more debauching, I plan to stop her."

"*More* debauching?"

He grinned despite his urgency to catch up to Maddie. "She's a wonderful debaucher."

Lace caught his arm. "Then why stop her?"

"Because she should be doing all her debauching with *me!*" Max reached his truck and jerked the door open. Cleo sprang inside and Max quickly buckled her into her doggy seat. He could just see the back of Maddie as she walked toward a small white compact parked on the opposite side of the street.

He turned to Lace, who leaned in his open door window. "I promise I'll only be a minute."

"This is my lunchtime, Max."

"I'll bring you back something Mexican."

Her eyes lit up. "Deal. But I only have an hour."

"Gotta go, sweets. I'll be back on time, I promise." Max gunned the truck and pulled out several lengths behind Maddie.

They didn't have far to go. In fact, they were still on the same street, but Max couldn't believe it when she pulled the little car into a parking space in front of a well-known fetish shop. Eyes agog, he said to himself, "No way."

Cleo whimpered.

"Can you believe this? What the hell is she up to?"

Cleo had no answer, only a worried frown.

"You stay put girl, and I'll go check it out. I'll only be a minute." Max adjusted both windows to let in enough breeze for Cleo to be comfortable, then slipped out of the truck. Maddie had indeed gone into the fetish shop, bold as you please.

Dashing across the street, Max sidled up to the enormous front window that was draped with a dark blue curtain, hiding all the scandalous material for sale. He could just barely see inside where the curtains didn't quite close all the way.

Maddie had gone down a long aisle, so Max opened the door and followed her in.

He heard her talking to a salesperson.

"I want it to be red leather. With colored gems and silver studs."

*Red leather! Studs?*

"I have just what you need," the salesman said. "Follow me."

*Ha!* Max thought to himself. He was the man who had what she needed, not some salesman. He slunk along, feeling like a very determined fool. When he peeked around the corner of a tall shelf holding a variety of adult magazines and books, he saw Maddie testing the strength of a thick red leather collar.

His stomach dropped to his knees.

He was outraged, scandalized—and horny as hell.

The salesman said, "Would you like to see the ankle and wrist cuffs as well?"

In her oh-so-innocent voice, Maddie asked, "Ankle and wrist cuffs? Really?"

The salesman—a young fellow with an array of earrings—gave her a smarmy grin. "They're padded with sheepskin so as not to abrade."

Maddie's beautiful blue eyes widened in fascination. "Show me."

Growling under his breath, Max made his way back up to the front of the store and skulked behind a display of soft velvet whips. Just what did Maddie think she was going to do with that paraphernalia? Max wondered. Then such an interesting parade of ideas flashed through his mind, he almost didn't notice when Maddie came to the counter to pay.

He was shaking too badly.

She had her back to him, so Max couldn't see her final purchases, but the bag she walked out with was enormous. Almost as enormous as the smile on her face.

Max stewed as he followed her, keeping a safe distance away so as not to be observed. She was actually humming. He could hear the happy, devil-may-care sound easily over the noise of the street.

He narrowed his eyes as he watched her get into her car. Oh, Maddie may have been making some fantasy-based plans in her creative little mind, but Max decided right then and there that her plans were about to change.

She'd just started the car when Max leaned into the window.

"Maddie."

She squealed and jumped a good foot. With a hand over her heart, she said, "Good grief, Max! What are you doing here?"

Max smiled. *I've got you now, sweetheart.* "I was just picking up some lunch for Lace."

He saw Maddie's smile turn into a frown. "She's having lunch with you?"

"Yes."

"What," she demanded, "does her husband think of that?"

"My brother's not an ogre who chains a woman to his side." Then he admitted, "Besides, he knows he can trust Lace."

That gave her pause, and rightfully so, because it was apparent she didn't trust Max at all.

All she said was, "Oh."

"What are you doing here?"

Her face turned beet red. "Max." She looked

around, as if someone might hear her, then said, "Actually, nosy, it's a surprise."

"A surprise for who?" That was the part that was getting to him. If she wanted to play sex games, Max was willing. As long as he was the only other player, and they played by his rules.

"For you, who else?"

Now that pleased him. Who else, indeed.

"Here, I have something for you." Max pulled her panties out of his back pocket and offered them to her.

With a horrified gasp, Maddie snatched the underwear from his hand and shoved them under the car seat. "You, Max Sawyers, are the most annoying, the most—"

Max cut off her diatribe with a smoldering kiss. When he finally pulled away, Maddie was soft and warm and smiling at him.

Amazing.

"I thought about keeping them," he murmured. "Sort of as a trophy."

Rather than taking offense, Maddie asked, "Like a notch on the bedpost?"

It was hard to smile. "Yeah. But then I kept thinking about you running around bare-assed all day and I knew it'd make me crazy."

Maddie looked at him through her lashes. "Crazy…how?"

"Crazy with lust. Crazy with wanting you again. The thing about nooners, they're the equivalent of an appetizer." He trailed one rough fingertip down the line of her throat to her shoulder, then to the swell of her right breast. "I want the full course."

Sighing, Maddie said, "Mmm. Me, too." But she added, "Not that this afternoon wasn't nice. Exceptional in fact." And with a small smile, "I loved it. Thank you."

Damn, she was about to bring him to his knees right there in the middle of the street. Max cleared his throat.

"I gotta go, babe," he said regretfully. "Lace only has so long for lunch."

As if only then realizing what he'd done to her, arousing her again then saying goodbye, Maddie scowled. "Cad. But I'm glad you're here. I meant to ask you two things before you made me mad enough to leave."

Max didn't want her dredging up her pique, so he said quickly, "Ask away."

Now, Max thought, he'd find out about the bondage stuff. She'd ask him how he felt about it, if he'd be willing. And of course, Max would be understanding, and cooperative and—

"Will you come to work with me tonight?"

Vivid sexual images faded away to nothingness. "Uh…to work?"

"Yes, I have meetings several times a week with different groups, and tonight's the night I get together with some really special women. I'd like you to meet them, and as we discussed, you could share some firsthand experiences."

"Uh, Maddie…" Max was positively horrified by the idea.

"Please Max." She blinked those sexy big blue eyes at him and Max felt himself melting. He'd have to remember to write a column warning men about the effects of big blue eyes.

"I already told them about you. And about the book. I'd appreciate it if you could bring it along, too, since you...distracted me when I was there and I forgot to get it."

Max grinned. "Is that what the women are calling it these days? A distraction?"

Maddie returned his humor. "A very pleasant distraction, to be sure."

"Pleasant?" He snorted at her and pretended to be insulted. "I thought it was more like mind-blowing, climactic—"

Maddie purred, "Definitely climactic."

Her tone made his nerve endings riot. Max eyed the tiny back seat of her car and wondered if they'd fit...but no. Cleo was waiting in his truck. Damn.

If talking with young women who were complete strangers about sexual variety was what it took to see her again, Max figured he could handle it. After all, he had altruistic motives. Cleo needed Maddie. Today was proof of that.

But he wouldn't like it.

Grousing, he asked, "Where and when?"

"Thank you, Max!" Maddie shuffled through the glove box then handed him a business card with the address of the clinic printed on it. "Five o'clock, okay?"

Still uncertain of the whole idea, Max hesitantly nodded his agreement and took the card. Maddie reached out and caught his hand. She lifted it to her mouth and kissed his palm.

"And Max?" she whispered. "Would you want to come over to my apartment afterward?"

Desire snaked through him, nearly curling his toes.

That had never happened to him before. If one of his male readers had written to Max about curling toes, Max would have called him a weenie.

Now he had to reevaluate, because his toes were indeed curled.

And Max Sawyers was definitely not a weenie.

"No." The seductive teasing left Maddie's gaze, until Max leaned close and murmured, "I want you in my bed this time, little tease."

Her lips parted.

Max kissed her gently, sealing their agreement. If Maddie wanted to try her dominatrix tricks, it'd be on his turf.

"We'll have dinner," Max told her, stroking her sun-warmed cheek, "then I'll drive you to my house." And he'd damn well keep her there all night, he decided. Maybe even for a week. Possibly for the rest of her life.

It was the least he could do for Cleo.

When Max got back to his truck, tapping the clinic's business card against his thigh, Cleo gave him a sullen look.

"I'm sorry, girl, did you miss me?"

Grudgingly, Cleo licked his chin.

"Thanks, Cleo. I needed that."

Max found out how true that sentiment was the

second he stepped back into the bookstore. Lace practically pounced on him.

"Okay, what's going on?"

In no hurry to bare his soul, Max carried the Mexican food into the back room and placed it on the table. Cleo, smelling the food, stayed hot on his heels. So did Lace.

"What's going on with what?"

When Lace didn't answer, Max looked up to see her staring at the small refrigerator. It sat out of alignment, crooked instead of flush against the wall. He grinned.

Shaking her head, Lace said, "You're such a rogue. And quit smiling. I refuse to ask you anything about it."

"Great. Then let's eat." Cleo barked in agreement, making Lace jump. The two females kept a good deal of space between them.

Max knew if Maddie had been there, Cleo would have still been sitting on her foot.

Lace had only eaten two bites of her burrito before she said, "Why are you dodging Dan and Daniel?"

*Oh hell,* Max thought. He didn't need this today. "Lace…"

"No, don't start with your excuses. You're needed at the business and you know it. I've been patient with all this middle-child moping, but Max, it's time to move on."

Max glared at her, wondering how in the world he'd run head on into two such bullheaded women in one day. Through his teeth, he said, "I do not mope." And his damn toes didn't curl either. "The simple fact of the matter is, there's nothing for me to do at the business."

"There's all kinds of things for you to do!"

"Okay, let me rephrase that. There's nothing that I'm needed to do. You know I'd go crazy sitting in an office, crunching numbers or sitting in on board meetings. That's not my speed, Lace. I'd be like a fish out of water."

After glancing at her watch, Lace gobbled down the last of her food and stood. She crossed her arms and gave Max a calculating stare.

"What?" he asked, feeling uneasy about the way she seemed to dissect him with her gaze.

"Guy wants to spend more time with Annie now. You know he worked extra long and hard trying to keep himself occupied so he wouldn't think of her."

"Yeah, so? I gather it worked, given how long it took him to wise up and admit he loved her."

Lace nodded. "And you know Daniel has no spare time with the hours he puts in at the hospital."

"You're not going to guilt me into anything here, sweetheart, so you might as well give it up."

Lace ignored his interruption. "A lot of the workload that Guy's looking to get rid of involves travel."

Max couldn't quite hide his sudden interest. Damn, he missed traveling. He'd been born with a heavy case of wanderlust and missed being on the road. Even the simplest trip was a pleasure for him.

But since bringing Cleo home, he'd curbed all those tendencies. Cleo needed him. He rubbed her ears as he said, "You know I can't leave my dog. And there's no one she'd be comfortable staying with."

They both heard the ding of the front door and knew a customer had come in. Max stood, ready to wrap up their conversation. And Lace needed to get back to the radio station.

"Maddie could watch her," Lace suggested as she gathered up her purse.

Max put his arm around Lace and headed her toward the door. "What makes you think I want to leave Maddie behind either?"

Suddenly a big male body, taking up the entire doorframe blocked them. A low voice said, "Then take her with you. Take the dog with you, too. I'll pay for arrangements that'll accommodate all three of you. But Max, I want you in my company."

Max stared at Dan Sawyers, his mostly absentee father, a man who until very recently had retreated from life. Annie's engagement had given him new purpose and forced him out of his self-imposed exile. Max was glad; he wanted his father happy.

Things had just gotten very complicated.

Distracted, Max watched Lace slip out of the shop in a hurry. Dan stood there, looking determined and somewhat uncertain.

Cleo, the traitor, abandoned him to chew on a rawhide bone.

Never before in his entire life could Max remember his father asking him for anything. His brother Daniel had been the father figure, filling in when their mother died and Dan retreated from everyone, including his children. He'd provided for them and seen that their physical, medical and monetary needs had been taken care of. But every holiday he'd sought isolation, leaving their emotional care to Daniel.

Max respected his brother more than any man he'd ever known. For most of his life, he'd resented his father.

"Can I get you anything, Dad? I think there's some coffee left."

Dan appeared to let out a breath he'd been holding. "Coffee would be great. A little conversation would be even better."

"Strange. I didn't think you cared for conversation." Max wanted to hold on to his resentment, to nurture it. But his thoughts were softened by Maddie, and he was in too mellow a mood to be angry.

They each pulled out chairs at the table Max and Lace had just abandoned. Max poured the strong, stale coffee.

"I owe you a lot of explanations."

"No. You owe Daniel, not me. And you owe him more than lip service."

"I know." Dan turned his coffee cup this way and that, took a sip and then winced at the bitterness. "Daniel and I are working things out. It was grossly unfair the way I abandoned him to deal with everything." In a softer voice he added, "He's an exceptional man. I'm so damn proud of him..."

Max gulped down his own coffee. All his life he'd been known as the difficult one. Daniel was the oldest, the most mature, the patriarch of the family from the time he was a kid. Annie was a sweetheart, the only girl, the most loving. But Max...he'd indulged in mischief for as long as he could remember and as soon as he'd gotten old enough, he'd taken to traveling.

As if reading his mind, his father said, "I'd always thought you'd outgrow your love of travel, but Lace tells me it's a part of you."

Max shrugged. "I enjoy it, but I've given it up."

"You don't need to give it up. I meant what I said. Guy has never liked traveling or dealing with the chore of buying from our manufacturers. In fact, he threatened to leave the company unless I took an equal share of the responsibility."

"I see." It figured that his father would find a way around accepting that agreement. "So you want me to fill in for you now?"

"Not at all."

Max held his cup a little more tightly. That wasn't what he'd been expecting to hear.

Smiling, Dan said, "Given the way I've behaved in the past, you have every right to your assumptions. But the fact is, I'm enjoying being involved again. I'm enjoying life again."

Heart softening, Max returned his smile. "I'm glad." Then he asked, "What brought about this drastic change?"

A small smile on his face, Dan said, "I got some good advice."

"That right?" Max sipped his coffee. "What kind of advice?"

Dan tugged on his ear. "Sexual advice." Before Max could quite assimilate that, he added, "I was assured that a little sex would improve my disposition greatly. I've decided it's worth a try."

Max choked on a swallow and was forced to spend several minutes regaining his breath. When he was finally able to wheeze again, he said, "Sex!" and with a rumble of blustering menace, "Did Lace fill your head with nonsense?"

"Nope." Dan grinned. "Got the advice straight out of the newspaper. From that guy who writes the column on sex."

Max promptly choked again. Dan stood to thwack him on the back several times, but it didn't help. Good God, he'd advised his own father to make whoopie!

The vague memory of an unsigned letter, which he'd answered in the column, slipped through Max's brain. It had been good advice, he thought. But not for his *Dad!*

"The thing is," Dan continued, as if his youngest son wasn't turning red and strangling to death, "I've been out of the loop too long, both personally and professionally. The personal end I can work on myself."

"Glad to hear it," Max managed. He knew for a fact he couldn't offer any more suggestions, so it was a good thing his father didn't want any.

"But I'm too old to start dealing with the entire workload all at once. You have a way with people, Max. Everyone respects you and likes you."

The praise not only distracted Max from his father's first bomb, but it also warmed him from the inside out. That didn't sit well with him. At his age, he shouldn't want or need a father's approval.

But it felt good to get it just the same.

Dan watched Max a moment, then continued. "Guy hates to travel, I'm not up to it, and you like it. Also, because of all your traveling, you're up on which supplies are quality, and what's needed where. You've hiked, skied, trekked through Africa, spent weeks alone in the wilds of Canada… You'd be the perfect one to make purchase recommendations."

Max glanced at his watch. The shop would close in an hour, then he'd head home and shower, make sure Cleo was fed and comfortable—and be with Maddie again. He could hardly wait.

Curiosity got the better of him and he asked, "How much travel are we talking?"

"In the States, pretty regularly. But as I said, the company can afford to accommodate you in whatever way you want."

"I won't have Cleo closed up in a damn storage area. She wouldn't understand and it would upset her."

Dan looked at Cleo, who was now snoring loudly. He grinned. "We have a small private plane. She can ride with you."

Damn but the idea was appealing. The need to be on the move had been eating at him for weeks. And Maddie had claimed she wanted to travel…

Of course, she'd also claimed to want him only to notch her bedpost. He'd have to work on her.

Tonight, he'd wrap her in such a hot, sensual spell, she'd become addicted and gladly follow him around the country.

Ha, and Cleo would learn to fly.

Max cursed low.

"What does that mean, Max? Are you considering it?"

"I don't know. I was actually thinking of something else."

"The foreign travel?" Dan asked anxiously. "Because there won't be much of that. Just one or two trips a year to Mexico, perhaps Taiwan or China."

If Maddie stuck around, Cleo could stay with her. It'd be nice to have them both to come home to.

Max flattened his hands on the tabletop. "Actually, I was thinking of a woman I've met recently. I'm not too keen on the idea of running off and leaving her unsupervised. She's…well, she's enticing as hell. Without me around, there'll be a line of guys trying to take my place."

Dan blinked at Max, then threw his head back and laughed.

Max couldn't remember the last time he'd seen his father laugh. "Care to share the joke?"

Dan wiped his eyes, still chuckling, and managed to say, "You're in love! By God, that's wonderful. And Max, don't misunderstand, I'm thrilled!"

*Love?* Max shook his head. "I don't know her that well."

"So? I met your mother and within minutes knew she was my life."

"Maddie makes me crazy."

"That's a good sign. When I first met your mother, I couldn't decide if I wanted to kiss her or throttle her."

"I guess kissing won out, huh?" Max found himself smiling, too.

"Absolutely. And she was worth all the effort it cost me to win her over." Dan looked at Max, his face again solemn. "There've been a lot of lost years, son. I hope you can forgive me, but I can understand if you can't."

Without a single hesitation, Max said, "I forgive you." In many ways, he was beginning to realize the loss was more his father's than his own. He'd had Daniel and Annie and Guy…but his father had had no one and nothing but his grief.

"Thank you." Dan smiled in relief, then released Max and stood. "You do love her, son. I can see it in your face."

Also coming to his feet, Max said, "I don't know. It's not that easy."

"Love never is! But you're a good catch, so I'm positive she feels the same." Dan clapped him on the shoulder. "Think about the job. We really do need you there."

Grinning, Max said, "I'll talk it over with Maddie." Who knows, he thought, Maddie said she wanted to travel. Maybe the job would be a lure to help get her to commit.

At this point, Max was willing to try anything.

# Chapter 7

Maddie waited outside the clinic for Max. She couldn't stop thinking about what he'd done to her, what they'd done together! It was so wonderful.

And she couldn't stop thinking about Cleo.

Darn it all, she missed the dog almost as much as she missed the man. They were both so special! How many young, handsome, virile, world-traveled men would have settled down to take care of a dog? A very needy dog.

Not many.

No two ways about it, Max was special.

And she was sunk.

Maddie collapsed back against the brick wall of the clinic. How much longer would she have with Max? A few days, a week? Admitting to herself that she'd gotten emotionally involved wasn't easy. She'd meant to keep things superficial, to gather up some memories without commitment, the same as so many others did. Her ex had accused her of being too prim, and she'd wanted to prove him wrong. But now, what he thought didn't matter.

Deep down where it really counted, which was in her own heart, Maddie had always known that she wasn't the type of woman for sexual flings.

Oh, flinging with Max was great. Superb in fact. But she also wanted him to hold her. She wanted to talk to him and ask about his travels. Most of what she knew of Max she'd learned from Annie. And it wasn't enough.

Bea and Carmilla and Mavis swore she needed to hold out on him. Not sex, because Max could get that anywhere and from just about any woman. She needed to hold out on all those things she so wanted to give to him; affection and caring and...*love*.

Maddie groaned, knowing she was already too deeply involved to hold back on anything.

A bright yellow dandelion grew up through a crack in the sidewalk in front of the clinic and Maddie ruthlessly brought her sandal down onto it.

She could not love Max Sawyers!

A long, low whistle brought her head up. Max stood there, grinning like the devil, his dark eyes full of teasing good humor. "You got a thing about weeds, I gather?"

Maddie stared at him blankly. "What?"

"You looked like you had murder on your mind."

Maddie devoured the sight of him. He looked

scrumptious in a casual white shirt and khaki slacks. His dark hair was windblown, his teeth white in his tanned face. Her heart did a flip-flop, and was followed by her stomach.

She couldn't give him love, but she could give him female appreciation.

Maddie threw herself at him. Max looked startled for just a second before Maddie got hold of his head and brought it down for her kiss. "I missed you, Max."

He gave a murmuring reply against her lips. "Hmm. I like this welcome."

"Everything we did this afternoon… I haven't been able to stop thinking about…it." She'd almost said *you* but that would have given too much away.

Max lifted his head, looked up and down the street and smiled at her. "We're being watched by about a dozen people."

"Oh!" Maddie quickly straightened. Good grief, she worked here. The last thing she wanted to do was put on a show.

"Did you put your panties back on?"

"Of course!"

"Spoilsport."

Oh, the way he said that. He could make her want him with just a whispered word. "Max, behave. You'll get me all flustered and then I won't be able to concentrate on the meeting."

When she started to turn away, he caught her hand. "Tonight, how do you want it? Conventional or kinky?"

"Max…"

"Hey, a man needs to make plans. So which is it to be, sweetheart?"

He obviously liked to fluster her, Maddie thought. She looked up at him, touched his bottom lip, and said, "How about both?"

Maddie felt his indrawn breath both from her touch and her reply.

"You little witch," Max said with something that bordered on admiration. "Both it is."

"I was just teasing!"

"I'm not." Max handed her the slim book she'd requested. "Have you read this thing?"

"Not yet. Why? Did you?"

"Bits and pieces. It was…interesting, but not always accurate."

"There you see! I knew your perspective would add a lot." She smiled at him.

Max groaned. "Let's go get this over with before I change my mind."

Catching his arm, Maddie led him into the old building and down the tiled hallways. "You're not nervous are you?"

"Nervous about speaking to a bunch of young women on sexual dos and don'ts? Why ever would I be nervous?"

His sarcasm was plain to hear.

"Um, Max, about the women…" Maddie started to explain to him that the women weren't exactly young, but as she pushed open the door to the conference room, Max froze. Her friends were already inside.

Mavis, dressed in a long flowing dress of bright

cherry red that nearly matched her hair, sat with her feet propped up on another chair. She wiggled her foot in time to whatever music was coming through a set of headphones plugged into a portable CD player.

Bea, wearing jeans and a white ruffled blouse, paced, obviously deep in thought. And Carmilla was secluded in the corner talking to someone who sat behind her. Maddie couldn't see who it was.

Maddie cleared her throat and drew everyone's attention.

Max looked around the room, then at Maddie. Bending close to her ear, he whispered, "These are not young women, Maddie."

"Uh, no."

Bea gave Max a thorough once-over, then let loose with a wolf whistle.

Nodding in agreement, Mavis said, "Ho, baby. He's a hottie."

Bea added, "Our girl knows how to pick 'em, doesn't she?"

"Neither," Max said, his face bright red, "do any of these women look the least bit confused about anything sexual."

Bea said, "Ha!"

Mavis added, "You got that right, sweet cheeks." And she gave him a cocky grin.

"They're very nice ladies, Max." Maddie tried glaring at Mavis and Bea so they'd back off just a little. Max looked ready to make a run for it. "I promise."

Carmilla finally stepped out of the corner and a

man rose up from behind her. He rose and rose and rose some more.

Easily six feet six inches, the man was enormously built and bald as an ostrich egg. He wore a black Harley-Davidson T-shirt with the sleeves cut off to show massive biceps. His right forearm sported an intricate tattoo of a naked lady. When he moved his arm—which he was doing now by flexing his knuckles—the naked lady danced.

Maddie gulped.

Max said with certainty, "That is no lady."

The big man started forward.

Mustering up her courage, Maddie tentatively tried to offer her hand, and instead found herself tossed behind Max's back.

Carmilla burst loose with a robust laugh. "Honey, your heart's in the right place, but you sure ain't up to taking on Tiny."

Maddie peeked around Max. "Tiny? That's really you?"

Eyes narrowed, Max turned to face her suspiciously. "Is this another one of your jokes, Maddie? Like that 'small pistol' business. Because there's nothing tiny about that guy. He's *huge.*"

Maddie giggled nervously. "You mean just like your roll of dimes?"

Max gave her a belligerent look and growled, *"Flashlight."* Then he jutted his chin and added, "Industrial size."

"Oh, yeah." She giggled again. "I remember now."

"I know him," Carmilla interjected, "and I can guarantee you he would never hurt Maddie." Then, just because Carmilla was so dang bloodthirsty, she added, "But I make no guarantees where you're concerned, young fellow."

Max snorted.

Scooting out from behind her erstwhile protector, Maddie said, "Tiny, it's so nice to finally meet you!" There had been times in the past year that she'd wondered if Tiny was real, or a romanticized figment of Carmilla's imagination.

The man was very real. Imposingly real.

And though he took Maddie's hand and kissed her knuckles in a curiously old-world gesture, he kept looking at Carmilla with adoring eyes.

Well, well, Maddie thought. She glanced at Bea, who winked, and then to Mavis, who was still eyeing Max's more interesting parts.

"*Down,* Mavis," Bea suddenly said. "Apparently our Maddie is the jealous sort. Just look at her, her eyes are turning red."

Mavis looked and said, "I'll be damned. Even her nostrils are flared." Then to Carmilla, "Quit playing touchy-feely with your boyfriend and come look at Maddie."

It wasn't just her eyes that were red after that comment. Especially when Max, wearing a huge grin, peered directly into her gaze.

"Are you jealous, sweetheart? And here I didn't say a word when Tiny kissed your hand."

"So," Mavis said, sauntering forward. "You're the young stud Maddie has been telling us all about."

Max stiffened, then glared at Maddie.

Shrugging, she whispered, "I didn't tell them *everything*. I just…"

"She bragged on you, is what she did. And after that worthless creep she almost married, we were more than glad to hear it."

Max gave a parody of a smile. "What exactly did she tell you?"

Bea stepped forward and gave Mavis a warning frown. Then she turned her smile to Max. "Why, she told us you'd made her happy." Her smile lit up just a bit more. "And Maddie definitely deserves some happiness."

Things were out of control, Maddie decided. "Are we having a meeting today or not?"

"Not," Carmilla said. "We want to get to know Max better. That's more important."

"And it's for certain he can't tell us anything about sex that we don't already know," Bea added.

"After all," Mavis said with a sniff, "we got paid for our expertise."

Maddie whipped around to face Max, giving the women and Tiny her back. In a pleading voice, she said, "I'm sorry!"

Surprising her, Max touched her cheek and said, "For what?"

"I…" She felt confused and lost her train of thought. "I meant to tell you about this, about my friends…"

"They are friends, aren't they?" She nodded and he said, "I think that shows what a special woman you are, that friendship has grown from counsel meetings."

"Damn right," Carmilla said, and Bea added, "Best friends. She's like a daughter to us, and you should remember that."

Mavis laughed. "Calm down, Maddie. He's not afraid of three little old ladies. Are you, young man?"

Max looked over Maddie's head at the others. His eyes were lit with challenge. "Why don't we all sit down?" He threw his arm around Maddie, almost making her drop the book. "I'll wager there's a few things I can still enlighten you on."

Tiny smiled.

Carmilla snorted.

Bea and Mavis said in unison, "You're dreamin'!"

Maddie wished she could just crawl away. But Max had hold of her hand and his grip was unbreakable.

Oh, dear. This wasn't at all what she'd planned.


Max wanted to laugh at the silly little sick look on Maddie's face.

Prostitutes! Who'd have thought she was counseling retired ladies of the night? He shook his head. One thing about Maddie, she never ceased to surprise him.

"You know," he said to Mavis, who seemed to be the most brazen, "I thought I was here to talk to young innocent girls who were either caught in an unexpected pregnancy or had troubled home lives."

"You didn't expect a bunch of old biddies, did you?"

"I didn't expect mature women, no."

"Maddie does counseling with women of all ages.

The poor young girls you're talking about meet with her on Tuesdays."

"And they're lucky to have her," Carmilla told him. "They don't come any more compassionate than Maddie."

"Not to mention how smart she is, and such a good listener." Bea smiled fondly at Maddie.

Maddie had slipped down in her chair until her face was almost hidden behind the fall of her hair. She looked miserable by the turn of events.

But her long legs, thrust out in front of her looked incredibly nice. Max wanted to start kissing her slim ankles and work his way up. All the way up.

Until she was panting and moaning and… He cleared his throat.

"How many nights a week does she do this?"

Bea, catching his distraction with Maddie's legs, raised a brow and asked, "This?"

Max shook his head. "Have these meetings."

Carmilla perched herself on Tiny's lap. Tiny didn't seem to mind, if his big grin was any indication. "Two to three times a week," she said, "depending. Truth is, we should have quit bugging her years ago, but she's so much fun to talk to. Like the daughter none of us ever had."

Maddie was a nurturer, Max thought, seeing it in the older women's eyes. She didn't pass judgment on people, and she looked beyond the obvious. He knew that much about her because of how she'd so readily accepted Cleo.

"Did you know," Max asked, more than willing to work to meet the women's standards, "that men can literally become addicted to a certain woman's smell?"

Maddie's head lifted, her eyes filled with fascination.

Bea scoffed.

Carmilla looked at Tiny, who delicately sniffed her shoulder.

Mavis shrugged. "Where'd you hear such a thing?"

"I've read about it in medical studies. My brother is a doctor and my sister-in-law is a sex therapist."

That got a few raised brows. Max hid his smile. "Every woman's skin has a unique scent. A man's body can get used to that scent, and if the woman leaves him—" or dies, Max thought, as his mother had, and suddenly he understood his father much, much better "—then the man will suffer withdrawal. It's probably where the term heartsick came from. You *do* feel like you have a broken heart. And it really does hurt."

Max looked at Maddie. How would he feel if he could never hold her again, never kiss her again? In such a short time he'd become very addicted to her, her laugh, her smile, her compassion. And her scent.

What exactly had his poor father gone through, knowing the woman he loved had been taken from him forever?

The women were quiet, watching Max with new respect. Max knew they'd expected him to orate on sexual positions or some such nonsense. But he was smarter than that.

"Did you know," he asked, watching them all closely, "that sex is a natural pain reliever?"

They all straightened up to listen.

"It's true. Sex releases endorphins that relieve pain."

"Fascinating," Maddie said. "Annie told me a little about this."

"Annie manipulated the facts so she could seduce poor Guy." Before that, Max thought, he'd never known how creatively sneaky his baby sister could be, or how determined she was to have Guy as her own.

"My knee *has* been botherin' me," Tiny rumbled, and everyone laughed as Carmilla swatted at him.

"Both men and women," Max continued, pleased that he had their rapt attention, "have testosterone. And testosterone is the only proven true aphrodisiac."

"All right," Bea said, "you win. I didn't know any of that."

Carmilla bobbed her slim eyebrows. "Want us to tell you some of what we know?"

Lounging back in his chair, his arms spread wide, Max said, "Sorry girls. I already know it all."

Maddie threw the book at him, which he handily caught, while the others all hooted and made lewd observations. Max blew a kiss at Maddie and said, "I'm having fun, doll. You should have introduced me to your friends earlier."

While Maddie sat there looking openly pleased with him, Max passed the book over to Tiny. "You should check that out. Especially chapter six."

Tiny looked at the book. Max hoped like hell the guy could read! Then Tiny flipped through a few pages and grinned. "Interesting stuff, huh?"

"Real interesting."

Carmilla tried to grab the book, but Tiny held it out of her reach. "If you want to know what it says, you'll have to let me read it to you."

"Is that a dare?" Carmilla asked.

Tiny looked at Maddie. "Would you mind if Carmilla and I took off a little early? Now that I'm finally with her again, I'd like to get her to myself just a bit."

Maddie looked at the couple with dreamy, romantic eyes. "Of course I don't mind!" She sighed. "I think it's very sweet of you."

Carmilla had silver hair and faded brown eyes, but in that moment, she looked like an excited young girl. Max wanted to imitate Tiny and pull Maddie into his lap, but she stayed out of reach for the next ten minutes.

It wasn't until after Carmilla had gone and Bea and Mavis and Maddie had shared speculation on what might come of the relationship, that Max was able to really get her attention again.

He caught her close and kissed her. The older women chuckled and urged Max with ribald suggestions.

Maddie hid her face in his chest once he released her.

"So," Max asked, "which of you lovely ladies does the incredible slogans?"

Bea, looking flattered, primped with her white hair. "That would be me."

"Care to talk business for a moment?"

Bea glanced at Mavis and Maddie and then, blushing like a schoolgirl, said, "Sure. That'd be fine," and with just a touch more hesitation, "right now?"

"It's a simple proposition."

"I know all about *those,* honey!"

Max smiled. "Not that kind." He really enjoyed the women's ease and comfort with their pasts. They were obviously no longer in the flesh business, and just as obviously not about to make apologies. They were strong, blunt women, and he respected that.

"I just agreed to do some work for my father," Max said. "It'll involve traveling and purchasing." Out of the corner of his eye, Max watched Maddie make a sudden jerky move. He glanced at her, and saw that her eyes had flared, her cheeks had gone pale. He started to ask her what was wrong, but then she lowered her head to stare at her hands.

Max cleared his throat. "Once I agreed to the job, I got to thinking about other parts of the business. We deal in sporting goods and outdoor recreations like rock climbing and kayaking and such. A lot of the equipment we advertise is geared toward a younger crowd. I'm thinking your slogans may be the perfect way to draw attention to them."

"Oh, this could be fun," Bea said, and her blue eyes were alight with excitement.

"Why don't you think on it, maybe come up with a couple of samples, and we'll present them to my father to see what he thinks."

"I'll get right on it!" Bea sauntered away, murmuring to herself, already working on thinking up ideas. Watching her, Max noticed that she was slim despite her age, and had a rather stately walk. It dawned on him that Carmilla and Mavis were the same, though Carmilla had a very lush figure and Mavis was bordering on petite. They each had to be in or near their early seventies, but they had the attitudes and personalities of women much younger.

He wondered what his dad would think of them. He could hardly wait to introduce him to Bea. Now that his father was reentering the world, he could use a little shock therapy.

Mavis held up her hands. "I guess this makes me the third wheel."

"Not at all!" Maddie tried to stop her from leaving, but Mavis waved her off.

"I have a date anyway, honey, so don't worry about me."

Max cocked a brow. "A date?"

Maddie gave him a look. "Mavis is very popular among the retirees."

"Mmm-hmm," Mavis agreed. "Tonight I'm doing up the town with a very handsome widower." She leaned forward and confided, "He's six years younger than me! Only sixty-two. Isn't that delicious?"

Max held his humor in check and gave Mavis a hug. She was an easily likeable woman and he wished her a good time. He imagined the widower would have his hands full this night.

Once they were alone, Max asked Maddie, "You all right?" She was still too quiet and far too distracted. If she was thinking of the coming night and what she'd do with the stuff she'd bought at the fetish store, he'd gladly enlighten her to new plans.

"Yes, I'm fine."

He didn't believe her. Something was making her clam up, and Max decided he'd find out exactly what it was once he had her safely ensconced at his house. He took her hand and started her toward the door.

"You ever frolicked in a hot tub, Maddie, honey?"

Her steps faltered. "A hot tub?"

"In my backyard."

"But…it's too cool for that."

"Oh ye of little faith. I promise to keep you plenty warm enough. Hot even." Max leaned down to her ear and nipped her earlobe. "Burning up, in fact," he rasped.

They walked outside and Max started to lead her to his truck. Maddie held back. "I'll drive myself and meet you there."

No way. Max intended to keep her until he returned her to her home himself. If she was without a car, his odds were a lot better of succeeding. "Why bother," he asked. "Your car will be safe enough here."

"But…" She hesitated, then said, "Okay, just a second." Jogging over to her car, she unlocked the trunk and got out the bag he'd seen her purchase at the fetish shop. He thought of that damn collar and wanted to howl.

"Whatcha got there?" Max asked as she approached him again, the bag clutched tightly in her little fist.

Maddie grinned. "It's a surprise, remember? I promise to show you later tonight."

Oh, she'd show him all right. Max could hardly wait.

Once she was seated inside, the bag on the floor at her feet, Maddie looked at him. "Max?"

"Yes?" He hoped she'd ask for details on the hot tub, and then he intended to tantalize her with a blow-by-blow description of what he'd do to her, how he'd do it. The fun they'd both have.

"Do you taste the same as I do?"

The truck lurched hard as he pulled out into traffic. "Do I *what?*"

"Taste the same?" Maddie smoothed her skirt and settled herself comfortably in the seat. "I've been thinking about it all day. I don't mind if we play in the hot tub for a while, but when I taste you, I think we should be inside." As if sharing a confidence, she said, "I don't want to take a chance on a neighbor seeing us or something."

Max said, "Uh…" his mind still way back there on the tasting business.

She peeked at him. "I'm shy."

Max almost missed the turn onto the main street. "You intend to—" the words were so arousing, they would barely leave his tight throat "—*taste* me?" He hoped like hell she meant what he thought she meant.

Leaning slightly closer, Maddie put her small hand on his thigh. "Yes. Just like you tasted me." And then her hand tightened, squeezing his leg perilously close to a now very noticeable hard-on, and she added in a whisper, "Everywhere."

Max pushed down on the gas pedal.

"Slowly, Max, just as you've shown me." Her fingers drifted up his thigh, and he held his breath. Then they moved down to his knee. He groaned in disappointment and relief.

"Faster at the end though." Her fingers drifted upward again. "That's the right way, isn't it?"

Max locked his jaw to keep from panting with sensual pain. He could almost feel her mouth on him, her small pink tongue playful. He gulped.

Okay, so she wanted to play with bondage. No big deal. He could handle that, especially if it got her this enthusiastic.

She wanted to taste him.

Max felt like a Victorian maiden, ready to swoon. He concentrated hard on keeping the truck on the road so they didn't end up in a ditch.

Other women had riled him, aroused him, made him burn. What Maddie proposed had been done to him before. Hell, he'd done just about everything a man could do with a woman, and always enjoyed himself. So why was he shaking now? Why was he going alternately hot and cold with the excitement of it, the utter lust?

And dammit, his toes had just curled again.

Admittedly, he was in deep—and worse, he loved every minute of it.

# Chapter 8

They snuck into his house like thieves. Cleo, proving herself to be a miserable guard dog, was snoring too loudly to hear them. One small light shone from the kitchen, and the glow filtered into the living room where the dog sprawled across an enormous beige leather couch. Her tongue lolled out one side of her mouth, with spittle running down the couch cushion.

"She gets nervous in the dark," Max said. "So I always leave a light on for her."

Maddie's heart again performed that strange little softening for this man and his beast. "She's not much good at protecting you."

Max gave her a solemn nod. "I'd rather protect her anyway."

He was such an incredible man. And she wanted him so much.

She was also falling in love with him. Damn. Double damn.

It had just about killed her when Max claimed he'd be traveling again. She wanted to travel, too, and see the whole world. But she'd gladly have stayed in Ohio the rest of her life with Max. At first that idea hadn't appealed at all. When he'd said he'd given up traveling, she'd wanted to bemoan his decision. She didn't understand how anyone could not want to see the world, especially a man known for his wanderlust. Now she hated it that he'd leave her.

Maybe his life wasn't as settled as he'd claimed.

Soon he wouldn't have time for her anymore.

Maddie held close to the waistband of his slacks and followed him down the darkened hallway. She was here with him now, and the night was still young. Rather than regret the coming future, she should take advantage of the moment to get the most out of every second she could.

Max's house was beautiful on the outside. A mixture of Mediterranean tiles and stucco and lush landscaping. It wasn't enormous, but it was isolated, on a cul-de-sac, apart from the other houses and far more private.

The inside was too dark to distinguish precise colors, but the rooms were open, flowing into one another. The furnishings were sparse and everything appeared to be spotless. Max pulled her into his bedroom and softly closed the door.

Maddie thought of what she wanted to do to him,

and how he'd react. Her stomach knotted with excitement and she licked her lips.

In the very next instant, she found herself pinned to a wall being kissed silly.

Max closed both hands over her breasts, moaned sharply, then parted her legs with his knee. He was hard, pulsing against her belly. Maddie tore her mouth away. "Max!"

Ruthlessly, he recaptured her lips. "I need you, Maddie. Right now."

She dodged him again. "I have plans!"

He groaned and pressed his face into her neck. "Your plans are what have me coming apart. Maddie, I don't know if I could bear it."

Smoothing his back, smiling quietly to herself, Maddie said, "Now Max. You're a stud, remember? Surely there's nothing I can do to you that you can't handle."

He bit her shoulder, making her yelp, then he straightened. "All right. If you're going to challenge me then I suppose I have to prove myself." He stepped away from her for a second to flip on a bedside lamp. The light was gentle, soft, just barely touching a king-size bed that was unmade and looked very comfortable.

She met Max's gaze and said, "Oh good. Now I can see you better."

His eyes nearly crossed. He took a deep breath, flexed his fingers, and then said, "Okay I think I'm ready." But as she reached for his belt he said, "No wait! It'd be better if you got undressed first."

Maddie blinked at him. "Why?"

Voice dropping an octave to where the guttural sounds stroked up and down her nerve endings, Max said, "I'll be distracted by your gorgeous bod and might be able to control myself better."

*Might be able to control himself?* Did that mean he was losing his control? Maddie smiled. She really liked the idea that she could push his buttons. "All right."

With Max watching her closely, his gaze a hot caress, she stripped off her clothes. She loved how he looked at her, how his muscles tensed and his high cheekbones colored with arousal.

She'd never experienced a man looking at her with so much intensity. Her fiancé never had, and she was very glad that she'd found out about him before she'd foolishly gotten married. Otherwise she wouldn't be here with Max now, and just the thought of that left her empty.

When she was completely naked she slowly stepped up to Max and undid his belt buckle. "You promise you're going to behave now, right?"

"Yes." Then he groaned as her hand slipped inside his open fly. "I'm such a liar," he gasped. "Hell no, I'm not going to behave. You're naked. You're talking about doing lecherous things to my body!"

"I'm not just talking Max. I'm going to do them."

He nodded, resigned and anxious. "Right now, I'm just concentrating on my legs."

Maddie slowly stroked him through his briefs. He was hard, throbbing and impossibly large. "Your legs?"

"Yes," he croaked. "I have to remember that I have them so I don't fall down."

Maddie chuckled. "Let's get rid of your shirt."

Before she could reach for it, Max had already whisked it over his head. It went sailing across the room to a darkened corner. Without her instruction, he kicked his shoes off and they thumped somewhere behind her.

Knowing she'd make him crazier, Maddie went to her knees in front of him. She removed his socks, teasing him by taking her time. Lastly, her hands curled around the waistband of his khaki slacks. She pulled both his pants and his underwear down, then ordered, "Step out."

He did, and Maddie looked up the tall, hard length of his body. Her nipples pulled tight and her belly tingled. He was so gorgeous, all male, rigid and strong and his scent…she leaned forward and kissed his abdomen, then drew his smell deeply inside her lungs.

Max's fingers settled into her hair, gently cradling her head. "Maddie." His voice was hoarse with strain.

Her fingers could barely circle him, holding him close at the base of his erection. She could feel his heartbeat there, matching her own. With her other hand she explored his firm backside, the iron hard muscles of his thighs, the soft tender weight below his shaft.

Max shook, his breath a gasping sound in the otherwise quiet room.

She kissed his right thigh, the smooth taut skin of his hipbone. His fingers tightened, inexorably guiding her to where he wanted to feel her mouth.

Suddenly overwhelmed with a need to please him and herself, Maddie obliged and without warning, without so much as a single peck to warn of her intent, she drew him deep. As deep as she could.

His taste was incredible, hot and salty and alive. She swirled her tongue around him, amazed at how seducing him was seducing her as well.

Max jerked hard, his head back, his fingers now tight, holding her close. He moved, once, twice, then cursed low. "I can't, Maddie."

She withdrew a bit, licked the very tip of him, and said, "Yes, you can."

He howled, sounding much like a wounded wolf. "You don't get it, baby." She could barely understand him, his words were so raw. "I'm about to—"

Thrilled with her success, Maddie said, "Please do," and enclosed him in her mouth once again.

A heavy beat of stillness enveloped them, not a sound, not a heartbeat. And then Max broke. Maddie nearly cried out with the excitement of it. She hadn't known a man could be so untamed in his pleasure, so hot and free.

Maddie continued tantalizing him until his legs went limp and he dropped to his knees in front of her. He sat back, still panting, then met her anxious gaze and gave her a breathy laugh.

"You're dangerous," he whispered, and pulled her close. There on the floor he held her, giving her all the cuddling she'd wanted, until the trembling had left his body and he could breathe again.

And then he got even.

* * *

Max watched Maddie sleeping the next day. It was early afternoon, but she showed no signs of waking. Her blond hair was twisted onto his pillow, and her bottom was beautifully bare. He smiled. He wanted to touch her, but more than that he knew he needed to let her sleep. After the stunt she'd pulled last night, he'd kept her awake till well past dawn.

And even then he hadn't been appeased.

Maddie was simply different. Better. More. Deeper and sweeter and more consuming. He'd never tire of her. He knew that now.

What to do? Having her around would provide the perfect home life for Cleo. And for him. He needed her to commit to him, but she claimed to be against marriage.

All night long, she'd reveled in their intimacy, but not once had she hinted at an emotional connection.

Quietly, Max slipped from the bed and went to the kitchen to get juice. He'd wake her, they'd talk, and hopefully he could find some chink in her armor, some way to make her stop distrusting marriage, and to give him a chance to bind her to him.

Maddie awoke to the shifting of the bed and warm breath drifting over her bare hip. She smiled even before she got her eyes open. "Mmm," she mumbled with a languid stretch that found plenty of sore muscles from the newest night of debauchery. Max was just so damn good at debauching. A master.

"Not again, Max," she moaned, knowing she needed a warm shower before she could even think of going another round.

She twisted to face him, then jumped a foot when Cleo met her with a loud bark. She was naked in front of the dog!

Dreadfully embarrassed, Maddie jerked the sheet up off the floor to cover herself. The bed was destroyed, the sheets pulled loose, the spread totally gone. Both pillows were in the middle of the bed and Maddie blushed when she remembered why. Max had propped her up like a pagan offering, then made her feel pagan with the carnal way he'd enjoyed her body.

Cleo came the rest of the way into the bed, a little hesitant, keeping her head low, her tail well hidden, and Maddie felt emotions rise to choke her.

Scooting so that she was more or less sitting in the bed with the sheet around her sarong-style, she opened her arms to Cleo and the dog lumbered onto her lap.

It was the first time Cleo had come to her so openly, and it broke Maddie's heart. Maddie squeezed the dog tight as tears seeped from her eyes. She loved the ugly beast as much as she loved the magnificent master.

She wanted them both. She wanted them forever.

Yet she'd argued with Max, insisting on no more than a notch on the bedpost.

"Oh Cleo," Maddie wailed softly, "what am I going to do?" Last night had been the stuff dreams were made of, and Max thought it was all a lark, a way for her to gain sexual experience.

She certainly didn't disdain what she was learning sexually. No way. Max was a remarkable lover, natural and intense and so clever. Very clever.

But she cared about more than their physical relationship. She cared about all of him, his humor and his honor and the way he loved. He gave Cleo his whole heart, and he hadn't hesitated at all to befriend Carmilla, Bea and Mavis.

He was so easy to love, darn it.

More tears trickled down her cheeks, and Cleo whined. She licked Maddie's face, then began to wail.

The dog had the worst morning breath Maddie had ever smelled, but it didn't matter. They comforted each other, and it broke Maddie's heart to admit she had played a dumb game and lost. She'd thought she could cavort in sexual frivolity with Max and just walk away more experienced. She should have known after seeing Max with Cleo that he wasn't a man who could be played with.

And he wasn't a man who women willingly walked away from.

Maddie rocked the dog, holding her pudgy body tight. Cleo shifted around anxiously, throwing her head back and really getting into the maudlin mood of it. The more Cleo whimpered, the more tears ran down Maddie's face to mat in the dog's scruffy fur. The more Maddie hugged and cuddled the dog, the more Cleo moaned and yowled.

Max came running into the room. He carried a tray with two glasses of orange juice on it and a look of befuddlement on his face. He stopped in the doorway and glared when he saw the two females huddled on the bed making enough racket to wake the entire street.

"What the hell is going on?"

Max looked at Maddie's tear-streaked face with alarm. Good God, she didn't cry well. Her nose was red and swollen, her eyes puffy. Her cheeks were blotchy.

He wanted to hold her in his lap and beg her not to cry. First she'd curled his toes, and now she was ripping his guts out.

More softly, he asked, "What's all the caterwauling about?" He set the tray down on the nightstand. "Maddie? Are you hurt?"

She hid her face in the dog's fur. When he started to touch her, Cleo issued a low growl of warning, then snuffled her nose into Maddie's neck.

"Well, I'll be." His damn dog had switched loyalties. Max shook his head. Good thing he loved Maddie, too. *Love.* What a tricky thing to happen to a guy.

From now on, when he wrote his column, he'd be a lot more understanding with the poor saps who got themselves tangled up in the emotion. It was damn hard to deal with, setting his heart on fire and turning his brain to mush. Everything he'd always thought he knew about women now seemed insignificant, all because he hadn't yet known Maddie. Which meant he hadn't known much at all.

Oh sure, he could make little Maddie scream with pleasure, but could he make her say, "I do"? He hadn't believed in love at first sight. He hadn't

been all that sure that love existed at all, at least
not the type of love that had stolen his father from
him, the type of love that had turned his sedate older
brother into a caveman and their friend, Guy, into a
ball of distraction.

Max had honestly believed that if love existed, it
needed time to grow, to stew and ferment and get real
sticky. But hell, almost from the second he'd seen
Maddie, his heart had known she was different. He
tried to claim it was just his body talking—because
she was one sexy little number—but no. It had been
his heart attempting to warn his head, and now he
had a wailing woman in bed with his dog and a bad
case of uncertainty.

When Maddie lifted her face again, Max stared
in horror. She had dog hairs stuck to the tear tracks
on her cheeks. She looked to be in the throes of a
transition from woman to werewolf.

She sniffed loudly. And wetly. "I'm sorry, Max."

Feeling his way, Max ventured, "For what exactly?"

"For—" She sniffed again and Cleo whined in
sympathy "—for carrying on so."

Max sat on the edge of the bed and ignored Cleo's
protective bluster to scratch her ear. "Care to tell me
what you're carrying on about?"

Maddie nodded, but then said, "You'll hate me."

"Oh, hon." He picked off a few of the dog hairs
clinging to her cheeks. "I could never hate you."

"I love you."

Max drew back, nonplussed. "What?"

"See! It's awful!" Her face went back into Cleo's fur and Cleo glared at him.

Max got his mouth to close while wondering if he'd heard right. He felt mired in confusion. Cleo continued to give him dirty looks.

Max needed to take this slowly. If Maddie really was confessing to what he thought she might be confessing to, she sure as hell wasn't happy about it.

"Here, sweetheart. Drink a little juice." A totally inane thing to suggest, but at the moment nothing more brilliant came to him.

Maddie wrinkled her red nose up and turned away. "I can't drink cold in the morning. I need coffee. Hot black coffee."

"Oh." Max frowned at her. "The caffeine is bad for you."

Maddie blinked spiked wet lashes and then her face crumbled again. "What does it matter," she wailed. "Everything is ruined now anyway and I love Cleo so much."

So now she loved Cleo, too? Max looked around his room for inspiration. There was none to be found.

Making a sudden decision, he said to Cleo, "You gotta go out, girl?"

The dog abandoned Maddie's secure hold in the blink of an eye and began anxiously circling Max's feet. Max threw the sheet off the bed, lifted Maddie in his arms, and started out of the room.

"Max! What are you doing?"

He didn't slow down. Cleo danced along beside him, her tubby body jiggling as he headed for the back door. "You look like hell in the morning, Maddie, did you know that?"

She pressed her face into his shoulder, sharing some of the tear-soaked dog hairs. "Yes. But it doesn't matter."

"Caffeine doesn't matter, how you look doesn't matter. What does matter, sweetheart?"

She started to answer, then gasped loudly as he slid the patio doors open and stepped outside. Cool April air washed over their naked bodies. Cleo shot past, running into the yard beyond the privacy fence and barking with the sheer joy of going outside. She found her deflated plastic ball in the yard and trotted it back to Max.

"Just a second, girl. I have my hands full."

Maddie clutched at him. Her red-rimmed eyes were huge and her face was pale. "What are you doing?"

She sounded squeaky, all aghast at being outside in the buff.

"I promised you the hot tub. But then you distracted me with that incredible mouth of yours." Color rushed back into her cheeks, making Max smile. "The water's warm, so prepare yourself."

Maddie tried to keep a death grip on his neck, but Max lowered her into the frothing water of the hot tub. She looked around, and when she realized they were hidden completely by tall trees and the fence, she relaxed. Her gaze was still anxious as she watched him throw the ball for Cleo.

Max climbed into the tub and joined her. "I forgot about this," he said as he lifted her into his lap and positioned her to recline back against his chest. "And didn't you forget about something, too?"

Maybe if he could distract her from her tears, Maddie would tell him she loved him again. More calmly this time, so that he could believe it.

Maddie held still as Max cupped her breasts beneath the churning water. She caught his wrists and pressed his hands closer still. "What did I forget?"

"You said you had a surprise for me," Max reminded her.

"Oh!" She twisted around to face him. "I forgot after...well, after you did what you did."

"What I did?" Max teased, glad to see she'd stopped crying for the moment. "What about what you did."

Her ravaged face softened. "I loved what I did. You taste so good, Max, and it was so extraordinary to watch you—" Max clapped his hand over her mouth. "Shh," he warned. "I always wake up horny, and having you here makes it especially bad because I've been wanting you since before I even opened my eyes. Don't torture me now, okay?"

Maddie nodded and when he lifted his hand she asked, "Always?"

He grinned. "Yeah."

She bit her lip, and her gaze tried to see him below the water, but the bubbles made that impossible. Finally she sighed. "Okay. Can I go get my surprise now?"

Max stalled. "Uh, now?" He looked around. The yard was secluded, but he wasn't sure he wanted to get into anything too frisky out in the open that way. "What about waiting until we—"

Before he could finish, she'd scrambled out of the hot tub—giving Max a delectable glimpse of her pale round bottom—then darted for the door. She was back in less than half a minute with her bag.

Max stiffened, anxious and turned on and curious.

To his surprise she called Cleo to her and the dog came running, her tooth-punctured ball clamped in her mouth. Cleo growled and grumbled and groused as she approached Maddie, but her tail was out and wagging. Max leaned back into the water and felt contentment swell inside him.

Life was good with his dog happy and his woman making him crazy with lust.

All he had to do was figure out this love business.

"Come here, Cleo," Maddie was saying and she seemed oblivious to her nakedness now. Max was far from unaware. The chill of being wet and in the cool air had Maddie's nipples drawn tight. He could almost taste her.

Reaching into the bag, Maddie lifted out the ornate collar. Red leather, with colorful studs, just as she'd ordered.

"Isn't it beautiful?" she asked Max. "I couldn't find anything pretty enough for Cleo at the pet store, but I'd noticed her collar was looking a little old."

Max stared at the decorative, gaudy fetish collar and wanted to roar in hilarity at his own misconceptions.

He also wanted to moan out his disappointment.

Though at first he hadn't been too keen on getting kinky, he'd kind of gotten used to it.

"She didn't like for me to mess with it," Max explained, nearly choking on his suppressed laughter.

Maddie nodded. "This one is pretty. I found it at a...specialty shop. She'll like it. It looks fit for a queen."

*A queen indeed,* Max thought.

Cleo held perfectly still as Maddie removed the old leather collar and replaced it with the new. Once Maddie was done, the dog cast a nervous, uncertain glance at Max, which made him wonder if she knew where it had come from.

He not only had a kinky woman, but now his dog looked a bit risqué as well.

Max was grinning too much to reassure Cleo, so she looked away and shook her head. The collar was butter-soft red leather and sparkled with multihued faux gems and shining studs.

Cleo's rough yellow fur stuck out in clumps around it.

Still clutching her bag and looking at the dog, Maddie backed up next to where Max lounged in the tub. She sighed dreamily. "Doesn't she look wonderful?"

Max looked at Maddie, his heart feeling as swollen as his male parts always did when she was around. The combination was explosive. "Yes, she does."

Cleo again shook her head to get a feel for the collar, woofed in acceptance, then grabbed up the hapless ball. With a snarl, she ran off to do battle, slinging the ball away then snatching it back again for more punishment.

Max reached out of the tub to hook his arm around Maddie's hips. "You'll never guess what I thought you had in that bag."

When he recalled his heated visions of bondage and dominance games, Max's pulse raced. There would still be time to play those games, he decided. He'd find the time.

Maddie's eyes were hot when she looked at him again. Of course, they were still swollen and red, too, and dog hair clung tenaciously to her cheeks and forehead. "You won't guess," she purred, "what I *do* have."

Lust surged upward, nearly obliterating everything else. Max sat up on the bench in the tub, retaining his hold on Maddie, and said, "Tell me."

Smiling wickedly, she pulled out a large white feather and whisked it around in the air. "I found this when I bought the collar and couldn't resist. I've decided I want to try it."

Max eyed the feather. "On what?"

"On *you*."

His stomach clenched hard and he met her gaze. "Because that's what your ex-fiancé was doing?"

"No." She leaned down and kissed the end of his nose, then whispered, "Because the idea of having you tied up and at my mercy is very appealing."

Max tried to peek into the bag. "What else do you have in there?" No way would he let her use the damn feather on him, but using it on her might be fun.

Maddie held the bag away, then lifted out a velvet mitt. "This is for stroking."

"Ah." He knew just where he'd use it on her, too. "Anything else?"

Not quite meeting his gaze, Maddie mumbled something, and Max said, "What's that?"

She mumbled again, scuffing her bare toe along the edge of the hot tub.

Max tipped up her chin, curiosity humming thickly through his veins. "What else did you buy, honey?"

Maddie hesitated, then reached defiantly into the bag and withdrew a sexy little barely there camisole of cream lace. It had interesting cutouts where her nipples would be, and ended at about her hipbones. Max shuddered, just imagining Maddie decorated with that bit of fluff.

"Nice," he rasped.

Maddie clutched the camisole to her chest. "Really?"

"Oh yeah." Forcing his gaze to her face, he said, "You'll look great." Then he added, "But no better than you do standing here right now, buck naked with dog hairs sticking to your skin and your hair all mussed."

She frowned.

He meant it.

Max reached for her. "Come here, sweetheart. I want to talk to you."

She dropped the feather and the lingerie onto a lawn chair and climbed back into the tub with a splash. When she started to sit beside him, Max again brought her onto his lap—facing him this time.

Max cupped the water in his palms and rinsed her cheeks, her chest, until the dog hairs were gone and all that was left was the effects of her tears. He supposed Maddie was one of those women whose eyes stayed puffy for hours after crying. He didn't mind.

He kissed her chin, her nose, her soft mouth. "Why were you crying, honey?"

Maddie played with his chest hair. "I already told you."

"Because you love me?" Max had never felt vulnerable before, but he felt totally exposed saying the words to Maddie now. If he had heard her wrong, if she denied them, he wasn't sure what he'd do. His heart rapped sharply, clapping against his ribs.

She bobbed her head. "Yes."

"And that's a bad thing?" He wanted her to look at him, but she kept averting her face.

"It hurts." She peeked at him, then pressed herself hard against him with a bear hug. "I don't want to put any other notches on my bedpost."

"Thank God." Max returned her hug.

"I don't want you to leave me, either, but I promise I won't be a pain about it. If you…if you want to see me occasionally still, I think I'd like that."

"Maddie, where is it you think I'm going?"

"You took the job with your father." She squeezed him so hard she nearly choked him. "You're going to be traveling again."

"A little." Max stroked her back, then her soft bottom. "And only if you and Cleo can come with me most of the time."

Maddie bolted back so hard she lost her balance and toppled off Max's lap. Her head went underwater then she reappeared with a sputter. Max caught her beneath the arms and lifted her.

"For crying out loud, Maddie! What are you doing? Trying to drown yourself?" He wasn't sure he liked such a volatile reaction to his suggestion.

Maddie spit out chlorinated water and wheezed, "You want us to travel with you? Really?"

The tension that had been squeezing his heart started to ease. Max grinned. "Yeah, really. Cleo needs me too much to be left behind very often. And I'd only leave her with you, anyway. No one else."

Her smile was beautiful, brighter than the afternoon sun lighting the yard. "You trust me that much?"

Max nodded. "When I go places too far for Cleo to go along, I'll have to leave her behind. I'd feel better knowing she's with you, because she loves you."

Maddie looked toward the yard where Cleo was performing the strange act of dragging herself forward with just her front legs, scratching her behind on the ground. Maddie chuckled. "I love her, too, and I'd be happy to watch her for you."

"Here?" Max ventured, pushing just a little. "Because she'd be most comfortable in her own house."

With a wary stillness, Maddie looked at Max. "Okay, if that's what you want."

Max shoved aside his uncertainty—as any manly man would do—and stated, "You know, if you're going to be staying here sometimes, you really ought to get over this silly aversion you have to marriage and give the idea some thought. I mean, you said you love me, and you said you love my dog. Right?"

Maddie's bottom lip quivered. Oh hell, Max thought. If she started crying again he didn't know what he'd do. Her eyes would end up swollen shut.

Maddie gulped. "You...you'd want to marry me?"

He never hesitated. "Yes. I told you all along that I was through with short-term affairs. But I swear, baby, I'd never cheat on you. Not like your ex did. So if that's what's worrying you—"

"Do you care about me, Max?"

She looked so uncertain, Max grabbed her up close and kissed her breathless.

"Care about you? I'm crazy nuts for you."

"You are? It's not just sex?"

"I've loved you," Max growled against her mouth, "almost from the moment you threw yourself against the bookstore's door. And by the time you fell inside on the floor, I was a goner."

Maddie made a small sound of surprise and he kissed her hard again. Damn, he didn't ever want to stop kissing her.

"I love how you taste, how you laugh, the crazy clothes you wear and the incredible things you do to my body. Hell, yes, I love the sex. And so much more. I especially love the way you take all the bluster away from Cleo and how you accept your friends and give so much of yourself. I kept telling myself that you'd be perfect for Cleo, but the fact is, you're perfect for me."

"Oh Max." She sniffled loudly.

"I need you, Maddie. I already told my father that I didn't want to travel and leave you behind. Not even for a few days. Not when I don't have to."

She pushed against his chest and sat up to face him. Being that she was on his lap, there was no way she could miss his erection.

She smiled. "I don't want you to put off a great job with your family just because of me. As long as I know you're coming back, I'll be happy."

Max cupped her cheek. "As long as I know you're here waiting for me, I'll be coming back."

Maddie reached beneath the water and encircled his erection. "Too bad I don't want to get the velvet glove wet."

Max groaned. But he caught himself before succumbing. That thought amused him enough that he could fight off the lust. For just a moment. "I have another job you should probably know about."

Dismayed, she paused in her attention to his body and said, "More travel?"

"No, writing." He explained about the column he did for the magazine and to his surprise, Maddie glared at him.

"I read that column! You're always so cynical!"

"I was uneducated."

"Ha! You know more about women—"

"Their bodies, yes. But you've taught me about my own heart."

Her frown melted away. "Oh, Max." She kissed him, then asked hesitantly, "No one knows you write that column?"

"No, and I'd like to keep it that way."

Maddie grinned in relief. "Me, too. I'm finding I'm the jealous sort—which is new for me—and I just know if anyone found out that you write—"

A familiar female voice intruded. "Well, well. Someone go get my shotgun." Mavis sounded highly amused.

Max looked up and saw two of Maddie's friends standing just inside the gate to the privacy fence.

Bea caught his eye and added, her own voice heavy with humor, "Is it legal to carry on out in the open like this?"

Maddie screeched and slipped neck deep into the water. Unfortunately, she went between Max's legs and used his left thigh as an added shield. There was no way he could duck. A quick survey showed that his modesty was intact, thanks to the bubbling water and Maddie's shoulders.

"Bea, Mavis," Max said, trying not to lose his cool at the sudden turn of events. "What are you two doing here?"

Bea held out her arms in a grand gesture. "We came to tell Maddie that Carmilla is eloping! She and Tiny are heading to Las Vegas tonight and Carmilla expects a party when she returns."

Maddie jostled around with joy, almost forgetting her state of undress. "That's wonderful!"

Mavis laughed. "Yeah, she always talked about Tiny, but she figured he'd forgotten about her. Not so. She used your young fellow here as an excuse to get in touch with him again, and nature took care of the rest."

Bea tipped her head at Max. "Looks like nature has been working on the both of you, too. So tell me, when's the wedding?"

"Just as soon as I can arrange it," Max said, and then his father stepped out of the house.

"Wedding! Why Max, that's wonderful." Dan didn't look the least bit surprised to see his youngest son making merry in a hot tub with a naked young lady. He stepped out of the open patio doors and then caught sight of Mavis and Bea. He stopped stock-still, looking spellbound and tongue-tied. "Uh, hello."

A very slow smile spread over Bea's face as she looked him over. She winked, then said in an aside to Mavis, "Dibs."

Cleo suddenly noticed the crowd and began barking. Deciding she needed to protect her master she not only charged the newcomers, she put herself between them and her human family.

She leaped right into the hot tub.

Maddie knew her face was still red. Red and swollen. But she was so happy, it didn't matter. Max loved her. He wanted to marry her. Life couldn't get much better.

She and Cleo were both drier now, except for their hair. Maddie had already combed her own and she sat on the floor, Cleo lying in front of her, while she untangled the dog's fur. Everyone else was gathered at Max's kitchen table. Dan had insisted on coffee and Mavis and Bea had seconded his vote. They all sipped a fresh cup, except for Max.

Dan, who could barely keep his eyes off Bea—

which she obviously loved—said, "I came by to see
if you'd be ready to travel as early as next weekend." Sheepishly he admitted, "Now that I've finally
gotten your agreement to join me in the business, I
don't want to take any chances on you backing out."

Max, wearing only a pair of jeans and looking
sexy enough to kill, leaned against the counter drink-
ing juice. "Where to?"

"Minnesota. You'd have this whole week to get
acquainted with the product and the price list." Dan
added hurriedly, "And of course your young lady and
the dog are more than welcome to go along."

Cleo snarled at Dan. She wasn't the least bit happy
having the house full, but Maddie was keeping her
calm.

Max glanced at Maddie and she smiled. "I'm
free."

Max smiled, too, his look intimate enough that
Bea and Mavis raised their brows and snickered. Dan
gave both women another quick glance, then shared
a small grin with Bea.

Max clapped his father on the back, drawing his
attention away from Bea. "That'd be fine, then. I'll
be there bright and early tomorrow."

Dan sent Maddie a look of gratitude. "I can't tell
you how wonderful it is to meet you, young lady.
And I'm thrilled you'll be joining our family. Annie
speaks very highly of you, and Lace has been sing-
ing your praises, too."

Maddie felt ready to burst with happiness. Then
Mavis stood. "All this lovey-dovey stuff is killing

me. I wish you all well, but I'm much happier playing the field."

Max grinned at her. "Another hot date tonight?"

"Every night, sweetie."

Bea clasped Dan's arm. "Why don't you let me take you to lunch, sugar? Your son suggested I show you some of my slogans."

Dan glanced at Max, his brow raised in question.

"She's good, Dad. Very good."

Bea gave a feline smile. "And I write great slogans, too."

Dan choked, but quickly recovered. "Why, yes, lunch sounds very nice."

Max shook his head. It seemed his whole world had gotten turned upside down in a relatively short time.

His brother had married, his sister had married—which included a long-time family friend getting hitched, too. Maddie had burst into his life and practically stolen his dog from him.

He glanced at her to see Cleo sprawled over her lap in bliss while Maddie bent to the task of combing out the tangles in the dog's seldom seen tail. Maddie's brows were drawn in concentration, her eyes still swollen, her nose still red.

Damn he loved her.

And now his father was actually smitten with a woman.

Max waited impatiently until everyone had left the house. Cleo whined at the back door and Maddie let her back out to fight with her ball. Dog hairs were all over Maddie's fresh clothes, but thankfully there were none on her face. She went directly to Max and held him.

Max said, "Will you marry me soon?"

"As soon as you like."

He grinned. "An agreeable woman. What a lucky cuss I am." Then he added, "Now, about that bag of goodies you brought…"

Maddie looked up at him and smiled. "Thank you, Max."

"For what, sweetheart?"

"For being a reprobate. For being a kinky, macho, adorable, loveable man." She kissed him gently. "And mostly for being all mine."

Max lifted her in his arms. "Being all yours is my pleasure. In fact, I insist on it." He started toward the bedroom. "As for the rest, I think we need to explore the kinky part just a bit more."

He bobbed his eyebrows at Maddie and she laughed, saying, "Now where did I leave my feather?"

His life was complete.

\* \* \* \* \*

*USA TODAY* bestselling author **Jules Bennett** has published over sixty books and never tires of writing happy endings. Writing strong heroines and alpha heroes is Jules's favorite way to spend her workdays. Jules hosts weekly contests on her Facebook fan page and loves chatting with readers on Twitter, Facebook and via email through her website. Stay up-to-date by signing up for her newsletter at julesbennett.com.

## Books by Jules Bennett

### Harlequin Desire

#### The Rancher's Heirs

*Twin Secrets*
*Claimed by the Rancher*
*Taming the Texan*
*A Texan for Christmas*

#### Lockwood Lightning

*An Unexpected Scandal*
*Scandalous Reunion*
*Scandalous Engagement*

#### Texas Cattleman's Club: Rags to Riches

*Tempted by the Boss*

Visit the Author Profile page at
Harlequin.com for more titles.

# SINGLE MAN MEETS SINGLE MOM

Jules Bennett

To Jill, Amy and Inez.
I love you three more than the frozen yogurt
we devour. Thanks for the road trip and all the
laughs. May we have many, many more!

# Chapter 1

*Oomph!*

Out of nowhere, Ian Shaffer had his arms full of woman. Curvy, petite woman. A mass of silky red hair half covered her face, and as she shoved the wayward strands back to look up, Ian was met with the most intriguing set of blue eyes he'd ever seen.

"You okay?" he asked, in no hurry to let her down.

He'd taken one step into the stables at Stony Ridge Acres and this beauty had literally fallen into his arms. Talk about perfect timing.

The delicate hand against his shoulder pushed gently, but he didn't budge. How could he, when all those curves felt perfect against his body and she was still trembling?

He may not know much about the horse industry, but women… Yeah, he knew women really well.

"Thank you for catching me."

Her low, husky voice washed over him, making him even more thankful he'd come to this movie set to see to his client's needs in person…and to hopefully sign another actress to his growing roster of A-listers.

Most agents didn't visit movie sets as regularly as he did, but he sure as hell wasn't missing the opportunity to keep Max Ford happy and allow prospective client Lily Beaumont to witness just what a kick-ass, hands-on agent he was. Given his young age, the fact that he was known as a shark in the industry happened to be good for business.

Ian glanced to the ladder that stretched up into the loft of the spacious stables. His eyes narrowed in on the rung that hung vertically, the culprit of the lady's fall.

"Looks like your ladder needs repairing," he told her, looking back to those big, expressive blue eyes.

"I've been meaning to fix it," she told him, studying his face, his mouth. "You know, you can let me down now."

Yeah, he was probably freaking her out by keeping her in his clutches. But that didn't stop him from easing her down slowly, allowing her body to glide against his.

Hey, he may be there to concentrate on work, but that didn't mean he couldn't enjoy the samplings of a tempting woman when an opportunity presented itself.

Keeping his hand on her arm, Ian allowed his gaze to sweep down her body. He justified the touch by telling himself he was looking for signs of injury, but in all honesty, he simply wanted to get a better look. If this was what they called taking in the local scenery, then sign him up.

"Are you hurt anywhere?" he asked.

"Just my pride." Stepping back, forcing his hand to fall away, she brushed her fingers down her button-up plaid shirt. "I'm Cassie Barrington. And you are?"

He held out his hand. "Ian Shaffer. I'm Max Ford's agent."

And if all went well, he'd be signing Max's costar Lily, too. There was no way he'd let her go to his rival agency without one hell of a fight first. And then maybe his very unimpressed father would see that Ian had become a success. He was a top agent in L.A. and not just hanging out at parties with women for a living. He'd become a powerful man in the industry.

Though the parties and women were a nice added bonus, Ian enjoyed stepping away from the glamour to be on set with his clients. And it was that extra touch that made him so successful. Between forging connections with producers and getting to know the writers and actors better, he could place his clients in the roles best suited to them.

The role Max was playing was perfect for him. The top actor was portraying the dynamic Damon Barrington, famous horse owner and former jockey. And for Ian, escaping L.A.'s hustle and bustle to spend time on a prestigious Virginia horse farm was a nice change of pace.

"Oh, Max mentioned you'd be coming. Sorry for falling on you." Her brows drew together as she gave him a quick assessment. "I didn't hurt you, did I?"

Ian shoved his hands into his pockets, offering her a smile. She could assess him anytime she wanted. "Not at all," he assured her. "I rather enjoyed the greeting."

Her chin tilted just enough to show defiance. "I don't make a habit of being clumsy...or throwing myself at men."

"That a fact?" he asked, trying not to laugh. "Such a shame."

"Do you make a habit of hitting on women?" she asked.

Unable to resist the gauntlet she'd thrown before him, Ian took a step forward, pleased when her eyes widened and she had to tip her head up to hold his gaze.

"Actually, no. But I'm making an exception in your case."

"Aren't I lucky?" Her tone told him she felt anything but. "Max should be in his trailer. His name is on the outside, and I believe another trailer was recently brought in for you."

Apparently she was in a hurry for him to be on his way—which only made him want to stay longer. Finding someone who didn't care about his Hollywood status, someone who wasn't impressed with his power and money, was a refreshing change. The fact that someone was curvy, wore jeans as though they were made to mold those curves and had expressive baby blues was the icing on the proverbial cake.

"So you're the trainer and your sister is the famous jockey?" he asked, crossing his arms over his chest.

The warm late-spring sun beat against his back as it came through the wide doors of the stable. Summer blockbuster season was just around the corner and, hopefully, once the film wrapped and he'd signed Lily, his agency would still be on top. His ex-partner-turned-rival would no longer be an issue.

He'd started working for an agency right out of college, thanks to a referral from a professor he'd impressed, but some lucky breaks and smart business sense had had him quickly moving to open his own. Unfortunately, he'd taken on a partner who had stabbed him in the back and secretly wooed most of their clients in the hopes they'd work exclusively with him in a new venture.

For the sake of his pride, he had to win Lily over and get her under contract. But how could his mind be on business with this voluptuous distraction before him?

"You've done your homework," she commented. "I'm impressed you know about me and my sister and our different roles."

"I do my research. You could say I'm pretty hands-on as an agent."

"Apparently you're hands-on with everything."

Oh, that was such a loaded statement—one he wouldn't mind exploring if he had the time. His eyes held hers as he closed the gap between them. The pulse at the base of her throat quickened and her breath caught as she stared, unblinking, at him.

Damn work responsibilities. But surely a little flirting, hell, even a fling, would make this an even more riveting trip.

"Everything," he whispered. "Let me know if you ever want an experience."

When her gaze dropped to his mouth again, Ian resisted the urge to grab her, to taste her. There would be plenty of time for…anything she was willing to give. Besides, wasn't the chase half the fun?

"I think you know where my trailer is."

And because he'd probably crossed some sort of moral, ethical boundary, Ian turned and walked from the barn, leaving her with her mouth open.

Well, this was already the most exciting movie set he'd ever visited and he hadn't even seen his client yet.

Cassie tightened her grip on MacDuff's lead line. He was still new, still skittish, but she was working with him every single day and he was showing improvement. Every now and then he'd let her father, Damon Barrington, ride him, but he had a touch that every horse seemed to love.

At least MacDuff had quit trying to run from her. Now, if she could just get him to understand her silent commands that he had to mimic her pace and direction when they walked.

Her work with MacDuff and the other horses was just one of the many issues that had ended her marriage. Derek had wanted her to stop spending so much time with the "strays" she brought in. He'd insisted she stop trying to save every animal, especially when she'd become pregnant.

Cassie would never stop trying to save animals… especially since she hadn't been able to save her marriage. Her husband had obviously loved women and liquor more than her and their baby. His loss, but the pain still cut deep.

She focused on the line, holding it tight and trying to keep up with the routine because she was running a tad behind now.

Of course, she'd been thrown off her game already this morning after falling into the arms of that handsome, bedroom-eyed stranger. For a split second she'd wanted to revel in the strength with which he held her, but then reality had slapped her in the face, reminding her that she'd fallen for a smooth talker once. Married him, had his child and hadn't seen him since.

Well, except when he'd shown up for the divorce proceedings, mistress in tow. As if that busty bleach blonde would ever play stepmom to Cassie's precious baby. Hell. No.

Cassie swore she'd never let another man play her for a fool again, and she sure as hell wouldn't get swept away by another pretty smile and sultry touch.

Unfortunately, when she'd fallen into Ian's arms, she'd forgotten all about that speech she'd given herself when her husband had left. How could she have a coherent thought when such strong arms were holding her flush against a taut body? No woman would blame her for the lapse in judgment.

But no more. Cassie had her daughter to consider now.

With sweet Emily just turning one, Cassie knew she'd definitely gotten the best part of her marriage, and if Derek didn't want to see their baby, he was the one missing out.

So, no more sexy men who thought they were God's magnificent gift to this world. Although Cassie had to admit, even if just to herself, that her insides had tingled at Ian's touch. He'd been so strong, had smelled so…manly and had looked in her eyes as if she truly was a beautiful, desirable woman.

She hadn't felt anything but frumpy and still a bit pudgy since having Emily. The extra weight that refused to go away coupled with her husband leaving her for another woman were damaging blows to her self-esteem. Yet, Ian had held her with ease, which wasn't helping her ignore the potency of the mesmerizing man.

Getting swept away by another handsome man with sultry eyes and a powerful presence wouldn't do her any good. She had to concentrate on helping her sister, Tessa, win her way to the Triple Crown. They'd worked side by side nearly their entire lives, always with the dream of being Triple Crown winners like their father. And here they were, about to make history, and Cassie couldn't be more excited.

When Cassie had been too far along with her pregnancy, her father had stepped up to train Tessa. This racing dynasty truly was a family affair.

One race down, two to go.

The fact that the Barrington estate had been

turned into a film set was icing on the cake. A script surrounding her father's legacy, legendary racing and past winning streak had piqued the interest of Hollywood A-listers, and, suddenly, the horse farm was all abuzz with lighting, sound guys, extras and security.

Cassie actually loved seeing her father's life played out by Max Ford, the handsome, newly married actor. And playing the role of her late mother was beautiful Southern belle and it-girl Lily Beaumont. So far the two were doing an amazing job, and Cassie couldn't wait to see the final product.

To cap off the racing season, Cassie was moving full throttle toward opening her own riding school for handicapped children. Since having her own child, Cassie wanted to slow down, and she'd always had a soft spot for kids anyway...something she'd thought she and her ex had in common.

Launching the school would be one more step in the healing process. So now she just needed to keep saving up—she wouldn't dream of asking her father or anyone else for money—to get it off the ground.

"Daydreaming?"

Keeping a firm grip on the lead line, Cassie glanced over her shoulder to see Tessa moving toward her in slow, cautious steps. MacDuff really did get treated with kid gloves by everyone until he learned they were his friends.

"Maybe just a little," Cassie admitted, gently pulling MacDuff into a soft trot. "Give me just a few minutes and we'll get to work."

Tessa shoved her hands into the pockets of her

jeans. "I'd rather hear what has my big sister so distracted this morning."

Cassie rolled her eyes at Tessa's smirk and quirked brow. She led MacDuff forward a few steps, stopped and moved back a few steps, pleased when the stallion kept up with her exact number and didn't try to fight her.

He was learning. Finally.

"I'm always amazed at how broken they seem to be," Tessa said softly. "You have this patience and gentleness. It's almost as if they know you're determined to help them."

"That's because I am." Cassie reached up to MacDuff's neck, offering him praise. "He's just misunderstood and nobody wanted to work properly with him."

"He was abused."

Cassie swallowed as she led MacDuff back to the stables. The thought of someone beating him because he hadn't had the right training sickened her. She'd known he'd been abused on some level, simply because of how he'd arrived all wide-eyed and nervous and then threw Tessa the first time she'd mounted him. But the second any horse, rescued or not, stepped onto Stony Ridge Acres, they were treated like royalty. No matter their heritage. Yes, they bred prizewinning horses and bought from a long lineage of winners, but it wasn't always about the win…. It was about the love and care of the animal. And since Stony Ridge was a massive farm, they could take in those strays Cassie had a soft spot for.

She'd always loved watching the trainers her father had for his horses. Years ago, female trainers had been frowned upon, but her father had insisted women were more gentle and less competitive by nature than men, thus producing better-tempered horses—and winners.

"You didn't happen to see a certain new hunk on the set this morning, did you?" Tessa asked as she pulled out the tack box and helped to brush MacDuff.

Cassie eyed her sister over the horse's back. "Aren't you engaged?"

"I'm not dead, Cass." Tessa brushed in large circular strokes. "I'll take your lack of answering to mean you did see him."

Saw him, fell into his arms, got lost in those sexy eyes that could make a woman forget she'd been burned...and maybe reveled in that powerful hold a tad too long.

"Even you have to admit he's one attractive man," Tessa went on.

"I can admit that, yes." Cassie switched from the currycomb to the dandy brush. "I may have had an incident this morning involving that loose rung on the ladder to the loft and Mr. Shaffer."

Tessa stepped around MacDuff's head, dropped the brush into the tack box and crossed her arms over her chest. "Okay, spill it. You know his name and you said 'incident.' I want all the details."

Cassie laughed. "It's no big deal, Tess. I fell off the ladder. Ian happened to be there, and he caught me."

"Oh, so we've gone from Mr. Shaffer to Ian."

"He's Max's agent and apparently visits his clients' film sets. We exchanged names," Cassie defended herself. "Seemed like the thing to do since he was holding me."

"I love where this story is going." Tessa all but beamed as she clasped her hands together.

Laughing, Cassie tossed her brush aside, as well. "No story. That was pretty much it."

"Honey, you haven't even mentioned a man's name since *you know who* left and—" Tessa held up a hand when Cassie tried to intervene "—your face seemed to brighten up a bit when you said his name."

"It did not," Cassie protested.

Tessa's smile softened. "If you want to argue, that's fine. But he's hot, you finally showed a spark of life about a man and I'm clinging to hope that you haven't given up on finding love. Or, for heaven's sake, at least allowing yourself a fling."

Cassie rolled her eyes and patted MacDuff's side. "Just because this romance business is working for you doesn't mean it will for me. I tried that once—it didn't last. Besides, I have no time for love or even a date between training with you and Emily."

"There's always time. And, romance aside, have a good time. A little romp with a sexy stranger might be just what you need," Tessa said with a naughty smile. "Aren't you the one who forced me to take a few days off last month? You have to make time for yourself."

Cassie had conspired with Tessa's now fiancé, producer Grant Carter, to whisk Tessa away during her training and the filming of the movie. Grant had wanted to get Tessa far from the limelight, the stress and the demands of their busy schedules, and Cassie had been all too happy to help because her sister needed a break.

Tess had found the right man, but Cassie seriously doubted there was a "right man" for her. All she required was someone who loved her and didn't mind her smelling like horses more often than not, someone who would offer stability in her life, make her feel desirable and love her daughter. Was that too tall of an order?

"I'm not looking for a fling," Cassie insisted, even though she'd pretty much already envisioned a steamy affair with Ian.

Tessa raised a brow. "Maybe a fling is looking for you."

"I just met the man. I'm sure he's not going to be around me that much anyway, so there's very little chance of seduction. Sorry to burst your bubble."

"Maybe you should show Ian around the estate," Tessa suggested as she went to grab a blanket and saddle for her racing horse, Don Pedro.

Cassie sighed, closing the gate to MacDuff's stall. "I don't want to show him around. Max is his client—he can do it."

"Max is going to be busy filming the scene with Lily down by the pond. I want to make sure we're there to see that taping."

Cassie smiled and nodded in agreement. She loved watching the two actors get into character, loved watching her father's reaction to reliving his life through the eyes of a director, and there was no way she'd miss such a monumental scene. This was the scene where Max would propose to Lily. The replay of such a special moment in her parents' lives was something she had to witness.

"I'll make sure we're done here about the time shooting starts," Cassie assured her sister. "All the more reason I don't have time to show Ian around."

"Now, that's a shame."

Cassie and Tessa both turned to see the man in question. And just like with their earlier encounter, the mere sight of him caused a flutter to fill her belly. Of course, now she couldn't blame the sensation on the scare from the fall…only the scare from the enticing man.

"I'd like to have a look around the grounds if you have time," he said, looking directly into her eyes, seeming to not even notice Tessa.

Cassie settled her hands on her hips, cursing herself when his gaze followed her movements. Great, now she'd drawn his attention to her hips…not an area a woman wanted a man looking.

"I thought you went to see Max," Cassie said, refusing to acknowledge his request.

"I saw him for a brief moment to let him know I was here. He actually was talking with Grant and Lily."

Cassie cast a glance at her sister, whose face had split into a very wide grin. *Darn her.*

With a gracefulness that would've pleased their late mother, Tessa turned, extended her hand and smiled. "I'm Tessa Barrington, Cassie's sister. We're so glad to have you here at the farm."

Ian shook Tessa's hand as the two exchanged pleasantries. He finally settled his gaze back on Cassie. Did those eyes have some magical power? Seriously, why did she have to feel a jolt every single time he looked at her?

"Go ahead and show Ian around, Cassie. I'm fine here."

If Cassie could've reached out and strangled her sister with the lead line she so would have, but then Ian would be a witness.

"It will have to be tomorrow or later this evening." No, she wasn't too busy right now, but she wouldn't allow Mr. Hollywood Hotshot to hold any control over her. "I'll come find you when I'm ready."

"Well, I'm going to walk Don Pedro out," Tessa said. "It was a pleasure to meet you, Ian. Cass, I'll see you later."

Great, now they were alone. Cassie would definitely kill her sister for that little stunt.

Ian stepped closer, and Cassie held her ground. This was her property and no matter how charming, how sexy and how...

Damn, he smelled good. She lost all train of thought; Ian's masculine scent was enough to render her mind blank. How long had it been since she'd been with a man, felt his touch?

Too long. So why did this man with an inflated ego turn her on? Could she not attract the right kind of guy just once?

"I can wait till tomorrow," he told her. His eyes searched her face as a hint of a smile played around his lips. "I'm a pretty patient man."

Placing a hand on his chest to stop him may have been a mistake. A jolt of awareness tingled up her arm. The strength, the chiseled pecs beneath her palm... Yeah, she was very aware of the sexiness that encompassed Ian Shaffer.

"I appreciate the fact you're taking the time to use your charm on me, but I'm too busy for games. Besides, I'm pretty sure I'm a lot older than you."

Ian shrugged. "Age hadn't entered my mind."

Cassie laughed. "I'm pretty sure I know what entered your mind."

He stepped forward again, giving her no choice but to back up until the gate to a stall stopped her. Ian put one hand on either side of her head, blocking her.

"Then I'm sure you're aware I find you attractive." His eyes dropped to her mouth, then traveled back up. "I can't wait for that tour, Cassie."

He pushed off the stall and walked out of the stable. When was the last time a man had caught her attention, inspired her sexual desire so fast? The danger of falling into lust scared her to death.

But she had to be realistic. There was nothing special about her. And if she did allow herself to act on these very new, very powerful emotions, she highly doubted he'd remember her name in a few months.

No way could she succumb to his charms.

# *Chapter 2*

Cassie's parents had been married nearly twenty years when her mother was killed suddenly in a car accident. She'd always admired the love her parents had for each other, always wanted a marriage like that for herself.

Unfortunately, a happy, loving marriage wasn't in the cards for her. And hindsight was a harsh slap in the face because Cassie realized she'd probably married Derek too quickly.

She'd craved the love her parents had had and thought for sure Derek—the Barringtons' onetime groom—had the same outlook on marriage.... As in, it was long-term and between only two people.

How could she trust her feelings for a man again? Cassie swiped the tear from her cheek as she headed back toward the stable. The sun was slowly sinking behind the hills surrounding the estate. Spring was gradually turning into summer, giving the evenings just a bit more light.

The day's filming was complete and the scene she'd just witnessed had left her raw and hopeful all at the same time.

Max Ford and Lily Beaumont had beautifully re-enacted Cassie's parents' proposal. Cassie had heard stories, had seen pictures of her parents' early love. But to witness that moment in person... Cassie had no words for how precious the experience had been.

She'd stood with Tessa off to the side, and even with the directors and producers stopping and starting and rearranging in the middle of the scene, the moment had captured her heart.

Added to that, each time she'd glanced at Ian, his gaze had been on hers. He hadn't even bothered trying to hide the heat that lurked in those dark, heavy-lidded eyes. Thankfully, at one point he'd slid on his aviator shades, but his dominating presence still captured her attention...and her hormones.

There went those lustful emotions again. She couldn't afford to get swept away by a sexy body and killer smile. Lust was the evil that had overtaken her once before and look where that had gotten her. Oh, she didn't regret her marriage because she had Emily, but the pain from the rejection and having her love blatantly thrown back in her face was humiliating. Who wanted to be rejected?

Cassie reached the stable, intending to work with

MacDuff again, but her eyes moved up to the rung of the ladder that still hung vertically.

She'd meant to mention the problem to Nash, the new groom, but between the emotional shoot and a certain hot agent plaguing her mind, she'd simply forgotten. Besides, he'd been so busy today cleaning out all the stalls, she really hated to add to his list.

Her father took pride in his stables, always making sure everything looked pristine and perfect. Cassie would bite the bullet and fix the ladder herself. At least working on something would keep her mind off Ian…hopefully. Her tendency to fix things and have everything in her life make sense would have to be satisfied with just this piece of wood for now. The Ian issue—and she feared he was fast becoming an issue—would have to wait.

She grabbed the hammer and several long nails from the toolbox in the equipment room. She shoved the nails in her back pocket and held on to the hammer as she climbed the ladder that stretched to the loft of the stable.

The setting sun cast a soft glow into the structure. Horses neighed, stomped hooves and rustled in their stalls. The sounds, the smells—none of it ever got old. Cassie loved her life here and she looked forward to bringing her daughter up in such a beautiful, serene environment.

During her four years of marriage, she'd been away from the estate. Even though she and Derek had lived only ten minutes away, it just wasn't the same as being on the grounds. Cassie loved living in the cottage, being with the horses and knowing her family was all right here helping with her emotional recovery.

With her tears mostly dry, Cassie sniffed. Crying had never been her thing. Anger fit more into her life, especially since she'd been abandoned only two months after giving birth. Tears hadn't brought her cheating husband back, not that she'd wanted him after the fact, and tears certainly weren't helping her raise her daughter or move on like the strong mother she needed to be.

Halfway up the ladder, she eyed the broken rung, then carefully slid it back into place. Widening her stance as far as she could to balance her body while holding the hammer, she reached around into her back pocket for a nail.

"I can help you with that."

Cassie glanced over her shoulder to see Ian at the base of the ladder, his watchful gaze raking over her body. *Great.* She had red-rimmed eyes and a red-tipped nose, she was sure. She was not a pretty crier. She always got the snot-running, red-splotchy-face and puffy-eyes look.

Cassie slid a nail out and turned back around to place it against the wood. "I've got it, but thanks."

She knew he hadn't left, but Cassie didn't say anything else as she worked quickly and repaired the rung. With a hefty tug on the wood, she made sure it was securely in place before she started her descent. Just as she'd gotten to the last rung, Ian moved his hard body against hers, trapping her between the ladder and a most impressive chest. Her body was perfectly aligned with his, causing ripples of heat to slide through her. They were both fully dressed, but the sensations spiraling through her had never occurred before, even when she'd been completely naked with her ex.

Yeah, she was doomed where this sexy stranger was concerned.

Cassie swallowed, closed her eyes. Ian made her aware of just how feminine she was. When was the last time she'd felt desirable? Was it so wrong to want a man to find her attractive? After being married to someone who kept looking elsewhere for his desires to be fulfilled, Cassie knew she was probably grasping at any attention at this point.

She also knew she didn't care—not when his body was so hard, so perfectly perfect against hers. Not when his soft, warm breath tickled the side of her neck, and not when his masculine aroma enveloped her.

"What are you doing here?" she whispered.

Ian slid his arms up to align with hers, his hands covering hers on the wood. "I saw you walking this way. You looked upset."

No. He didn't care. He couldn't. Not this soon and not about her. Sexual desires were clouding his mind…and hers, too, apparently, because she was enjoying the heat of his body a little too much.

What man would follow a woman into a stable just because she looked upset? No. He'd followed her for one reason and one reason only. A reason she certainly didn't think she was ready for.

"I'm fine," she lied.

Ian nuzzled her hair. Oh…when he did that she

forgot all arguments about why being attracted to someone so full of himself was wrong. Her mind completely voided out any pep talks she'd given in regard to steering clear of lustful feelings and attractive charmers.

"You're a very beautiful woman, Cassie." His soft voice slid over her body, reinforcing those tremors that were becoming the norm where he was concerned. "I tried to ignore this pull I have toward you, but it was damn hard when I saw you during the shoot. How do you do that to a guy?"

Um…she had no clue. Power over men had certainly never been something she'd mastered. If it had, she'd still be married.

"Ian, we just met and…"

He used one hand and slid the hammer from her grasp, letting it fall to the concrete floor with a loud thud.

"And I'm older than you," she continued. "I'm thirty-four. You can't even be thirty."

With an arm around her waist, he hauled her off the ladder and spun her around until she faced him—their mouths inches apart.

"I'm twenty-nine, and I assure you I'm old enough to not only know what I want, but to act on it."

His mouth came down on hers, hard, fast, hungry. Cassie didn't have time to think or refuse because her body was already melting into his.

The passion pouring from him stirred her desire even more as she gripped his thick biceps. Giving in to just a few seconds of bliss wouldn't hurt.

And when Ian's mouth traveled from her mouth

down the column of her throat, Cassie tipped her head back as her breath caught. What was he doing to her? A full-on body attack. His mouth may be in one spot, but Cassie could feel every inch of her body tingling and wanting more.

Wait...this wasn't right. She couldn't do this.

Pushing him away, Cassie slid her hand up over the exposed skin peeking out of her shirt...the skin his mouth had just explored.

"Ian, I can't... We can't..." Words were useless because her mind was telling her one thing and her body was telling her another. "I just met you."

"You're attracted to me."

She couldn't deny the statement. "That doesn't mean I should act on it. I don't just go around kissing strangers."

"After you learned my name this morning, I was no longer a stranger."

Those dark eyes held her gaze. Even without a word the man exuded power, control. Derek had been so laid-back, so uncaring about everything that this was quite a change.

And Cassie would be lying if she didn't admit the fact that Ian was the polar opposite of her ex turned her on even more.

"You're only here for a short time," she went on, crossing her arms over her chest. "We can't just... you know."

"Have sex?" he asked, quirking a brow.

*Oh, mercy.* The words were now out, hovering in the air, and from the smirk on his face, she was the only one feeling awkward at this moment.

"Yes, that." *Dear Lord.* It wasn't as if she hadn't had sex before; she'd had a baby, for crying out loud. But she couldn't discuss something like that with him. Now she felt foolish and juvenile. "Acting on sexual attraction isn't something I normally do."

That was an understatement, considering she'd had sex with one man and that had been her husband. What if she did throw caution to the wind? What if she had some sordid affair?

Seriously? Was she contemplating that? She was a mother—a mother to a little girl. What kind of example was she?

"You're thinking too hard." Ian started to step forward, but he stopped when Cassie held up a hand.

"Don't. I can't think when you're touching me."

"I'll take that as a compliment."

Cassie rolled her eyes. "You would."

"See? You know me already."

One of them had to think rationally. Apparently it would be her. She maneuvered around him toward the opening of the stable.

"You're going to have to keep your hands and your mouth to yourself."

Those tempting lips curved into a smile. "You're no fun."

"I don't have time for fun, Ian."

And more than likely he was the proverbial good time back in L.A. She could easily see him hopping from one party to the next, beautiful women draped over his arm, falling into his bed.

Cassie flicked the main switch to light up the pathways between the stalls. The brightness from the antique horseshoe-style chandeliers put a screeching halt to any romantic ambience that had been lurking in the darkening stable.

When she turned back around, Ian had his hands on his narrow hips, his focus still locked on her. There was a hunger in his eyes she'd never seen from any man before.

Without a word, he closed the gap between them. Cassie's heart had just started to settle, but now it picked back up again. She should've known better than to think the intense moment would pass.

Ian framed her face with his hands and brought his mouth to within a fraction of an inch of hers. "A woman who kisses, who responds to my touch without hesitation, has pent-up passion that needs to be released."

His lips barely brushed hers. "Come find me when you're ready."

Ian walked around her, leaving her still surrounded by that masculine scent, his arousing words and the tingling from his touch still on her lips.

She'd known the man twelve hours. There was no way she could handle him being on the grounds for two more months. She was a woman—a woman with needs.

And a part of her wondered just what would happen if she allowed herself to put those needs first for once.

# Chapter 3

Two days had passed since she'd been up close and personal with Ian, but Cassie was more than aware of his quiet, yet dominating, presence on the estate. She'd seen him from a distance as he talked with Max. She'd found out she'd just missed him on the set of one scene she'd gone to watch, but she refused to admit she was wondering about his schedule, about when she'd see him again. Feel his body against hers.

She refused to fall for another man who set her hormones into overdrive, so where did that leave her? Considering a fling?

Groaning, she made her way from the stables to the main house. The sun was making its descent behind the mountains and Emily was at her weekly sleepover with Tessa and Grant. After witnessing the shooting of the engagement scene over the past couple of days, Cassie was feeling more and more nostalgic.

She missed her mother with each passing day; seeing Rose's life depicted in the film had Cassie wanting to feel closer to her. And with Emily away for the night, this was the perfect opportunity to reminisce and head up to the attic, where all her mother's things were stored.

Rose's unexpected death had shaken up the family in ways they'd never even imagined. As teen girls, Tessa and Cassie had really taken it hard, but they'd all been there for each other, forming an even stronger bond. But Cassie still ached for her mother's sweet smile, her encouraging words and her patient guidance.

Because right now she truly wanted a mother's advice. Ian had her completely tied in knots. When he'd left her in the stables two days ago, Cassie had never felt so torn, so conflicted in her life. And he hadn't approached her since. What was up with that? Had he changed his mind? Had he decided she wasn't worth the trouble?

Why was she even worried about this anyway? No doubt Ian was used to those flawless women who had been surgically perfected. More than likely Cassie's extra pounds and shapelier curves were not what Ian was looking for in a...fling? What was he doing exactly with his flirting? Where had he expected this to go?

Never mind. He'd thrown out the word *sex* like

nothing. Cassie knew exactly where he was headed with his flirting.

Leaving the attic door propped open, Cassie headed up the narrow wooden staircase. At the top she flicked on the small light that was so soft, it really only set off a glow on one wall. But that was the wall where her mother's boxes were stacked.

In the silence of the evening, Cassie was all alone with her thoughts, her memories. She pulled the lid off the first bin and choked back tears.

How could anyone's life, especially that of her beautiful, loving, vivacious mother, be condensed to a few boxes? All the memories, all the smiles, all the comfort Rose Barrington had offered to the world... all gone. Only tangible items remained stored neatly in plastic bins.

Cassie couldn't help but smile. Her very organized mother wouldn't have had it any other way.

After going through pictures from her parents' simple, elegant wedding day, Cassie knew the wedding dress was around. Tessa actually planned on wearing it for her upcoming vows, and Cassie couldn't wait to see her baby sister in their mother's gown. Just that image was enough to have her tearing up again.

This film was certainly wreaking havoc on her emotions, that was for sure.

Cassie kept searching through storage bins, looking for a box or a folded garment bag. Would the crew need to duplicate that dress for the wedding scene? More than likely they'd already researched pictures to find inspiration for the costumes, just as they had for the settings.

Cassie had been itching for a chance to look through the old photos again herself.

Moving from the bins, Cassie went and looked inside the narrow antique wardrobe, where she discovered a white garment bag. Slowly unzipping, so as not to tear the precious material inside, Cassie peeled back the bag and pulled out the classy gown she'd been hunting for.

The dress had been preserved so that the cream-colored material was still perfect. Tessa would be just as beautiful a bride as their mother had been.

Cassie had thought about wearing it for her own wedding, but her ex had insisted on getting married at the courthouse. She should've known then that he wasn't the one. Not that there was anything wrong with a small civil ceremony, but Derek had known she'd always wanted a wedding in the small church where her parents had married. She'd wanted the lacy gown, the rice in her hair as they ran to their awaiting car...the special wedding night.

None of those young-girl dreams had come true.

Unable to resist, Cassie stripped from her jeans, boots, button-up and bra and pulled on the strapless floor-length dress. A straight cut with lace overlay may be simple to some, but the design was perfect to Cassie.

Smoothing a hand down the snug bodice, Cassie went to the antique mirror in the corner. If she fell in love one day—real love this time—maybe she could wear it. Wouldn't that be a beautiful tradition? Rose,

Tessa and Cassie all wearing the same gown. Perhaps if the material held up and the gown was well preserved again, little Emily would one day walk down the aisle wearing the dress her grandmother had.

If it weren't for baby weight, the frock would fit perfectly. Unfortunately, right now her boobs threatened to spill out the top and lace was definitely not a forgiving material, so her curves were very…prominent.

Behind her, the attic door clicked. Cassie turned, her hand to her beating heart as footsteps sounded up the stairs. No time to cover up all her goods, so she kept her hand in place over her generous cleavage.

"Hello?" she called.

Ian rounded the landing and froze. He took in her state of dress—or undress, really—of course zeroing in on where her hand had settled.

So much for her evening of reminiscing. Could fate be any more mocking? Dangling this sexy stranger in her face when she knew full well that nothing could or should happen?

"What are you doing?" she asked, keeping her hand in place and trying to remain calm. Kind of hard when she was on display and just the sight of the man had her heart accelerating.

"I wanted to apologize for the other day," he told her, coming up the last couple of steps. "I never force myself on a woman, and I didn't want you to have that impression of me. But if I'm going to be here any length of time, and I am, we need to clear the air."

*Clear the air?* Cassie sighed and prayed because

she had a sinking feeling they may be there for a while.

"Well, now's the perfect time because if that door latched all the way, we're locked in here."

Ian drew his brows together. "Locked in?"

"The door locks from the outside. That's why I had left it standing open."

Pulling up the hem of the dress with one hand and trying to keep the bodice up with the other, she moved around him down the steps and tugged on the handle. She leaned her forehead against the door and groaned.

"I didn't know," he murmured behind her.

Cassie turned and looked up the steps to see Ian looking menacing and dangerous—in that sexy way only he could—standing at the top. His muscles filled out his long-sleeved T, those wide shoulders stretching the material, and his dark jeans fit his narrow hips beautifully.

She knew firsthand exactly how that body felt against hers. Knew just how well he could kiss a woman into forgetting her morals.

In a house this size, with only her father living here and his bedroom on the first floor, no one would hear them yell until morning, when they could open the small window and catch someone's attention.

Risking another full-body glance at Ian, Cassie knew she was in big, big trouble. Her attraction to him was the strongest she'd ever felt toward a man. But it wasn't so much the level of heat between them that scared her; it was the quick onset of it. It felt as if she had no control over her own reaction. She'd been helplessly drawn to this intriguing man. How could she trust her emotions right now? He was honestly the first man to find her desirable since her ex. Was he just a sexy diversion or were her feelings more in-depth than that?

Earlier tonight she'd flirted with the idea of a fling, but now the reality of being trapped with Ian made her heart flutter and nerves dance in her belly.

Her gaze met his. Crackling tension vibrated between them in the soft glow and the silence.

And Cassie had all night to decide what to do with all her attraction and the hungry look in Ian's eyes…

Ian stared down at Cassie, struck by those creamy exposed shoulders, that poured-on, vintage-style wedding gown molded to her sweet curves. From his vantage point, he could see even more of her very exposed breasts and most impressive cleavage—even though she was trying her hardest to keep gravity from taking over the top of that dress.

*Mercy.* Being straight in front of her had been torture, but this angle offered a much more interesting, gut-clenching view. Not that he was complaining.

Being stuck in an attic with Cassie would be no hardship because he'd caught a glimpse of the passion she held beneath her vulnerability. And there wasn't a doubt in his mind that her war with herself stemmed from some past hurt.

Cassie attempted to cross her arms over her breasts, which only tortured him further, because she failed to cover the goods and actually ended up offering him an even more enticing view. Was she doing this as punishment?

"Text Max and have him come to the main house and ring the doorbell. Dad won't be in bed yet."

Ian shook his head. "Sorry. I only came over to apologize to you, so I left my phone in my trailer to charge."

Groaning, Cassie tipped her head back against the door and closed her eyes. "This isn't happening to me," she muttered. "This cannot be happening."

Ian had to smile. Of all the scenarios he'd envisioned on his short walk from his trailer to the main house, he hadn't once thought of being stuck for hours with someone so sexy, so unexpected, and wearing a wedding dress to boot.

This couldn't have been scripted any worse…or better, depending on the point of view.

Cassie lifted the dress and stomped back up the steps, her shoulder slamming into him as she stormed by.

"Wipe that smirk off your face, Ian. Nothing about this is comical."

"Can't you call someone with your phone?" he asked, turning to face her.

Cassie propped her hands on her hips. "No. I came up here to be alone, to think."

Damn, she was even sexier when she was angry. But getting too wrapped up with Cassie Barrington was a dangerous move. She wasn't a fling type of girl and he'd pushed too hard in the stables. Had she given in to his blatant advances, he knew she would've regretted it later.

He needed to do the right thing and keep his hands off her. He was here for two main purposes: keep Max happy and sign Lily so she didn't go to his rival. Period.

But his hormones didn't get the memo, because the more he was around Cassie, the more alluring and sexy she became. Of course, now that he'd seen a sample, he had to admit, he wanted to see more. That dress… Yeah, she looked like a 1950s pinup. Sexy as hell, with all the right curves and none of that stick-thin, anorexic nonsense, and she was even hotter with a slight flush from anger.

For the past two days he'd seen her working with her sister, training the horses and driving him unbelievably mad with the way her lush body filled out a pair of jeans. He'd seriously had to get his damn hormones in check and then approach her with a much-needed apology for his Neanderthal tendencies.

But now that he was here, those hormones were front and center once again, overriding all common sense and rational thoughts.

"How did you know I was up here?" she asked. "I figured all the crew was either in their trailers or back at the hotel."

"I ran into Grant on my way to your cottage. He told me you were here. As I was coming in the back door, your cook, Linda, was going out for the night and she said you mentioned coming to the attic."

"You came all this way just to apologize? I'm sure you would've seen me tomorrow."

Ian shrugged, shoving his hands into his pockets.

"True, but I knew too many people would be around tomorrow. I assumed you wouldn't want to discuss this in front of an audience. Besides, I think we need to address this spark between us and figure out what to do with it since I'll be here several weeks."

Cassie threw her hands in the air. "Could you at least turn around so I can put my clothes back on?"

His eyes traveled down her body, darting to the pile of clothes behind her, zeroing in on the leopard-print bra lying on top.

"Sure," he said, trying to get the visual of her in that leopard bra out of his mind before he went insane.

Fate may have landed him up here with the sassy, sexy Ms. Barrington, and fate also provided a window directly in front of him, where he was afforded a glorious view of Cassie's reflection as she changed. Of course, that made him a bit of a jerk, but no man with air in his lungs would look away from that enticing view. This evening just kept getting better and better.

Cassie would probably die before she asked for help with the zipper, so he didn't offer. And she didn't have any trouble. As the dress slid down her body, Ian's knees nearly buckled.

*Lush* didn't even begin to describe her. Her full breasts, rounded belly and the slight flare of her hips were a lethal combination.

"As I was saying," he went on, cursing his voice when it cracked like that of an adolescent. "I realize that neither of us was prepared for the instant physical attraction—"

"You're delusional," she muttered as she tugged her jeans up over her hips and matching bikini panties.

"But just because I find you sexy as hell doesn't mean I can't control myself."

Her hands froze on her back as she fastened her bra. Apparently his words had struck a chord. She glanced up and caught his gaze in the reflection. Busted.

"Seriously?" she asked with a half laugh. "Why did you even turn around?"

"I didn't know the window was there." That was the truth.

"And you weren't going to say anything?"

Ian spun around—no point in being subtle now. "I'm a guy. What do you think?"

Rolling her eyes, Cassie shrugged into her shirt and buttoned it up with jerky, hurried motions.

Fighting the urge to cross the room and undress her again, Ian slid his hands into his pockets and met her gaze.

"You are stunning," he told her, suddenly feeling the need to drive that point home. "I'm not sure why that statement caught you off guard."

Most women in Hollywood would pause at such a comment, try to deny it in order to hear more pretty words in a vain attempt to boost their own egos, but Ian knew Cassie was different. She truly didn't believe she was beautiful, and he had a feeling all that insecurity circled back to whatever the basis was for her vulnerability.

Damn, he didn't have time to delve into distressed damsels. But there was a desire in him, something primal, almost possessive that made him want to dig deeper, to uncover more of Cassie Barrington. And not just physically.

That revelation alone scared the hell out of him.

"I don't need to be charmed, Ian." She propped her hands on her hips. "We're stuck up here and lying or trying to make me want you isn't going to work."

"I don't lie, Cassie." When she quirked a brow, he merely shrugged. "I find you sexy. Any man would be insane or blind not to."

Cassie shook her head. After zipping the dress into a white garment bag, she headed over to a storage box and popped off the lid. She flopped down on the floor, crossing her legs and offering him the view of her back.

He waited for her to say something, but she seemed to have dismissed him or was so wrapped up in the memories of the photos she was pulling out, she just didn't care that he was there.

"You ever look at a picture and remember that moment so well, you can actually feel it?" she asked, her soft voice carrying across the room.

Ian took that as his invitation to join her. He closed the distance between them, taking a seat directly beside her. Cassie held a picture. A young girl, he presumed it was her, sat atop a horse, and a dark-haired beauty, who he assumed was her mother, held the lead line.

"That was my first horse," she told him, her eyes still on the picture. "I'd always ridden with Dad and helped him around the stables, but this one was all mine. I'd picked him out at auction and Mom and Dad told me I had to care for him all by myself."

Ian looked at the image of a young Cassie. "How old were you?"

"Eight. But I knew as soon as I saw him that I'd want him. He was skittish and shied away from the men, but when I approached him, against my father's advice, he came right to me and actually nuzzled my neck."

Ian listened to her, refusing to let himself fall into her sea of emotions. He'd noticed her and Tessa holding hands at the shoot, tears swimming in both of their eyes.

"I've never ridden a horse," he admitted.

Cassie dropped the picture back into the bin and turned to stare at him. "Seriously? We'll have to rectify that while you're here."

Ian laughed. "I wasn't asking for an invitation. Just stating a fact."

She turned a bit more to face him, her thigh rubbing against his. Did she have a clue that she was playing with fire? She may be older than him, but something told him she wasn't necessarily more experienced.

Arrogance had him believing they weren't on a level playing field. He had plenty he wanted to show her.

"I love teaching people how to ride," she went on,

oblivious to his thoughts. "It's such an exhilarating experience."

Cassie's wide smile lit up her entire face. The room had a soft glow from the single-bulb sconce on the wall and Ian could resist those full lips for only so long…especially now that he knew exactly how they tasted.

Without warning, he slid his hands through her hair and captured her lips. She opened freely, just like when they'd been in the stables.

Ian tipped her head, taking the kiss deeper. He wanted more, so much more. He wanted to feel her hands on him as he explored her mouth, relishing her taste, but she didn't touch him. Maybe she did know how to play this age-old game of catch and release.

Easing back, Ian took in her swollen lips, her heavy lids and flushed cheeks and smiled. "Actually, *that's* an exhilarating experience."

And God help them both because between the interlude in the stables and that kiss, he had the whole night to think about how this sexual chemistry would play out.

The real question was: Could he make it all night without finding out?

# Chapter 4

Cassie jumped to her feet, instantly feeling the chill without Ian's powerful touch. The man was beyond potent and he damn well knew it.

"You seriously think because we're locked in here and we kissed a few times that I'll just have sex with you?" Cassie ran a shaky hand through her hair, cursing her nerves for overtaking her as fast as those heated kisses had. "I don't know what lifestyle you lead in L.A., but that's not how I work."

Ian stared up at her, desire still lurking in those dark-as-sin eyes. "Are you denying you were just as involved in those kisses as I was?"

"You had your hands all over me," she threw back. "Just because I like kissing doesn't mean I always use it as a stepping-stone for sex. I technically just met you, for crying out loud. I don't know anything about you."

Moving as slowly as a panther hunting its prey, Ian came to his feet and crossed to her. "You know how quick you respond to my touch, you know how your heartbeat quickens when you wonder what my next move will be and you know you're fighting this pull between us."

Cassie raised a brow, trying for her best bored look. "That has nothing to do with Ian Shaffer. That's all chemistry."

"So you don't deny you want me?" he asked with a smirk.

Crossing her arms and taking a step back, Cassie narrowed her eyes. "Drop the ego down a notch. You just proved how very little we know about each other. You may sleep with virtual strangers, but I don't."

Ian laughed, throwing his arms in the air. "Okay. What do you want to know?"

"Are you married?"

Shock slid over his face. "Hell no. Never plan to be."

Commitment issues? Lovely. Hadn't she just gotten out of a relationship with a man of the same nature?

On the other hand, Ian wasn't cheating on a wife back in California. That was at least one mark in his favor. Okay, the toe-curling kisses were major positive points in his favor, but she'd never confess that out loud. And she wasn't actually looking to jump back into another relationship anyway.

"No girlfriend?" she asked.

"Would I be all over you if I did?"

Cassie shrugged. "Some guys wouldn't care."

That heated gaze glided over her and was just as effective as a lover's touch. Her body trembled.

"I'm not like a lot of other guys."

He was powerful, sexy and wanted in her pants. Yeah, he was just like some guys.

With a sigh, Cassie laughed. "I can't believe this," she muttered more to herself than to Ian. "I'm actually playing twenty questions because I want to have sex."

"Sweetheart, I don't care a bit to answer a hundred questions if you're considering sex."

Lord have mercy, it was hot up there. Not just because of the ridiculous way her body responded to this charmer, but literally. The heat in the attic was stifling.

Cassie unbuttoned the top two buttons of her shirt, exposing her cleavage area, but she needed air. She rolled her sleeves up and caught Ian's eyes taking in her actions.

"Don't get excited there, hotshot. I'm just trying to cool off."

Sweat trickled between her shoulder blades and she so wished she'd at least pulled her hair up earlier. There had to be something up here. As she started to look around in boxes for a rubber band of any type, she tried not to think of Ian and if he had sweat on the taut muscles beneath his shirt.

Okay, that mental blocker was broken because all she could see was glistening bronzed skin. And while she hadn't seen him without a shirt, she had a very good imagination.

"Can I help you find something?" he asked.

Throwing a glance over her shoulder, she caught his smirk as he crossed his arms over his chest. "I just need something to pull my hair up. I'm sweating."

There, that should douse his oversexed status a little. What man found a sweaty woman attractive? And she was pretty sure her wavy red hair was starting to look like Bozo the Clown's after a motorcycle ride...sans helmet. She lifted the flap off a box in the far corner and shuffled things around in her hunt.

"So, why is an agent needed on a film set?" she asked, truly wondering but also wanting to keep his mind on work—which was what he should be doing anyway.

"Max is one of my top clients." Ian unbuttoned his shirt halfway. "I often visit my clients on set to make sure they're taken care of. And with this being a very impressive script and plot, I knew I had to be here. I've actually blocked off a good bit of time to spend at Stony Ridge."

And wasn't that just the news she needed to hear? Mr. Tall, Dark and Tempting would be spending "a good bit of time" here. Just what her very inactive sexual life needed...temptation.

"Yes," she shouted as she grabbed a rubber band off a stack of school papers from her primary days.

"Max is a great guy, from what I've seen." After pulling her hair into a knot on top of her head, she turned to Ian. "He and Lily are doing an amazing job, too. Lily seems like a sweetheart."

Nodding his agreement, Ian rested a hip against an old dresser. "She's rare in the industry. L.A. hasn't jaded her or sucked the goodness out of her. She had a rough patch with a scandal at the start of her career, but she's overcome it. She's a rare gem."

"And I'm sure you've tried to get her into bed."

Rich laughter filled the space. The fact he was mocking her only ticked Cassie off more. But, if she were honest, she was ticked at herself for wanting him.

"I've never slept with Lily," he told her, a grin still spread across his handsome face. "I've never even tried to. I'm actually hoping to sign her to my agency. I respect my clients and they respect me. This business is too risky and too exposed for anything like that to remain a secret. There are no secrets in Hollywood."

"Is that all that's stopped you? The fact that people could find out?"

Ian straightened to his full height and took a step toward her. *Great.* She'd awoken the sex beast again.

"What stopped me," he said as he took slow steps toward her, "was the fact that, yes, she's beautiful, but I'm not attracted to her. Added to that, I want a professional relationship with her, not a sexual one. If I want a woman in my bed, she won't be on my client list. Plain and simple."

He'd come close enough that Cassie had to tip her head back. Thankfully, he hadn't touched her. Too much more touching—or, heaven forbid, kissing—and she feared her self-control would be totally shot.

Cassie swiped a hand over her damp neck. "Is everything a business strategy with you?"

"Not at all. Right now, I'm not thinking anything about business."

The way his eyes held hers, as if she was the only person that mattered right now, made her wonder…

She may be naive and she was certainly still recovering from Derek walking out on her, but what would a fling hurt? Tessa had even verbally expressed Cassie's thoughts on the matter. She'd married for "love," or so she'd thought. Hell, she'd even saved herself for marriage and look how that had turned out.

"I promise I won't ravage you if you'd like to take something off," he told her with a naughty grin. "I'm sure your shirt will be long enough to cover things if you need to get out of those jeans. If not, I've seen naked women before."

Yeah? Well, not *this* naked woman, and with that last bit of baby weight still hanging on for dear life, she most definitely wasn't comfortable enough with her body to flaunt it. Even if she did indulge in a fling with the sexy agent—and she couldn't believe she was seriously considering such a thing—she wasn't going to make the catch so easy for him. What fun would that be?

Deciding to teach him a lesson, Cassie reached up and patted the side of his face. "You're so sweet to sacrifice yourself that way."

Cassie knew her mother had a box of old clothes

up here. Perhaps something could be used to cool her off and make Ian squirm just a bit more.

As she went toward the area with the clothing boxes, she opted to keep Ian talking.

"So, tell me more about Lily." Cassie pulled the lid off an oblong box and nearly wept with relief at the colorful summer dresses inside. "She's very striking and has a strong resemblance to my mother."

"When this film came across my desk, I knew I wanted Max to try for it and I was sincerely hoping they paired him with Lily. This role was made for her. She's already got that Southern-belle charm your mother had, according to everyone on set. Lily has the sweet little twang in her voice like all of you Barringtons do."

Cassie turned, clutching a simple strapless cotton dress to her chest. "I do not have a twang."

Ian quirked a brow. "It's actually even more prominent when you get ticked. Very cute and sexy."

Rolling her eyes, Cassie turned back to the box and placed the lid back on. "I'm going to change. Could you try not to stare at me through the reflection again?"

Ian shrugged one broad shoulder. "I promise."

Cassie waited for him to turn around or move, but he just sat there smiling. Damn that man. Now that she'd reminded him he'd seen her pretty much naked, Cassie had no doubt she'd just thrown gasoline on the fire.

"Aren't you going to turn around?" she finally asked.

"Oh, when you just said not to look at you through

the reflection, I assumed you wanted to let me in on the full viewing."

"I didn't want to let you into this room...let alone treat you to a viewing."

Cassie resisted the urge to kiss that smirk off his face. He knew he was getting to her, and she wondered just how much longer she'd deny it to herself.

"I'll move, then," she told him, stomping to the other end of the attic behind a tall stack of boxes. "And don't you follow me."

"Wouldn't dream of it." He chuckled. "But you're just putting off the inevitable, you know."

She quickly wrestled out of her clothes and yanked the strapless dress up over her heated body. Her bare arms and legs cooled instantly.

"I'm not putting anything off," she informed him as she came back around the boxes. "I know your type, Ian. Sex shouldn't just be a way to pass the time. It should mean something, and the couple should have feelings for each other."

"Oh, I feel something for you. And I plan on making you feel something, too."

Why did her body have to respond to him? And why did she always have to be so goody-goody all the time?

She didn't even have the ability to make him squirm. No wonder her husband had left her for another woman.

"I'm not sure what put that look on your face, but I hope it wasn't me."

Cassie drew her attention back to Ian, who had now moved in closer and was very much in her personal space. His dark eyes stared at her mouth and Cassie really tried to remember why she was putting up such a fight.

Had her husband ever looked at her like this? As though he was so turned on that all that mattered was the two of them? Had he ever made her tingle like this or feel so feminine and sexy?

No to all the above.

Cassie swallowed. If she was really going to do this, she needed to be in control. She'd been dominated enough in her marriage and right now she wanted something totally different. She wanted sex and she wanted Ian.

Mustering up all her courage, Cassie looked up at him with a wide smile and said, "Strip."

# Chapter 5

It wasn't often Ian was shocked—he did live in Hollywood, after all. But that one word that had just slid from Cassie's lips truly took his breath and left him utterly speechless.

"Excuse me?"

Raising a brow, she crossed her arms as if she dared him to refuse. "I said strip. You want this, fine. But on my terms."

"I don't do sex with rules."

Cassie shrugged. "I don't do flings, but here we both are, stepping outside of our comfort zones."

Damn, she was hot. He never would've guessed the shy, quiet sister had this vixen streak. Of course, she admitted she was stepping outside her comfort zone, so perhaps this was all new territory. He had to hand it to her—she was doing a spectacular job. But he couldn't let her have all the control.

Reaching behind his neck, Ian fisted his shirt and tugged it off, flinging it to the side. Hands on his hips, he offered a grin.

"Now you."

Cassie laughed. "You're not done yet."

"No, but I'm ahead of you." He met her gaze, the silent challenge thrown down between them. "I'm waiting."

Even though her eyes never left his, he didn't miss the way her hands shook as she reached beneath the dress and pulled her panties down her bare legs.

Just that simple piece of silk lying discarded at her feet had his pulse racing, his body responding.

She quirked a brow again, as if waiting for him to proceed.

Without hesitation he toed off his shoes and ripped off his socks. "Looks like you're down to only one garment now," he told her, taking in the strapless dress she'd donned.

And it was about to get a whole hell of a lot hotter in here.

She eyed the lamp across the room and started for it.

"No," he told her. "Leave it on."

Glancing over her shoulder, she met his stare. "Trust me when I say you'll want that off."

"And why is that?"

Turning fully to face him, she pointed to her body. "In case you haven't noticed, I'm not one of those

Hollywood types who starve themselves for the sake of being ultrathin."

Crossing the narrow space between them, Ian ran both his hands up her bare arms and tucked his fingers in the elastic of the top of the dress, causing her arms to fall to her side.

"Oh, I've noticed." He yanked the dress down until it puddled at her feet, leaving her bare to him. "And that's precisely why I want that light on."

Her body trembled beneath his. No way did he want her questioning her gorgeous curves or the fact that he wanted the hell out of her.

Without a word he shucked off his pants and boxer briefs and tossed them aside.

Her eyes drank him in, causing the same effect as if she'd touched his entire body with her bare hands. Dying to touch her, to run his fingers along her curves, Ian snaked his arms around her waist and tugged her against him.

"As much as I want to explore that sexy body of yours, I'm hanging on by a thread here," he admitted as his mouth slammed down onto hers.

Cassie wrapped her arms around his neck. Their damp bodies molded together from torso to thigh, and she felt so perfect against him.

Perfect? No, she couldn't be perfect for him. Perfect for right now, which was all either of them was after.

They were simply taking advantage of the moment…of the sexual attraction that had enveloped them since she'd literally fallen into his arms only a few days ago.

Ian gripped her waist and lifted her.

"Ian, don't—"

"Shh," he whispered against her mouth. "I've got you."

Her lips curved into a smile. "What about a condom? Do you have that, too?"

*Condom, yes.* They needed a condom. His mind had been on the subtle moans escaping from her lips and getting those curves beneath his hands.

He eased her down his body and went to his jeans, where he pulled a condom from his wallet and in record time had it on.

When he turned back to her, he fully expected her to have her arms wrapped around her waist, maybe even be biting her lip out of nerves. But what he saw was a secure woman, hands on her hips, head tilted and a naughty grin on her face.

"Your confidence is sexy," he told her as he came back to her.

"You make me feel sexy."

Yeah, she wasn't a Hollywood size zero. Cassie Barrington was more old-school Hollywood starlet. She was a natural, stunning, vibrant woman, and now that she'd agreed to leave the light on, he could fully appreciate the beauty she was.

And when she reached for him and nearly wrapped herself around him as she claimed his mouth, her sexy status soared even higher.

Damn, he wasn't going to make it through this night.

Ian backed her against the wall and lifted her once again. This time her legs went around his waist and he had no control. None. The second he'd shucked that dress off her he'd been holding on by that proverbial thin thread.

Ian took her, causing her body to bow back, and her head tilted, eyes closed as she groaned once again.

As their hips moved together, Ian took the opportunity to kiss his way across her shoulders and the column of her throat before taking her face between his palms and claiming her mouth.

Sweat slick between them, the air around them grew even hotter as Cassie gripped his bare shoulders. Her nails bit into his skin; her heels dug into his back.

He wouldn't have it any other way.

She tore her mouth from his. "Ian, I—"

Yeah, he knew. He was right there with her as her body stilled, trembled. Following her over the edge, watching her face as she succumbed to the passion was one of the most erotic moments of his life.

Her body slid down his and he was pretty sure she would've collapsed to the floor had he not been leaning against her. He needed to lean into her or he'd be a puddle, too.

And the night had just begun.

Cassie slid back into her dress, ignoring the panties. Why bother with modesty at this point?

She may not live in Hollywood, but she'd put on one hell of an acting display. Ian thought her confident? She'd played along simply because she secretly wanted to be that wanton, take-charge woman, that woman who claimed what she wanted. And if he thought she was so comfortable with her body in this situation, then who was she to tell him different?

She'd been meek in her marriage, not a sex goddess in any way. But the way Ian had looked at her, touched her, was nothing like she'd ever experienced.

How could a man she'd known only a handful of days provide so much self-assurance? He'd awakened something within her she hadn't even known existed.

Cassie was certainly not used to one-night stands or flings, but she couldn't regret what had just happened. A virtual stranger had just given her one of the greatest gifts…self-esteem. Not too long ago she'd thought she'd never have that back, but right now, with her body still tingling from his talented hands and lips, Cassie knew without a doubt that she was better than the husband who had left her for another woman.

She'd just scooped up her discarded panties from the floor when Ian placed his hands around her waist and tugged her back against his bare chest.

"How's that age thing now?" he asked, nipping her ear. "Any complaints about how young I am?"

Laughing, Cassie shook her head. "You certainly know what you're doing."

His lips trailed over her neck. "I'm not done, either."

*Oh, mercy.* Her entire body shivered as she let her head fall back against his shoulder, enjoying the kisses he sprinkled across her heated skin.

"I'm not sure why you put this dress back on," he told her between kisses. "It's so hot in here and all."

*Yes, yes, it is.*

Cassie turned in his arms, noticing he was still completely naked. Those ripped muscles beneath taut, tanned skin begged for her touch.

"I didn't get to appreciate all of this a moment ago, before you attacked me," she told him, trailing her fingertips along his biceps and across his pecs.

"Appreciate me all you want," he told her with a crooked grin. "But let it be known, I didn't attack. You ordered me to strip, so I believe you started this."

Cassie playfully smacked his chest. "Who started what? You were the one who propositioned me in the stables."

"How's a man supposed to react when a sexy woman falls into his arms?"

"Yes, naturally that's what most people would do," she said, rolling her eyes.

Ian reached down, cupped her backside and widened his sexy smile. "I'm glad this little incident happened with the lock."

Cassie had to admit she was, too. There was no way she would've been able to focus on work with all her emotions fluttering around inside her. Now hopefully she wouldn't have to worry about this overwhelming physical attraction to Ian. They'd had sex, gotten it out of their systems and could move on.

His body stirred against hers. Okay, maybe they hadn't gotten it out of their systems.

"We still have hours before anyone will find us." He started backing her up again. "I have so many ideas to fill the time."

The backs of Cassie's thighs hit the edge of an old table. Ian wasted no time hoisting her up onto the smooth wooden surface.

"Do you have more condoms?" she asked.

His heavy-lidded gaze combined with that Cheshire-cat smile had her quivering before he even spoke.

"I may be out of condoms, but not out of ways to pleasure you."

And when he proceeded to show her, Cassie was suddenly in no hurry for daylight to come.

# Chapter 6

Unable to sleep for appreciating the feel of this sexy woman tangled all around him on the old chaise, Ian smoothed a hand down Cassie's bare back. Trailing down the dip in her waist, up over the curve of her hip had his body stirring again.

What on earth was he doing? Sex was one thing, but to lie awake most of the night rehashing it over and over in his head like some lovesick fool was, well…for fools. Not that he was any expert on relationships.

His mother was gearing up to divorce husband number four, no doubt with number five waiting in the wings, and his father… Ian sighed. His father probably wasn't even capable of love. Ian hadn't spoken to his father in years and rarely talked with his mother. He had nothing to say to either and it was obvious both of his parents were battling their own issues that didn't include him.

It shouldn't come as a surprise that Ian didn't do relationships.

He was great at his job, however, and what he wanted was to take his client roster to the next level. Lily Beaumont was the key.

Yet here he was, getting involved with Cassie Barrington. And, yes, they'd just had sex, but during the moments in between their intimacy, he'd gotten a brief glimpse of a playful, confident woman and he couldn't deny he liked what he saw.

The sound of a car door jarred him from his thoughts. He eased out from beneath Cassie's warm, lush body and moved over to the small window that faced the side of the house.

Tessa and Grant had arrived. He didn't know if he wanted to call for their attention or crawl back over to Cassie and give her a proper good-morning wake-up.

But their night was over, and he had responsibilities. He honestly had no clue how she'd react once she woke up. Would she regret what they'd done? Would she want more and expect some sort of relationship?

Ian gave the window a tug and it rose slowly with a groan.

"Hey," he yelled down. "Up here."

Tessa and Grant both looked around and Ian eased his arm out to wave. "We're locked in the attic," he called.

"Ian?" Grant shouted. "What on earth? We'll be right up."

Of course, now it dawned on him that both he and Cassie were as naked as the day they were born, and he turned around to see her already getting up. Shame that he hadn't ignored the rescue party and gone with his original idea of waking her, especially now that she was covering that made-for-sex body.

"Was that Tessa and Grant?" she asked, tugging on her jeans from the previous day.

"Uh-huh." He pulled on his own clothes, trying to keep his eyes off her as she wrestled into her bra.

Several moments later, the door below creaked open and Ian rushed over to the top of the stairs to see Tessa.

"We'll be right down," he told her, hoping to save Cassie some time to finish dressing.

He didn't know if she wanted it public knowledge that they'd slept together. This was all her call. He was much more comfortable with a fling than he figured she was. Plus this was her home, her family, and the last thing he wanted to do was put her in an awkward position.

"Who's up there with you?" Tessa asked, her brows drawn together.

"Your sister."

Tessa smiled. "Really? Well, we'll meet you all down in the kitchen. Take your time."

Once she walked away, Ian glanced up to Cassie, who was wearing a lovely shade of red over her neck and face.

"I tried," he defended, holding out his hands. "But I'd say your sister knows."

Cassie nodded. "That's okay. Tessa won't say anything."

Okay, maybe he hadn't wanted a relationship, but her statement hit a nerve. Seconds ago he'd thought he was fine with a fling and she wasn't, but perhaps he'd had that scenario backward.

"Is that what we're going to do? Keep this quiet?"

Smoothing her tousled hair away from her face, Cassie eyed him from across the room and sighed. "I don't know. This is all new to me. Can we just go downstairs and talk later?"

The voice of reason had him nodding. He didn't want to analyze what had happened too much. They both needed to concentrate on their jobs. After all, he had a mission and she was in the middle of the biggest racing season of her life.

Cassie started to ease by him when he stepped in front of her, blocking her exit. Her eyes went wide, then dropped to his mouth. Why was he doing this?

*Quit stalling and let her go.*

But he needed one more taste before their night officially came to an end.

He shoved his hands into her hair, tilting her head as he closed the distance between them. "Before you go," he whispered as his mouth slid across hers.

She melted into him as she returned the kiss. Her hands gripped his wrists as he held on to her. As much as Ian wanted her naked once again, he knew that was not an option.

Easing back, he smiled when her eyes took a moment to open. He released her, and, without a word, she walked by him and down the stairs.

And like some nostalgic sap, he glanced around the attic and smiled. This was definitely his favorite place on the estate.

Ian met up with Cassie in the kitchen. As soon as he entered the open room, he took in several things at once.

Tessa and Grant were seated at the bar, where Linda was serving cinnamon rolls. Both Tessa and Grant were eyeing Ian with knowing grins on their faces.

But it was Cassie, yet again, who captured his attention.

The woman he'd spent the night with was currently squatting down in front of a little girl with soft blond curls. The little girl looked nothing like Cassie, but the interaction didn't lie. The way she clung to Cassie, Cassie's sweet smile and laughter as she kissed her—it all had a sickening feeling settling deep in his gut.

"And who's this?" he asked, hoping it was Linda's grandchild or something because he knew Tessa and Grant had no children.

Coming to her feet with the little girl wrapped in her arms, Cassie still wore that vibrant smile as she turned to face him. "This is my daughter, Emily."

All eyes were on Ian. Granted, they were watching him because of the unspoken fact that he and Cassie had spent the night together, but they couldn't know the turmoil that flooded him. Cassie had a child and hadn't told him.

Not that they'd played the getting-to-know-you game before they'd shed their clothes, but wasn't that something that would come up?

Cassie's smile faded as Ian remained silent. Her protective hands held Emily close to her chest.

"Why don't you have some breakfast?" Linda asked, breaking the silence.

His eyes darted to her, then back to Cassie, who still watched him with a questioning look. Tessa and Grant had yet to move as they also took in the unfolding scene.

"I have things to do," he said as he walked by Cassie, ignoring the hurt in her eyes, and out the back door.

He couldn't stay in there another second. Rage filled him at the idea that Cassie had kept such a vital part of her life a secret. Was she the mother who pawned her kid off on other people so she could go have a good time? She'd been so confident, so eager to please him last night. Perhaps he was just the latest in a long line of men she threaded into her web.

No, he hadn't wanted anything beyond sex. And he sure as hell didn't want to discover that the woman he'd spent the night with was manipulative and selfish, looking for attention…just like his mother.


Humiliation flooded her.

The look of utter shock layered with anger had consumed Ian when she'd announced Emily was her daughter.

"Cass?"

Swallowing the hurt, Cassie turned to see her

sister watching her. Because this awkward moment didn't need any more fuel added to the fire, Cassie smiled.

"Thanks for watching her last night," Cassie said as she held Emily with one arm and grabbed the overnight bag off the counter. "I need to go change and then I'll meet you at the stables."

"Cassie." Tessa slid from the stool and crossed to her. "Don't do this."

"Do what?"

Blue eyes stared back at her and Cassie wanted nothing more than to sit and cry, but feeling sorry for herself wouldn't accomplish anything. She'd tried that when Derek had left her.

"I just want to go feed Emily and change." Cassie blinked back the burn of tears. "I'll meet you in an hour."

"Leave Emily here," Linda said. "I'm keeping her today anyway. Do what you need to do. I'll make sure she's fed."

As much as Cassie wanted to keep Emily with her, she knew it was silly. She'd just have to put her in her crib with toys while she grabbed a shower.

"All right," she conceded, dropping the bag back onto the counter and easing Emily into the wooden high chair next to the wide granite island. "Thanks, guys."

Barely keeping it together, she started for the door. When Tessa called her name again, Cassie raised a hand and waved her off. She just wanted to be alone for a minute, to compose herself.

How could she be so naive? Of course some big-city bachelor would be turned off by kids, but to act so repulsed by the fact made her flat-out angry.

She'd sworn when Derek had left she wouldn't allow herself to get hurt again. So, what did she do? Sleep with the first man who showed her any kind of affection.

Seriously, she thought she had more self-respect than that.

More angry at herself now, Cassie marched across the Barrington estate to her cottage next to the stables. Swatting at her damp cheeks, she squinted against the bright early-morning sun.

And because of the light in her eyes she didn't see Ian until she was in the shadow of her house. There he stood, resting against one of the porch posts as if he belonged there.

"Don't you have a client who needs your attention?" she asked, not stopping as she brushed past him and slid her key from her pocket to let herself in.

When she tried to close the door behind her, Ian's muscular arm shot out and his hand gripped the edge.

Those dark eyes leveled hers as she reined in her tears. No way would she let him see just how upset she truly was.

Tension crackled between them as Ian stood on the threshold, making no move to come in or leave.

"What do you want?" she asked.

"I want to know why you didn't tell me you had a daughter."

"Do you have kids?" she retorted.

He blinked. "No."

"Why didn't you tell me you didn't?"

"It never came up."

She threw her arms out. "Exactly. We didn't discuss too much personal stuff before…"

Shaking her head, Cassie looked up to the ceiling and sighed. "Just go. I made a mistake—it's over."

When her front door slammed, she jumped.

"I don't like being played." Ian fisted his hands on his narrow hips.

"This is my life, Ian." She gestured toward the Pack 'n Play in the corner and the toys in a basket next to the sofa. "I'm a mom. I'm not apologizing for it, and you won't make me feel bad."

When he continued to stare, muscle ticking in his jaw, Cassie tried her hardest not to wilt under his powerful presence. His gray T-shirt stretched over taut muscles, and she instantly recalled him taking her against the wall.

"Look, you're going to be here for a while," she said, reality sinking in. "I'm going to be here for the most part except during races. We're going to see each other."

His eyes roamed over her as if he were recalling last night, too. A shiver crept through her, but she remained still, waiting on his response.

"I wish you were different," he told her, his voice low.

Stunned, Cassie crossed her arms. "What?"

Cursing, Ian turned for the door. "Nothing. You're right," he said, gripping the handle and glancing over his shoulder. "We have to see each other, so why make this harder than necessary? Last night was a mistake, so let's just forget it happened."

He walked out the door and Cassie resisted the urge to throw something. For a second, when he'd said he wished she were different, she'd seen a sliver of vulnerability in his eyes. But he'd quickly masked it with his cruel, hurtful words. *Fine.* She didn't need anybody, especially someone who acted as if her child was a burden. Emily came first in her life. Period.

And no man, not her ex-husband and certainly not this sexy stranger, would make her feel ashamed.

Cassie turned toward her bedroom and cursed her body. She hated Ian Shaffer for his words, his actions, but her body still tingled from everything he'd done to her last night. How could someone so passionate and gentle turn into someone so hurtful?

Something about Emily had triggered such a dramatic turnaround. Unfortunately, Cassie didn't have the time or the energy to care. Whatever issues Ian had didn't concern her.

Now she just had to figure out how to see him on a daily basis and block out the fact he'd made her so alive, so confident for a brief time. Because now she didn't feel confident at all. She wished she could have a do-over of last night.

This time she'd keep her clothes on.

# Chapter 7

Ian may have had the best sexual experience of his life last night, but any desire he felt for Cassie was quickly squelched when he'd discovered her with a baby. A baby, for crying out loud.

It wasn't that he didn't like children. Kids were innocent in life, innocent in the actions of adults. How could he not love them? He just didn't see any in his future. And Cassie having a child certainly wasn't a problem in and of itself.

No, the issue had been when he'd seen her holding her child and he'd instantly flashed back to his mother, who would drag him from sitter to sitter while she went out at night.

But he wouldn't blame his past for his present problems. His body seemed to forget how angry he was and continued to betray him. Cassie was still sexy as hell and he'd forever be replaying just how hot their encounter had been.

But now that he knew she had a daughter, messing around on a whim was definitely out. He wasn't cut out for the long term, and he refused to be the lover floating in and out of a kid's life the way his mother's lovers had floated through his.

Shaking off the unpleasant memories seeing Cassie with her baby had inspired, Ian approached Max Ford. His client had recently married his high school sweetheart and the couple had adopted a little girl. Ian couldn't be happier for the guy, but he wanted no part in the happily-ever-after myth himself.

"Hey," Max greeted him as he headed toward the makeup trailer. "Coming in with me?"

"Yeah."

Ian fell into step behind Max. The actor tugged on the narrow door and gestured for Ian to enter first. After climbing the three metal steps, Ian entered the cool trailer and nodded a greeting to the makeup artist.

Max closed the door behind him and exchanged pleasantries with the young lady. Ian took a seat on the small sofa across from the workstation and waited until the two finished their discussion of the day's events.

"You're working out in the stables and field today?" Ian asked. "I saw the script. Looked like the scene with you and Lily when the first horses were brought onto the estate after the wedding."

Max nodded as the makeup artist swiped over his face with a sponge full of foundation. "Yeah. It's a short scene. This afternoon and evening we'll be shooting some of the wedding scenes at the small church in town."

Ian settled deeper into the sofa, resting an arm across the back of the cushion. "Everything going okay so far?"

"Great," Max told him. "Raine is planning on joining me in a few days. She was excited I was shooting on the East Coast."

Ian knew Max and Raine had been through hell after years apart before finally finding their way back to each other in Max's hometown of Lenox, Massachusetts. Ian couldn't imagine trying to juggle a family while working in this crazy industry, let alone from across the country. Speaking of crazy, Ian never thought Hollywood heartthrob Max Ford would settle down, much less on some goat and chicken farm in New England, but to each his own and all that. Love apparently made you do some strange things.

"You talking to Lily soon?" Max asked.

Max had been one of Ian's first clients. They'd both taken a chance on each other, the risk had paid off and here they were, at the top of their games. They had no secrets and oftentimes their relationship was more like friends than business associates.

"Yeah. Hoping to get a few more minutes with her today."

The makeup artist reached for a brush and started stroking a shadow across Max's lids. Yeah, Ian would much rather stay on this side of the industry…the side where his face stayed makeup-free.

"I'll keep you posted," Ian said, not wanting to get too detailed since there were other ears in the room. "I plan on being on set for the next several weeks, so hopefully something will come from that."

Something positive. There was no way Ian wanted his ex-partner to get his clutches on Lily. Not to mention Ian was selfish and now that Lily was between agents, he wanted her because she was one of the top Hollywood leading ladies.

Added to that, she was the rare celebrity who hadn't been jaded or swayed by the limelight. Lily was the real deal who made a point to keep her nose out of trouble.

Any agent's dream client.

"I've discussed some things with her," Max stated. "She's interested in hearing your terms and ideas, so hopefully she makes the right decision."

Ian was counting on it. Lily was smart enough to know the industry. After all, she'd just left her agent, who'd been a bit shady with her career. She'd put a stop to that immediately.

Ian could only hope she saw the hands-on way he worked and how invested he was as an agent. Visiting movie sets was his favorite job perk. Getting out of a stuffy office and being on location was always the highlight. Plus he wanted to make sure his clients were comfortable and there were no glitches.

"I'll be around if you need me." Ian came to his feet and moved toward the trailer door, pulling his phone from his pocket to check his emails. "I plan on being at both scenes today."

"Sounds good. I assume you've met all the Barringtons?" Max asked as the makeup artist ran the powder brush over his neck.

Ian swallowed. "Yeah. I've met them."

Met them, slept with one and still felt the stirrings from the continuous play of memories.

"They're one impressive family," Max went on, oblivious to the turmoil within Ian. "Damon is an amazing man with all of his accomplishments, but I swear, Cassie and Tessa are a force to be reckoned with."

Ian bit the inside of his cheek to avoid commenting on one of those "forces." The image of her in that body-hugging dress still made his knees weak, his heart quicken.

"That's why this movie is going to kick ass," Ian said, circling back to work, where his mind needed to stay. "Everyone loves a story like this, and having it on the big screen with two of Hollywood's top stars will only make it pull in that much more at the box office."

"I hope you're right."

Ian was confident this movie would be one of the biggest for both Max and Lily. Hollywood's heart-throb and sweetheart playing a married couple in a true story? It was a guaranteed slam dunk for everybody.

Which reminded him, he needed to check his emails and hopefully line up another client's role.

"I'll see you in a bit," Ian said as he exited the trailer.

He refused to glance toward Cassie's cottage. He wasn't some love-struck teen who'd slept with a woman and now wondered what she was doing every waking minute.

Okay, so he did wonder what she was doing, but love had absolutely nothing to do with it. His hormones were stuck in overdrive and they would just have to stay there because he refused to see her in any type of personal atmosphere again.

Even flings warranted a certain type of honesty, and getting involved, in any manner, with a woman who reminded him of the past he'd outrun was simply not an option.

A flash of movement from the field in the distance caught his eye. He headed toward the white fence stretching over the Barrington estate. As he neared, his gut tightened.

Cassie sat atop a chestnut-colored horse flying through the open field. Her hair danced unrestrained in the wind behind her and the breeze carried her rich laughter straight to him...and his body responded... work and emails instantly forgotten.

Ian stood frozen and admired the beauty. From behind her came Tessa on her own horse, but Ian's gaze was riveted on Cassie. He hadn't heard that deep laugh. She all but screamed sex with that throaty sound, her curves bouncing in the saddle, hair a wild mass of deep crimson curls.

Her carefree attitude would've been such a turn-on, but in the back of his mind he couldn't forget where he came from. From a father who had standards so high nobody could reach them and a mother who spent her time entertaining boyfriends and husbands, leaving a young Ian a distant second in her life.

He never wanted to go back to that emotional place again.

"You've got an audience."

Breathless and smiling, Cassie turned to her sister as Tessa came to a stop beside her. This felt good, to get out and not worry about training or anything else for a few minutes. Just getting back to their roots and racing was something she and her sister didn't do nearly often enough.

"Who's the audience?" Cassie asked, fully expecting to see some of the film crew. The cameramen and lighting people seemed to be all over the estate, moving things around, making the place their own for the sake of the film. The Hollywood scene was definitely a far cry from the usual relaxed atmosphere of Stony Ridge.

A sense of pride welled deep within her at the fact that Hollywood loved her family's story as much as she did. Horses, racing and family... That was what it meant to be a Barrington, and they excelled at it all because they worked hard and loved harder.

"Your agent," Tessa replied, nodding back toward the fence line. "I saw him stop when you raced by. He hasn't moved."

Cassie risked a glance and, sure enough, Ian stood turned in her direction. He was just far enough away that she couldn't make out his facial expression...not that she cared. But damn, why did he have to be a jumbled mess? He'd wanted her with such passion last night, had made her feel so special and wanted. How dare he pull such emotions out of her when she was still trying to piece the shards of her heart back together after her divorce?

Today when he'd seen Emily, he'd become detached, angry and not at all the same man she'd been with last night. His silence had hurt her, had made the night before instantly ugly.

And after coming home, she'd checked her phone and found a missed call from Derek. Seriously? After months of no contact whatsoever, now he decided to call? Cassie had deleted the message without listening. She didn't care what he had to say, and, after her emotional morning with Ian, she wasn't in the mood.

"He's not my anything." Cassie turned back toward Tessa, turning her back on Ian and willing him to go away.

"He was something to you last night."

Squinting against the sun, Cassie shrugged. "He was my temporary mistake. Nothing more."

Leaning across the gap between the horses, Tessa slid her hand over Cassie's. "I'm not judging at all. I just want you to know people aren't perfect. We all make rash decisions, and beating yourself up won't change what happened."

Cassie knew Tessa would be the last person to judge her, but that didn't stop the embarrassment from settling in her gut.

"I just hate that I gave in to the first man to show

me any attention since being divorced," Cassie explained, gripping the reins.

Tessa's warm smile spread across her face. "Honey, Ian is a very attractive man, you're a beautiful woman and you all were locked in an attic all night. Instant attraction is hard to ignore, especially when you have nothing else to focus on."

"Self-control is a beautiful thing," Cassie murmured. "Too bad I didn't have any."

Laughing, Tessa squeezed Cassie's hand before pulling back. "Yeah, well, I didn't have any where Grant was concerned, either, and look how well it worked out for us."

Cassie's eyes darted down to the impressive diamond band surrounding Tessa's ring finger. Grant had gotten a flat band because of Tessa's riding career; he knew she wouldn't want to work with anything too bulky.

And that proved just how beautiful a relationship her sister and Grant had. The man knew Tessa inside and out, loved her and her career. He'd even overcome his own personal demons to be with her.

Cassie couldn't be happier for the two of them, but her situation was different.

"I'm pretty sure my attic rendezvous will not be leading to any proposals," Cassie joked. She had to joke with Tessa, otherwise she'd cry, and she refused to let this experience pull her down and make her feel guilty for having needs. "Besides, I think seeing Emily was like a bucket of cold water in Ian's face. I won't be with anybody who can't accept that I'm a package deal."

"I saw Ian's face when he found out Emily was yours," Tessa said, shoving her hair behind her ear. "He was definitely caught off guard, but the man wasn't unaffected by whatever happened between the two of you or he wouldn't have just stopped to watch you ride by. He may be torn, but he's still interested. You can't blame him for being shocked you're a mother."

Yeah, well, Ian's interest more than likely consisted of getting in her pants again…which she wouldn't allow.

But the memory of last night still played through her mind. His touch had been perfect. His words had seduced her until she'd forgotten about anything else but the moment they were locked in.

No matter how her body craved to be touched by his talented hands again, Cassie knew she deserved better than the way she'd been treated afterward.

So if Ian wanted her, that was his problem and he'd have to deal with it. She had enough on her plate without worrying about some big-time Hollywood agent who was only looking for only a fling.

She had a racing season to finish and a school for handicapped children to get started.

Her soon-to-be brother-in-law, Grant, had a paralyzed sister who used to ride, and her story had inspired Cassie on so many levels. Even though they hadn't met yet, just her story alone was enough to drive Cassie to want more for the next chapter of life. And what better way to teach her daughter to give back and love and care for others? Instilling love in young children made all the difference. She and Tessa were evidence of that.

Throwing a glance over her shoulder, Cassie had mixed emotions when she saw Ian was nowhere in sight. On one hand, she was glad he'd moved on. On the other, she kind of liked knowing she'd left some sort of impression on him.

No matter how things were now, for a time last night, she'd been in a sexy man's arms and that man had been attentive and giving and had made her feel more self-worth than ever.

Having regrets at this point was kind of in vain.

Besides, no matter what common sense played through her mind, she couldn't deny the physical pull she still felt toward Ian. And she was positive she hadn't seen the last of him.

# Chapter 8

After shooting wrapped for the day, Ian headed toward the stables to see if Lily was in there. He hadn't seen her for two days, and Max had mentioned he'd seen her heading that way. Ian hadn't had a chance to speak with her yet. The chaos of filming and so many people around had gotten in the way. Other than the usual small talk, he'd not been able to catch her alone.

Hopefully he could find her and perhaps they could arrange for a time to sit down and talk.

The sun was just at the edge of the horizon, casting a vibrant orange glow across the sky. The air had turned warmer as spring approached summer. Soon they'd be off to the Preakness Stakes, where Tessa would try to win the second race on her way toward the coveted Triple Crown.

The entire crew was riding the high of the shoot as well as getting sucked into the excitement of cheering the Barrington girls on toward victory. He had no doubt Tessa and Cassie were a jumble of anticipation and nerves.

Ian shoved his hands into his pockets as he approached the stables. He wasn't letting his mind wander to Cassie, because if he thought of her, he'd think of her sweet curves, her tempting smile and the fact he still wanted her.

Before he could travel too far down that path of mixed emotions, Ian rounded the corner of the open stable door and froze.

Lily was in the stable all right. But she wasn't alone. The groom, Ian believed his name was Nash, had his back to Lily, and Lily's hand rested on his shoulder, a look of concern marring her beautiful face.

She whispered something Ian couldn't make out and Nash's head dropped at the same time Lily's arms slid around his waist and she rested her forehead on his back. The intimate, private moment shocked Ian and he really had no clue what he'd walked in on.

The old-fashioned lanterns suspended from the ceiling cast a perfect glow on them and Ian quickly stepped out of the stable before he could be spotted... or interrupt whatever was happening.

He had a feeling whatever was going on between the groom and the star of the film was on the down low...especially since an affair had nearly cost Grant Carter his job when he'd been sneaking to see Tessa.

But that had all worked out and the two were headed down the aisle in the near future.

Their secret would be safe with him. For one, he wanted Lily to trust him and sign with his agency. And for another, why stir up trouble? Ian couldn't help but laugh. He and Cassie were pretty far-fetched in terms of the possibility of getting together, but look where they were now after a heated night in the attic.

Heading back toward his on-site trailer, Ian stopped when a scream cut through the evening. It was loud enough to have him trying to figure out where the sound was coming from.

He heard it again and moved toward the row of cottages settled beyond the main house. The grounds were deserted now since the entire crew had left for the hotel in town. Only a handful of people were staying on the property in trailers like the one Max had requested for him. The scream split through the air once more and Ian quickly found the culprit.

Just behind Cassie's cottage there was a small patio area and suspended from the pergola was a child's swing.

Cassie pushed her daughter, and each time the child went high, she let out a squeal. Ian's heart dropped at the sight. He didn't recall ever having that one-on-one playful time with either of his parents. Perhaps when he'd been a toddler, but he doubted it, considering they weren't affectionate when he'd been old enough to recall.

The sweet little girl with blond curls blowing in the breeze giggled and kicked her feet when Cassie grabbed the back of the plastic seat on the swing and held it back.

"Hold on," Cassie warned. "Here comes the biggest push of all."

When she let go of the swing, Cassie laughed right along with her daughter and Ian found himself rooted to his spot at the edge of her concrete patio.

The man in him watched, admiring Cassie's laid-back style, with her hair in a ponytail and wearing leggings and an oversize T-shirt that slid off one delicate, creamy shoulder. Her feet were bare and her face was void of any makeup, which was how he'd seen her since he'd arrived. Everything about her screamed country girl.

While the man in him watched, the lost little boy in him turned his attention to Emily. He took in all the delight from the sweet girl still clutching the rope holding up her swing and wondered where her father was. Did the man even know he had a child? Did Cassie have any contact with him?

All the questions forming in his head were absolutely none of his business, yet he couldn't help but want to know more.

Ian's gaze traveled from Emily back to Cassie... and he found her looking right back at him with those impressive blue eyes.

"What are you doing here?" she asked, giving the swing another light push.

Ian tried not to focus on the fact that her shirt had slipped in the front, giving him a glimpse of the swell of her breast.

"I heard screaming." He stepped onto the concrete

pad, cursing himself for being drawn in even more. "I wasn't sure who it was."

Cassie's eyes held his for a second before she turned her attention back to the swing. She held on to the ropes, thus bringing Emily's fun to a screeching halt.

The little girl twisted in her seat to look back at Cassie. Cassie went to the front of the swing, unfastened the safety harness and lifted Emily out.

"We were just heading in for dinner," Cassie said, propping Emily up on her hip.

Damn if her tilted, defiant chin didn't make him want to stay longer. Why torture himself? He wanted her physically, nothing more. Yet he found himself being pulled ever so slowly toward her.

"Don't go in just because of me."

Emily stared at him with bright, expressive blue eyes like her mother's. Her hand reached toward him and he couldn't stop himself from reaching back. The moment he looked into those little baby blues something unidentifiable slid over his heart.

Emily's tiny hand encircled his finger as a smile spread across her baby face. That innocent gesture touched so many places in him: the child who'd craved attention, the teen who'd needed guidance and the adult who still secretly wished he had a parent who gave a damn without being judgmental.

Ian didn't miss the way Cassie tensed at the sight of Emily holding on to his finger, but he wasn't pulling back. How could he deny such an innocent little girl human touch? She was smiling, happy and had no clue the turmoil that surrounded her right now.

"Don't you have a client you should tend to?" Cassie asked, her meaning that he was not welcome all too clear.

"I already talked with Max after the shooting wrapped and we came back here." The crew had taken a few shots of the wedding scene in town. "I didn't see you at the church earlier."

Cassie reached up, smoothing away blond curls from Emily's forehead. "I was there. I stayed in the back with Tessa. We didn't want to get in the way."

"What did you think of the shoot?"

Why was he still here talking to her? Why didn't he just leave? He had calls to return, emails to answer, contracts to look over.

Besides the fact a little cherublike toddler had his finger in a vise grip, he could walk away. Cassie had made it clear she didn't like him, and he certainly wasn't looking for a woman with a child.

Yet here he stood, talking to her and eagerly awaiting her answer.

"It was perfect," she said, a soft smile dancing across her lips. "Lily looked exactly like the pictures I've always seen of my mother on that day. My father teared up, so I know Lily and Max hit that scene beautifully."

Ian wiggled his finger, making Emily giggle as she tugged on him. He took a step forward, now being drawn in by two intriguing ladies.

"I think the fans will fall in love with this film,"

he told Cassie as his eyes settled on hers. "And your family."

The pulse at the base of her throat quickened and Ian couldn't help but smile. Good to know she wasn't so unaffected. What they'd shared the other night was nothing short of amazing. No matter what transpired afterward, he couldn't deny that had been the most intense night of his life.

Damn it. Cassie and her innocent daughter were the exact picture of the commitment he could never make.

So how could he be drawn to this woman?

"I just want my father to be happy with the end result," she told him. "I want people to see what a hard worker he is and that everything didn't get handed to him."

Ian couldn't help but admire her for wanting people to see the other side of Damon Barrington. The man was a phenomenon, and Ian had no doubt whatsoever that this film would be a mega blockbuster.

Emily let go of his finger and started patting her mother's cheeks. Instantly Ian missed the innocent touch, but he stepped back and shoved his hands into his pockets.

"Was there something else you wanted?" she asked.

Clearing his throat, Ian shoved pride aside and nodded. "Actually, yeah. I'm sorry for how I handled the other morning."

Cassie's brows rose as she reached up to try to pull Emily's hands from her face. "I never expected you to apologize."

He hadn't expected it, either, but he couldn't deny the fact he'd been a jerk. If he'd learned anything from growing up, it was to know when to apologize. He'd never seen his parents say they were sorry to each other, and he'd always wondered if such a simple gesture would have made a difference.

"I can admit when I make a mistake," he informed her.

Those bright eyes darted down as she sighed. "This is a first for me."

"What's that?"

Glancing back up, she shook her head. "Nothing. I appreciate you apologizing. Since you're going to be here awhile, I really don't want tension. Between you working and me training, I just can't handle more stress."

Ian noticed the soft lines between her brows, the dark circles beneath her eyes. This single mother was worn-out and he'd added to her worry because she hadn't wanted any awkwardness between them.

"Who helps you with Emily?"

Great, now he was asking questions before he could fully process them. He needed a filter on his mouth and he needed to mind his own business. The last thing he wanted was to worry about Cassie and her daughter. He certainly wasn't applying for the position of caregiver.

"My family." Her chin tilted as she held his gaze, unblinking. "Why?"

Yeah, why indeed? Why was this his concern? They'd slept together one night after days of intense sexual tension and now he was all up in her personal space…a space that hit too close to home and touched his heart way too deeply.

He pushed aside the unwanted emotions. He would be here only a short time. Even if his past hadn't mixed him all up, he still couldn't get too involved with Cassie Barrington.

Besides, she had her hands full and they'd definitely done a complete one-eighty since they'd spent the night together. That night had been full of passion and surrender. Now Cassie had erected walls, thanks to him, and the only thing he saw in her eyes was exhaustion.

"I'll let you get in to dinner," he told her, not answering her question. "See you tomorrow."

When he turned away, Cassie called his name. He glanced over his shoulder and found two sets of beautiful blue eyes staring at him.

"We're not having much, but you're welcome to join us."

The olive branch had been extended and he wondered if this was her manners and upbringing talking or if she truly wanted him to stay.

"I'd be a fool to turn down dinner with two pretty ladies," he told her, turning back to face her. "Are you sure?"

With a shaky nod, Cassie smiled. "I'm sure."

*Well, hell.* Looked as if he was getting in deeper after all. But he followed her through the back door like the lost man that he was.

They could be friends, he thought. Friends ate dinner together; friends apologized when they were wrong. That was where they were at now because

Cassie and her little girl deserved a commitment, a family life—things he couldn't offer.

As Cassie slid Emily into her high chair, Ian watched her delicate skin as her shoulder peeked from her shirt once again. Anything he was feeling right now went way beyond friendship and ventured down the path at warp speed toward carnal desire.

# Chapter 9

Cassie had no clue what had prompted her to invite Ian inside. She wasn't weak. She didn't need a man and had been just fine on her own for the better part of a year now. But something about Ian kept pulling her toward him, as if some invisible force tugged on her heart.

And when Emily had reached for him, Cassie had waited to see his reaction. Thankfully, he'd played right along. She'd barely noticed his hesitation and hard swallow, but he hadn't disappointed Emily. Maybe kids weren't the issue with him; perhaps he was just upset because she hadn't said anything. But really, when would that conversation have occurred? When she had fallen into his arms that first day or when she'd told him to strip in the attic?

The image of him doing just that flooded her mind. Cassie was thankful her back was to him as she turned on the oven.

"Hope you like grilled cheese and French fries." Cassie reached into the narrow cabinet beside the oven and pulled out a cookie sheet.

"Considering I was going to probably have microwave popcorn back in my trailer, grilled cheese and fries sounds gourmet."

Her phone vibrated on the counter next to the stove. She saw Derek's name flash across the screen. No and no. If he was so determined to talk to her, he knew where she was.

Right where he'd left her months ago. Pompous jerk.

As she busied herself getting the meager dinner ready for the other man who was driving her out of her mind in a totally different way, she mentally cursed. Ian was probably used to fine dining, glamorous parties and beautiful women wearing slinky dresses and dripping in diamonds. Unfortunately, tonight he was getting a single mother throwing together cheese sandwiches while wearing an old, oversize T-shirt to hide her extra weight.

More than likely he'd said yes because he felt sorry for her. Regardless, he was in her house now. Surprisingly he'd pulled up a kitchen chair next to the high chair and was feeding puff snacks to Emily.

The sight had Cassie blinking back tears. Emily's father should be doing that. He should be here having dinner with them, as a family. He should've stuck it out and kept his pants zipped.

But he'd decided a wife and a baby were too much of a commitment and put a damper on his lifestyle.

In the back of her mind, Cassie knew she was better off without him. Any man that didn't put his family first was a coward. Not suitable material for a husband or father to her child.

But the reality of being rejected still hurt. Cassie could honestly say she'd gotten over her love, but the betrayal… That was something she would probably never recover from. Because he'd not just left her; he'd left a precious, innocent baby behind without even attempting to fight for what he'd created.

Being rejected by Ian was just another blow to her already battered self-esteem.

"You okay?"

Cassie jerked back to the moment and realized two things. One, Ian was staring at her, his brows drawn together, and two, she'd worn a hole in the bread from being too aggressive applying the butter.

Laughing, Cassie tossed the torn bread onto the counter and grabbed another piece from the bag. "Yeah. My mind was elsewhere for a minute."

"Were you angry with that slice of bread?" he asked with a teasing grin.

"I may have had a little aggression I needed to take out." Cassie couldn't help but laugh again. "You're pretty good with her. Do you have nieces or nephews?"

Ian shook his head. "I'm an only child. But there was a set I visited not too long ago that had a baby about Emily's age. He was the cutest little guy and instantly wanted me over anyone else. I guess kids just like me."

*Great.* Now he had a soft spot for kids. Wasn't that the exact opposite of the image he'd portrayed the other morning when seeing Emily for the first time?

Ian Shaffer had many facets and she hated that she wanted to figure out who the real Ian was deep down inside.

Dinner was ready in no time, and thankfully, the silence wasn't too awkward. Eating and caring for a baby helped fill the void of conversation. When they were done, Ian went to clear the table and Cassie stopped him.

"I'll get it," she told him, picking up her own plate. "It's not that much."

"You cooked. The least I could do is help clean." He picked up his plate and took it to the sink. "Besides, if you cook more often, I'll gladly clean up after."

Cassie froze in the midst of lifting Emily from her high chair. "You want to come back for dinner?" she asked.

"I wouldn't say no if you asked."

Cassie settled Emily on her hip and turned to Ian, who was putting the pitcher of tea into the refrigerator. Okay, now she knew this wasn't pity. He obviously wanted to spend time with her. But why? Did he think she'd be that easy to get into bed again? Of course he did. She'd barely known his name when she'd shed her clothes for him. What man wouldn't get the impression she was easy?

Cassie turned and went into the living room,

placed Emily in her Pack 'n Play and handed her her favorite stuffed horse. Footsteps shuffled over the carpet behind her and Cassie swallowed, knowing she'd have to be up front with Ian.

"Listen," she said as she straightened and faced the man who stood only a few feet away. "I have a feeling you think I'm somebody that I'm not."

Crossing his arms over his wide chest, Ian tilted his head and leveled those dark eyes right on her. "And what do you believe I think of you?"

Well, now she felt stupid. Why did he make this sound like a challenge? And why was she getting all heated over the fact he was standing in her living room? No man had been there other than her father and her soon-to-be brother-in-law. She'd moved into the guest cottage on the estate after Derek had left her so she could be closer to the family for support with Emily.

So seeing such a big, powerful man in her house was a little…arousing. Which just negated the whole point she was trying to make. Yeah, she was a juxtaposition of nerves and emotions.

"I think because we slept together you think I'm eager to do it again." She rested her hands on her hips, willing them to stop shaking. She had to be strong, no matter her physical attraction to Ian. "I'm really not the aggressive, confident woman who was locked in that attic."

Ian's gaze roamed down her body, traveled back up and landed on her mouth as he stepped forward. "You look like the same woman to me," he said, closing the gap between them. "What makes you think you're so different from the woman I spent the night with?"

She couldn't think with him this close, the way his eyes studied her, the woodsy scent of his cologne, the way she felt his body when he wasn't even touching her.

"Well, I..." She smoothed her hair back behind her ears and tipped her head to look him in the eye. "I'm afraid you think that I look for a good time and that I'm easy."

A ghost of a smile flirted around those full lips of his. "I rushed to judgment. I don't think you're easy, Cassie. Sexy, intriguing and confident, but not easy."

Sighing, she shook her head. "I'm anything but confident."

Now his hands came up, framed her face and sent an insane amount of electrical charges coursing through her. As much as she wanted his touch, she couldn't allow herself to crave such things. Hadn't she learned her lesson? Physical attraction and sexual chemistry did not make for a solid base for family, and, right now, all she could focus on was her family. Between Emily and the race with her sister, Cassie had no time for anything else.

But, oh, how she loved the feel of those strong, warm palms covering her face, fingertips slipping into her hair.

"You were amazing and strong in the attic," he told her. He placed a finger over her lips when she tried to speak. "You may not be like that all the time, but you were then. And that tells me that the real you came out that night. You had no reason to put on a front with me and you were comfortable being yourself. Your passion and ability to control the situation was the biggest turn-on I've ever experienced."

Cassie wanted to tell him he was wrong, that she wasn't the powerful, confident woman he thought she was.

But she couldn't say a word when he leaned in just a bit more, tickling his lips across hers so slowly that Cassie feared she'd have to clutch on to his thick biceps to stay upright.

She didn't reach up, though. Didn't encourage Ian in tormenting her any further.

But when his mouth opened over hers so gently, coaxing hers open, as well, Cassie didn't stop him. Still not reaching for him, she allowed him to claim her. His hands still gripped her face, his body pressed perfectly against hers and she flashed back instantly to when they'd had nothing between them. He'd felt so strong, so powerful.

More than anything to do with his looks or his charming words, he made her feel more alive than she'd ever felt.

Ian's lips nipped at hers once, twice, before he lifted his head and looked her straight in the eyes.

The muscle ticked in his jaw as he slowly lowered his hands from her face and stepped back. "No, Cassie. Nothing about you or this situation is easy."

Without another word, he turned and walked through her house and out the back door. Cassie gripped the edge of the sofa and let out a sigh. She had no clue what had just happened, but something beyond desire lurked in Ian's dark eyes. The way he'd looked at her, as if he was wrestling his own personal demon…

Cassie shook her head. This was not her problem. Sleeping with the man had brought up so many complications—the main reason she never did flings.

Was that why she kept feeling this pull? Because sex just wasn't sex to her? For her to sleep with someone meant she had some sort of deeper bond than just lust. How could she not feel attached to the man who made her feel this alive?

Glancing down to sweet Emily, who was chewing on her stuffed horse, Cassie rested her hip against the couch. This baby was her world and no way would she be that mother who needed to cling to men or have a revolving door of them.

Better to get her head on straight and forget just how much Mr. Hollywood Agent affected her mind.

Trouble was, she was seriously afraid he'd already affected her heart.

# Chapter 10

"My girls ready for next week?"

Cassie slid the saddle off Don Pedro and threw a glance over her shoulder to her father. Damon Barrington stalked through the stables that he not only owned, but at one time had spent nearly every waking hour in.

Even though the Barringtons' planned to retire from the scene after this racing season, Damon still wasn't ready to sell the prizewinning horses. He'd had generous offers, including one from his biggest rival in the industry, Jake Mason, but so far no deal had been made. Cassie highly doubted her father would ever sell to Jake. The two had been competitors for years and had never gotten along on the track…or off it.

"We're as ready as we'll ever be," Tessa said as she started brushing down the Thoroughbred. "My time is even better than before. I'm pretty confident about the Preakness."

Damon smiled, slipping his hands into the pockets of his worn jeans. The man may be a millionaire and near royalty in the horse industry because of his Triple Crown win nearly two decades ago, but he still was down-to-earth and very much involved in his daughters' careers.

"I know you'll do the Barrington name proud, Tess." He reached up and stroked the horse's mane as Cassie slid in beside her father.

"What are you doing down here?" Cassie asked. "Thought you'd be keeping your eye on the film crew."

Damon patted the horse and reached over to wrap an arm around Cassie's shoulders. A wide grin spread across his tanned, aged face. His bright blue eyes landed on hers.

"The lighting guys are reworking the living room right now," he explained. "The scene they shot the other day wasn't quite what they wanted. They're shooting a small portion again this afternoon."

This whole new world of filming was so foreign to her, but the process was rather fascinating. "I plan on heading into town and picking up some feed later," she told him. "I guess I'll miss watching that."

And more than likely miss seeing Ian again—which was probably for the best. She needed space after that simple dinner and arousing kiss last night. He hadn't been by the stables and she hadn't seen him

around the grounds, so he was probably working…
which was what she needed to concentrate on.

"I thought I'd take Emily with me and maybe run
her by that new toy store in town," Cassie went on.
"She's learning to walk now and maybe I can find
her something she can hold on to and push around
to strengthen her little legs."

Damon laughed. "Once she starts walking, she'll
be all over this place."

Cassie smiled. "I can't wait to see how she looks
in a saddle."

Tessa came around Don Pedro and started brushing his other side. "Why don't you take her for a ride
now? I'm sure she'd love it and it's such a nice day
out. We're done for a while anyway."

The idea was tempting. "I still need to get feed,
though."

"I'll send Nash to get it," Damon spoke up. "He
won't mind."

Cassie leaned her head against her father's strong
shoulder. "Thanks, Dad."

Patting her arm, Damon placed a kiss on top of
her head. "Anytime. Now go get my granddaughter
and start training her right."

Excited for Emily's first ride, Cassie nearly
sprinted to the main house and through the back
door to the kitchen, where Linda was washing dishes.

"Hey, Linda." Cassie glanced over the island to
see Emily in her Pack 'n Play clapping her hands and
gibbering to her animals. "I'm going to take Emily
off your hands for a bit."

"Oh, she's no trouble at all." Linda rinsed a pan and set it in the drainer before drying her hands and turning. "I actually just sat her in there. We've been watching the action in the living room. She likes all the lights."

Cassie scooped up her girl and kissed her cheek. "I'm sure she does. She'd probably like to crawl all over and knock them down."

Laughing, Linda crossed to the double ovens in the wall and peeked inside the top one. "I'm sure she would, but I held on tight. The cranberry muffins are almost done if you'd like one."

Yeah, she'd love about six warm, gooey muffins dripping with butter, but she'd resist for the sake of her backside.

"Maybe later. I'm taking Emily for her first ride."

A wide smile blossomed across Linda's face. "Oh, how fun. She's going to love it."

"I hope so," Cassie said. "I'll be back in a bit."

When Cassie stepped back into the barn, Tessa had already saddled up Oliver, the oldest, most gentle horse in the stables. Cassie absolutely couldn't wait to see Emily's excitement as she took her first horseback ride.

"He's all ready for you," Tessa exclaimed, reaching for Emily.

Cassie mounted the horse and lifted Emily from Tessa's arms. Settling her daughter in front of her and wrapping an arm around her waist, Cassie reached for the rein and smiled down to Tessa.

"Get a few pics of us when we're in the field, would you?"

Tessa slid her hand into her pocket and held up her phone. "I'm set. You guys look so cute up there," she said, still grinning. "My niece already looks like a pro."

Cassie tugged on the line and steered Oliver out of the barn and into the field. The warm late-spring sunshine beat down on them and Cassie couldn't help but smile when Emily clapped her hands and squealed as the horse started a light trot.

"This is fun, isn't it, sweetie?" Cassie asked. "When you get big, Mommy will buy you your own horse and he will be your best friend."

Cassie didn't know how long they were riding, and she didn't really care. Memories were being made, and even though Emily wouldn't recall this day at all, Cassie would cherish it forever. She thought of her own mother and held Emily a little tighter. Her mom lived in her heart and there was an attic full of pictures and mementos to remember her by.

Turning Oliver to head back toward the front fields, Cassie swallowed as new memories overtook her. That attic wasn't just a room to store boxes and old furniture. Now the attic was a place where she'd given herself to a man…a dangerous man. He made her feel too much, want too much.

And what was with him wanting to eat dinner with her and Emily? Not that she minded, but having him in her house just once was enough to have her envisioning so much more than just a friendly encounter.

She had to admit, at least to herself, that Ian intrigued her. And if she was going that far, she also had to admit that every part of her wished he weren't just passing through. She missed the company of a man…and not just sex. She missed the conversation, the spark of excitement in harmless flirting… Okay, fine, she missed the sex, too.

But it really was so much more than that. There was a special connection, a certain bond that strengthened after being intimate. At least there was for her. Perhaps that was why she couldn't dismiss what had happened between her and Ian so easily.

As she neared the stables, she caught sight of Ian walking toward the main house with the beautiful Lily Beaumont at his side. The gorgeous actress was laughing and Cassie had to ignore the sliver of jealousy that shot through her. Ian wasn't hers by any means, no matter what she may wish for.

And Lily was a very sweet woman, from what Cassie had experienced on the set. As Cassie watched the two head toward the front door, she couldn't help but get a swift kick back into reality. Ian and Lily were from the same world. They were near the same age, for crying out loud.

In comparison, Cassie was just a worn-out single mom. Squeezing Emily tight and placing a kiss on her little mop of curls, Cassie knew she wouldn't wish to be anything else. Being the solid foundation for Emily was the most important job of her life, and for now, all her daughter's needs had to come first. One day, Cassie vowed, she'd take time for herself and perhaps find love.

* * *

"I'm actually considering your offer and one other," Lily stated.

Ian rested his hand on the knob of the front door. "You don't have to tell me the other agency. I already know."

And damn if he'd lose this starlet to his rival. They'd ruin her and not give a damn about reputation, only the bottom line, which was money to them.

"It's not a decision I'm going to make overnight." Lily lifted her hand to shield her eyes from the afternoon sun. "I am glad you're on set, though, because that will give us more of a chance to discuss terms and what I'm looking for in an agency."

*Good.* That sounded as though she was interested in him. "I'm ready to talk anytime you are."

A bright smile spread across her face. "Well, right now I'm needed for a scene, but perhaps we could have lunch or dinner one day while we're both here?"

Returning her smile, Ian nodded and opened the door for her, gesturing her in. "Let me know when you're not filming and we'll make that happen."

Nodding her thanks, Lily headed into the house. Ian wasn't sticking around for the short scene retake. He had other pressing matters to attend to. Like the beauty he'd seen out in the field moments ago. With red hair blazing past her shoulders and a heart-clenching smile on her face, Cassie had captured his attention instantly. So what else was new? The woman managed to turn him inside out without even being near. More times than not she consumed his thoughts, but when he'd seen her taking her daughter on a horseback ride, Ian had to admit that the sight had damn near stopped him in his tracks.

Emily's sweet squeals of delight, the loving expression on Cassie's face… The combination had shifted something in Ian's heart, something he wasn't quite ready to identify.

But he did know one thing. He'd been wrong. He was wrong about Cassie in thinking she was just like his mother. His mother never would've taken the time to have precious moments with him like the ones he'd seen with Cassie and Emily. His mother had been too busy on her quest for love and Mr. Right.

Ian ran a hand over his hair and sighed. He'd turned out just fine, no thanks to Mom and Dad, but getting involved with a woman and an innocent child was a hazardous mistake that would leave all parties vulnerable and in a risky position. What did he know about children or how to care for them?

And why was he even thinking this way? He was leaving in a few weeks. No matter his attraction and growing interest in Cassie Barrington, he couldn't afford to get personally involved.

Hours later, after he'd drafted a contract he hoped would entice Lily Beaumont into signing with his agency, Ian found himself leaving his trailer and heading toward Cassie's cottage.

Night had settled over the grounds and all was quiet. No bustling crew or noisy conversation. Max's wife and baby had shown up earlier in the evening, so they were probably holed up in his trailer for family time. And the producer's and director's families had arrived the day before. Bronson Dane and Anthony Price were at the top 1 percent of the film industry and still made time for their growing families.

Everyone had a family, a connection and the promise of love.

Ignoring the pang of envy he didn't want to feel, Ian stepped up onto Cassie's porch, which was illuminated with a lantern-style light on either side of the door. As soon as he knocked, he glanced down to his watch. Damn, maybe it was too late to be making a social call.

The door swung open and Ian took in the sight of Cassie wearing a long T-shirt and her hair down, curling around her shoulders. Long legs left uncovered tempted him to linger, but he brought his eyes back up to her surprised face.

"I'm sorry," he said, shoving his hands into his pockets. "I just realized how late it was."

"Oh, um…it's fine." She rested her hand on the edge of the oak door and tilted her head. "Is everything okay?"

Nodding, Ian suddenly felt like an idiot. "Yeah, I was working and lost track of time. Then I started walking and ended up here."

A sweet smile lit up her features. "Come on in," she told him, opening the door and stepping aside. "I just put Emily to bed, so this is fine."

He stepped inside and inhaled a scent of something sweet. "Is that cookies I smell?"

Cassie shut the door and turned to face him. "I thought I'd make some goodies for the wives who arrived. This way they can stock their trailers with snacks. I already made a batch of caramel corn."

His heart flipped in his chest. He hated the fact he kept going back to his mother, but he honestly couldn't recall a time when his mother had baked anything or even reached out to others by doing a kind act.

A shrink would have a field day in his head with all his Mommy and Daddy issues. *Jeez.* And here he'd thought once he'd left for L.A. he'd left all of those years behind.

"They will really appreciate that," he told her.

Shrugging, Cassie maneuvered around him and grabbed a small blanket from the couch and started folding it. "I'm no Linda, but I do enjoy baking when I have the time."

She laid the folded blanket across the back of the couch and looked back at him. He couldn't stop his eyes from traveling over her again. How could he help the fact he found her sexier than any woman he'd ever met? She probably wouldn't believe him if he told her that her curves were enticing, her low maintenance a refreshing change.

Cassie tugged on the hem of her shirt. "I should probably go change."

"No." He held up his hand to stop her. "This is your house—you should be comfortable. Besides, I've seen it all."

Her eyes flared with remembrance and passion as Ian closed the space between them and looked down at her mouth. "I've tasted it all, too, if you recall."

With a shaky nod, she said, "I remember."

The pulse at the base of her throat increased and

Ian ran a hand over his face as he took a step back. "I swear, I didn't come here for this."

Cassie's bright blue eyes darted away. "I understand."

"No, you don't." Great, now she thought he was rejecting her. "It's not that I don't want you, Cassie. That's the furthest from the truth."

Shoving her hair back from her shoulders, Cassie shook her head. "Ian, it's okay. You don't have to make excuses. I'm a big girl. I can handle the truth. Besides, we're past this awkward stage, right?"

"Yeah," he agreed because right now he was feeling anything but awkward. Excited and aroused, but not awkward. "I don't know what possessed me to show up at your door this late, but…"

Cassie produced that punch-to-the-gut smile. "You can stop by anytime."

How did she do that? Instantly make him feel welcome, wanted…needed. There was so much more to Cassie Barrington than he'd first perceived. There were sides to the confident vixen, the single mother and the overworked trainer he had yet to discover.

Cassie was giving, loving and patient. He'd known instantly that she was special, but maybe he just hadn't realized how special. This woman embodied everything he hadn't known he'd been looking for.

"Why are you looking at me like that?" she asked, brows drawn together, smile all but gone.

Ian took a step toward her. He'd been mentally dancing around her for days and now he was physically doing it as he made up his mind on how to approach her.

"Because I just realized that all of your layers are starting to reveal themselves, one at a time." He slid his fingertips up her arms and back down, relishing the goose bumps he produced with such a simple touch. "I didn't want to see all of that before. I wanted you to be unattainable. I wanted you to be all wrong and someone I could easily forget."

Those vibrant eyes remained locked on his as her breath caught.

"But there's no way I could ever forget you, Cassie. Or us."

He didn't give her time to object. He claimed her lips and instantly she responded—opening her mouth to him, wrapping her arms around his neck and plunging her fingers into his hair.

Ian knew he wasn't leaving anytime soon. He also knew her T-shirt had to go.

# *Chapter 11*

Cassie had no idea what she was doing. Okay, she knew what she was doing and who she was doing it with, but hadn't she just had a mental talk with herself about the hazards of getting wrapped up in Ian's seductive ways? Hadn't she told herself she'd already been burned once and was still recovering?

But the way his mouth captured hers, the way he held her as if she were the rarest of gems, Cassie couldn't help but take pleasure in the fact that Ian pulled out a passion in her that she'd never known existed.

When Ian's hands gripped the hem of her T-shirt and tugged up, she eased back and in an instant the unwanted garment was up and over her head, flung to the side without a care.

Dark-as-sin eyes raked over her body, which was now bare of everything except a pair of red lacy panties. The old Cassie wanted to shield herself with her hands, but the way Ian visually sampled her gave her the confidence of a goddess.

"I could look at you forever," he said, his voice husky.

*Forever.* The word hovered in the air, but Cassie knew he was speaking only from lust, not in the happily-ever-after term.

Ian pulled his own shirt off and Cassie reached out, quickly unfastening his pants. In no time he was reaching for her, wearing only a smile.

"Tell me you know this is more than sex," he muttered against her lips. "I want you to know that to me, this is so much more."

Tears pricked the backs of her eyes as she nodded. The lump in her throat left her speechless. She really didn't know what label he wanted to put on this relationship, but right now, she couldn't think beyond the fact that Ian's hands were sliding into her panties and gliding them down her shaky legs.

Cassie wrapped her arms around his broad shoulders and kicked aside the flimsy material. Ian's hands cupped her bottom as he guided her backward.

"Tell me where your room is," he muttered against her lips.

"Last door on the right."

He kissed her on the throat, across the swells of her breasts, all the while keeping his hands firmly gripped on her backside as he maneuvered her down the hallway and into her room.

302    *Single Man Meets Single Mom*

A small bedside lamp gave the room a soft glow. Ian gently shut the door behind him and looked her right in the eyes. There was an underlying vulnerability looking back at her, and Cassie knew what he was thinking.

"I've never had a man in this room," she told him. "And there's no other man I want here."

As if the dam had broken, Ian reached for her, capturing her lips once again and lifting her by the waist.

When she locked her legs around his hips and they tumbled onto the bed, Ian broke free of her lips and kissed a path down to her breasts. Leaning back, Cassie gripped his hair as he tasted her.

"Ian," she panted. "I don't have any protection."

His dark gaze lifted to hers. "I didn't bring any. I hadn't planned on ending up here."

Biting her lip, Cassie said, "I'm on birth control and I'm clean. I've only been with my ex-husband and you."

Ian's hands slid up to cup her face as he kissed her lips. "I've never been without protection and I know I'm clean, too."

She smiled. "Then why are we still talking?"

Cassie moved her hands to his waist. Before she could say another word, Ian slid into her. Closing her eyes, Cassie let out a soft groan as he began to move above her.

"Look at me," he demanded in that low tone. "I want you to see me and only me."

As if any other man could take his place? But as she stared into his eyes, she saw so much more than lust, than sex and passion. This man was falling for her. He may not even recognize the emotion himself, but it was there, plain as day, looking back at her.

When his pace increased, Cassie gripped his shoulders and arched her back. "Ian… I…"

Eyes still locked on to her, he clenched the muscle in his jaw. "Go ahead, baby."

Her body trembled with her release, but she refused to close her eyes. She wanted him to see just how affected she was by his touch…his love.

When his arms stiffened and his body quivered against hers, Cassie held on, swallowing back the tears that clogged her throat.

One thing was very certain. The night in the attic may have been all about lust, but this moment right here in her bed, Cassie had gone and fallen in love with Ian Shaffer.

"I have to be on set early," Ian whispered into her ear.

Pulling himself away from the warm bed they'd spent the night in, Ian quickly gathered his clothes and dressed. Cassie eased up onto one elbow, and the sheet slipped down to stop just at the slope of her breasts. All that creamy exposed skin had him clenching his jaw and reliving what had just transpired hours before between those sheets.

"How early?" she asked, her voice thick with sleep.

"I'd like to see Max before he starts."

Okay, so the lie rolled easily off his tongue, but he couldn't stay. He couldn't remain in her bed, smelling her sweet scent, playing house in her little cottage, with her innocent baby sleeping in the next room.

What did he know about family or children…or whatever emotion was stirring within him? His career had always taken precedence over any social life or any feelings. With his parents' example of the epitome of failed marriages and love, he knew he wanted something completely different for his own life, so perfecting his career was the path he'd chosen.

How could he put his career, his agency and the impending addition of Lily to his client roster in jeopardy simply because he'd become entangled with Cassie Barrington? She was the poster child for commitment, and an instant family was something he couldn't get wrapped up in.

Cassie was a beautiful, intriguing complication. His eyes darted to the bed, where she studied him with a hint of desire layered with curiosity.

"Everything okay?" she asked.

Nodding, he shoved his feet into his shoes. "Of course. I'll lock the door behind me."

Unable to avoid temptation completely, Ian crossed the room, leaned down and kissed her lips. Just as her hand came up to his stubbled jaw, he pulled away and left her alone.

He stepped onto the front porch, closed the door behind him and leaned against it to catch his breath. The easy way Cassie welcomed him into her bed— and into her life with Emily—terrified him. Last night she'd accepted him without question and she'd given him everything she had…including love. He'd seen it in her eyes, but even more worrisome was what she may have seen reflected in his.

Because in those moments, when they were one and her bright blue eyes sought his, Ian had found himself completely and utterly lost. He wanted so much, but fear of everything he'd ever known regarding love and family made him question his emotions and his intentions.

Damn it. His intentions? What the hell was this? He wasn't the kind of man who had dreams of driving a minivan or heading up a household. He was a top Hollywood agent and if he didn't get his head on straight, he could lose one of the most important clients he'd ever had the chance of snagging.

Shaking his head, Ian pushed off the door and forced himself to walk toward his trailer. Twenty-nine years old and doing the walk of shame? *Classy, Shaffer. Real classy.*

Darkness and early-morning fog settled low over the estate. He shoved his hands into his pockets and decided he needed to shower and change before seeing Max…especially considering he was wearing the same clothes as yesterday.

He hadn't totally lied when he'd left Cassie's bed. He would talk to Max, but it wasn't dire and they could always talk later. Yet he worried if he stayed, he'd give Cassie false hope.

Okay, he worried he'd give himself false hope, too, because being with her was like nothing he'd ever experienced before and he wanted to hold on to those moments.

But the reality was, he was passing through.

Ian took his time getting ready for the day, answered a few emails and jotted down notes for calls he needed to make later in the week. He hated to admit he was shaken up by this newfound flood of emotions, but he had to come to grips with the fact that whatever he was feeling for Cassie Barrington was most definitely not going away.... It was only getting stronger.

By the time he exited his trailer, he had a plan of action, and today would be all about work and focusing on the big picture and his agency.

Crew members were gathered around the entrance of the stables, and off to the side were Max and Lily, holding their scripts and chatting. Ian headed in their direction, eager to get the day started.

"Morning," he greeted them as he approached.

Max nodded. "Came by your trailer last night to discuss something. Have a late night?"

The smile on Max's face was devilish—and all-knowing.

"What did you need?" Ian asked, dodging the question.

With a shrug, Max shook his head. "It can wait. I'm going to talk to Bronson before we start filming. Excuse me."

Ian figured Max left so Ian could chat with Lily. *Good boy.*

"I glanced over today's filming schedule." Ian stepped in front of Lily to shade her face from the sun. "Looks like after three today you guys are free."

Lily smiled. "We are indeed. Are you available to talk then?"

He'd be available anytime she wanted if it meant persuading her to sign with him. "I am. Would you like to stay here or go out to grab something for dinner?"

"I say go out," she replied. "Hopefully we can talk privately without everyone around."

Before he could respond, Lily's gaze darted from his to a spot over his left shoulder. A smile like he'd never seen before lit up her face and Ian couldn't help but glance around to see who she was connecting with.

Nash.

More confirmation that this Hollywood starlet and the groom on the Barrington estate had something going on.

Ian only hoped whatever was happening with the two of them was kept quiet and didn't interfere with filming or hinder her judgment in signing with him.

"Going out is fine," he told her.

Blinking, she focused back on him. "I'm sorry. What?"

Yeah, definitely something going on there.

"I said we could go out for a bite to eat. I can come by your trailer about five. Does that work?"

"Of course," she replied with a nod. "I'll see you then."

As she walked away, Ian turned and caught Nash still staring as Lily entered the stable. Nash had the look of a man totally and utterly smitten and Ian couldn't help but feel a twinge of remorse for the guy. Nash and Lily were worlds apart.

Exactly like Ian and Cassie.

What a mess. A complicated, passion-induced mess.

Ian stood to the side as lighting and people were set in place to prepare for filming. Bronson was talking with Max, and Lily's hair was being smoothed one last time. Grant and Anthony were adjusting the bales of hay at the end of the aisle.

Ian wasn't sure what Cassie's plans were for the day, but he intended to keep his distance for now. He needed to figure out exactly how to handle this situation because the last thing she needed was more heartache. And he, who knew nothing about real intimacy, would most certainly break her heart if he wasn't careful.

Damon Barrington settled in beside him and whispered, "Their chemistry on set is amazing."

Ian watched Max and Lily embrace in the middle of the aisle, horses' heads popping out over their stalls. The set was utterly quiet except for Lily's staged tears as she clung to Max. The couple was the perfect image of a younger Damon and Rose Barrington, according to the pictures Ian had seen.

As soon as Anthony yelled, "Cut!" the couple broke apart and Lily dabbed at her damp cheeks.

Damon glanced around. "I can't believe my girls aren't down here. You haven't seen Cassie or Tessa, have you?"

Ian shook his head. "I haven't."

No need to tell Cassie's father that just a few hours

ago Ian had slipped from her bed. Best not bring that up.

"I'm sure they'll be along shortly." Damon looked over at Ian and grinned. "My girls haven't let too many scenes slip by. They've enjoyed this process."

"And you?" Ian asked. "Have you enjoyed the Hollywood invasion?"

Nodding, Damon crossed his arms over his chest. "It's not what I thought it would be. The scenes vary in length and everything is shot out of order. But I'm very interested in seeing how they piece this all together."

Ian liked Damon, appreciated the way the man had taken charge of his life, made something of it and encouraged his children to do the same. And when his wife had passed, the man had taken over the roles of both parents and loved his children to the point where both women were now two of the most amazing people he'd met.

Ian had never received encouragement from his father and couldn't help but wonder what his life would've been like had his father been more hands-on.

Shrugging off years that couldn't be changed, Ian excused himself from Damon. If Cassie was going to come watch the filming, he needed to be elsewhere.

Because he had no doubt that if he hung around and had to look Cassie in the eye in front of all these people, there would be no hiding the fact that he'd developed some serious feelings for her.

# Chapter 12

Who was he kidding? There was no way he could stay away from Cassie. All during the business dinner with Lily, his mind had been on Cassie and what she was doing.

By the end of the night he'd nearly driven himself crazy with curiosity about what Cassie and Emily had done all day. Added to that, Lily hadn't signed with him. Not yet. She'd looked over his proposed contract and agreed with most of it, but she'd also said she needed to look over one other contract before deciding.

He was still in the running, but he'd rather have this deal signed and completed so he could move on to other deals waiting in the wings…not so he could focus on the woman who had his head spinning and his gut tied in knots.

After walking Lily to her trailer, Ian crossed the estate toward the two cottages. Only one of Cassie's outdoor lights was on and she was on her porch switching out the bulb in the other.

"Hey," he greeted her as he stepped onto the top step. "Need help?"

"I can manage just fine."

As she stood on her tiptoes and reached, her red tank top slid up over her torso, exposing a tantalizing band of flesh.

"I can get that so you don't have to stretch so far," he told her.

She quickly changed out the bulb and turned to face him, tapping the dead bulb against her palm. "I've been doing things on my own for a while now. Besides, I won't be anybody's second choice. I figured you were smart enough to know that."

"I'm sorry?"

Somehow he was not on the same page as her and she was mad at someone. From the daggers she was throwing him, he'd done something to upset her. Considering he hadn't sneaked out of her bed that morning without saying goodbye, he really had no clue what was going on.

"Forget it." She shook her head and opened her front door, then turned before he could enter. "I'm pretty tired, but thanks for stopping by."

*Oh, hell no.* He wasn't going to just let her be mad and not tell him what was going on. More than that, did she really believe he'd just leave her when she was this upset?

His hand smacked against the door as she tried to close it. "I'm coming in."

Cassie stepped back and let him pass. Emily sat in her Pack 'n Play and chattered with a stuffed horse, oblivious to the world around her.

"I need to get Emily ready for bed." Cassie maneuvered around him and picked up Emily. "I may be a while."

Code for "I'm going to take my time and let you worry." That was fine; he had no intention of going anywhere.

If Cassie was gearing up for a fight, he was ready. Seeing her pain, masked by anger, had a vise gripping his heart, and he cared too much about her to just brush her feelings aside.

Ian glanced around the somewhat tidy living area and started picking up toys before he thought better of it. He tossed them into the Pack 'n Play; then he folded the throw and laid it on the back of the sofa, neatened the pillows and took a plate and cup into the kitchen and placed them in the dishwasher.

By the time he'd taken a seat on the couch, he found himself smiling. Where had this little domestic streak come from? He hadn't even thought twice about helping Cassie, and not just because she was angry. He found himself wanting to do things to make her life easier.

Ian had no clue what had happened with her life before he'd come along, but he knew she was divorced and assumed the ex had done a number on her.

Well, Ian intended to stick this out, at least for

as long as he was here. He would make her smile again, because she deserved nothing less.

Cassie wasn't jealous. Just because she'd heard Ian and Lily had had dinner didn't mean a thing. Really.

But that green-eyed monster reared its ugly head and reminded Cassie that she'd fallen for a cheating man once before.

On the other hand, what hold did she have over Ian? He wasn't staying and he'd never confessed his undying love to her. But she'd seen his eyes last night, she'd seen how he looked at her, and she'd experienced lovemaking like she never had before. How could he deny that they'd formed an unspoken bond?

Cassie quickly dried off Emily and got her dressed in her footed bunny pajamas. After giving her a bottle and rocking her gently, Cassie began to sing.

This was the time of night she enjoyed most. Just her and her precious baby girl. Cassie might sing off-key, she might even get an occasional word wrong, but Emily didn't care. She just reached her little hands up and patted Cassie's hand or touched her lips.

They had a nightly ritual and just because Ian was out in her living room didn't mean she would change her routine. Before Emily fell asleep in her arms, Cassie laid her in her crib, giving her a soft kiss on her forehead, then left the room.

Cassie took a moment to straighten her tank and smooth her hair over her shoulders before she started down the hallway. As she entered the living room, she noticed that Ian was reclined on her sofa, head tilted back, eyes closed, with his hands laced across his abdomen. He'd picked up the toys and neatly piled them in the Pack 'n Play in the corner.

No. She didn't want that unwelcome tumble of her heart where this man was concerned. She couldn't risk everything again on the chance that he could love her the way she loved him.

Tears pricked her eyes as she fully confessed just how much she did love this man. But he could never know.

Her feet shuffled over the hardwood floors, and Ian lifted his lids, his gaze seeking hers.

"Thank you for picking up," she told him, still standing because she intended to show him out the door.

Shifting to fully sit up, Ian patted the cushion beside him. "Come here, Cassie."

She didn't like being told what to do, but she wasn't going to act like a teenager who pouted over a boy, either.

She was a big girl, but that didn't exempt her from a broken heart.

Taking a seat on the opposite end of the couch, she gripped her hands in her lap. "What do you want, Ian? I don't have time for games."

His eyes locked on to hers. "I don't play games, Cassie, and I have no idea what you're so upset about."

Of course he didn't. Neither had her ex when he'd cheated.

She eased back against the arm of the sofa and returned his stare. "Do you know why I'm divorced?"

Ian shook his head and slid his arm along the back of the couch as if to reach for her.

"My husband got tired of me," she told him, tamping down the sliver of hurt and betrayal that threatened to make her vulnerable. Never again. "The whole marriage-baby thing was cramping his style. Apparently he'd been cheating on me for most of our marriage and I was too naive and dumb to realize it. You see, I assumed that when we took our vows they meant something to him."

"Cassie—"

"No," she said, holding up her hand. "I'm not finished. After Emily was born, Derek left. She was barely two months old. He left me a note and was just…gone. It seems the sexy wife he once knew was no longer there for him, so, in turn, his cheating and the divorce were my fault. I know now that he was a coward and I'm glad he's gone because I never want Emily to see me settle for someone who treats me like I'm not worth everything.

"I want my daughter to see a worthy example of how love should be," she went on, cursing her eyes for misting up. "I want her to see that love does exist. My parents had it, and I will find it. But I won't be played for a fool while I wait for love to come into my life."

Ian swallowed, his eyes never leaving hers as he scooted closer. He wasn't stupid; he could put the pieces together and know she'd assumed the worst about his dinner meeting with Lily.

"I didn't play you for a fool, Cassie." His tone was light as he settled his hand over both of hers, which were still clasped together in her lap. "I have never lied to a woman and I've never pretended to be something I wasn't."

With a deep sigh, Cassie shook her head. "Forget I said anything. I mean, it's not like we're committed to each other," she said as she got to her feet.

But Ian jumped right up with her and gripped her shoulders before she could turn from him.

"Do you seriously think for one second that I believe you're so laid-back about the idea of me seeing you and another woman?" he demanded. "I had a business meeting with Lily. I told you I've wanted to sign her to my agency for months. She's the main reason I came to the set and why I'm staying so long."

Cassie's eyes widened, but he didn't give her a chance to speak. He needed her to know she didn't come in second…and she should never have to.

"I spent the entire evening trying to win her over, outlining every detail of the contract and all the perks of having me as her agent." Ian loosened his grip as he stepped closer to Cassie and slid his hands up to frame her face. "But the entire evening, I was thinking of you. Wondering what you were doing, how long it would be until I could see you again."

Her shoulders relaxed and her face softened as she kept those stunning baby blues locked on his. The hope he saw in her eyes nearly melted him on the spot. He knew she wanted to trust. He knew she'd been burned once and he completely understood that need, the yearning for that solid foundation.

"I'm sorry," she whispered. Cassie's lids lowered as she shook her head before she raised her gaze to his once more. "I don't want to be that woman. I seriously have no hold on you, Ian. You've promised me nothing and I don't expect you to check in."

Ian kissed her gently, then rested his forehead against hers. A soft shudder rippled through her and Ian wanted nothing more than to reassure her everything would be all right.

But how could he, when he knew he wasn't staying? How could they move forward with emotions overtaking them both?

"I hate what he did to me," she whispered, reaching up to clasp his wrists as he continued to cup her face. "I hate that I've turned bitter. That's not who I want to be."

Ian eased back and tipped her face up to his. "That's not who you are. You're not bitter. You're cautious and nobody blames you. You not only have yourself to think of—you have Emily, too."

Cassie's sweet smile never failed to squeeze his heart, and Ian had no clue how a man could leave behind a wife and child. Ian wouldn't mind getting ahold of Cassie's ex. He obviously was no man, but a coward. Selfishly, Ian was glad Derek was out of the picture. If the man could throw away his family so easily, he wasn't worthy.

"What's that look for?" she asked. "You're very intense all of a sudden."

He had to be honest because she was worth everything he had inside him.

"Where is this going?" he asked. "I care about

you, Cassie. More than I thought I would, and I think we need to discuss what's happening between us."

A soft laugh escaped her. "You sound like a woman."

Ian smiled with a shrug. "I assure you I've never said this to anyone else, but I don't want you getting hurt."

Cassie nodded and a shield came over her eyes as if she was already steeling herself. "Honestly, I don't know. I care for you, too. I question myself because I'm still so scarred from the divorce and I told myself I wouldn't get involved again. Yet, here we are and I can't stop myself."

Her inner battle shouldn't make him happy, but he couldn't help but admit he liked the fact she had no control over her feelings for him.... At least he wasn't in this boat of emotions alone.

"I don't want you to be the rebound guy," she murmured. "But I'm so afraid of how you make me feel."

Stroking her silky skin, wanting to kiss her trembling lips, Ian asked, "How do I make you feel?"

He shouldn't have asked. Cassie pursed her lips together as if contemplating her response, and Ian worried he'd put her on the spot. But he had to know. This mattered too much. *She* mattered too much.

"Like I'm special."

She couldn't have zeroed in on a better word that would hit him straight in the heart. *Special.* She was special to him on so many levels. She was special because he'd never felt more alive than he did with her. He'd never let his career come second to anything before her, and he sure as hell had never thought, with his family issues, that he'd be falling for a woman with a child.

Cassie inspired him to be a better person, to want to care for others and put his needs last.

But most of all he understood that need to feel special. He'd craved it his entire life, and until this very moment, he hadn't realized that was what he'd been missing.

"You make me feel special, too." Before now he never would've felt comfortable opening up, showing how vulnerable he was on the inside. "I don't want to be the rebound guy, either."

Her eyes widened as she tried to blink back the moisture. "So what does that mean?"

Hell if he knew. Suddenly he wanted it all—his career, the Hollywood lifestyle, Cassie and Emily. Cassie had him rethinking what family could be.

There was that other part of him that was absolutely terrified and wanted to hightail it back to Hollywood. But for now, he would relish their time together until he could come to grips with this mess of emotions.

"It means for now, you're mine." He kissed the corners of her mouth. "It means you are more to me than any other woman has ever been." He kissed her directly on the mouth, coaxing her lips apart before murmuring, "It means I'm taking you to bed to show you just how much you mean to me."

Only wanting to keep her smiling, keep her happy for as long as he was here, Ian slid his arms around her waist and pulled her body flush against his own.

When Cassie's fingers slid up around his neck

and threaded into his hair, Ian claimed her mouth and lifted her off the ground. She wrapped her legs around his waist and he carried her toward the bedroom, where he fully intended to make good on his promise.

# Chapter 13

The day couldn't be more perfect. God had painted a beautiful setting with the sun high in the sky and the temperature an ideal sixty degrees. The stage was set for Tessa to win the Preakness and take the second step toward the Triple Crown.

But no matter the weather, the thrill that always slid through Cassie at each race had to do with the stomp of the hooves in the stalls as the horses eagerly awaited their shining moment, the thick aroma of straw, the colorful silks adorning each horse, the tangible excitement of the jockeys as they shared last-minute talks with their trainers.

Which was exactly what Cassie and Tessa had just finished doing. Cassie had the utmost confidence that this race would go in their favor, but strange things always happened and they both knew better than to get cocky—especially at this point.

The first third of the Triple Crown was theirs, but this was a new day, a new race and a whole other level of adrenaline rushes.

Cassie followed behind as Tessa rode Don Pedro from the stables through the paddock and entered the track. No matter the outcome, Cassie was proud of her sister, of what they'd accomplished in their years together.

Soon their racing season would come to an end and Cassie would move on with her goal of opening a riding camp for handicapped children. Training a Triple Crown winner would put her in high demand in the horse-breeding world, but she hoped to use that reputation as a launching point for her school.

And beyond the school worries, her father was getting offers from his most heated rival, Jake Mason, to buy the prizewinning horses. Their season wasn't even over yet, for heaven's sake.

But those thoughts would have to wait until after the competition.

As would her thoughts of a certain Hollywood agent who had stayed behind on the estate to get some work done without distractions. The majority of the film crew had accompanied the Barringtons to Baltimore, Maryland, but today they were spectators, enjoying the race. They'd gotten many great shots from Louisville a couple of weeks ago, so now they were able to relax…somewhat. Cassie knew they were still taking still shots for the ad campaign, but not as many as at the derby.

As Tessa rode onto the track, Cassie couldn't help but smile. There was so much to be thankful for right now in her life. One chapter of her career was coming to an end. Another was going to begin in a few months. Her daughter was happy and healthy and nearing her first birthday.

And, delicious icing on the cake, Ian Shaffer had entered her life. For how long she didn't know. But she did know that, for now, they were together and he had admitted his feelings were strong. But did that mean he'd want to try something long distance? Or would he stay around a little longer after the film was finished?

So many questions and none of them would be answered today. She needed to concentrate and be there for Tessa. All else could wait until this race was over.

In no time the horses were in their places and Cassie felt her father's presence beside her. His arm snaked around her waist, the silent support a welcome comfort. Each race had nerves balling up in her stomach, but nothing could be done now. The training for the Preakness was complete and now they waited for the fastest, most exciting moment in sports.

Cassie glanced toward the grandstands, and the colorful array of hats and suits had her smile widening. Excitement settled heavily over the track as everyone's gaze was drawn to the starting gate.

"You're trembling," her father whispered into her ear.

Cassie let out a shaky laugh. "I think that's you."

His arm tightened around her waist as a robust chuckle escaped. "I believe you're right, my dear."

The gun sounded and Cassie had no time for nerves. She couldn't keep her eyes off the places switching, the colored numbers on the board swapping out as horses passed each other and inched toward the lead.

Don Pedro was in forth. Cassie fisted her hands so tight, her short nails bit into her palms.

"Come on. Come on," she muttered.

Tessa eased past third and into second on the last turn.

The announcer's tone raised in excitement as Tessa inched even farther toward the head of the race. Cassie wanted to close her eyes to pray, but she couldn't take her gaze off the board.

Just as the first two horses headed to the finish line, Cassie started jumping up and down. Excitement, fear, nerves... They all had her unable to stand still.

And when the announcer blared that the winner was Don Pedro by a nose, Cassie jumped even higher, wrapped her arms around her father's neck and squealed like a little girl.

"We did it," he yelled, embracing her. "My girls did it!"

Damon jerked back, gripped her hand and tugged her toward the winner's circle, where Tessa met them. Her radiant smile, the mass of people surrounding her and the flash of cameras all announced there was a new winner.

Grant was right there in the throng of people, his

grin so wide there was no way to hide the pride beaming off him.

Cassie's heart lurched. She loved that Tessa had found the man of her dreams, couldn't be happier for the couple. But, for the first time, Cassie was not the first one Tessa turned to after a race.

And that was not jealousy talking…. Cassie loved seeing Tessa and Grant so happy, and sharing Tessa's affection was fine. It was the fact that Cassie still felt empty when monumental things happened. Whom did she turn to to celebrate or for a shoulder to cry on?

Tessa turned her head, caught Cassie's eye and winked down at her. Returning the wink, Cassie smiled to hide her sad thoughts.

Soon reporters were thrusting microphones in her face, as well. Very few ever won the Triple Crown, and a team of females was practically unheard of. History was definitely in the making.

The Barrington sisters had done it again, and with only one more race to go to round out the season and secure the coveted Triple Crown, Cassie knew she needed to focus now more than ever on training for the Belmont.

Which meant keeping her heart shielded from Ian, because if he penetrated too much more, she feared she'd never be able to recover if it all fell apart.

They were gone for days, weeks.

Okay, maybe it wasn't weeks, but Ian felt as if he hadn't seen Cassie forever. Which told him he was going to be in trouble when it came time for him to head back to L.A.

She'd arrived home late last night and he'd known she'd be tired, so he had stayed away to let her rest and spend time with Emily. But knowing she was so close was hard.

As he headed toward the stables just as the sun peeked overtop the hilltops, Ian wanted to spend some time with her. He'd actually ached for her while she'd been away. Like most of the nation, he'd watched with eyes glued to the television during the Preakness and he'd jumped out of his seat and cheered when Don Pedro crossed the finish line for the win.

The familiar smell of hay greeted him before he even hit the entrance. As soon as he crossed the threshold, Ian spotted Nash cleaning out a stall.

"Morning," Ian greeted him.

Nash nodded a good-morning and continued raking old hay. "Cassie isn't here yet," he said without looking up.

Ian grinned. Apparently he and Cassie weren't very discreet…not that they'd tried to be, but they also hadn't been blatant about their relationship, either.

"Hey, Ian."

He turned to see Tessa striding into the stables, all smiles with her hair pulled back.

"Congrats on the win." Ian couldn't help but offer a quick hug with a pat on her back. "That was one intense race."

Tessa laughed. "You should've seen it from my point of view."

Her eyes darted to Nash, then back to Ian. "What brings you out this early?"

Ian shrugged, sliding his hands into his pockets. "Just looking for Cassie."

Tessa's grin went into that all-knowing mode as she quirked a brow. "She actually was up most of the night with Emily. Poor baby is teething and nobody is getting any sleep."

"But Cassie has to be exhausted. You just got back late last night," he argued, realizing he was stating nothing new to Tessa.

Shrugging, Tessa sighed. "I know. I offered to take Emily for the night, but Cassie wouldn't hear of it."

Probably because the last time Cassie had been without her child, she had been locked in the attic with him.

"She's spreading herself too thin," Ian muttered.

Nash walked around them and pulled a bale of hay from the stack against the wall, then moved back into the stall. Ian shifted closer to the doorway to get out of the quiet groom's way.

"Follow me," Tessa said with a nod.

Intrigued, Ian fell into step behind the famous jockey. She stopped just outside the stables, but away from where Nash could overhear.

"This isn't where you tell me if I hurt your sister you'll kill me, is it?" he asked with a smile.

Tessa laughed and shook her head, eyes sparkling with amusement. "You're smart enough to know that goes without saying. I wanted to discuss something else, actually."

"And what's that?"

"Did Cassie ever tell you about the little getaway she and Grant came up with for me? Grant felt I was pushing myself too hard, never taking time for myself to regroup and recharge."

Ian grinned. "Must run in the family."

"Yeah, we Barringtons are all made of the same stubborn stuff."

Ian had no doubt the almighty Damon Barrington had instilled all his work ethic into his girls and that hard work and determination were paying off in spades.

"I'd like to return the favor," Tessa went on. "Are you up for taking a few days away from here?"

Was he? Did he want to leave Lily when they were still negotiating a contract? He didn't mind leaving Max. The actor could handle anything and Ian was very confident with their working relationship.

It was Lily that worried him. But he couldn't be in her face all the time. He'd spoken with her a few times since their dinner meeting. She'd promised a decision once she realized which agency would offer her the most and which one she'd feel most at home with.

He had to believe she'd see that his company was hands down the front-runner.

And a few days away with Cassie? He had deals and meetings to get back to, but after days without her, how could he not want to jump at that chance?

"Should I take that smile to mean you're going to take me up on this offer?"

Ian nodded. "I think I will. What did you have in mind?"

# Chapter 14

How long could a baby be angry and how many teeth would be popping through?

Cassie had just collapsed onto the couch for the first time all day when someone knocked on her door. She threw a glance to Emily, who was playing on the floor and crawling from toy to toy...content for now.

Stepping over plush toys and blankets, Cassie opened the door and froze. Ian stood on her porch looking as handsome as ever, sporting aviator sunglasses and a navy T-shirt pulled taut across his wide shoulders and tucked into dark jeans.

She didn't need to look down at her own outfit to know she was just a step above homeless chic with her mismatched lounge pants with margarita glasses on them and her oversize T-shirt with a giant smiley face in the middle.

And her hair? She'd pulled it up into a ponytail for bed and hadn't touched it since. Half was falling around her face; the other half was in a nest on the side of her head.

Yeah, she exuded sex appeal.

"Um…are you going to invite me in?"

Cassie shoved a clump of hair behind her ear. "Are you sure you want to come in? Emily is teething. She's cranky more often than not since last night, and I'm…well…"

Ian closed the gap between them, laying a gentle kiss on her lips. "Beautiful."

Okay, there was no way she couldn't melt at that sweet declaration even if he was just trying to score points. He'd succeeded.

When he stepped into the house, Cassie stepped back and closed the door behind him. Emily grabbed hold of the couch cushion and pulled herself to her feet, throwing an innocent smile over her shoulder to Ian.

Cassie laughed. "Seriously? She smiles for you and I've had screaming for over twelve hours?"

"What can I say? I'm irresistible."

No denying that. Cassie still wasn't used to his powerful presence in her home, but she was growing to love it more and more each time he came for a visit.

"Hey, sweetheart," he said, squatting down beside Emily. "Did you have your mommy up last night?"

Emily let go of the couch to clap her hands and

immediately fell down onto her diaper-covered butt. She giggled and looked up at Ian to see his reaction.

Cassie waited, too. She couldn't help but want to know how Ian would be around Emily. He hadn't spent too much time with her, considering he stopped by at night and he'd gone straight to Cassie's bed.

Reaching forward, Ian slid his big hands beneath Emily's delicate arms and lifted her as he came to his full height.

Cassie couldn't deny the lurch of her heart at the sight of this powerful man holding her precious baby. Was there a sexier sight than this? Not in Cassie's opinion.

"I know we talked on the phone, but congratulations." A smile lit up his already handsome face. "I'm so happy for you and Tessa."

Cassie still couldn't believe it herself. Of course they'd trained to win, but what trainer and jockey didn't? The fact they were that much closer to winning that coveted Triple Crown still seemed surreal.

"I'm still recovering from all the celebrating we did in Baltimore," she told him. "I've never been so happy in all my life. Well, except for when Emily was born."

"I have a surprise for you," Ian told her as Emily reached up and grabbed his nose.

Cassie went to reach for Emily, but Ian stepped back. "She's fine," he told her. "I love having my nose held so my voice can sound a little more like a chipmunk when I ask a sexy woman to go away with me for a few days."

Shocked at his invitation, Cassie shook her head, trying to make sense of it. "Go away with you?"

Ian nodded as Emily reached up on his head and tugged his glasses off. Immediately they went to her mouth.

"She's still fine," Ian told Cassie as he dodged her again. "They're sunglasses. She can chew on them all she wants."

"They'll have drool on them."

Ian's eyes darted to the lenses, but he just sighed. "Oh, well. So, what do you say? You up for getting away for a few days?"

Oh, how Cassie would love to get away. To not worry or train or do anything but be with Ian because their time together was coming to an end and she was certainly not ready to let go.

"Ian, going away with you sounds amazing, but I can't."

Ian glanced at Emily. "She's going to use you as an excuse, isn't she?"

Cassie laughed. "Actually, yes. But she's not an excuse. I mean, I can't ask anyone to keep her for days, especially with her teething and upset."

Bringing his gaze back to Cassie, Ian crossed the space between them until he stood so close she could see the flecks of amber in his dark eyes.

"I'm not asking you to hand her off to anybody. I want to take you both away."

Cassie stared back at him, sure she'd heard him wrong. He wanted to take her and a baby? A cranky baby?

"But...but...are you sure?"

Ian dipped his head and gently kissed her before easing back and giving her that heart-melting grin. "I wouldn't have asked if I wasn't sure."

A million things ran through her mind. Could she actually take off and be with Ian for a few days? Did he honestly know what he was asking? Because she really didn't think he knew how difficult playing house could be.

"Stop thinking so hard." He shifted Emily to his other side and reached out to cup the side of Cassie's face. "Do you want to go?"

Cassie nodded. "Of course I do. It's just—"

"Yes, you want to go. That's what I need to hear. Everything else is taken care of."

Intrigued, Cassie raised her brows. "Oh, is it?"

A corner of Ian's mouth quirked into a devilish half smile. "Absolutely. How about I come back and get you in an hour. Just pack simple clothing and whatever Emily can't live without. I'll be back to help you finish up and then we'll go."

"Where are we going?" she asked.

Handing Emily back to Cassie, Ian shrugged. "I guess you'll find out when we get there."

She tried to get the sunglasses away from Emily and noticed slobber bubbles along the lenses. Ian waved a hand and laughed.

"No, really, keep them," he said as he headed toward the door. "She apparently gets more use out of them than I did."

Cassie was still laughing after he'd closed the door behind him. A getaway with Ian and Emily? How could she not want to jump at this chance?

And how could she not read more into it? Was Ian silently telling her he wanted more? Or was he getting in all the time he could before he said his final goodbye?

Ian didn't know if he was making a mistake or if he was finally taking a leap of faith by bringing Cassie and Emily to his beachfront home. They'd flown from the East Coast to the West and he'd questioned himself the entire way.

Tessa had suggested he take Cassie to Grant's mountain home for a getaway, but Ian wanted Cassie on his turf. Deep down inside he wanted her to see how he lived, see part of his world.

And he wanted to find out how well she fit into his home. Would she feel out of place or would she enjoy the breathtaking views from his bedroom, which overlooked the Pacific Ocean?

Surprisingly, Emily was wonderful on the plane ride, thanks to the pain reliever aiding in her teething process. As Ian maneuvered his car—it had been waiting for him at the airport—into his drive, he risked a glance over to Cassie. He wanted to see her initial reaction.

And he wasn't disappointed. Her eyes widened at the two-story white beach house with the porch stretching across the first floor and the balcony wrapping around the house on the second. He'd had that same reaction when his Realtor had shown him the property a few years ago. Love at first sight.

"Ian, this is gorgeous," she exclaimed. "I can't

believe you managed to get a beach house on such short notice."

He hadn't told her he was bringing her to his home. He'd wanted to surprise her, and he was afraid if he told her, then she'd back out.

As he pulled into the garage and killed the engine, Ian turned to face her. "Actually, this is my house."

Cassie gasped, jerking her head toward him. "Your house? Why didn't you tell me we were coming to your house?"

He honestly didn't have an excuse unless he wanted to delve way down and dig up the commitment issues he still faced. His fear of having her reject his plan, his fear of how fast they'd progressed and his fear of where the hell all of this would lead had kept him silent.

"I can't believe you live on the beach," she said, still smiling. "You must love it here."

Yeah, he did, but for the first time in his life, he suddenly found himself loving another location, as well. Who knew he'd fall in love with a horse farm on the other side of the country?

While Cassie got Emily out of the car, Ian took all the luggage into the house. He put his and Cassie's in the master bedroom and took Emily's bag into the room across the hall.

Thankfully, he'd called ahead and had his housekeeper pick up a few items and set them up in the makeshift nursery. Since she was a new grandmother, she knew exactly what a baby would need. And judging from the looks of the room, she'd gone all out.

Ian chuckled. The woman was a saint and deserved a raise...as always.

"Ian, this house is—"

He turned around to see Cassie in the doorway, Emily on her hip, eyes wide, mouth open.

"I had a little help getting the place ready," he informed her, moving aside so she could enter. "I hope you don't mind that I had my housekeeper get Emily some things to make her comfortable while you guys are here."

Cassie's gaze roamed around the room, pausing on the crib in the corner. "I don't know what to say," she whispered as her eyes sought his. "This is... Thank you."

Warmth spread through him. Cassie was absolutely speechless over a package of diapers, a bed and some toys. Cost hadn't even factored into his plan; Emily's comfort and easing Cassie's mind even a little had been his top priorities.

Before he could respond, Emily started fussing. Cassie kissed her forehead and patted her back. "It's okay, baby. You're all right."

The low cries turned into a full-fledged wail and a sense of helplessness overtook him. Yes, he could buy anything for her, but what did he know about consoling a child or what to do when they were hurting or sick?

With a soft smile, Cassie looked back to him. "Sorry. I'm sure this isn't the getaway you'd hoped for."

Ian returned her smile and reached out to slide his hand over Emily's back. "The only expectation

I had was spending time with both of you. She can't help that she's teething."

Her eyes studied him for a moment before she said, "I don't know what I did to deserve you, Ian."

"You deserve everything you've ever wanted."

He wanted to say more, he wanted to do more and give more to her, but they were both in uncharted territory, and taking things slow was the best approach. God knew they hadn't started out slow. Working backward might not have been the most conventional approach, but it was all they had to work with.

"Can you get in the side of her diaper bag and get out the Tylenol?" she asked.

While Cassie got Emily settled with pain medication and started to sing to her, Ian watched from the doorway. Had his father ever felt this way about him? Had the man wanted to be hands-on? Because Ian desperately found himself wanting to be more in not just Cassie's life, but Emily's, as well. He didn't have the first clue about caring for children, but he wanted to learn.

How could he ever be what they needed?

But how could he ever let either of them go?

# Chapter 15

Thankfully, after a round of medicine and a short nap, Emily was back to her happy self. Cassie put on her bathing suit, wrapping a sheer sarong around her waist, then put Emily into her suit, as well.

Why waste time indoors when there was a beach and rolling waves just steps away?

"You ready to play in the ocean?" Cassie asked Emily as she carried her toward the back door. "You're going to love it, baby girl."

The open-concept living room and kitchen spread across the entire back of the house, and two sets of French doors led out onto the patio. Cassie stepped out into the warm sunshine and stopped.

At the edge of the water, Ian stood with his back to her wearing black trunks and flaunting his excellent muscle tone. The fabric clinging to the back of his well-toned thighs, his slicked-back hair and the water droplets glistening on his tanned shoulders and back indicated he'd already tested the waters.

The man was sinful. He tempted her in ways she never thought possible, made her want things that could never be. They couldn't be more opposite, yet they'd somehow found each other. And they'd grown so close since their encounter in the attic.

The night of the lock-in had been filled with nothing but lust and desire. Now, though, Cassie was wrestling with so many more emotions. At the top of her list was one she'd futilely guarded her heart against...love.

She completely loved this man who had brought her to his home, shown her his piece of the world. But the clincher was when he'd assumed Emily would accompany them. He knew Cassie and Emily were a package deal, and he'd embraced the fact and still welcomed them.

How could she not fall hard for this intriguing man? He was nothing like her ex, nothing like any man she'd ever known, really. And that was what made him so special.

Emily started clapping and pointing toward Ian. Cassie laughed. "Yeah, we're going, baby."

Sand shifted beneath her toes as she made her way toward the man who'd taught her heart to trust again. Just the sight of him had her anticipating their night alone after Emily went to bed.

It wasn't as if she hadn't seen or touched him all over, but still, his sexiness never got old.

Emily squealed and Ian turned to face her. His gaze traveled over her modest suit and Cassie tamped down that inner demon that tried to tell her that her extra baby weight was hideous. Ian never, ever made her feel less than beautiful, so that inner voice could just shut the hell up.

"You look good in a suit, Cass."

His low voice, combined with that heavy-lidded gaze, had her insides doing an amazing little dance number.

"I was thinking the same thing about you," she told him with a grin.

"Mom, Mom, Mom," Emily squealed again, clapping her little hands and staring out at the water.

"Can I?" Ian asked, reaching for Emily.

Handing Emily over, Cassie watched as Ian stepped into the water. Slowly, he waded in deeper, all the while taking his hand and cupping water to splash up onto her little pudgy legs. Emily's laughter, her arms around Ian's neck and seeing Ian bounce around in the water like a complete goofball had Cassie laughing herself.

This getaway was exactly what she needed. Coming off the win at the Preakness and rolling right into a special weekend had Cassie realizing that her life was pretty near perfect right now. For this moment, she would relish the fact that Ian had to care for her on some deep level…possibly even love her. If he only had feelings of lust, he wouldn't have brought her to his home, wouldn't have invited a teething, sometimes cranky kid, and he certainly wouldn't be playing in the water with Emily like a proud daddy.

Cassie hated to place all her hope, all her heart, on one man…but how could she not, when he'd captured her heart the instant they'd been intimate in that attic?

Not wanting to miss out on a single moment, Cassie jumped into the ocean, reached beneath the water and pinched Ian on the butt.

The grin he threw over his shoulder at her told her she was in for a fun night.

Rocking a now peaceful baby had Ian truly wishing for so much. He'd convinced Cassie that he could put Emily to bed. He figured the little one was so tired from the day of playing in the ocean and taking a stroller ride around his neighborhood that she'd fall fast asleep.

She'd been fussy at first and Cassie had shown Ian how to rub some numbing ointment onto Emily's gums. He'd given Emily a bottle, even burped her, and rocked her until her sweet breath evened out.

He glanced down to the puckered lips, the pink cheeks from the sun—even though they'd slathered her with sunscreen—and smiled. Was it any wonder Cassie worked herself to death? How could a parent not want to sacrifice herself to make such an innocent child happy?

Cassie worked so hard with her sister, worked harder in the stables caring for horses, and she busted her butt to make a secure life and happy home for Emily…all without a husband.

Oh, she'd be ticked if she knew he worried about her not having someone in her life to help her. Granted, she had her father, Tessa and Linda, but whom did she have at night? Who helped her at home?

God help him, but Ian wanted to be that man. The weight of a sleeping baby in his arms, the sweet smell of her skin after her bath and the thought that this innocent child had complete and total trust in him were truly humbling.

Once he knew she was asleep, Ian eased from the rocking chair and laid Emily into the new crib, complete with pink-and-white-striped sheets. When he stood up, she stirred a little, but she settled right in.

A sigh of relief escaped Ian. He'd mastered numerous multimillion-dollar movie deals, he rubbed elbows with A-list actors and he'd managed to start his own agency at the age of twenty-four. But putting a child to sleep all by himself felt like quite an accomplishment.

He glanced at the monitor beside the crib and made sure it was on before he stepped out into the hall and quietly shut the door behind him.

He barely managed not to jump when he noticed Cassie across the hall, leaning against the doorway to his bedroom.

"You did it," she said with a wide smile. "I'm impressed."

All thoughts fled his mind as he took in the muted glow that surrounded her from the small lamp in his room. Her long red curls slid around her shoulders, lying against the stark white silk robe she wore—and what she wasn't wearing beneath. The V in the front plunged so deep, the swells of her breasts begged for his touch.

"I like your pajamas," he told her, crossing the hallway and immediately going to the belt on her robe. "Reminds me of something…"

Cassie lifted her arms to wrap around his neck. "What's that?"

"The fact I haven't seen you naked in several days."

She shifted, allowing the material to slide from her shoulders and puddle at her feet. Ian's hands roamed over the soft, lush curves he'd come to love and crave.

"You feel so good," he groaned as he trailed his lips from her jawline down the smooth column of her neck. "So perfect."

When she trembled beneath his touch, Ian cupped her behind and pulled her flush against his body. Nothing had ever felt so right. Every time Cassie was in his arms, contentment settled deeper and deeper into his heart.

She undressed him rapidly, matching his own frenzy. Ian had brought other women to his home. Not many, but a few. Yet he knew the second he laid Cassie beneath him and looked down into her blue eyes…he never wanted another woman in this bed.

He knew she wasn't asleep. The full moon shone through the wide expanse of windows across the room from the king-size bed and directly across their tangled bodies.

Cassie's breathing wasn't even and he'd felt the

soft flutter of her lashes against his arm. Whatever thoughts consumed her mind, they were keeping her awake.

More than likely they were the same things that had him awake hours after they'd made love…twice.

Ian trailed his fingertips over her hip, down into the dip of her waist and back again. Goose bumps prickled beneath his touch.

"Talk to me," she whispered in the darkened room.

Words that had frightened him on more than one occasion after sex. But this was so different from any other time. First, Cassie was like no other woman. Second, what had just happened between them was so far beyond sex. And third, he actually didn't cringe as the words hovered in the air between them.

Moreover, he *wanted* to talk to her. He wanted her to know about his past, his life and what had brought him to this point…and why the thought of commitment scared the hell out of him.

Part of him truly wanted to try for her. Never before had he even considered permanent anything in his life, let alone a woman and a child. Cassie changed everything for him, because she was starting to *be* everything for him.

Of course, there was that devil on his shoulder that kept telling him he couldn't just try out playing house with this woman. She was genuine, with real feelings and a heart of gold that she had to protect. If he attempted to try for a long-term spot in her life and things didn't work out, he would never be able to forgive himself.

"My childhood wasn't quite as rosy and enjoyable as yours." The words tumbled out before he thought better of opening up about the past he hated to even think about. "My father was a military man. Things had to be perfect, and not just perfect, but done five minutes ago. When he was home on leave, if I had a chore, I had better get to it the second he told me or I would face punishment."

Cassie gasped next to him. "He hit you?"

Ian stared up at the darkened ceiling as he continued to trail his fingertips over her lush, naked curves. "On occasion. But it wasn't a beating. He was old-school and a hand to my backside wasn't unheard of. But then he came home less and less because he and my mother divorced. That's when she started bringing her male friends into the house."

Ian recalled how weird it felt having a strange man at the breakfast table when he woke up, but eventually he didn't question his mother…and he didn't ask the names of the men. Would it matter? They'd be gone when she finished with them anyway.

"My mom is currently in the middle of her fourth divorce and I've no doubt number five is waiting in the wings absolutely convinced he's the one."

Cassie's arm tightened around his abdomen. "I'm sorry. I can't imagine."

Her warm breath tickled his chest, but Ian wouldn't have it any other way. He loved the feel of her tucked perfectly against him, her hair falling over his shoulder, the flutter of her lashes against his side.

"Don't be sorry," he told her. "There are kids way worse off than I was. But I always wished I had parents who loved each other, who loved me. A family was everything to me when I was younger, but I wanted the impossible."

A drop of moisture slid down his side. Ian shifted his body, folding Cassie closer as he half loomed over her.

"Don't cry for me." In the pale moonlight, her eyes glistened. Had anyone ever cried for him before? "I'm fine, Cassie. I guess I just wanted you to know what I came from."

Soft fingertips came up to trail down his cheek. Her thumb caressed his bottom lip, and his body responded instantly.

"I'm crying for the little boy who needed love and attention," she whispered. "And I'm crying for the man who fits so perfectly into my family, I'm terrified of how we'll get along without him."

Her declaration was a punch to his gut. The fact that they'd never mentioned his leaving after the film wrapped hung heavy in the air between them. And knowing she not only worried about his absence, but she'd cried over it had him hating himself on so many levels.

"I don't want to hurt you," he murmured as he slid his lips across hers. "That's the last thing I'd ever want."

Adjusting her body so she could frame his face with her hands, Cassie looked up at him with those damn misty eyes and smiled. "I know. I went into this with my eyes wide-open. For right now, though, you're mine and I don't want to think about tomorrow, Ian. I don't want to worry about that void that will inevitably come when you're gone."

Her hips tilted against his. "I just want you. Here. Now."

As he kissed her lips he had a hard time reining in his own emotions, because Cassie was dead-on about one thing.... There would most definitely be a void—the one he would feel without her by his side.

# Chapter 16

Cassie reached across the bed, only to encounter cool sheets. Quickly she sat up, clutching the material to her chest and glancing to the nightstand clock.

How on earth had she slept until nine? Between having a career set around a working horse farm and being a single mother, sleeping in was a foreign concept and a luxury she simply couldn't afford.

Another reality hit her hard as she jerked to look at the baby monitor on the dresser across the room. The red light wasn't on, which meant at some point the device had been turned off. Throwing the covers aside, Cassie grabbed the first available article of clothing—which happened to be Ian's T-shirt—and pulled the soft cotton over her head. She inhaled the embedded masculine scent of Ian as she darted across the hall.

The nursery was empty. Giggling erupted from downstairs, so Cassie turned and headed toward the sweet sound. At the base of the steps, Cassie froze as she stared into the living room. Ian stood behind Emily, her little hands held high, clutching on to his as he helped her walk across the open space. He'd pushed the coffee table against one wall, leaving the dark hardwood floor completely open.

Emily squealed as she waddled through the area, and Cassie, who still stood unnoticed, had to bite her lip to control the trembling and wash of emotions that instantly consumed her.

Ian Shaffer had officially stolen her heart, and there was no way she could go back to her life before she'd ever met him. The man had opened his home to her and her daughter. He wasn't just interested in having her in his bed. Granted, that was how they'd started out, but over a brief period of time they'd grown together and meshed in such a way that had Cassie hopeful and wishing. Dare she set her sights so high and dream for things that once seemed unattainable?

"Mamamama," Emily cried when she saw Cassie in the doorway.

Cassie stepped toward her daughter and squatted down. "Hey, sweet pea. Are you making Ian work this morning?"

Emily's precious two-toothed grin melted her heart. When she glanced up to meet Ian's gaze, her breath literally caught. He still clung to Emily's fingers and he'd been hunched over so he could accommodate her height, but he just looked so at peace and happy.

"What time did she get up?"

Ian shrugged. "Maybe around seven."

Cassie straightened. "Why didn't you get me up?"

Scooping Emily into his arms, Ian smiled. "Because you needed to sleep, so I turned the monitor off and got her out of the crib. She's been changed and fed—probably not how you'd do it, but it's done nonetheless."

Cassie was utterly speechless. The man had taken such care of her daughter all so Cassie could sleep in. He'd been watching and loving over Emily…over another man's baby, and all without a care or second thought. And now he stood holding her as if the act were the most natural thing in the world.

"Don't look at me like that," he told her. Emily turned her head into Ian's shoulder and his wide, tanned hand patted her tiny back. "I wanted to help and I knew you'd refuse if you even thought she was awake. Besides, I kind of wanted to see how Emily and I would get along. I'm pretty sure she loves me."

Cassie couldn't help but laugh. "I'm sure she does love you. She knows a good thing when she sees it."

Ian's eyes widened, and the muscle in his jaw moved as if he were hiding his words deep within. Had she said too much? At this point, with time against them, Cassie truly believed she couldn't hold back. She needed to be up front and honest.

"I'm not saying that to make you uncomfortable," she informed him, crossing her arms over her chest.

"But you have to know this is so much more than physical for me, Ian."

Those dark eyes studied her a second before he nodded. "I'd be lying if I said this was all sexual for me. You and Emily…"

He shook his head as his words died on his lips. Cassie wanted him to go on, but she knew the internal battle he waged with himself and she didn't want to push him. He'd opened up to her last night, bared his soul, and she knew what he'd shared hadn't come easy for him.

Placing a hand on his arm, Cassie smiled. "We don't need to define anything right now," she assured him. "I just wanted you to know this thing between us—it matters so much to me."

With Emily lying against one shoulder, Ian pulled Cassie to his other side and wrapped an arm around her. "Everything in my arms right now matters more to me than I ever thought possible," he told her with a kiss to the top of her head.

Before she could completely melt into a puddle at his feet over his raw, heartfelt words, Ian's hand slid down her side and cupped her bottom beneath his T-shirt.

"This shirt never looked this sexy on me," he growled into her ear. "So unless you want to end up back in bed, you better go get some clothes on."

Shivers of arousal swept through her. Would she ever get enough of him? More so, would he get enough of her?

Tipping her head back, she stared up into his eyes. Desire and, dare she say, love stared back at her. No, she didn't think they'd get enough of each other, which meant whatever they were building wouldn't come crumbling down when he left Virginia after the film was done shooting. But how they would manage was a whole other hurdle to jump.

Extracting herself from his side, Cassie pulled Emily from his arms. "How about we spend the day on the beach?" she suggested.

Emily's little hand went into Cassie's hair, and she started winding the strands around her baby fingers.

"You in a suit?" Ian's gaze raked over her once more. "I'd never say no to that."

With this being their last day of complete relaxation, Cassie wanted to live for the moment, this day, and not worry about what obstacles they faced tomorrow or even next week. She was completely in love with Ian. He wasn't a rebound; he wasn't a filler or a stepping-stone until the next chapter of her life.

Ian Shaffer *was* the next chapter of her life.

# Chapter 17

"I just need someone who's good with advertising," Cassie muttered as she stared down at the new plans for her riding school for handicapped children.

"How about that hunky agent you're shacking up with?"

Cassie threw a glare across the room at her sister. Tessa silently volleyed back a wicked grin.

"We're not shacking up." Not technically, anyway. "And that's not his job."

"Maybe not," Tessa replied, coming to her feet. "But he'd know more about it than we would, and I guarantee he'd do anything to help you."

More than likely, but Cassie wasn't going to ask. Venturing into personal favors would imply something…something they'd yet to identify in their relationship.

Yes, they'd admitted they had strong feelings for each other, but after the giant leap into intimacy, they'd pulled back the emotional roller coaster and examined where they were going.

And they still didn't know.

Cassie spoon-fed another bite of squash and rice to Emily. Right now she needed to focus on the final race of the season, getting her school properly advertised and caring for her daughter. Ian, unfortunately, would have to fall in line behind all of that and she highly doubted he would want to. What man would? He deserved more than waiting on her leftover time.

"You're scowling." Tessa came to stand beside the high chair and leaned against the wall. "What's really bothering you?"

Sisters. They always knew when to dig deeper and pull the truth from the depths of hell just to make you say the words aloud.

"Ian is out to dinner with Lily."

A quirk of a smile danced around Tessa's mouth. "You're jealous? Honey, the man is absolutely crazy about you. All you'd have to do is see how he looks at you when you aren't paying attention."

The idea that he studied her enough to show emotion on his face for others to see made her way more thrilled than she should be. She wanted to tell him she'd fallen for him—she wanted to tell everybody. But there was that annoying little voice that kept telling her this was too good to be true and that she needed to come back to reality before she ended up hurt.

"He's not like Derek," Tessa informed her as if she were reading her mind. "Ian may be younger, but he's all man and he's only got eyes for you."

Cassie smiled with a nod and scooped up the last bite, shoving it into Emily's waiting mouth. "I know. There's just that thread of doubt that gets to me, and I know it's not Ian's fault. He can't help the mess that is my life."

Laying a hand over Cassie's arm, Tessa squeezed. "Your life is beautiful. You have a precious baby, an awesome career and the best sister anyone could ever ask for. What more could a girl want?"

*To be loved.* The words remained in her head, in her heart.

"So where's your guy tonight?" Cassie asked, wiping off the orange, messy mouth, hoping to unearth her daughter. "You two aren't normally separated for more than an hour at a time."

With a smile that could only be equated to love, Tessa positively beamed. "He's going over some things with Bronson and Anthony. I'm pretty sure Dad weaseled his way into that meeting, as well."

Cassie scooped Emily from the high chair and settled her on her hip. "I've no doubt Dad is weighing in with his opinion. I need to give her a bath. You sticking around?"

Shaking her head, Tessa sighed and started across the living room. "I think I'll head home and make some dinner. It's not often I get to cook for Grant, and he's worked so hard lately. He needs to relax."

Cassie squeezed her eyes shut. "I don't want

to hear about you two relaxing. Just a simple no would've answered my question."

With a naughty laugh, Tessa grabbed her keys from the entry table and waved. "See you tomorrow."

Once Cassie was alone, she couldn't help that her thoughts drifted to Ian, to the days they'd spent at his home in L.A. and to the fact he'd taken such good care of her sweet Emily.

Yes, the man may be five years her junior, but so what? Her ex-husband had been two years older and look how well that had turned out. Cassie couldn't hang a single argument on age, not when Ian went above and beyond to show her just what type of man he was.

After Emily was bathed and dressed in her light-weight sleeper, Cassie set some toys on a blanket and let her daughter have some playtime before bed. Settling on the couch, curling her legs to the side, Cassie rested her elbow on the arm of the sofa and watched Emily smack soft yellow and red cubes together, making them jingle.

Exhaustion consumed her, but how could she not be tired? Her plate was not only full—it was over-flowing. Physically, mentally, she was drained. Her head was actually pounding so fiercely her eyes ached. Maybe she could just lay her head on the arm of the couch while Emily played for a bit longer.

Adjusting her arm beneath her head, Cassie closed her eyes, hoping to chase away the dull throb.

After the flash of panic in seeing Cassie slumped over the arm of the couch and Emily holding herself up against the edge of the couch by her mama, Ian realized Cassie had merely fallen asleep.

"Hey, sweetie," he said softly when Emily smiled up at him, flashing her two little baby teeth. "Your mama is pretty tired. Why don't we let her sleep?"

Ian scooped Emily up, set her in her Pack 'n Play across the room and made sure she had her favorite stuffed horse. He had to ignore her slight protesting as he crossed back and gently lifted Cassie into his arms. Murmuring something, she tilted her head against his chest and let out a deep sigh. She was exhausted and apparently couldn't even keep her eyes open. It was so unlike her to fall asleep with Emily still up and not confined to one area.

A small bedside lamp sent a soft glow through her bedroom. After gently laying her down, he pulled the folded blanket from the foot of the bed and draped it over her curled form. Smoothing her hair from her face, Ian frowned and leaned in closer to rest his palm across her forehead.

She wasn't burning up, but she wasn't far from it. Careful not to wake her, he peeled the throw back off her to hopefully get her fever down. Her cheeks were pink and the dark circles beneath her eyes were telltale signs of an illness settling in. He had a feeling Cassie would only be angry to know she was getting sick.

He went into her adjoining bath, got a cool cloth and brought it back out, carefully laying it across her forehead. She stirred and her lids fluttered open as she tried to focus.

"Ian?"

"Shh." He curled a hand over her shoulder to get her to remain down. "It's all right. You need to rest."

"Emily…" Cassie's eyes closed for a moment before she looked back up at him. "I don't feel very well."

"I know, baby. I'm not going anywhere and Emily is fine. Just rest."

He had no clue if she heard him; her eyes were closed and her soft, even breathing had resumed.

The woman worked herself too hard. Not that he could judge. After all, he hadn't grown to be one of Hollywood's most sought-out agents at such a young age by playing assistant and errand boy. No, he'd done grunt work, made his career his since he'd left home determined to prove to his free-spirited mother and domineering father that he could manage on his own and succeed way above anything they'd ever dreamed.

And he'd done just that.

But now that he looked down at Cassie resting peacefully, he couldn't help but wonder if there wasn't more in store for him. Work was satisfying on so many levels, but it didn't keep his bed warm, didn't look to him for support and compassion and sure as hell didn't make his heart swell to the point of bursting.

Cassie and Emily, on the other hand…

After clicking off the bedside lamp, he went straight to the hall bath to wash his hands. If Cassie was contagious, he didn't want to get her daughter sick. Granted, the child had been with her mother all evening, but still. Weren't people supposed to wash their hands before dealing with kids?

Yeah, he had a lot to learn. As he lathered up

and rinsed, he glanced across the open floor plan to Emily, who had long since forgotten she was angry with being confined. Ian dried his hands on a plaid towel and smiled. Definitely had a lot to learn about little people.

And suddenly it hit him that he actually wanted to do just that. Who knew that when he came out here to sway Lily into signing with his agency that he'd completely get sidetracked by a beauty who literally fell into his arms?

After getting a bottle ready—thank God he'd had those alone days with Cassie and Emily in California so he knew a bit more about Emily's care—Ian set it on the end table and went to retrieve one happy baby.

"Are you always in a good mood?" he asked as he lifted her from the baby prison. "Your mama isn't feeling good, so it's just you and me."

Emily patted his face and smiled. "Dadadada."

Ian froze. *Oh, no. No, no, no.* As if a vise was being tightened around his chest, Ian's breath left him.

"No, baby. Ian."

Emily patted his cheek again. "Dadada."

Okay, he had to put his own issues aside at the thought of someone calling him Daddy because this poor girl honestly didn't know her daddy. She didn't remember the man who was supposed to be here for her and her mother.

Ian held her closer, silently wanting to reassure her that she was not alone. But was he also silently telling himself that he'd be here beyond the rough night right now? Would he be here after the film wrapped up?

Since he was alone with his thoughts he might as well admit to himself that being with Cassie and Emily for the long term was something he wanted and, dare he say…ached for?

As he settled into the corner of the couch with Emily, he slid the bottle between her little puckered lips and smiled as those expressive blue eyes looked back up at him. Eyes like her mother's. Both ladies had him wrapped around their fingers.

Emily drifted off to sleep about the time the bottle was empty. He set it back on the table and shifted her gently up onto his shoulder. If she spit up on his dress shirt, so be it. He hadn't taken the time to change after his dinner meeting with Lily. She was pretty confident she'd be signing with his agency.

And the fact this was the first time he'd thought of that monumental career development since he'd come in and discovered Cassie ill should tell him exactly how quickly his priorities had changed where the Barrington females were concerned.

Once Emily had fallen asleep, he figured it was okay for him to rest on the couch with her. He carefully got up and turned off the lights in the living room, leaving on only the small light over the stove in the kitchen. Pulling the throw off the back of the sofa with one hand and holding Emily firmly with the other, Ian toed off his shoes and laid the little girl against the back of the sofa before he eased down onto his side beside her. Not the most comfortable of positions, but he was so tired he could've slept standing up, and there was no way he'd leave Cassie alone with the baby tonight.

Resting with the baby on a couch was probably some sort of Parenting 101 no-no, but since he'd taken no crash courses in this gig, he was totally winging it.

The next thing he knew someone was ringing the doorbell. Ian jerked up, taking in the sunlight streaming in through the windows. It was Sunday and the crew was taking the day off. Was someone looking for him? The doorbell chimed again and Emily's eyes popped open, too.

Ian picked her up and raked a hand over his hair as he padded to the door. The last thing he needed was for someone to ring that bell again and wake Cassie. Apparently they'd all slept uneventfully through the night.

As he flicked the lock, Ian glanced out the sidelight, frowning when he didn't recognize the stranger on the porch.

Easing the door open slightly, Ian met the other man's gaze. "Can I help you?"

The stranger's eyes went from Emily back to Ian before the muscle in his jaw jumped. "Who the hell are you, and where is Cassie?"

Shocked at the immediate anger, Ian instantly felt defensive. "I should be asking you who you are, considering you're on the outside."

Narrowed eyes pierced Ian. "I'm Cassie's husband. I'll ask again. Who the hell are you?"

*Husband.* Ian didn't miss the fact the prick left out the "ex" part.

"I'm her lover," Ian said, mentally high-fiving himself for wiping that smug look off the man's face.

# Chapter 18

Cassie held on to the side of her head, which was still pounding, but now she had a new problem.

Frozen at the end of her hallway, she had full view of Ian holding Emily and the front door wide-open with Derek standing on the other side looking beyond pissed. This was the dead-last thing she wanted to deal with in her life, particularly at this moment.

"Derek, what are you doing here?" she asked, slowly crossing the room, praying she didn't collapse.

"Go back to bed, honey." Ian turned to her, his face softening as he took in what she knew was impressive bed head. "Emily is fine and he can come back later."

"Don't tell my wife what to do," Derek practically shouted as he shouldered his way past Ian and into the living room.

"She's not your wife." Ian's eyes narrowed. When Emily started to fidget, Ian patted her back and murmured something to her. "I need to feed her and change her diaper."

Derek's gaze darted from Ian to Cassie and back to Ian. "What the hell is this? You move in your lover to shack up? Never took you for a whore."

Cassie didn't think she could feel worse. She was wrong. But before she could defend herself, Ian had turned back, clenching the muscle in his jaw.

"Apologize," Ian said in a low, threatening tone.

Cassie had no doubt if Ian hadn't been holding the baby, he would've been across the room in an instant.

"This has nothing to do with you," Derek shot back. "Why don't you give me my daughter and get out."

No matter how awful Cassie felt, she raised her hand to silence Ian and moved closer to Derek. Too bad whatever bug she'd picked up couldn't be fast-acting or she'd so exhale all over him.

"You relinquished any right you had when you walked out on us." Cassie laid a hand on the back of the couch for support. She'd be a little more intimidating if she wasn't freezing and ready to fall onto her face. "You can't just barge into my house and try to take control. I don't know why you're here, but I don't really care."

Cassie felt Ian's hard body behind her, his strong hand settled around her waist. The man offered support both physically and emotionally with one simple, selfless touch. And the sea of differences between the two men in this room was evident without so much as a spoken word.

Ian had watched her with care, concern and, yes, even love. Derek stood glaring, judging and hating. When he'd first walked out she would've done anything to get her family back, but now that he was here, she loathed the sight of him.

"I'm here to see my wife and daughter," Derek told her.

"I'm not your wife," Cassie fired back. "And if you want to see Emily, you can contact your attorney and he can call mine. You can't just charge in here after being gone for nearly a year and expect me to just let you see her. Did you think she'd be comfortable with you?"

"She seems fine with him." Derek nodded his chin in Ian's direction.

"That's because she knows who I am," Ian stated from behind her. "Now, Cassie has asked you to leave. She's not feeling good and my patience has just about run out. Leave now or I'll escort you out personally, then notify the crew's security to take you off the estate property."

Derek looked as if he wanted to say more, but Ian stepped around Cassie, keeping his arm wrapped around her waist. He said nothing and kept his gaze on Derek until Derek stepped back toward the front door.

"I plan on seeing my daughter," Derek threatened. "And my wife. I'll go through my lawyer, but I will be getting my family back."

He slammed the door, leaving the echoing sound

to fill the silence. Cassie hadn't seen Derek in so long, she had no idea how to feel, how to react. She didn't feel like battling him.

And had he threatened to take Emily? Was that what he'd implied?

Cassie sank onto the back of the couch and wrapped her arms around her waist. Maybe she should have listened to those voice mails.

"Go back to bed, Cass. Don't think about him— just go rest for now."

Cassie looked up at Ian, still holding Emily. The image just seemed so…right. The three of them *felt* right. They'd all been random puzzle pieces and when they'd come together they'd instantly clicked into place without question.

Shoving her wayward hair behind her ears, Cassie shook her head. "I can't rest, Ian. He just made a veiled threat to take Emily. He can't do that, right? I mean, what judge would let him have my baby after he walked out on us?"

Tears pricked her eyes. She couldn't fathom sharing custody of her baby. Emily belonged here.

"She doesn't even know him," Cassie murmured, thinking aloud. "There's no way he could take her. Emily would be terrified."

Ian rested a hand on her shoulder and held on to Emily with his other strong arm. "You're jumping the gun here. He didn't say he was going to ask for custody. I honestly think those were just hollow words. He wants to scare you because he's angry I was here. I guarantee had you been alone, his attitude would've been completely different. One look at me, especially holding his daughter, and he was instantly on the defensive."

Emily started to reach for Cassie, but Ian shifted his arm away. "Go on back to rest. I'll feed her breakfast and then I'll check on you to see if you feel like eating. You're exhausted and working too hard."

Cassie raised a brow. "Working too hard? Are you the pot or the kettle?"

Laughing, Ian shrugged. "Does it matter?"

Cassie pushed away from the couch and sighed. "Thanks, Ian. Really. I don't know what I would've done without you here last night."

After a light kiss across her forehead, Ian looked into her eyes. "There's nowhere else I would've rather been."

As Cassie got back into bed, she knew Ian wasn't just saying pretty words to try to win her over. The man was full of surprises, and she found herself falling harder with each passing revelation.

And now here she was, 100 percent in love with a man who lived on the other side of the country, who would be leaving in a couple of weeks to go back to his life. And, of all the rotten timing, her ex had decided to show up now.

Cassie curled into her pillow and fisted her hands beside her face as the tears threatened to fall. Somehow this would all work out. She had faith, she had hope and, for the first time in her life, she had love. All of that had to count for something…didn't it?

Once Cassie had gotten a little food in her, she seemed even more tired, so Ian insisted on taking

Emily for a few hours and then checking back. There was no way he could leave her alone with a baby, but he still had work to do.

Single parents worked while caring for their babies all the time, right? Shouldn't be too hard to send some emails and make a few phone calls.

After fighting with the straps on the stroller and narrowly missing pinching Emily's soft skin in the buckle, he finally had her secured and ready to go. Diaper bag over his shoulder, Ian set out across the estate, pushing Emily toward his trailer.

Bright purple flats covered her feet as she kicked her little legs the entire way. Ian knew he was smiling like an idiot, but how could he not? Emily was an absolute doll and she was such a sweet kid. He was actually looking forward to spending time with her.

Max Ford and his wife, Raine, were just stepping out of their trailer as he passed by. Max held their little girl, Abby, who was almost two now.

"Look at this," Max said with a wide grin. "You seeing how the family life fits you?"

Ian didn't mind the question. Actually, he kind of warmed at the idea of it. "Cassie isn't feeling too great, so I told her I'd take Emily for the day."

Max's daughter pointed down to Emily. "Baby."

Laughing, Raine took the little girl and squatted down to the stroller to see Emily. "Her name is Emily," Raine explained.

"You're pretty serious about Cassie," Max said in a softer tone. "Happened pretty quick."

Ian shook his head and raked a hand over his hair, which was probably still sporting a messy look after sleeping on the sofa all night. "Yeah, it did. But I can't help it, man. I didn't see this coming."

"You plan on staying after the film is done?" Max asked.

Ian watched the interaction between the two little girls and Raine and his heart swelled. "I honestly don't know," Ian said, looking back to Max. "How hard was it for you with the transition?"

Max's gaze drifted to his family, and a genuine smile, not what he used for the cameras or his on-screen love interests, but the one that Ian had seen directed only at Raine, transformed his face. "When you want something so bad you'd die without it, there's no transition. It's the easiest and best decision I've ever made."

Yeah, that was kind of where Ian's mind was going. Having Cassie and Emily in his life made him feel things on a level he hadn't even known existed inside him.

Ian said his goodbyes to Max and his family and stepped inside his trailer. After settling Emily on a pink fuzzy blanket from her house, Ian placed her favorite toys all around her. Standing back to admire his feat of babysitting, he went to boot up his laptop, grabbed his phone and sat at the small kitchenette. Thankfully, the trailer was all open and small, so Emily couldn't leave his sight.

After answering a few emails, Ian glanced at the little girl, who was chewing on one toy and pounding the other one against the side of her rainbow-striped leggings. So far so good.

As he dialed one of his clients, rising star Bran-

don Crowe, who was on his way to Texas for filming, Ian scrolled back through his emails, deleting
the junk so he could wade through and find things
that actually needed his attention.

"Hello."

"Brandon, glad I caught you." Ian closed out his
email and opened the document with his client's
name on it to make notes. "You arrive in Houston
yet?"

"About an hour ago. I'm ready for a beer, my hotel
room and about five days of sleep. In that order."

Ian chuckled. His client had been filming all over
with a tight schedule; the crew had literally been running from one location to another.

"What's up?" Brandon asked.

"I know your mind is on overload right now, but
I need to discuss the next script. I have a film that
will be set in Alaska and the producer has specifically asked for you. I'd like to send this script to you
and see what you think."

Brandon sighed. "Sure. Did you look it over?"

"Yeah. I think this character would be a perfect
fit for you. I can see why they want you for the role."

"Who's the producer?" Brandon asked.

Ian told him more specifics and turned to see
Emily…only she wasn't there. Panic rushed through
him as he jerked to his feet, sending his chair top-
pling to the floor behind him.

"Emily," he called, glancing around the very tiny
area.

"Excuse me?"

Ian glanced at the phone. For a second he'd forgotten about the call. "I need to call you back. The baby is gone."

"Baby?"

Ian disconnected the call and tossed his phone on the table. Stepping over the toys and blanket, Ian crossed to the other end of the trailer. He peeked into the tiny bathroom: no Emily.

"Emily," he called. "Sweetheart?"

In the small bedroom, Ian saw bright rainbow material sticking out from the side of the bed. He rounded the bed. Emily sat on her bottom, still chewing her favorite stuffed horse. Of course, when she saw him she looked up and gave that heart-melting smile.

"You're rotten," he told her. "Your mom is not going to let you come play with me anymore if you give me a heart attack."

He scooped her up and was rewarded with a wet, sloppy horse to the side of the face. *Nice.*

The next hour went about as stellar as the first, and by the end of hour two, Ian knew he was an amateur and needed reinforcements. There was just no way he could do this on his own.

How the hell did Cassie manage? Not only manage, but still put up the front of keeping it together and succeeding at each job: mother, sister, daughter, trainer. She did it all.

Of course, now she was home, in bed, flat-out exhausted and literally making herself sick.

As Ian gathered up all Emily's things, she started crying. The crying turned into a wail in about 2.5

seconds, so Ian figured she was hungry. Wrong. He changed her diaper. Still not happy.

He picked up the bag and Emily, stepped outside and strapped her into the stroller. Perhaps a walk around the estate would help.

Keeping toward the back of the main house, Ian quickly realized this also wasn't making her very happy. That was it. Reinforcements were past due.

He made his way to the back door, unfastened the very angry Emily and carried her into the house, where—*thank you, God*—Linda greeted him with a smile and some heavenly aroma that could only be her cinnamon rolls.

"I've done something wrong," Ian yelled over Emily's tantrum. "We were fine." A slight lie. "But then she started screaming. She's not hungry. She has a clean diaper. We took a walk. I don't know what to do."

Linda wiped her hand on a plaid towel and tossed it onto the granite counter before circling the island and holding her hands out for Emily. The baby eagerly went to the middle-aged woman and Ian nearly wept with gratitude that someone else surely knew what they were doing.

"She probably needs a nap," Linda told him as she jostled and tried to calm Emily.

Ian laughed and pushed a hand through his hair. "After all of that, I need one, too."

Smiling, Linda patted Emily's back. "You say you fed her?"

Ian nodded. "She took a bottle. I have some jar food, but Cassie said to save that for a bit later."

"If she's had her bottle, then her little belly is full and she's ready to rest. I'll just take her into the master bedroom. Damon has a crib set up in there for when Cassie is over here."

Ian sank to the bar stool, rested his elbow on the island and held his head in his hands. Good grief, being in charge of one tiny little being was the hardest job he'd ever had...and he'd had the job only a few hours.

Hands down, parenting was not for wimps.

A slither of guilt crept through him. Had he been too hard on his parents all those years? His free-spirited mother who was always seeking attention and his by-the-book father who could never be pleased... were they just struggling at this whole parenting thing, too?

Ian didn't have the answers and he couldn't go back in time and analyze each and every moment. The most pressing matter right now was the fact that he was in love with Cassie and her sweet baby, and the ex had just stepped back into the picture.

*Great freakin' timing.*

But Ian needed to wait, to let Cassie deal with this matter in her own way. He wasn't stepping aside, not by any means. He'd offer support any way she wanted it, but this was her past to handle, and with a baby involved, Ian had a bad feeling things were about to get worse before they could get better.

# *Chapter 19*

Cassie jerked when the loud knock on her door pulled her out of her sleep. Glancing to the clock on the bedside table, she realized she'd slept most of the day. Damn, she'd never slept that much.

Throwing off the covers and coming to her feet, Cassie was thrilled when she didn't sway and within moments knew she was feeling better. Perhaps her body was just telling her she needed to slow it down every now and then. The pounding on her door continued and Cassie rolled her eyes. There wasn't a doubt in her mind who stood on the other side of the door. Ian wouldn't pound on her door. He'd knock or just come on in, and so would her father and Tessa.

And that left only one rude, unwanted guest.

Shuffling down the hall, probably looking even

more stellar than earlier today when Derek had stopped by, Cassie actually laughed. Was he really here to plead for his family back when she looked like death and after he'd left her for some young, hot bimbo? Oh, the irony was not lost on her.

Cassie took her time flipping the lock on the knob and opening the door. Sure enough, Derek stood there, clutching a newspaper. Disapproval settled in his eyes.

"Funny," she told him, leaning against the edge of the door. "That's the same look you wore when you left me. What do you want now?"

He slapped the paper to her chest and pushed past her to enter.

"Come on in," she muttered, holding on to the paper and closing the door. "I thought I told you to have your lawyer contact mine."

Derek scanned the living area, then stretched his neck to see down the hall. "Where's Emily?"

"With Ian." Crossing her arms, crinkling the paper, Cassie sighed. "What do you want, Derek?"

"First of all, I don't want my daughter with a stranger."

Hysterical laughter bubbled out before she could even try to control it. "Seriously? If anyone is a stranger to her, it's you. We've already established what you think of Ian, so state your reason for this unwanted visit or that threat of calling security will become a fast reality."

He pointed toward the paper. "Apparently you haven't seen today's local paper. Maybe your pretty boy is a stranger to you, as well."

Cassie unfolded the paper. She'd play his game if it meant he'd leave sooner.

Her eyes settled on the picture of Lily and Ian. Cassie had known they were having a business meeting the evening before, she'd known they were discussing a major career move for both of them, but she hadn't known the media would spin the story into something…romantic.

Her eyes landed on the headline: Hollywood Starlet on Location Still Finds Time for Romance.

The way their two heads were angled together in the grainy picture did imply something more than a business meeting. The intimate table for two complete with bouquet and candles also added to the ambience of love.

Cassie glanced back up to Derek. "What about it?"

She would not give her ex the satisfaction of letting it get to her, of coming between something she and Ian had built and worked hard at.

"Looks like your boy toy has someone else on the side." Derek smirked. "Is this really what you've moved on to?"

"Why are you here?" she demanded. "What do you want from me?"

"If you'd answered my calls or texts you'd know I want my family back. I had no idea you opted to replace me with such a younger man."

Cassie smacked the paper down on the table beside the door. "Don't you dare judge me. You left me, remember? And if we're casting stones, I'll remind you that when you left, you moved on with a much younger woman with boobs as her only major asset."

Fired up and more than geared for a fight, Cassie advanced on him. "You're just upset because Ian is a real man. He cares about me, about Emily. My looks don't matter, my size doesn't matter and he's taken to Emily like she is his own, which is a hell of a lot more than you ever did for either of us."

Derek clenched his jaw as he loomed over her and held her gaze. "I just want you to know that this man, this kid, really, will get bored with the family life. He'll move on, and then where will you be? I'm man enough to admit I was wrong and that I'm willing to try again."

She hated that she felt a small tug, hated that for months she'd prayed for this moment. But she loved Ian. How could she deny herself the man she felt she'd been waiting for her whole life?

But on the other hand, how could she deny her daughter the bond of her parents raising her in the same house?

Cassie shook her head, refusing to listen to the conflicting voices in her head. She needed to think, needed to be alone.

"I waited for months for you to come back," she told him, hoping her words would make him squirm, make him feel the heavy dose of guilt he was due. "I cried myself to sleep when I thought of Emily not knowing her father. But you know what? After the tears were spent, I realized that Emily was better off. Both of us were, actually. Neither of us needed a man in our life who didn't put us first. We needed a man who would love us, put our needs above his own selfish ones and be there for us no matter what."

When he opened his mouth, Cassie raised a hand to silence him. "I would've given you the same in return. I married you thinking we were both in love, but I was wrong. You didn't love me, because if you did, you wouldn't have found it so easy to leave me."

"I'm back, though." He reached out, touched her face. "I want my family back, my wife back. I know I made a mistake, but you can't tell me you're ready to throw everything away."

When the door opened behind her, Cassie didn't have to turn to know Ian stood just at the threshold. She closed her eyes and sighed.

"Actually," she whispered. "You already threw it all away."

Derek's eyes darted from hers to just over her shoulder before he dropped his hands. "You can keep the paper. Maybe it will give you something to think about."

She didn't move as he skirted around her. When the door shut once again, Cassie turned slowly to see Ian, hands on his hips. Even with the space between them, Cassie saw so many emotions dancing in his eyes: confusion, hurt, love.

"Where's Emily?" she asked, hoping to keep the conversation on safer ground.

"I actually just left her with Linda. She's taking a nap."

Cassie nodded, worry lacing through her. "What you just saw was—"

"I know what I saw," he murmured. "I know he wants you back. He'd be a fool not to. It's just—"

Ian glanced down, smoothing a hand over the

back of his neck, then froze when his gaze landed on the paper. Slowly he picked it up, skimming the front page.

Cassie waited, wondering how he would react.

When he muttered a curse and slammed the paper down, Cassie jumped.

"Tell me this wasn't Derek's defense," Ian begged. "He surely wasn't using me as his battle to win you back."

Shrugging, Cassie crossed her arms around her waist. "It's a pretty damning photograph."

Closing the spacious gap between them, Ian stood within a breath of her and tipped her chin up so she looked him in the eyes. "The media is known for spinning stories to create the best reaction from viewers. It's how they stay in business."

Cassie nodded. "I'm aware of that."

Ian studied her for a moment before he plunged his fingers through her disheveled hair and claimed her lips. The passion, desire and fury all poured from him, and Cassie had to grip his biceps to hold on for the ride.

He attacked her mouth, a man on a mission of proving something, of taking what was his and damning the consequences.

When he pulled away, Ian rested his forehead against hers. "Tell me you believe that I could kiss you like that and have feelings for another woman. Tell me that you don't trust me and all we have here is built on lies. Because if that's the case, I'll leave right now and never come back."

Cassie's throat tightened as she continued to

clutch his arms. "I don't believe that, Ian. I know you wouldn't lie to me. You've shown me what a real man is, how a real man treats a lady."

Taking a deep breath, she finally stepped back, away from his hold. "But I also know that this is something I'm going to have to deal with if we're together. The media spinning stories, always being in the limelight."

"I'm an agent, Cassie. Nobody cares about me. If I had been out alone, nobody would've known who I was."

Cassie smiled. "But you were out with the breathtaking Lily Beaumont. All of your clients are famous, Ian. There will be other times, other photos."

Shaking her head, she walked around and finally sank onto the sofa. Ian joined her but didn't touch her. She hated this wedge that had settled between them…a wedge that had formed only once Derek had entered the picture.

"I want to be with you, Cassie," he told her. "As in beyond the movie, beyond next month or even next year. I want to see where this can go, but if the idea of my work will hold you back, maybe we both need to reevaluate what we're doing."

Tears pricked her eyes as she turned to face him fully. "You want to be with me?"

Reaching out to swipe the pad of his thumb across her cheek to clear the rogue tear, Ian smiled. "Yes. I know it's crazy and we've only known each other a short time, but I do want to be with you."

"Is this because my ex is back? Are you feeling threatened?"

Shaking his head, Ian took her shoulders and squeezed. "This has nothing to do with Derek. His appearance is just bad timing, that's all. I can't deny myself the fact that being with you has made me a better person. Finding myself wrapped around yours and Emily's lives makes me want more for myself. I never thought about a family before, but I want to see where this will lead and how we can make it work."

Hope filled Cassie as she threw her arms around Ian's neck and sniffed. "I know I'm a hot mess right now," she told him. "I have no idea how I was lucky enough to get you, but I want to see where we go, too. I'm just sorry you'll have to deal with Derek." Cassie eased back and wiped her cheeks. "He's Emily's father, and even though he abandoned us, I can't deny him if he wants to see her."

"What if he wants custody? Did he mention that again?"

"No. I hope he was just trying to scare me, like you said."

Smoothing her hair behind her ear, Ian smiled and settled his palm against her cheek. "No matter what, I'm here for you. Okay?"

For the first time in a long time, Cassie knew there was something to be hopeful about, something more than her career and Emily to fight for. And that was the love of a good man.

Ian was right. Damn if Derek's visit hadn't come at the worst possible time. Not only was the estate covered in film crew and actors, but Ian had settled so perfectly into her life and now the Belmont Stakes was upon them.

The final of the three most prestigious races in the horse world. There was no way Cassie could possibly think of Derek and his threats right now...and yet he had left her with a doozy last night.

He'd called her and issued an ultimatum—either she take him back and give their marriage another go or he would go to his lawyer with a plea to get full custody. Of course, she doubted he could, but the threat was there, and even if he didn't get full, there was always a chance he could get shared. And then where would she be?

Cassie sank down onto the bed in her hotel room and rested her head in her hands. Crying would be of no use, but she so wished she could cut loose and absolutely throw a fit. Being an adult flat-out sucked sometimes.

The adjoining door to the bedroom next to hers creaked open and Cassie glanced up to see Tessa standing in the doorway wearing a gray tank top and black yoga pants.

"I know you're not in a good spot, and as much as I think you could use a drink, that won't help us any in tomorrow's race." Tessa held up a shiny gold bag. "But I do have chocolates and I'm willing to share."

Cassie attempted a smile. "Are they at least rum balls?"

Laughing, Tessa crossed the room and sank onto the bed, bumping Cassie's hip. "Sorry. Just decadent white-chocolate truffles. You ready to talk about Derek being back and wreaking havoc? Because it's been all I could do not to say something to you, but I figured you'd tell me on your own."

Cassie took the bag and dug out a chocolate. No, the sweetness wouldn't cure all, but it would certainly take the edge off her rage.

"I was hoping if I ignored the fact he was in town he'd just go away," Cassie said as she bit into the chocolate.

"How's that working?"

"Not well. How did you find out anyway? He's only been in town two days."

Tessa reached into the bag and pulled out a piece for herself. "Ian and Max were discussing the problem, and I may have eavesdropped on their conversation."

Swallowing the bite and reaching for another truffle, Cassie shifted on the bed to face her sister, settling the bag between them. "I planned on telling you. I was just trying to focus on Ian, make sure Emily was all settled with Linda before we left and praying Derek didn't try to get back onto Stony Ridge while we were gone. I've got security keeping an eye out for him."

"Can you legally do that?" Tessa asked.

Shrugging, Cassie smoothed her hair back and tugged the rubber band from her wrist to secure the knotty mess. "I have no clue. But if he's trespassing on the property, that's all the guards need to know to have him escorted off. If he wants to play the poor-father card, I doubt he'll have a leg to stand on."

"After the race tomorrow, go on home." Tessa reached in the bag and offered Cassie another chocolate, but Cassie wasn't in the mood anymore. "Nash and I will make sure everything is handled and taken care of. Take the truck Nash brought, and he and I can take the trailer and other truck."

Cassie bit her lip when tears threatened. "I don't want him to ruin this, Tessa. We've worked too hard, come too far, and we're both retiring after this season. I can't let him destroy our dreams of going out on top."

Reaching between them to take Cassie's hand, Tessa smiled. "Derek won't destroy anything. You won't give him that power. He's a jerk and he'll probably be gone when we get back because you weren't falling all over yourself to take him back when he appeared on your doorstep."

"He's threatening to file for custody," Cassie whispered.

Tessa let out a string of words that would've made their mother's face turn red. "He's an ass, Cassie. No judge will let him take Emily."

"What about joint custody?"

With a shrug, Tessa shook her head. "Honestly, I don't know, but the man has been gone almost a year, so I would certainly hope no judge would allow someone so restless to help raise a child."

Cassie had the same thoughts, but life and the legal system weren't always fair.

Flinging herself onto the bed, Cassie crossed her arms over her head. "I just never thought I'd be in this situation, you know? I mean, I married Derek thinking we'd be together forever. Then when we had Emily I really thought my family was complete and we were happy. Derek leaving was a bomb I hadn't expected, but now that he's back, I don't want him. I feel nothing but anger and resentment."

Tessa lay on her back next to Cassie and sighed. "You know, between me, Dad, Grant, Linda and Ian, Derek doesn't stand a chance. There's no way we'd let him just take Emily without a fight. If the man wants to play daddy, he'll have to actually stick around and prove he can man up."

"I agree," Cassie told her, lacing her fingers behind her head and staring up at the ceiling. "I won't deny my daughter the chance of knowing her father if I truly believe he won't desert her in a year just when she's getting used to him. I will do everything in my power to protect her heart from him."

And wasn't that just the saddest statement? Protecting a little girl's heart from her own father. But Derek had given her little choice.

"So, you want to tell me what you and Ian are doing?" Tessa asked. "Because I'm pretty sure the two of you are much more than a fling."

Cassie laughed. "Yeah, we're definitely much more than a fling."

"Who knew when you got locked in that attic the man of your dreams would come to your rescue?"

"Technically he didn't rescue me," Cassie clarified.

Tessa glanced over, patted Cassie's leg and smiled. "Oh, honey. He's rescued you—you just might not see it yet."

She was right. Ian had come along at a time in her life when the last thing she'd wanted was a man. But he'd shown her love, shown her daughter love. He'd shown her what true intimacy was all about.

When she'd been sick he hadn't thought twice about taking Emily, even though he knew next to nothing about babies.

He made Cassie's life better.

There was no way that she could not fight for what they had. Maybe she should look into a riding school in California. With her income and her knowledge, she technically could start it anywhere.

She had to deal with Derek first; then she would figure out how being far away from her family would work.

Tessa's brows lifted. "I know that look," she said. "You're plotting something. Share or I'll take my chocolates back to my room."

"Just thinking of the future," Cassie replied with a smile. "Thinking of my school. I've already started putting the wheels in motion for Stony Ridge, but who's to say that's where it has to be?"

Tessa hugged her. "I was so afraid this is what you'd do. Damn, I'm going to miss you if you move."

"Don't go tearing up on me," Cassie ordered. "Ian hasn't asked me, but if he did, I can't say that I would tell him no. On the other hand, Grant has a home out in L.A., too, so I'm sure you'd spend time out there."

"It wouldn't be the same." Tessa sniffed, blinked back tears. "But I want you happy and this is truly the happiest I've seen you in your entire life. I'll support any decision you make."

Cassie reached out, grabbed Tessa's hand and settled in with the fact she'd move heaven and earth to be with Ian. And now she couldn't wait to get home to tell him just that.

# Chapter 20

Ian had a wonderful surprise planned for Cassie. He couldn't wait for her to get home.

Not only had Tessa and Cassie taken the Belmont Stakes and the coveted Triple Crown, but Cassie was on her way back and Ian had to get the stage set. They had so much to celebrate.

Very few had ever taken home the Triple Crown title, and Tessa was the first female jockey to own the honor. The Barrington sisters had officially made history and Ian was so proud he'd been able to witness a small portion of their success. He hated he wasn't there in person, though.

Ian had opted to stay behind for two reasons. So they could both concentrate on their own work without distractions and to see if he could handle being without her.

He couldn't.

After a perfect morning in which Lily officially signed with his agency, he was now in town hitting up the quaint little florist, about to buy an exorbitant amount of flowers in a variety of colors and styles. He wanted her cottage to be drowning in bouquets for the evening he had planned. Not only because he had high hopes about their future, but because she deserved to be placed on a pedestal after such a milestone win.

He may have also had Linda's help in the matter of planning.

The days they'd been apart had been a smack of reality to the face. He didn't want to be without her, without Emily. He was ready to make a family with them.

He also realized that love and marriage—and fatherhood—weren't scary at all once you found the person who totally completed you.

This family had instantly been so welcoming, so loving, and Ian couldn't be happier. From Linda to sweet Emily, he was so overwhelmed by how easily they accepted him. And now Cassie was about to get the surprise of her life.

As Ian rounded the building that housed the flower shop, he smacked into someone... Derek. *Great.*

"You're still in town?" Ian asked, eyeing the man clutching a massive bouquet of roses.

Derek shielded his eyes from the warm afternoon sun. "I'm not leaving until I get what I want."

Becoming more irritated by the moment, and a tad amused, Ian crossed his arms over his chest. "That will be a while, considering what you want is mine."

"Yours? My family is not your property," Derek clarified.

"They're also not your family. Not anymore. Cassie made her choice."

"Did she? Because the Cassie I know loves family." Derek adjusted the flowers to his other hand and shifted beneath the awning of the flower shop to shield himself from the sun. "It means more to her than anything. Do you think she'd honestly choose some young guy who she just met over the father of her child? Because I can assure you, she'll put Emily's needs ahead of her own."

There was a ring of truth to Derek's words, but there was also no way Ian would show any emotion or allow this guy to step into the life he was trying to build.

"Don't blame me or Cassie because you realized too late that you made a mistake," Ian said, propping his hands on his hips and resisting the urge to take those flowers, throw them on the ground and crush them. "Cassie and I have something, and there's no way you're going to come charging in like you belong. You missed your chance."

Derek smiled. "I didn't miss anything. You see, no matter how much you hate me, I am Emily's father. She will want to know me and I will make damn sure my lawyer does everything he can to get my baby girl in my life. Now, if Cassie wants to come, too, that's her decision, but I'll fight dirty to get what I want. Considering the fact that you are a Hollywood playboy, combined with the perfectly timed image in the paper, I don't see how I can't use that against Cassie. Obviously she's eager to get any man's attention—"

All control snapped as Ian fisted Derek's shirt and slammed him against the old brick building. Petals flew everywhere as the bouquet also smacked against the wall.

"Listen here, you little prick." It was all Ian could do not to pummel the jerk. "I will not be bullied into giving up what I want, and Cassie will not be blackmailed, either. If you want to see your daughter, then go through your attorney the proper way, but don't you dare use your own child as a pawn. Only a sick ass would do that."

Stepping back, Ian jerked the bouquet from Derek's hand and threw it down on the sidewalk. He'd held back long enough and Ian knew full well whom that arrangement was meant for.

Ian issued one final warning through gritted teeth. "Stay away from me and mine."

As he walked away, he didn't go into the flower store as originally intended. He had some thinking to do.

No, he wouldn't be intimidated by some jerk who thought he could blackmail his way back into Cassie's life, but if Ian's presence was going to cause issues with custody of Emily, Ian knew he had a difficult decision to make.

As he headed back to his sporty rental car, the small box in his pocket felt heavier than ever.

* * *

Cassie had never been so eager to return from a race, especially one as important as this one.

They'd done it. The Barrington women had conquered the racing world and brought home the Triple Crown. Cassie was pretty sure she'd be smiling in her sleep for years to come. She and Tessa had worked so hard, prayed even harder, and all their endless hours and years of training had paid off.

But beyond the joy of the racing season coming to an amazing end, Cassie couldn't wait to celebrate with Emily and Ian and wanted to get Derek taken care of so he would leave her alone once and for all.

Because she'd gotten home later than intended, Linda had stayed in the cottage and put Emily to bed. Now Cassie was alone, her baby sleeping down the hall and unpacked bags still just inside the door where she'd dropped them.

She had to see Ian now. Too many days had passed since she'd seen him, touched him. Each day she was away from him she realized just how much she truly loved him.

A gentle tap on her front door had her jerking around. The glow of the porch light illuminated Ian's frame through the frosted glass. She'd know that build anywhere and a shiver of excitement crept over her at the thought of seeing him again. She hadn't realized she could miss someone so much.

But the second she flung the door open, ready to launch into his strong hold, she froze. Something was wrong. He wasn't smiling, wasn't even reaching for her. Actually, his hands were shoved in his pockets.

"What's wrong?" she asked, clutching the door frame.

Ian said nothing as his gaze moved over her. Something flashed through his eyes as he settled back on her face…regret?

"Ian?"

He stepped over the threshold, paused within a breath of her and then scooted around her. After closing the door behind her, she leaned against it, unsure of what to say or how to act.

Her eyes locked on to Ian's as silence quickly became the third party present. Moments ago she'd had nothing but hope filling her heart. Now fear had laid a heavy blanket over that hope.

"This is so much harder than I thought it would be," he whispered, his eyes glistening. "I had tonight planned so different."

"You're scaring me, Ian."

Wrapping her arms around her waist, Cassie rubbed her hands up and down her bare arms to ward off the chill.

"I love you, Cassie. I've never said that to another human being, not even my own parents." Ian stepped closer but didn't touch her. "Tonight I thought I would tell you I loved you, show you that I can't live without you and Emily, but I've thought about it all evening and came to the hardest decision of my life."

Cassie wasn't a fool. She knew exactly what he was going to say. "How dare you," she whispered through tears clogging her throat. "You tell me you love me a breath before you're about to break things off? Because that's what this is, right?"

Ian ran a hand over his face. "Damn it, Cassie. I'm letting you go to make things easier. I can't keep you in my life, knowing I could be the one thing that stands between you and keeping custody of your daughter."

Realization quickly dawned on Cassie. "You bastard. You let Derek get to you, didn't you? I never took you for a coward, Ian."

"I'm not a coward, and if Emily weren't in the picture I would stay and fight for you...and I'd win. But Emily deserves a chance to know her father, and I can't stand the thought of you sharing custody or possibly losing because Derek is going to fight dirty. He said it himself. This way, with me gone, maybe you two can come to some sort of peaceful middle ground."

Torn between hurt, love and anger, Cassie tried to rein in her emotions. "You're leaving me because you're afraid. I understand that you didn't have a great childhood, which makes me respect you all the more for stepping up and loving Emily the way you have. But don't you dare leave now when things get tough. I thought you were more of a man than that."

He jerked as if she'd slapped him. "Trust me, Cass. In the long run, this is the best for Emily."

"What about me?" she cried. "I love my daughter and her needs will always come first, but you say you love me. So what about that? What about us?"

The glistening in his eyes intensified a second before a tear slid down his cheek. He didn't make a move to swipe it away and Cassie couldn't stop staring at the wet track.

Her heart literally ached for the man who was

trying to be strong and, in his own way, do the right thing. But damn it, she wanted more and she thought she'd found it with him.

As she stepped forward, Ian took a step back. And that lone action severed any thread of hope she had been holding on to.

"I'm barely hanging on here," he whispered. "You can't touch me. I have to be strong for both of us. Just think about what I said. You'll know that I'm right. There's no other way if you want to keep Emily. Derek won't play fair, and if I'm in your life, he'll use that against you."

He took in a deep, shuddering breath. "I want to be part of your life, Cass. I want to be part of Emily's. But it's because I want so much to be a part of your family that I must protect you both, and unfortunately, that means I need to step aside."

Cassie hated the emotions whirling about inside her. So much love for this man and so much hatred toward another. Damn Ian for being noble.

"If you're not staying to fight for me and with me, then leave." Blinking back tears and clenching her fists at her side to keep from wrapping her arms around him, Cassie held his gaze. "You've done what you came to do, so go."

Ian slid a hand from his pocket, clutched something and reached out to place it on the end table by the sofa. "What I came to do was quite the opposite," he told her as he took a step toward her. "But I want you to have that and remember that I do love you, Cassie. No matter what you think right now. I'll always love you."

Without touching her, without even a kiss goodbye, Ian stepped around her and quietly walked out of her life. Drawing in a shaky breath, she took a step toward the end table and saw a blue box. Her heart in her throat, Cassie reached for the box. Her hands shook because she knew exactly what would be beneath that velvety lid.

Lifting the lid with a slow creak, Cassie gasped. Three square-cut stones nestled perfectly in a pewter band had tears spilling down both cheeks. Cassie's hand came to her mouth to hold back the sob that threatened to escape.

Ian had put all of their birthstones in the ring... a ring he'd planned on giving her when he told her he loved her.

Unable to help herself, she pulled the band from the box and slid it on. A perfect fit—just like the man who had walked out the door moments ago.

As she studied the ring on her finger, Cassie knew there was no way she would go down without a fight. No way at all. Emily would come first, as always, but who said she couldn't have the man of her dreams *and* her family?

If Derek wanted to fight dirty, well, bring it on, because Cassie had just gotten a whole new level of motivation to fuel her fire. And there was no way in hell Derek would take her child or the dreams Cassie had for a future with Ian.

The depth of Ian's love was so far beyond what she'd dared to imagine. His strength as a man and father was exactly what she needed, wanted...deserved. She wouldn't let his sacrifice go to waste.

# Chapter 21

Ian wasn't sure why he didn't book a trip somewhere exotic to just get away. He'd come back to L.A. after breaking things off with Cassie. Max had more than understood his need to leave, but his friend had also had some choice words for him regarding the stupidity of his decision.

Ian wished there'd been another way. He'd had many sleepless nights looking for another way to protect Cassie and Emily, but it was because he loved them so much—because they *were* his family—he knew he needed to remove himself from their lives.

The pain after he'd left was unlike anything he'd ever known. Sharp, piercing pain had settled into the void in his heart that Cassie and Emily had left.

But he also knew, in the long run, this was the best for the ladies he'd quickly grown to love.

Now, back in his beachfront home, he saw Cassie and that precious baby. How had two females he'd known only a short time infiltrated every single corner of his life? There wasn't a spot in his house, his mind or his heart that they hadn't left their imprint on.

He'd been home almost a month, and in the phone calls and texts between Max and Lily, he knew the filming was nearing the end. He hadn't asked about Cassie.... He just couldn't. The thought of her possibly playing house with Derek to keep the peace for Emily nearly crippled him.

Ian sank down onto the sand and pulled his knees up to his chest. The orange glow from the sunset made for a beautiful backdrop and not for the first time was he elated to have all of this for his backyard.

But he'd give it up in a heartbeat for a chance at happiness with Cassie. Letting her go was hands down the hardest thing he'd ever done in his entire life.

He hadn't been lying when he'd said this decision was better for Emily in the long run. When he'd been younger he would've given anything for his parents to have stayed together. Perhaps his father would've been a little more relaxed and his mother not so much of a free spirit always seeking attention from men.

Ian couldn't alter Emily's future by coming between her parents. His broken heart was minor in comparison to their safety. All that mattered was that sweet Emily wasn't a pawn, that he gave her the best chance to know her father. A chance he'd never had.

Damn it, he loved that little girl. He missed those little fingers wrapped around his thumb as he gave her a nighttime bottle. He missed that little two-toothed grin she'd offer for no apparent reason.

He missed everything…even the diaper changes.

"Beautiful place you have here."

Ian jerked his head over his shoulder, his heart nearly stopping at the sight of Cassie in a little green sundress, her hair whipping about her shoulders and Emily on her hip.

"I was just in the neighborhood and was curious if you had room for two more," she went on, not coming any closer.

In an instant, Ian was on his feet. "Room for two? Were you wanting to stay here?"

Cassie shrugged, her face tipped up to hold his gaze as he moved in closer. "Your house, your heart. Wherever you have room."

Ian's knees weakened. She'd come for him. When he'd thought they were finished, when he'd thought he'd done the right thing by setting her free, she'd come to him.

"I'll always have room in my heart for you and Emily." Ian reached out, slid a crimson curl behind her ear. "But my house? That depends on what's going on with you and Derek."

Cassie grabbed his hand before he could pull away from her. "Derek is being taken care of by my team of attorneys. I hired three to make sure he didn't blackmail me, you or use Emily as a bargaining chip.

He's agreed to supervised visitation because Emily is young and would view him as a stranger. He's not allowed to take her from the state for any reason and I have approval over any and all visits."

Shocked, Ian merely stared. When Emily reached for him, his heart tumbled. Pulling her into his arms, he held her tight, breathing in her sweet scent.

"I've missed you," he whispered into her ear. Her little arms came around his neck and Ian had to physically fight back tears.

"We've missed *you,*" Cassie told him. "But I had to make sure Derek was being handled before I could come to you."

Ian lifted his head, slid his arm around Cassie's waist and pulled her against his side. This right here was worth everything. The heartache he'd felt, the worry, the sleepless nights.

"If you ever try to be noble again, I'll go to the press with horrid lies." Cassie smiled up at him. "I know why you left—I even admire your decision on some level—but being without you for weeks was a nightmare. I never want to be without you again."

Ian slid his lips over hers. "What about your family? What about the school?"

Reaching up to pat his cheek, Cassie smiled. "Emily and I are staying here for a while. As for the school, I'd really like to open it on the estate, but I'll move it to California if you're needed here."

Ian couldn't believe what he was hearing. She was willing to part with her life, live across the country from her family, her rock, all because of him.

"I'd never ask you to leave your family," he told

her. "I actually want to be near them. What do you say we keep this home for our getaways and vacations? We can live on the estate or build nearby. The choice is totally up to you, but I want you to have the school at Stony Ridge."

Cassie's smile widened, those sparkling blue eyes glistening. "Sounds like a plan. Of course, we're missing something, you know."

Curious, Ian drew back slightly. "What's that?"

"Well, I've worn my ring since you left." She held up her left ring finger and the sight had his heart jumping. "I assumed that this ring had a question that went along with it. I mean, I'm assuming the man I've fallen in love with plans on carrying out his intentions."

Ian looked to Emily. "What do you think, sweetheart? Should I ask your mommy to marry me?"

Emily clapped her hands and grinned. "Mom-mom-mom."

Laughing, Ian glanced back to Cassie. So many emotions swam in her eyes. So much hope and love, and it was all for him.

"How did I get to be so lucky?" he murmured.

Shrugging, Cassie said, "I'd say fate has been pushing us together since the moment I fell into your arms."

Pulling her tighter against him, he held the two most precious ladies. "This right here, in my arms, is my world. Nothing will come between us again. Not an ex, not my tendency to be noble, nothing. You're mine, Cassie."

Easing back to look down into her eyes, Ian saw

his entire future looking back at him. "Tell me you'll marry me. Tell me you'll let me be Em's dad. That you'll even teach me all about horses. I want to be part of everything in your life."

"I wouldn't have it any other way," she told him, wiping a lone tear that had slid down her cheek. "Besides, I still owe you that horseback ride you've never been on."

Ian laughed. "How about we lay Emily down for a nap and we'll discuss other plans for our family?"

The gleam in her eye told him she hadn't missed his hidden meaning. "*Our family.* Those are two of the most beautiful words I've ever heard."

He kissed her once again. "Then let's get started on building it."

\* \* \* \* \*